HALFWAY HOUSE

A COMEDY OF DEGREES

HALFWAY HOUSE

A COMEDY OF DEGREES

BY

MAURICE HEWLETT

CHARLES SCRIBNER'S SONS
NEW YORK : : : : 1908

CONTENTS

BOOK I

BOOK II

v

BOOK I

HALFWAY HOUSE

A COMEDY OF DEGREES

I

MR. GERMAIN TAKES NOTICE

IT was when Mr. John Germain, a gentleman of fifty, and of fine landed estate in Berks—head of his family, Deputy-Lieutenant, Chairman of Quarter Sessions, and I don't know what not—was paying one of his yearly visits to his brother James, who was Rector of Misperton Brand, in Somerset, that an adventure of a sentimental kind presented itself to him, engaged him, carried him into mid-air upon a winged horse, and set him treading clouds and such-like filmy footing. Chance-caught combinations, associations tenderly touched—what do I know? He had a vision and located it; he dreamed a dream, and began to live it out; out of a simple maid he read a young goddess, into a lover's ardent form he pressed his leanness and grey hairs. Bluntly, he, a widower of ten years' standing, fell in love with a

young person half his age, and of no estate at all—
but quite the contrary; and, after an interval of
time which he chose to ignore, applied himself earnestly to the practice of poetry. There ensued certain
curious relationships between quite ordinary people
which justify me in calling my book a Comedy of
Degrees.

This sudden seizure of the heart overtook him
one afternoon in July, on the occasion of a Sunday-
school feast, an annual affair. He had lent himself
to that because, while he claimed his mornings, his
afternoons were always at the disposition of his
hostess and sister-in-law, the Hon. Mrs. James
Germain, who naturally made the most of them.
She, of course, must be present at the affair, must
have a tea-party for the notables. The Cantacutes
always came, and the Binghams; there might be
others: John must really consent to be bored. There
would be no occasion to pass the railing which sepa-
rated the revellers in the paddock from the Rectory
lawn; all he had to do was to show himself and allow
Mrs. Bingham to talk round about him. True, the
afternoon was very hot; but the Rectory garden was
at its best, velvet-lawned, shady and trim. Mr. Germain confessed that it was the very day for out-of-
door merrymaking—by other people—and smilingly
added that the exertion of the school-feasters would
lend a savour to the leisure he was promised. He
appeared—somewhat late—in a suit of summer
coolness, and white spats, and was charming with
Lady Cantacute, an old friend; perfect with Mrs.

Bingham, whose fault was that she was too anxious to please. In the absence of the Rector and Lord Cantacute, who were conferring on parish business, these ladies made much of their cavalier. He had a comfortable chair, which allowed him to stretch his long legs before him at the right and only angle. Leisurely and measured in all that he did, talking but little, he was allowed to feel that his presence was the utmost that would be asked of him, and that leisure and measure were at his disposal. When, therefore, he had said all that seemed proper, he adjusted his glasses, gave one glance to the white spat upon the foot of his crossed leg, put his elbows on the arms of his chair, clasped his hands, and set himself to observe the sports. All was well with the world so far, and he—the handsome, fine-featured, thin gentleman—as good a thing as this fraction of a world contained. He was in the mood to receive impressions and be charitable to them. This was the moment chosen by the Blind God.

The flags drooped lazily about their poles, the great elms beyond the paddock seemed muffled in their July wrappage, and a swoon; but over the sward the figures of the children and their friends flashed and darted, and crossed each other as on a scene. A stentorian curate in black and white cap directed the cricket. Mr. Germain marked his flying coat-tails and approved them. "Ha! my excellent friend Soames!" he reflected aloud, and added that years left no marks upon Soames. The swiping boys were young England at play—our future was safe in their hands, Soames to urge them. He had his own ideas about our future, and called himself a Liberal in politics; but confessed that Young England was all the better for a Soames or two to guide it. He was a sound Churchman.

His benevolent eye, seeking other objects of interest, was now turned to the girls.

Oranges and Lemons was the cry with them: a pretty game, as elaborate and rhythmical as an old-world dance, with a romp interposed. Two of the tallest hold the gate—their raised arms make it. About the skirts of each you see the clustered bevy of her capture; the doomed ones creep in a file beneath their hands; the sing-song swells, rises, grows, holds—and presently falls with the blow.

The gate-keepers stoop, they clasp, they catch close some struggling prisoner; hot cheek lies fast to pillowing breast, laughing child to laughing maid. It is the strife of love in a dream; like all figure-dances, it figures that; for what cuddling girl but mimics there the transports she is to know one day? Sometimes the captive breaks away and runs; then must the taker give chase: and as the race is swift, and may be long, so is the end the sweeter both for huntress and for quarry. Kisses mark the end; you die of a surfeit of kisses. The strife of love in a dream—a gentle, innocent parody of it!

Whether these amiable musings were cause or consequence of what happened to catch Mr. Germain's eye more than once or twice, there's no telling. I content myself with recording that the most

eyes, the better to regard Miss Cecily from the Rectory party. Presently, after an eager colloquy, expressive on one side of dismay and disarray, Miss Cecily was seen returning with her convoy, talking gaily. The captive nymph, though still busy with hat and hairpins, or fanning herself with her pocket handkerchief, walked confidently, carried her head well, and joined happily in the laugh. This until within hail. But then she changed. Her tongue was still, her head was bent the least in the world, and her eyes became guarded and watchful. At the railing, which Miss Cecily again neatly vaulted, Miss Middleham paused, and blushed before she climbed. But she had nothing to be afraid of, for Mr. Germain was looking at his white spats. When she stood before her betters, however, he, following her example, stood before her. And now he observed her sedately.

He was struck first by a caution in her fine eyes which caused them to loom as with reproach, to peer as if she doubted. Her colour, heightened by exertion and, perhaps, by shyness, was very becoming to her. She glowed like a peach burnt by the sun. She looked wholesome and healthy, and her voice did not belie her appearance—a fresh, confident, young voice. She kept her hands behind her—as if she were a catechumen—and with her shoulders back, looked watchfully at you as she listened and replied. The attitude showed her figure to be charming—softly, tenderly curved; a budding figure. Undoubtedly she was pleasant to behold, but she would have

been no more to any one but a confirmed amorist had
it not been for her eyes.

Mr. Germain was little of an amorist by temperament, though time and the hour had led him to
muse over maids at play. And that being so, he was
shocked rather than struck by the discrepancy between the playing nymph of his fancies and this
healthy sunburnt girl with peering eyes. It almost
shocked him to see her so wary. It gave her a guilty
look as if she feared detection momently. He thought
of a squirrel in leafage, of a dormouse by a tree-bole;
he thought, above all, of flinching, of harsh treatment, of the whip. "Great God," he cried to himself, "what a state of things is this when, upon a sum-
mons suddenly, flashing limbs grow stiff and sparkling eyes burn large with apprehension!" And then
he said in his heart, "To woo the confidence back to
such eyes, to still the doubts in such a breast, were
work for a true man."

From the height of his argument to the flat of the
facts is a longish drop. The Catechism had taken
this simple form. "Mary," Mrs. Germain had said
with something, but very little after all, of the air of a
proprietor, "I see that they are bringing out the tea."

"Yes, Mrs. Germain." A young, fresh, confident
voice.

"Surely, it is not time?"

"Tea was to be at four, Mrs. Germain."

"Oh. Well, the Rector is busy with his lordship
and cannot be disturbed. Tea must not begin until
he can say Grace."

"Very well, Mrs. Germain. But Mr. Soames——"

"No doubt. But I don't wish Mr. Soames to say Grace." This was explained to Mrs. Bingham. "Mr. Soames is a most worthy young man—we are fortunate in him. But he knows only two forms of Grace—*Benedictus benedicat*, which is of course, absurd, and *For these and all Thy mercies*."

"Oh," said Lady Cantacute, "and won't that do?"

Mrs. James looked to the tree-tops. "We think that village children should be taught to expect other things besides mercies. James always says *For what we are about to receive*, which of course might be anything."

"I suppose it might, poor things," said Lady Cantacute, comfortably; and Mrs. Bingham whispered, "So sensible!" to her eldest daughter.

"Besides, the Rector is the proper person on such a day. See to it, if you please, Mary."

"Very well, Mrs. Germain." She lowered her eyes again directly she had spoken, as she was apt to do before her notables.

"My dear," said Lady Cantacute suddenly, "you look very hot." She now looked hotter, but she laughed as she admitted the fact. Laughing became her. Mr. Germain admired her teeth—small, white, and, so far as he could see, perfect. He formed a higher opinion of Lady Cantacute's character—an old friend. To make a young girl smile and show her teeth is to use both tact and benevolence—natural benevolence.

"It is a very hot afternoon," he said, as if delivering a considered judgment, and as he blinked upon her she flashed him one of her hasty looks.

"Yes, it is, Mr. Germain."

"And I think you must be a most unselfish young lady."

"Oh, no, Mr. Germain, indeed." She was quite pleased, and looked very pretty when pleased.

"But I must maintain that you are. You put us luxurious people to shame. Now, Miss Cecily and I will undertake to help you after tea. Is that a bargain, Miss Cecily?" Cecily looked dogged, and said, If he liked."

"All well at home, dear child?" Mrs. Bingham asked here, and made Cecily snort. I am afraid, too, that she nudged her sister Agatha.

"Quite well, thank you, Mrs. ——." She stopped, her voice tailing off into breath, as if she guessed that she had been using too many names just now, and yet knew that, from her sort, the full title was expected. Conversation not being resumed, Mrs. James said shortly, "That will do, Mary, I think. See about the tea, will you?"

Miss Middleham promised, and retired with veiled eyes and an inclination of the head; but Cecily asked, "May I go with her, mother?" and went without the answer.

Their backs turned, the rail safely over, there was a different Miss Middleham to be found, the sparkling, audacious, merry Miss Middleham of Oranges and Lemons who, to Cecily Bingham's "I say, I can

too. Her tennis dress had the air of a riding habit,
and her person that of a young Amazon. She was
not only sumptuous, but severe, a golden beauty, as
nearly indifferent to the fact as a girl may be. "Helen
of Troy, fancy-free, before Paris beguiled her," she
had been called—but the *Diana* of the Louvre comes
readiest to mind.

Mr. John Germain, seeing his chair in possession
—and in that of Duplessis—crossed the railing and
walked over the field towards the trestle-tables where
the scholars feasted. Miss Bingham—the eldest—
and Duplessis were now side by side. "Your young
lady has made another conquest," she told him, and
nodded towards the severe, retreating form. Duplessis observed her calmly. "It's no good, Mildred,"
he said. "You can't get a rise out of me, you know."
She laughed. "I think I've been saved the trouble,
I was only calling your attention to it. He is greatly
interested." The young man's answer was to look
at Mr. Germain, retreating still in a stately manner,
and then at Mildred Bingham. Graphic commentary
enough.

When Mr. Germain approached the tables, Miss
Middleham, who had been very aware of his coming,
became instantly circumspect. He advanced deliberately and stood by her side for a while without
speaking: he then offered himself to hand tea-cups,
and when she assured him that the work was done,
held to his post without any more words or seeming
embarrassment. He was affable to Mr. Soames, if
somewhat lofty; spoke of cricket and cricketers, the

performances of Somerset, and of its champion, whom he was careful to call Mr. Palairet. For Berks, his own county, he apologized. He had a theory, not fully worked out yet, that the Scandinavian blood in us produced the best athletes. Consider Yorkshire and Lancashire. Kent, too: there was an undoubted strain of the Norseman in Kent. Surrey was against him—apparently; but he could not admit it. Of course, London gave the pick of everything; Surrey, a metropolitan shire, could hardly be reckoned, nor, by a parity of reasoning, Middlesex. Mr. Soames, who had not hitherto considered the ethnological side of his game, shook his head and said, "No, by jingo!" then plunged to another table and appeared to be busy. Mr. Germain turned to Miss Middleham and begged to know how he could be of service. "I must make good my boast: I rely upon the loyalty of Miss Cecily Bingham. Do you play after tea?" She said that there would be games. "For instance?" he inquired, and Mr. Soames, who was now hovering near again, said, "We shall finish the match. Perhaps you would care to umpire?" But Mr. Germain had picked up a small wooden implement and was turning it about like a fan. Bat, trap, and ball, he supposed? She laughed him yes. "Very well, then," said he, "you shall allow me to help you in bat, trap, and ball." Cecily Bingham's eyes had now to be avoided at all costs.

The tall, stiff-shouldered gentleman made good his word—if that can be called playing the game where a player never hits the ball, frequently himself, and once (with a resounding smack) the boy fielding behind him. Grouped girls admired with open mouths; but the temptation to giggle when he caught himself for the second time upon the elbow and betrayed something of the torment he suffered was not to be resisted. Miss Middleham bit her lip, but turned to rend one of her pupils. "Gracie," she said in a fierce whisper, "if you dare to laugh I'll never speak to you again."

"Here comes Tristram," said Cecily, but Miss Middleham had no need to be told that. She was very busy teaching a small boy how to wield the bat which Mr. Germain now hastened to discard. "Thank you, Mr. Germain," she said sincerely. "It's very kind of you."

"I am delighted to have been of the least service to you," he replied with a bow. "You set us all an example which I, for one, am proud to follow."

The games languished, flickered out under the calm eyes of Mr. Duplessis, but he took no part in reviving them. Nor did Miss Middleham do more than pretend to instruct. He stood, hands in pockets, for a while, looking at nothing, whistling softly to himself, then strolled towards Mary Middleham and, without looking at her, said two or three words. She listened to them intently without turning her head, said, "Yes," and went on with her business of the moment. Still whistling, Duplessis strolled away, and, in passing, tweaked Cecily Bingham's straight hair.

Mr. Germain, after salutations of a courtly kind, had returned leisurely to the Rectory Garden—to help his sister-in-law feel the early peaches on the wall.

III

MR. DUPLESSIS PREVARICATES

THAT evening there was a vacant place at the Rectory dinner-table. Tristram Duplessis was to have filled it, but did not appear until dessert. He entered then with smiles and light-hearted apologies.

"It isn't often that I work, you'll say, but when I do, I believe I'm not to be restrained. Thanks, Molesworth, anything will do for me." This was how he put it, first to his hostess, next to the anxious butler, each of whom knew better. He chose to add, for the general benefit, "As a matter of fact, I got interested, and entirely forgot that a man must eat."

"Or behave himself," said the Rector, with lifted brows.

Duplessis paused, soup-spoon in air. "He should, no doubt. That's why I'm so late. I had to dress, you see. Anon Soames must needs come in and talk his cricket. They play Cromberton to-morrow, and are two short. Will I be one, and bring another man? says Soames." The spoon was emptied and put down. "I half promised to bring you, you know, Germain." This was suavely addressed to Mr. John Germain, who unblinkingly received it.

23

"Where is your match?" Mr. Germain was peeling a peach, and did not look up. He was told, a home match, and then, without faltering before the "You play?" of as rude a young man as these islands can contain, replied deliberately, "I am very ready to oblige Mr. Soames." The hush upon the dinner-table which followed this declaration was its most eloquent commentary. Mrs. James Germain surveyed the walls, as if calling them to witness her secret thoughts. The Rector drained his glass of sherry, and took another.

"My dear fellow, you make me feel an old fogey," he said. "Do you know that I've not had a bat in my hand since I left Cambridge? And you'll forgive me for remarking that you haven't either, to the best of my belief."

Mr. Germain, whose serenity was proof, reflected before he replied that that seemed an excellent reason for having one to-morrow. "Assuredly," he said, "I shall rally to Mr. Soames, with whom I had a little chat this afternoon. He seemed an amiable and intelligent young man."

"I like Soames," the Rector agreed. "He's a worker."

Mrs. James said sharply, "He needs to be," and received a bow. "My dear, it is now you who put me to shame."

"Not in the least, James," cried the lady. "You are as incapable of the feeling as I am of the action."

The Rector twinkled. "Shameless? Really, my dear——"

"While Soames plays cricket, Cousin James writes sound theology," said Duplessis, and got the lady off the rocks.

Mr. John Germain was now sedately sipping his port.

"That was a pleasant girl you had here," he said, and got his sister-in-law's attention. Duplessis did not look up from his plate, but he listened.

"You mean, I suppose——?"

"I mean Mrs. Bingham's girl—the youngest of the three. I had a little chat with her, too—over our games. I was pleased with her friendly ways. They sit charmingly upon young ladies who are so apt to think that because their frocks are short their manners may be."

Mrs. James spoke to her plate. "I think I understand, but am not altogether prepared to agree with you. Of course, at such gatherings one welcomes help; but I doubt whether it is wise to put ideas into heads which——"

"Which are not capable of holding 'em?" asked the Rector, using his eyebrows.

"Which can have little or no use for them, perhaps."

Mr. Germain, having given this oracle due attention, pronounced upon it as if he were admonishing a poacher. "I am constrained to say that I did not observe a preponderance of ideas in Miss Cecily's conversation."

"Took the rails very neatly, I thought," Duplessis put in, but Mrs. James was not to be balked.

"I don't object to her taking rails or anything else of the sort. But I certainly think it a pity that she should take Mary Middleham's arm, and walk among the children as if they were bosom friends."

Mr. Germain squared his shoulders and lifted his head to reply. "Miss Middleham—" he said; but he was a slow beginner; Mrs. James had risen. It was her husband who fired the parting shot, that he would as soon take Mary Middleham's arm as that of any one in the parish; and it was Duplessis, with his hand on the door, who received her answering shake of the head, and peered after her with quizzical eyes.

Conversation at her exit was between those two. John Germain never spoke to the young man if he could help it, and if he had occasion to look at him always blinked as he did so. Just now he had no occasion, being occupied with his thoughts, smiling quietly at them, drumming time to them with his thin fingers on the table.

We must inquire into Mr. Tristram's avowed labours, and may not, perhaps, he surprised to find out of what nature they were. They had taken him, not to the study and the lamp, but into Lord Canta-cute's fine park by a wicket in the wall, to a largely spreading oak-tree and a seat upon the roots, to el-bows on knees, a cigar, and some moments of frown-ing meditation, from which a light step upon the acorns caused him to look up, but not to rise. Miss Middleham, very flushed and bright-eyed, ap-proached. She wore a cloak over her white dress.

whispered as he stooped. "No, no," she said, and put up her lips. That was the way of it, the saying and doing not without a pathetic simplicity, relished by him to the full.

Exquisite little triumph! which he was too wise to repeat. He spent another twenty minutes discoursing of himself, his works, and plans. Believing her to be interested—as he was himself—he became extremely kind, forgot to be jealous of John Germain's notice, forgot to require or exact anything from her, forgot even to be rude. Really, he parted from her with more politeness than he would have shown to one of his own class—say, to Miss de Speyne. He sought no more favours. "I shall see you in the distance to-morrow, perhaps. I play cricket for Soames—I think he wants me. I don't forget the book, you may be sure. Good night."

It was nine o'clock before he reached his mother's house, and by that time Miss Middleham's person and his pleasure in it were absorbed into the vague physical comfort which a healthy young man feels in changing his clothes. They gave a zest to his bath and clean linen, quickened his brains, and strung him to activity of a sort. He sketched out an article for the weekly review which helped to support him, chaffed Soames, and comfortably dressed himself for the Rectory. There, as we know, he prevaricated, but there also he received some impressions which caused the image of Mary Middleham to visit him in the watches of the night.

He played with the thought of her, as she now

appeared to him. A hint was enough; she was no saint, he had told her; and he knew that, for his purposes, she was all the better for that. Old Germain was clearly a victim—old Germain, of all men possible! How she attracted men—with her pallor, and heavy lids, and those peering, looming, speaking eyes beneath them. What did she want of them? Love, love, and more love—insatiable, was she—and unappeasable? A small, secret, pale, and careworn little huntress; hunting to be hunted, never caught and never catching. Strange! But there were women like that, nympholepts—and wherein lay their charm for men? Oh, well, he knew. He ought to know. And Germain—old Germain—great Heaven! A little Venus—*Venus toute entière* . . . and raised in a suburb, earning her bread as a nursery-governess! Stuff for a sonnet here! He laughed, and sketched it by the open window.

The thought was good. It pleased, excited him, kept him wakeful. A cigar into the still dark seemed reasonable.

She was charming. Her transparency was charming, which made it so easy to see her little shifts and designs; the casting of her home-made nets, and setting of her primitive snares. She betrayed her need so simply. When once you had her confidence there were no more drawbacks, no reticences. By George, she was as simply pagan as a South Sea Islander; not a stitch on her—and a scarlet flower between her teeth. One might drown one's self in love—for a season—if one were a fool. But one was not, you see.

This simple creature, this little Suburban Venus, showed such extraordinary aptitude for the rarer thing, was so susceptible to the finer shades of the business, that one would need be a tearing fool if he —No, and it would be a shame. He would never do that. Better on all accounts to be free—better not commit one's self. She would always be there, could be counted upon. He knew women, he told himself.

They will wait for you—wait for ever, helped on by a little kindness. It's not love they want from you —they have more than enough of that themselves; it's tenderness, once the imagination is really struck. She! Oh, there was no doubt about her. She was his for all time, sensitive, flushing, and paling creature, alternately too bold and too coy. Bold when she ought not—coy when she need not; these were flaws, but he protested that they charmed him. Flaws there must be; it was not reasonable to suppose himself pioneer in that little thicket; and, while the knowledge must cheapen, yet it endeared her to him. Some subtle excitation of sense was stirred by that. What now?

He probed, but gave over the analysis. "Damn it, I'm too curious," he said. "Sonnets don't come this way. I must compose her, not dissect."

But there was to be no more composition of sonnets. He had warped his mood, so threw away his cigar, and went to bed.

IV

A MISS AND A CATCH

As for Mr. Germain, whatever his nightly medita-
tions or dreams may have been, he was as good as
his word, and stoutly took the field on the morrow
when Misperton Brand, having lost the toss, spread
itself over the greensward under Mr. Soames's eye
and imperative hand. Mr. Soames was a bowler
and desperately in earnest; to see him marshal his
field was a study in statesmanship. Knowledge of
men went to it. "Can you throw?" he had asked
the stately gentleman who had somehow to be accounted for; and when Mr. Germain replied that he
would do his best to oblige him—"*Verbum sap*," he
said afterwards to Duplessis, "I knew what that
meant all right, and put him cover. He only missed
two catches, you know, and one of 'em was old
Blacklock who simply *has* to make a run. I don't
call that so bad!"

The game was played in the Rectory field, where
the tent and trestle-tables, and in truth some of the
baked meats of a recent festival did duty for to-day.
Behind the railings, as before, sat Mrs. James and
her Cantacutes. Miss de Speyne was not there, but

Mrs. Duplessis was—a carefully preserved lady,
handsome and fatigued. On the further side of the
field were benches, and here also spectators clustered
—farmers' ladies, the doctor and his wife, Mr.
Nunn, the retired solicitor, who lived at The Sanctuary and employed Miss Middleham to look after
his children; young Perivale, the auctioneer's son,
from Townham, the Misses Finch, of Stockfield
Peverel, the Misses Wake; and Mary Middleham
was undoubtedly there, with white sunshade, her
young charges about her, or running from her to
papa and back as needs might be. And to Miss
Middleham it undoubtedly was that Mr. Germain,
on an occasion of attempting to retrieve a slashing
cut by the butcher's man—and fruitlessly, seeing he
was outpaced by the second gardener from the
Rectory—paid the distinction of a salute before he
returned leisurely to the fray.

She had been standing with a group of acquaintances, of whom Miss Kitty Wake, Miss Sally Wake,
and Miss Letty Wake—all of Whiteacre Farm—
formed three, and young Perivale a fourth. Upon
these young people the courtesy smote like a puff of
wind. Perivale blinked, and "Gracious! Who's
that?" escaped Miss Sally, and was caught and ex-
pounded by her sister Kitty. "Stupid. It's Mr.
Germain, the Rector's brother."

"Then he bowed to you, Mary," said Miss Sally,
and, as Mary blushed, young Perivale ground his
heel into a dandelion.

"I don't wonder," said this youth, whose complaint was not hard to diagnose; but the compliment was ignored by the Misses Wake.

"Whatever makes him play village cricket? Why, his lordship never does, nor the Rector—and Mr. Germain could buy up the pair of them, I hear. Don't you call it singular, Mr. Perivale? I do."

"Doesn't make much of it, does he?" says Perivale, drily.

"No, certainly not. Why should he? An old gentleman like that!"

Friendship required a protest, and so Miss Kitty cried, "Oh, Sally, he's not a bit old!" Mary's corroboration being called for, she said that she should not call him old.

"Well, whatever he is, he's very polite. That bow of his! My dear, you might have been Miss de Speyne! However did he know it was you, at this distance?"

"Perhaps he took his hat off to you, Sally," Mary said, but Miss Sally would have none of that.

"He looks straight at you, as if he knew you by heart, and then stiffens himself, and off with his hat. Cricket! He's no cricketer—but he's a gentleman."

So much all must admit. Mary, mildly elated, had no objection to further inquiries. The former encounter, Mr. Germain's deliberate advance into the school-treat: these wonders were revealed, rolled on the tongue, absorbed. Young Mr. Perivale took a stroll and fiercely, in the course of it, asked a small boy what he was looking at, hey? But more won-

ders were to come. Mr. Germain refreshed himself
with the players, during the tea interval, introduced
himself to Mr. Nunn, of The Sanctuary, patted the
heads of his brood, and meeting Miss Middleham by
the trestle-table, shook hands with her and held her
in talk. He deprecated his cricket with simplicity.
"I reflect that it is five-and-twenty years since I
chased a cricket ball; but you may see the force of
your example, Miss Middleham. Had you not inspired me to effort the other day I should hardly
have embarked upon to-day's adventure."

She was prettily confused—her friends' eyes upon
her; but he ambled on in his kindly way.

"I put myself in the hands of my friend Mr.
Soames. I was sure of his charitable discretion.
Therefore, when he asked me whether I could do
this or that, I did not tell him the facts, because I did
not know them and was so confident that he did.
I said that I should be happy to serve him, which
was perfectly true. I based myself upon a famous
French exemplar. You know the anecdote? A gentleman of that nation was asked whether he could take
the violin part in a quartette. He said that he did
not know, but that he would try. One may admire
his courage."

Miss Middleham was in this difficulty, that she
did not know whether the anecdote was amusing or
not. "I suppose that he was not sure of the part,"
she said.

"No," Mr. Germain corrected her; "he meant
that he did not know how to play the violin." Then

she laughed, more to cover her confusion than because she was tickled.

"I like his attitude of mind, I must say," Mr. Germain continued, talking in the air. "The sonata doubtless mattered as little as this cricket match, but neighbourliness is the great thing. We have too little of that in England. We segregate too willingly I fear. I have no notion of—I beg your pardon. While I have no notions, you have no tea. Pray allow me to get you some."

He was a long time on this errand—for short sight and a complete absence of assertion do not help one to tea in a crowd; but nobody dare engage Miss Middleham while she stood there, so to speak, earmarked for the great man's. Mr. Nunn, her employer, kept his flock carefully about him; Duplessis was over the railings in the Rectory garden; Mr. Soames was exercising the hospitalities due from a captain to his rival. The Perivales, Wakes, Finches, could but look on respectfully. That they did.

Her cup of tea, her plate of bread and butter were handed to her with another fine bow; but even then her cavalier did not consider himself discharged. He stood to his post, tall, unperturbed, using his *pince-nez* to observe with gentle interest the audience which stood about, not for a single moment realizing that it was an audience indeed. But as he talked his amiable commonplaces, he was very conscious of the young woman, object of his attentions; little escaped him there. It was evident to him that she was pleased, softly, quietly thrilled by them; and it gratified him extremely to feel that he could confer pleasure upon her while he took his own. Pleasure, you see, costs nothing, therefore it is priceless. It cannot be bought, and yet can only be got by giving. The distinction seemed to him material, but he could not remember to have remarked it until the other day, when Lady Cantacute—a kind woman—by a trivial remark had made this child forget her wariness and smile enchantingly.

Since that moment he had pursued the thought, and verified it. He was verifying it now; there was no possible doubt that he was giving and taking pleasure. Had there been any—of this you may be sure—he would have known it; he was sensitive in such matters. He would have retired with a fine bow, and resumed his isolation and his dreams, the nursing of his secret fire. I shall have described Mr. Germain ill if I do not make it plain that he was perfectly honest, simple, very solemn, rather dull, a gentleman from the bone outwards. Miss Sally was quite right there. It was, I am sure, rather his education than his breeding which made him look upon his world, his village, native land, the continent he happened to be visiting as either in his employment (like his valet) or a negligible quantity. The same straightness of categories, with an offensive twist, has been observed in Mr. Duplessis and is common to gentlemen by inheritance. Mr. Germain had that sickness mildly, but unmistakably. Take the weather. If the day was fine, he was not insensible to that: he wore white spats and took abroad a silver-headed

cane; he snuffed the genial gale, said Ha! and perhaps gave sixpence to a little boy. All was as it
should be; he was excellently served. But if the
morn broke stormily, with a wailing, wet, west wind,
with scudding rain or whirling snow, all that escaped
his lips was "Provoking!" He ordered the brougham. And you may think that, in effect, these things
are what any gentleman may do, and yet not be exactly right. Other gentlemen may damn the rain;
but Mr. Germain, more in sorrow than in anger,
gave nature a month's warning. If there is offence
to Miss Mary Middleham in likening her to the
weather, I am sorry for it. There's no doubt that
that is how she stood in Mr. Germain's regard,
though he would have gone to the stake denying it.

No misgiving, therefore, disturbed his serenity
while he talked to her of the art of teaching, which
he understood she practised. It was truly, he
thought, one of the great arts, to give it no prouder
title. What more wonderful material could be put
under the hands of any artist than humanity? More
plastic than paint, more durable than the potter's clay
or the builder's stone, more subtly responsive than
the vibrations with which the musician must cope.
He had been reading the other day a very excellent
Life of Vittorino da Feltre, a great Italian educa-
tionist. He should he happy to send it to Miss Middleham. The man was as proud as a prince; and to
the credit of the princes of Italy it must be said that
he was treated as their peer. A remarkable career,
full of suggestion.

A certain scare, faintly discernible in Miss Middleham's open eyes, recalled him from so wide a cast.
He told her that he had been renewing acquaintance
with Mr. Nunn—"a worthy friend of some years'
standing"—and had received that gentleman's testimony to her value, to the affection which all his children had for her. He had a great respect for Mr.
Nunn—a widower with six young children. "I,"
said he, "am a widower—but yet I can envy Mr.
Nunn. I am childless and much alone. You are
fond of children, Miss Middleham?"

She owned to that gladly. "I was sure of it," he
said. "You betrayed yourself at the school-treat.
Not so much by what you did—though you worked
nobly—as by what was done to you. I watched the
children; they could not let you alone. They must
touch you—children express themselves by their *an-
tennæ*. Again I envy you, Miss Middleham."

At this point Mr. Soames most happily, if abruptly,
intervened. We were to go in. Mr. Germain
started, ha'd for his mental balance, poised so for an
uncertain moment, and then broke away as desired.
"My stout commander! Ha, yes. I am ready.
Lead, leader, and I follow." He bowed to his late
captive, left her rosily confused, and bent himself to
his duty in the field.

He faced the bowling of the lower end, with carefully adjusted glasses and a resolute chin. He out-
lived four balls, and actually hit two of them, but
forgot to run the first—to the discomfiture of Wilcox,
the saddler, who did run for it, and lost his wicket.

The second he ran when he should not, though Soames's hand and "No! No!" pealed coming disaster; and then he walked back to the tent, and thence to the Rectory garden, while Duplessis, joining Soames, made vigourous practice of the Cromberton bowling. His enthusiasm held out to the end; he marked every ball, cheered every notch. He was impartial—the fall of Soames's wicket received his plaudits, the hundred on the telegraph got no more. For so sedate a personage he was in great spirits; he rallied the Rector on his timidity, urged Lord Cantacute to put James to the blush. He went so far, even, as to congratulate Duplessis upon his 76 not out; and when all was over reverted more than once during a leisurely stroll among the box-edged walks to the pleasures of village life. He deplored his "great, shut-up Southover." We were too fond of our fenced enclosures. According to Tacitus the trick must be inveterate, but just now there were signs of its losing hold. Our American kindred would have none of it—a park-pale, even a garden hedge was an offence against public conscience over there. The convenience of *appartements* was gaining upon London, and in the country allotments were recalling the old days of the common fields. Well, he was good Liberal enough to welcome the breaking down of our grudging defences. Why should an Englishman's house be his castle, while England, surrounded by its briny moat, was sufficient castle for us all? Merry England! England might be merry enough if Englishmen could forget themselves, and remember each other. Mrs. James did not agree with him, and shortly said so, but Lord Cantacute, who may have seen further than she cared to look, said it would never do. "It's been tried over and over again, you know. You can't mix people up, because they won't meet you. If you go and make a fuss with a fellow, you'll gratify him, you know; but what will he do? Will he make a fuss with his next-door neighbour? Not he! He'll kick him. You've made him feel that he's somebody, d'you see? So he can afford himself the luxury. No, no, Germain. I wish you were right—you ought to be—but you're not."

"There's a queer kind of fellow," his lordship went on, while Mr. Germain seemed to be holding his opinion firmly in his clasped hands behind his back, "who lives in a tilt-cart and mends kettles when the fancy takes him. Paints a good picture, too, and has plenty to say for himself. Hertha found him at that the other day, out riding—but the kettles were not far off, and the sawder bubbling in a pot on a fire. From what she says, he's come as near to your standard as any one. No hedges there. And he's a gentleman, mind you. Hertha says that's clear. But look at the difference. He steps down you see. You are for pulling 'em up. That don't do, as I say."

Mr. Germain explained himself. "I deny the imputation; I cannot admit the possibility. Pulling up, my dear Cantacute! How can you pull up, when there is no eminence? I spoke of enclosures, of artificial barriers—a very different matter."

"Same thing," said my lord. "We didn't plant 'em. They grew."

"I met to-day again," said Mr. Germain, pointedly to his sister-in-law, "your Miss Middleham—a charming girl—with whom I gave myself the pleasure of some little talk during the interval allowed me by my stalwart friend Soames. I became a hedge-breaker, my dear Constantia, deliberately"—Lord Cantacute's shrewd eye being upon him, he turned to the attack—"and I can assure you that I found her in every respect worthy of my homage, in every respect. We discussed her art——"

"What's that?" asked the lord.

"The art of teaching, my dear friend. I maintained that it was the finest art—and Miss Middleham quite agreed with me."

Mrs. James asked him tartly what else Mary Middleham could have done, or been supposed to do. Lord Cantacute contented himself by saying that he believed she was a nice young woman.

"There are, at any rate, no hedges about her," said Mrs. James.

V

HOW TO BREAK A HEDGE

Mr. JOHN GERMAIN, of Southover House, in Berkshire—since it is time to be particular about him—was five years older than his brother—a man of fifty, of habits as settled as his income, and like his income, too, mostly in land. Yet he had literary tastes, a fine library, for instance, of which the nucleus only had been inherited, and the rest selected, bound, and mostly read by himself. He was said to have corresponded with the late Mr. Herbert Spencer, and when he was in town invariably to lunch at the Athenæum, sometimes in the company of that philosopher. In person he was tall, distinguished, very erect, very lean, near-sighted, impassive, and leisurely in his movements. One could not well imagine him running for a train—and indeed the appointments of his household service must have precluded the possibility. His coachman had been with him five-and-twenty years, his butler thirty, and the rest to correspond. I believe there was not an upper servant in his employ who had not either seen him grow up or been so seen by himself. He lived mostly in the country, upon his estate, and there fulfilled its duties

as he conceived them to be—was Chairman of Quarter Sessions, Deputy-Lieutenant, had been Sheriff,
was Chairman of the Board of Guardians. At these
things he worked, to lesser incumbencies he stooped,
to meet them halfway and no more—as if he deprecated the fashion which insisted on them.   Thus he
was patron of sport rather than sportsman, subscribed
liberally to the hounds, but never hunted, offered
excellent shooting to his county, but never handled
a gun. A very dignified man—with his high, fastidious face—you had to look hard to discern the character he was. He masked his features as he subdued
his movements to express deliberately measured
advance; and yet, in his own way and within his
own limits, he had never failed of having what he
wanted, as he wanted it. And if he had to pay, as
we mostly do, he paid without turning a visible
hair. I say that with the remembrance of his marriage to Lady Di Wymondesley in my mind.

That had, at first, seemed a stroke of Fortune
with which he was not to cope. He had married
her—when she was the fashion of the day, the day's
last expression—early in life, so soon as he had gone
down from Cambridge and entered upon his inheritance. She had brought him little money—but he
wanted none of her money; he wanted her, as every
enthusiast for the ideal then did. A beautiful, haggard, swift, violent creature, tearing life to tatters
that she might find some excitement in the lining,
there came a year when Clytemnestra threatened to
be her proper name—that year when her husband

returned from a solitary tour in Palestine, Syria, and the Trojan plain, and when Ægisthus, they say, had not been wanting, to make the trio of them. But he, this immovable, triple-armoured man of thirty—he was no more—had shown what his fibre was when he had lived Ægisthus down, lived him out of Berks, out of his clubs, out of London, out of England, and then had set himself to work to live the devil out of his Clytemnestra. What he suffered will never be known, for he took good care of that; and what she may have suffered can hardly be guessed, for she talked too much and too bitterly to be believed. There's no doubt that these were terrible years; there were fifteen of them, and of every one you would have sworn it must be the last. Providence finally justified that wonderful grit in the man—that panoply of esteem which no sword could bite on— by breaking Lady Di's back in the hunting-field.

He had been forty when that crowning mercy came to him, and had spent the ten following years in getting his affairs into order. Changing out-wardly none of his habits, such as his yearly visit to London, his yearly visit to Misperton Rectory, he was none the less conscious of a departed zest; his panoply was frayed if not rent; and wherever he was during those ten orderly years carried his hope about with him—a treasured, if dim, a real, if unde-fined, presence. He called it Hestia, and wrote verses about it in secret; he had a positive taste for certain forms of poetry—the Court pastoral, the shepherd-in-satin, beribboned lamb sort of poetry—

but not a soul knew that, not even his butler. Hestia
was not a woman—at least, she had no members; she
appeared in his verses unwooing and unwooed. She
was, rather, the vision of an Influence; she was an
Aura, a rhythm, a tone. She involved, implied, a domestic calm which had never been his, though
Southover's walls were fair and many; she was a
melodious beat added to his ordered goings; at her
touch the clockwork of Southover chimed silvern
instead of steely. The hope of this Hestia, if I may
say so, he carried always about with him at the half-
cock. It was the secret of his life. You would never
have suspected him of a musical ear; yet there it
was. You would have said that any spring of poetry
in him would have been sealed at the fount by that
panoply which could turn a sword-edge—but no!
The eye of such a man may never betray its content
and his heart be incapable of voicing its desire. But
what heart covets eye will hold, and ear strain after.
The man will burn within and make no sign—to
fellow man.

And now, the stateliest hedge-breaker that ever,
surely, wrought in Somerset, Mr. Germain proceeded
on his declared purpose with an absence of parade
which, while it robbed it of all sting, must also have
threatened its value. Unless you shout Liberty as
you trample barriers down, the prisoners may well
remain within their pinfolds. There was no shouting
in Misperton Brand. It was Mr. Germain's habit
to take breakfast in his own room and keep a solitary
morning. He was not visible to the Rectory party

until luncheon time; after tea he was accustomed also to withdraw himself until dinner. During these times of seclusion, as I collect, he devoted himself to the emancipation of Miss Middleham.

Sobered as such a young lady could not fail to be by the unimpeachable testimony of Thursday's school treat and Saturday's cricket, it was on the Monday following that a series of encounters began, which struck, excited, and ended by enthralling her. Walking to her work in the mornings, she must needs overtake him, returning late in the evenings, behold him strolling a few yards in front of her. This may be done once and be a transient glory, twice and be for remembrance—a comfort when things go awry; let it happen three times, and you will be frightened. After that it may colour each day beforehand as it comes. Miss Middleham had reached the stage where her heart began to beat as she approached the corner of Love-lane, at the end of which stood The Sanctuary behind its defences of laurela, white gates and laurustinus—when another shock was given her, one of those shocks which you get when you put two and two together, as the saying is. It did not take her a second to do the sum—but it had to be done.

On this occasion lessons had been rolling for an hour—long enough to discover how hot it was and how interesting a bee in a window could make himself; more than long enough for Tommy to yawn and squeak his slate-pencil, for Elsie to sigh and look appealingly at Miss Middleham—when the door opened and papa appeared, and behind papa, tall and benevolent, Mr. Germain, the great gentleman from the Rectory.

At this sudden invasion of her sanctuary, Miss Middleham rose startled in her place, and her hand unconsciously sought her side. As Dian surprised with her nymphs might have covered her unveiled breast, so she her heart. At least, so the visitor interpreted the act. If the children stared clear-eyed, Miss Middleham's fine eyes were misty. Altogether a pretty commotion without and within.

Mr. Nunn—Mr. T. Albert Nunn, as he was pleased to sign himself—was a hale, elderly, and plump gentleman, in colouring rather like a greenhouse plant, so vividly white and feathery was he in the whiskers, so fleshily pink in the cheeks. He now showed considerable elation, though modesty rode it, as it were, on the curb.

"Miss Middleham—pray let me not disturb you. Mr. Germain, Sir, our preceptress, Miss Middleham—who is so kind as to take charge of my nestlings—ha, Sir! my motherless babes—" As he waved them into acquaintance with each other Miss Middleham became deeply suffused, but Mr. Germain was ready to help her.

"Miss Middleham and I are old acquaintances," he said. "Indeed, I presume upon that at the moment." He turned to her, excusing himself. "Mr. Nunn assured me that we should not disturb you, and I hope you will support him. You know my interest in educational matters——"

"Yes, Mr. Germain," she said, faintly. "You have spoken of it."

"I thought it due to you, when I learned what an honourable charge you profess, that you should know me an admirer of it from afar—unfortunately from afar. Your little pupils, too, I have met—" Mr. Nunn, who had a good ear for sentiment, had his cue.

"My motherless—! Ha, Miss Middleham, what can we show Mr. Germain—what have we of interest? My Gertrude, now, writes a good essay—I have heard you say so. Hey?"

"Very good, indeed, Mr. Nunn," said Miss Middleham, while Miss Gertrude swallowed hard.

"I should enjoy a sight of it of all things," said Mr. Germain; so the essay was produced—in all its round and becapitalled script, with Miss Middleham's corrections in red ink. "The Character of John Lackland, King of England."

Mr. Germain read between the lines, studied the corrections, and mused as he read. At the end, it happened there was a model essay in the teacher's hand, not hard to discover as the teacher's composition. He read this, too, and interpreted it in the light of his vision of the girl. He read into it her confident, natural voice, saw behind it her trim figure, her expressive eyes and softly rich colour. The entire absence of anything remarkable in itself gave him no dismay. He was not looking for that, but for confirmation of his emotions, for a reasoned basis to them. It was clear to him in a moment that the

Kings of England were counters in a game—a game,
to the teacher, only a shade less dreary, because
much more familiar, than to her pupils. This was
what he wanted to find. It corroborated his first
vision: the vision held. Had she shown talent, to
say nothing of genius, for her profession, he would
have been greatly disconcerted. Handing the book
back, he patted Miss Gertrude on the head for a
quick little pupil, and her beaming parent on the
back, in a manner of speaking, for possessing her.
"You are happy, Mr. Nunn," he said, "in your children's promise, and I am sure that their instructress
may be satisfied with their performance."

"You are very good, Sir," replied Mr. Nunn.
"It is naturally gratifying to me—highly gratifying
—when a gentleman in your position takes notice of
my little brood. Ha! my little seed-plots, as I may
truly say. Miss Middleham reports favourably of
progress—steady progress. I hear that little Margaret's sewing is somewhat remarkable——"

But Mr. Germain did not pursue his researches,
having no need.

Heaven and Earth! he thought, as he had intended
all along to think, were ever labours more jejune
compelled upon a fresh and budding young life?
Was ever yoke more galling laid upon yearling shoulders? To set a being so delicate at liberty, there can
be no hammer and pick laid to the barrier; nay, it
must be rather by enlarging from within. The butterfly lies so in a prison house, his iris wings close-
folded to his sides. Break into the shell, you either

crush the filmy thing, or usher it untimely into a chill
world. No, no. Breathe tenderness, shed warmth
about the lovely prisoner; it grows in grace and
strength to free itself. Then be at hand to see the
dawning of life, share in the contemplative ecstasy of
a God, rejoice with Him in a fair work—behold it
very good!

"What is exquisite here," he told himself as he
thought of Mary standing at her work, "is the bend-
ing to the yoke, and the resiliency, the strain for release which is irrepressible in so ardent and strong
a nature. I remember the proud youths in the Pan-
athenaic frieze, the noble maidens bearing baskets
on their heads. Obedience, willingness, patience on
the curb—can anything be more beautiful? You
ride a perfect horse; he throbs under your hand. A
touch will guide him, but brutality will make a mad
thing of him. The gentle hand, the gentle hand!
He who is privileged enough to have that in his gift,
within his faculty, is surely blessed above his fellows!

"And does not that quality of beauty, indeed, depend upon the curb? Can it exist, as such, without
it? No: the head cannot bow so meekly without the
burden laid, the neck cannot spring until it has been
bent. Ah, but the curb is wielded by the hand, and
must never be in unwise or brutal employ. Here
there is not brutality, but a stupidity beyond belief,
something horrible to me, and deeply touching, that
one so young, so highly graced, so little advantaged,
should be drudging to prepare for others a lot no
better than her own—drudging without aptitude,

without reason, without hope to realize or ambition to gratify—desiring merely to live and grow and be happy! Horrible, most horrible. Surely so fair a spirit should be more thriftily expended! Transplant that sweet humour, that really beautiful submissiveness into a room more gracious, an atmosphere more appreciative, and how could it fail to thrive, to bear flower and fruit?"

Flower and fruit—ah, me! There leapt up in his heart an answering fire, and he cried to himself, "Hestia! The Hearth!"

VI

MISS MIDDLEHAM IS INVITED TO CONFIRM A VISION

THE object of these sentimental and persistent excursions—circular tours, in fact, since, however far they wandered, whether to the Parthenon or to the shrouded Hestia of the Hearth, they always returned to their starting place—by no means filled the scene at Misperton Brand, which, when she crossed it at all, approved or disapproved according to taste and opportunity. Lady Cantacute had no doubt but she was a good little soul, and young Perivale would confidently wager her a girl with whom you could have fun. Her pupils adored her, Miss de Speyne had not yet realized her existence. Tristram Duplessis believed her waiting for him. The Rector had once called her a sun child, it appears; and that sounds like a compliment, but her good looks were denied. Yet "sun child" is apt, from a friendly tongue. Her colour was quick to come and go; no doubt she was burnt becomingly by the weather. She had—he might have said—a dewy freshness upon her, rather the appearance of having been newly kissed. No doubt, she had a figure, no doubt, the hot, full eyes of the South. Here her soul, if she

had one, spoke to those who could hear. Excitement made her eyes to shine like large stars, apprehension opened them like a hare's. Reproach made
them loom upon you all black. If you interested her,
they peered. They filled readily with tears, and
could laugh like wavelets in the sun. But you can't
build a beauty upon eyes alone, and a beauty she had
no claim to be. And yet she was well finished off—
with small hands and feet, pointed fingers, small
ears, quick nostrils, a smooth throat, running from
dusk to ivory as the sun held or fainted in his chase.
Then she had "pretty ways"—admitted—and there's
enough title for your sun child.

But the Rector, you see, liked her, while his wife
disapproved of her fundamentally. Pretty ways,
forsooth! "She's a flirt, James, and I have no patience with Mr. Soames. The Eastward position is
perfectly harmless, of course. Many clergymen
adopt it—Lord Victor for one. But it was never
done here, as you know very well, until Mr. Soames
discovered that he could see the Sunday-school
benches that way."

The Rector shrugged with his eyebrows. "*Scan-
dalum magnatum*, my dear, and dire nonsense at that.
Soames is a good fellow with a conscience, and may
say his creed in my church to whatever wall he finds
helpful."

Mrs. James retorted that a magnet was quite out
of place in a church, and set him gently chuckling.
That, as she knew, was final for the day; but she
kept her eye steadily upon Miss Middleham, and

had her small rewards. What was not discoverable
could be guessed at by what was. She lighted by
chance upon one crowning episode when, on a Sunday afternoon, she found her cousin Tristram de-
claiming Shelley's *Prometheus* under the apple tree
in the garden of Mary's lodging—not to the apples
and birds of the bough, but to the young person herself, snug in an easy chair, her Sunday pleats neatly
disposed, no ankle showing, to speak of, but—and
this did stamp a fatal air of domesticity upon the
whole exhibition—but *without a hat*. This, if you
come to think of it, means the worst kind of behaviour,
a perverted mind. Shelley was an atheist, and his
Prometheus was probably subversive of every kind
of decency—but that is nothing beside the point of
the hat, which might be missed by any man, but by
no woman. For consider. If a little nursery governess were to be read to by the cousin of a person of good
family—a young man who might be engaged to a
peer's daughter by a nod of the head—one might
think little of it, *had there been evidence of its being
an event*. But there had been none—far from that.
Mrs. James knew her Misperton Brand very well;
events there were hailed by young persons *in their
best hats*. Here, nothing of the kind. On the contrary, there was an every-day air about it which
showed that the girl was at home with Tristram,
Tristram much at home with the girl. That Tristram should be at ease was nothing; it would have
been ridiculous had he not been—a nursery governess! But was it not disastrous flippancy—to say no

harsher thing—in Mary that she, too, could be at ease; hatless, in a rocking chair; not rocking herself —no, not that! but able to rock at any moment! The enormity was reported, and the Rector said that so long as young women wore their hats in his church he cared nothing what they did with them elsewhere. He threatened to chuckle, so no more could be said; but to Mrs. James, what had been dark surmise before was now garishly plain. The girl was——

But all this takes us far from the schoolroom where Miss Middleham was blamelessly expounding the Plantagenet Kings of England, or from the shady lime-tree walk where Mr. Germain was rhapsodizing upon yokes, submissiveness, and young necks resilient.

He met her, as had now become his habit, on the next morning, and the next. The same bewildering, gentle monologues were delivered—or he paced by her side without speaking, without constraint or any sign that betrayed he was not doing an every-day thing. He was doing a thing which held her spellbound; but shortly afterwards he did another which made her brain spin. He proposed "a little walk" in the course of that afternoon—"Let us say, at six o'clock, if that would be perfectly agreeable to you." An appointment! It must needs be agreeable; perhaps it was. He called for her at her woodbine-covered lodging, asked for her by name, and stood uncovered in the porch until she appeared; and then they walked by field-ways some couple of miles in the direction of Stockfield Peverel.

Upon this occasion she was invited, if not directed, to talk. It was a little catechism. Mr. Germain asked her of her family and prospects, and she replied readily enough. There was neither disguise, nor pretence about what she had to tell him. She was what Mrs. James would have thought—and did think—frankly *canaille*. Her father was cashier in the London and Suburban Bank at Blackheath, and her mother was alive. This Mary was the second child of a family of six—all girls. Jane—"We call her Jinny"—was the eldest, and a typewriter in a City office: "We shall never be anything more than we are now, because we aren't clever, and are quite poor." Jinny was seven-and-twenty; then came herself, Mary Susan, twenty-four years ago. A hiatus represented two boys who had died in infancy —"they mean more than all of us to Mother"—and then in succession four more girls, the eldest sixteen and "finishing." "Ready to go out in the world, just as I did." She knew nothing of her father's father; but had heard that he had come from the West Country, Gloucestershire, she thought. Her mother's maiden name had been Unthank. Really, that was all—except that she had been much what she was now—a nursery governess—since she was seventeen. "Seven years—yes, a long time; but one gets accustomed to it." He tried, but could get no more out of her concerning herself; and he remarked upon it that, so surely as she began to talk of her own affairs, she compared them with Jinny's and allowed them to fade out in Jinny's favour. He judged that, as a child, she had been overshadowed. Jinny's beauty, accomplishments, audacity were much upon Mary's tongue. Jinny knew French, and could sing French songs. She was tall—"a head taller than me"—not engaged to be married, but able to be so whenever she chose. Not easy to please, however. "Father thinks a great deal of Jinny. We are all proud of her. Perhaps you might not admire her style. Everybody looks at her in Blackheath." Mr. Germain thought to himself that in that case, he should not admire her style.

It is not to be denied that these details had to be digested under protest. They were perfectly innocent, but they did not help the ideal. She was much more attractive when she was fluttered and whirled off her feet, rather breathless, with a good deal of colour, rather scared—as she had been at first. Now, however, she was at ease, tripping by his side, full of the charms of a dashing Jinny at Blackheath —and it came into his mind with a pang that, at this rate, she—the ideal, first-seen She—might disappear altogether behind that young lady's whisking skirts. This he could not afford: his inquiries became more personal, and she immediately more coy. There came almost naturally into his attitude towards her an air of patronage—tender, diffident, very respectful patronage, under which she soon showed him that his interest in her was moving her pleasantly. A man of more experience than he—who had none— would have seen in a moment that the attention of the other sex was indeed her supreme interest, the

mainspring of her being; would have noticed that
every filament in her young frame was sensitive to
that. A man of gallantry and *expertise* could have
played upon her as on a harp. Mr. Germain could
not do this, but his feelings were strongly attracted.
So young, so simple, so ardent a creature! he said to
himself, and—"God be good to all of us!—living,
breathing delicately, exquisitely, daintily indeed
before my eyes upon sixty-five pounds a year!"

This fact had truly taken his breath away. Sixty-
five pounds a year—mere wages—for the hire of a
girl like a flower. "It was a great rise for me," she
had said. "I had never expected to earn more than
£45—Jinny herself only gets a pound a week, and
French is required in her office. But Mr. Nunn said
that he would pay me £15 more than his usual allowance for governesses because it would not be convenient to have me in the house, and I must therefore pay for a lodging in the village. So I must think
myself a very fortunate girl, to have my evenings to
myself, and £15 a year into the bargain."

Mr. Germain, reflecting upon the wages of his
butler, valet, cook, head-housemaid, head-gardener,
head-keeper, head-coachman, felt himself—though
he did not know it—knocked off his feet. This comes
of mingling interests under glamour. The beglamoured would wiselier postpone practical inquiries.

But as it was, his interest in the young girl was
quickened by admiration and pity to a dangerous
height. He more than admired, he respected her.
To make so gallant, so enchanting a figure on sixty-

five pounds a year! And oh, the scheming and shifts that the effort must involve. His fine lips twitched, his fine, benevolent eyes grew dim; he blinked and raised his brows. Summer lightning seemed to play incessantly over his pale face. "My poor child, my poor, brave child!" he murmured to himself: but aloud he said,

"You interest me extremely—I am greatly touched, somewhat moved. Believe me, I value the confidence you have shown me. I do believe I shall not be unworthy of it. I must think—I must take time to consider—a little time, to see whether I cannot— whether I might presume—Sixty-five pounds a year —God bless me, it is astounding!"

Then, to complete the enchantment, she looked quickly up at him, gave him a full quiver from those deep homes of wonder, her unsearchable eyes. "It's wonderful to me," she said, simply, without any pretence, "that you should interest yourself in me. I cannot understand it."

He schooled himself to smile, to be the patron again. "What do you find so wonderful in that, my dear?"

"That you should find time—that you should care—take notice—oh, I don't know how to say it. I'm only a poor girl, you know, a nursery governess and a dunce. I was so terrified when you came into lessons that morning—I couldn't tell you, really. My knees knocked."

He felt more at his ease. "That was very foolish of your knees, my dear. I was greatly interested. And

pray do not think me inquisitive: that is not one of
my vices. It is far from my wish to—to patronize one
for whom I have so high a respect. Your poverty is
as it may be—at any rate, you earn your bread; and
in that you are a head and shoulders above myself.
And if you are a dunce, which I cannot admit—well,
that can be mended, you know. Are we not all
dunces? I remember a very wise man saying once
that we know nothing until we know that we know
nothing. Do you understand that?"

"Yes, I think so. But even then—Oh, no! It is
very wonderful, I think." And then, as he looked
down at her smiling, he received again her full-
orbed attack, and she said in a low voice, "Thank
you for being so kind to me." He had to turn away
his head lest he should betray himself, and wreck
what was to him a moment of ridiculous happiness.
He could not trust himself to speak.

At the turnstile between the smithy and the Rising
Sun beershop their ways should have diverged; but,
although he had fallen entirely silent, he accompanied
her to Orient Cottage, where she lodged. At the
gate he held her hand for a minute while he somewhat breathlessly committed himself. "Let us, if
you will be so good, repeat our little walk the day
after to-morrow—that is, on Saturday. I leave this
place on Monday, and should value another conversation with you. On Saturday you will be free,
I think? Shall we then say the morning, at
eleven?"

She would not allow him to see her eyes now.

She murmured her "Yes—thank you," and he went on.

"It is very kind of you. I may have something to say—but, be that as it may, to an old fogy of my sort the companionship of a young lady is flattering. I hope I may believe that I have not wearied you, since you are willing to indulge me again."

"No, indeed, Mr. Germain. I shall be proud to come." And then he let her hand go, and she slipped through the gate. As she entered her door she looked over her shoulder a shy good-night; he saluted her and paced slowly back to the Rectory. Combustible matter had been handled; had she been less simple or he more sure, there's no saying what might not have been ablaze. As it was he betrayed by no outward sign at all how stirred he was, though he was not very talkative at the dinner-table. The Rectory people dined at the Park. Tristram, it was told, was off again, He had gone to Pau, at a moment's notice, with young Lord Branleigh.

VII

MISS MIDDLEHAM HAS VISIONS OF HER OWN

As for Mary Middleham, it behoved her to cool her hot cheeks and quench the fires in her eyes as soon as she might, for within a few minutes of Mr. Germain's departure she must set out again. She had been bidden to the Wakes for supper, and the Wakes lived five miles away. Without changing her dress, she mounted her bicycle and was off. She rode fast, but her thoughts outstripped her. She tried to look cool, but the fire throbbed and gleamed. It was not possible but she must recall every stage in the journey of the week that was passing—a week in which there had not been a day without some signal mark of Mr. Germain's attention.

He had "noticed" her; he had "noticed" her and her peddling affairs every day since the school-treat. His interest had increased, and was increasing; she could not credit it, but still less could doubt it. What in the world did the good gentleman mean? What did he see in her, what want of such as she was? Things of the sort had happened before; Mr. Duplessis was a gentleman, but he was different, quite different. He was, to say the least of it, a younger

gentleman, and age was a leveller. "Fun" was to
be expected from such as he; but no more. Her
conscience had to be put to sleep where Mr. Duplessis
was concerned. But Mr. Germain was good and
great, wise and—well, middle-aged—a landlord,
almost a nobleman. There was no question of
"fun" there, or of conscience either—it was all wild
surmise. Could he mean anything? One answer
to that only: he must. Then, what under Heaven
could he mean but one thing? And that was flat
absurdity—impossible of belief. And yet—! So her
little careful mind, scared out of its bearings, beat
and boxed the compass as her heart drove it.

She had a shrewd eye for that form of flattery
which girls call "attentions"; for the education of
her world cultivates the fibres of sense, and she had
been upon it from her seventeenth to this her four-
and-twentieth year. Never a year of the seven but
her wits had been strung by some affair or another,
scarcely one but she had supposed herself within hail
of that hour of moment, had seen before her a point
beyond which there was no seeing. "If he asks me,
I must answer him. And how?" Mostly he had
not; and, after a drowning interval, she had presently discovered herself heart-whole, conscience-
clean, with no wounds visible, no weals or bruises to
ache their reminders. Then it had all begun again—
da capo.

She was very woman to the extremities. Nothing
more feminine than she had ever been taken from
the side of man, or been more strongly inclined to go

back again. Nothing else in life really interested her but the attitude of men—of this man or that man —towards her. That was why work was task-work, and daily intercourse (without an implication) like meat without salt. Instinct had swallowed her up; her mind was a slave, her heart not yet born. She knew nothing whatever of passion; nobody had ever evoked that. She had been touched, interested, flattered, excited, but never in love in her whole life. Love, indeed, in its real sense, was a sealed book; but curiosity absorbed her, and she was as responsive to the flatteries of attention as a looking-glass to breath. Though she was what we call a coquette by nature, she had no vanities, no vulgar delight in flaunting her conquests before the envious. On the contrary, she was secretive, hoarded her love-affairs, preferred to be wooed in the dark. Her philosophy was really very simple and, I say, perfectly innocent. She loved to be loved, sought out, desired. If she was pretty, it was good to be claimed; if she was not, it was better. So all was for the best.

Sitting erect in her saddle, with squared shoulders, open-breasted to the fanning airs, it was clear that she was pleased, and that throbbing heart and coursing blood became her. She had never looked so well or so modest. Her lips were parted, but her eyes were veiled by those heavy lids and deep lashes which to Duplessis spoke strongly of desire, and to Mr. Germain of virgin bashfulness. A smile lay lurking at the corners of her mouth, ready to flash and dart as her thought was stirred. She was not

thinking—perhaps she was incapable of it—she was
playing with thought. What had he been doing
with her to-day? What was he going to do with her
the day after to-morrow? It was all very extraordinary. He liked her, he tried to please her—and so
far well; but he was not like Mr. Duplessis, never
looked at you as he did, as if he was angry that you
were not a morsel. It wasn't that at all: well then,
what was it? The milestones flew by between Misperton and Whiteacre; she was received by the
buxom Miss Wakes with kisses and smiles; but her
questions were not solved, and her excitement must
vent itself in sallies.

So it did. Young Mr. Perivale, the auctioneer's
son, was dumb before her, went down like a stricken
steer. She teased him, dazzled him, inflamed his
face and tied his tongue. She chattered, sang snatches
of songs, scribbled on the piano, flashed and loomed,
dared greatly to a point, and then turned to fly. She
sat on Sally's lap and ate apples, allowed Letty to
whisper secrets in a corner and quarrel with Kitty
who should have her next; sedately conscious of her
good looks, she sat downcast all of a sudden and let
herself be adored—and then of the suddenest she
fled them all and went with Mr. Wake to visit a sick
mare, to pity and to serve, to hold the twitch for him
while he administered a ball. The end of such
flights may be imagined; a pursuit, a capture in the
shrubbery, her waist a prisoner, and a panting dec-
·laration from young Perivale of the state of his
feelings.

She seemed heartless to him. She escaped his
arm, and, "Oh, no, Mr. Perivale, I really couldn't,"
she told him, when he asked, "Could she care for
him?" and looked to snatch a kiss. Which did she
mean—that she couldn't? Both, it seemed. She
handled him lightly; but she thoroughly understood
the game, and her ease was that of a skilled practi-
tioner. Mr. Perivale was hurt, and, it may be, forgot
himself. He told her fairly that her head had been
turned. "That's what it is," he said, with hot eyes
and a sore tongue, "we're not good enough for you
now. The great folks have taken you up. You
think they mean something—and perhaps they do.
But it's not what you think it is."

"I think nothing about it, I assure you," she
cried, with her head high.

"You think nothing of Mr. Germain in the cricket-
field—like a codfish on a bank? Nothing of Mr.
Duplessis glaring at you fit to break you? You think
these very fine attentions? You'll excuse me, Miss
Middleham, but I know the world."

"Oh, you may believe what you please of me,"
said she, flushing up; "but I hope you'll believe
what I've told you just now."

"I'll accept it, whether or no—," said Mr. Perivale, and bade her good-night. Left to herself, in
the shrubbery, she shed some tears: *spretæ injuria
formæ*. The result of the scene was a supper eaten
in subdued silence and the prospect of five miles
home, unescorted. She disliked being about in the
dark; imagination pictured beauty defenceless and

man ranging hungrily. There was a moon, which made it worse. You can only see how dark it is on a moonlight night. No question, however, but she must go.

She made her farewells and set out, her spirits quelled, her little joys all dashed by the quarter-hour's strife, and a victory which seemed not worth the having. The wind had died down; it was a per-fectly still night, close and hot. The very moon seemed hot—heavy, full and burnt yellow—midway up its path. Soon she too was hot, and walking up Faraway Hill got hotter. Her hair loosened and sagged on her neck; her thin muslin gown clung about her knees; she felt tumbled and blowsed, was as near cross as she could ever be, and had spirits like lead—no elation to be got out of the wonderful week, no high-heart hopes for the day after to-morrow, no wild surmises. Atop of the great hill she stopped for breath, fanned herself with her handkerchief, and put up her hair again. Then she mounted and began the short descent to Cubbingdean.

She had not gone a hundred yards before she felt the dull shock and gritty strain which betokens a punctured wheel. This seemed too much, but, dis-mounting, she found it too true. Disaster on the heels of discomfort; here she was with four fine miles to walk, alone, in the dark, the scorn and re-proof of a young Perivale! And part of her way led over Mere Common, where gipsies often encamped, and lay abroad at this season of the year, sleeping, lurking with dogs, doing wickedness in couples.

Her heart began to beat at the thought of all this—
and what wickedness they might do, and how the
dogs would scuffle and tear; but there was no help
for it. She had passed this way but three hours ago
—and how gay it had looked in the golden sunlight
of the late afternoon! Ah, but then her thoughts had
been golden, and music in her heart. A snatch came
back of the song which had been on her lips; stale
jingle it seemed to her now. There had been no gipsies, though, on the Common; comfort in that.

After Cubbingdean, where a little river runs over
the road, you climb again between hedgerows and
orchards; then comes a piece of woodland on either
side, and beyond that you are on Mere Common,
which is more than a mile across and half as much
again in length. Mary tiptoed through the wood
with a knocking heart and, taking breath, addressed
herself to the proof before her. She had not, so far,
met a living soul, unless pheasants have souls, and
hares. These light-foot beasts had made her jump
more than enough, and set the pulses at her temples
beating like kettle-drums. Her mind was beset by
terrors; she had to bite her lip sharply to keep herself to her task.

The wooded road opened, the trees thinned out;
now she was on the Common, indeed, and saw the
ghostly lumps of furze—each in its shroud—on either
hand, with the mist irradiate upon them. She saw
the ribbon of white road tapering to a point—and
midway of that, beside it, dead in her way, a bright
and steady light. At this apparition she stopped

short, gazing in panic, her eyes wide, lips apart. Somebody was there! somebody was there—and what could she do?

She had plenty of spirit for the ordinary encounters of daylight. Over-confident young Mr. Perivale, impudent Sunday scholars, young men who took liberties, found their level; Mrs. James herself would not care to go too far. But in the dark her imagination rode her; she then became what indeed she seemed to one at least of her admirers—the hunted nymph cowering in covert, appealing only for the mercy of men. So now, before this terrible light, glimmering there steady and on the watch, her knees began to shake, her eyes to grow dim. She dared not pass it—so much she confessed; she must make a wide cast, and slip by it through the furze.

She plunged desperately in and struck out to the left of the road. Almost immediately the furze was level with her head, often over it; and she had but one arm free to fend it off. It scratched her cheeks, tore her frock, pulled her hair all about her shoulders; she felt the hairpins part and fall. As for the accursed bicycle, it seemed to be battling on its own account like a mad thing, contesting every inch of ground, clinging to every root, sticking in every hollow. Her breath went, and her strength after it, but still she fought and panted. Amazing contrast between what she had been at seven o'clock, and was now at half-past ten! Impossibly fair seemed the spent day, impossibly serene her panic heart. Bitter regret for what was so lovely and so far away started the tears again; she bit her lip, forced herself on; but at last, pushing with all her might between two ragged clumps, she was caught up sharp, felt a stinging pain on her shin, her ankle gripped by something which cut to the bone. She tottered and fell forward upon her bicycle, and as she went down the ring of fire holding her ankle bit and burned—and Mary shrieked.

She had done herself no service by her *détour*, for she heard a man cry, "Hulloa—I'm coming," and resigned herself to utter fate. God send him kind! —what were these terrible teeth at her ankle? She felt out to reach it—a wire! She was in a hare-wire, set, no doubt by this ruffian who was coming to her now. She heard him labouring through the bushes, and held her breath; and then again he called— "Where are you? Don't be afraid." That was a good voice surely! That was a young man's voice— not a gipsy's. Comforted, perhaps interested, she crouched, holding her caught ankle, and waited.

VIII

FRIENDSHIP'S GARLAND

THE beam of a lantern enveloped her and her gossamered surroundings; presently it blazed full upon her, discovered her flushed and reproachful face, curtained in hair. She saw a tall person, bareheaded, in what seemed to be white clothes, and, by a chance ray, that he was sallow, black-haired, smiling, and had black eyes. A young man! She had no fears left; she was on her own ground again.

"What under the sky are you doing here?" he said. She almost laughed.

"I'm caught in a hare-wire. It hurts very much."

"It would, you know. Let me look." He knelt beside her, and then his quick fingers searched for the wire. As they touched hers she felt them cool and nervous. "I've got it. I say! it's nearly through your stocking. No wonder you cried—but now you know why a hare cries. Quiet now—I'll have it off in a minute." He dived for a knife, talking all the time. "I dare say you think that I set that wire for a hare, and caught you. You're quite wrong. I don't kill hares, and I don't eat 'em; too nearly related to us, I believe. One minute more—" and he nipped the wire. "There—you are free. You can leap and you can run. Perhaps you'd care to tell me why you battle in these brakes, tearing your frock to ribbons and scratching your eyes out, when you might walk that road like a Christian lady. Just as you please— why, good Lord, you've got a bike! It beats cock-fighting. But don't tell me unless you care to; perhaps it's a secret."

She stiffened her shoulders for the fray. "I wish to tell you because I'm ashamed of myself now. Of course, it's not a secret. I have punctured my bicycle, and have to walk home—three miles more. And I saw your light in front of me, and was frightened."

His eyes were as bright as her own, but much more mischievous. "Frightened?" he said. "What, of the light?"

"No, no, of course not. But some one must have lit it."

"Do you mean to say that you were frightened of *me?* The most harmless creature on God's earth?"

She laughed. "How could I know how harmless you were? I thought you were gipsies."

"I couldn't be gipsies. Perhaps I am a gipsy— I'm not sure that I know what I am. My father might, poor man—and he's an alderman. That light, let me tell you, was going to cook my supper; and now it shall cook yours, if you'll have some."

An invitation suggested in that way can only have one answer from a young woman. "No, thank you. I must go on if I can. It's dreadfully late." He reflected.

"It's late, but it's not dreadful at all. These summer nights are made to live in. Look at the moon on those misty bushes! Nothing lovelier can be dreamed of by poets than the hours from now to dawn. Sightseers always go for daylight—and in July everything's blotted up in sap green. There's no drawing in July—I say, you might get up, don't you think?"

"Yes, I might." She tried, and sat down again with a wry face. "It hurts awfully." He had watched the performance.

"I guessed it would. Well, look here. I'll help you." He put out his two hands, met hers, and pulled her gently up by the wrists. "Lean on my shoulder—lean as hard as you like." So she did, because she must.

She limped by his side through the brake, and he talked on. It seemed to her afterwards that she had never heard so much talk in her life. Singular talk too—as if to himself—no hint of her in it—no affected gallantry or solicitude—no consciousness of her presence, not even of her contact; and yet, when she stumbled and clung to his shoulder, he took her round the waist and supported her whole weight with his arm, and so held her until he had her safely by his fire.

He made her sit down upon his rug, took off her shoe and told her to take her stocking off while he got a rag. She obeyed without question, and presently had her ankle in a bandage, which smelt aromatic and stung her, but gave strength and was pleasant. She was very grateful, and entirely at her ease. "I think I'm glad that I was afraid of you," she told him. "Do you know that I've never been so taken care of in my life?" He was putting her shoe on at the moment, pulling tight the laces. "I don't believe you," he said. "You are the sort that was made to be taken care of—abominably feminine. The odds are that you'll put my picture out of my head for at least three days—so I shall have to stop here until it comes back again."

"Then I'm very sorry—" she began, but stopped, as if puzzled.

"You need not be. I shall be perfectly happy. And it will give you a chance of biking out here to report yourself."

Was this an invitation? Did he—? No; it was never done in that tone.

"I shall certainly come," she said. "Perhaps you'll show me the picture. Are you an artist?"

He nodded, busy preparing a dish for the fire, a little silver dish, into which he was breaking eggs. "I'm going to make an omelette; you are to eat half of it. I'm an artist in omelettes, I do believe. Yes, I'm a sort of artist; a bad one, you know. But we're all bad unless we're the best of all—and there's only one best. However, it's all the same. You have your fun."

"But—" She was looking about her with animation—"But where do you—? I mean, do you—?"

He chuckled, but mostly with his black eyes. "I know what you mean. Everybody asks the same questions, and breaks them off at the same point. I'll tell you. I live here, at this moment. I do travel in that cart—and this is my tent—and that ghost over there is my white horse—and hulloa! you've woken Bingo." A lithe grey dog came delicately forward into the light, with lowly head and lowly wagging tail. He was like a terrier, with hound's ears, soft and sleek and silver grey. He sniffed at Mary's dress and feet, sneezed over the bandage, and, edging up, put a cool nose against her neck, and then a warm tongue.

"Oh, what a darling!" she cried softly, and made much of him.

"He's a Bedlington," said his owner, above the sizzling eggs, "a beauty and a devil. He likes you evidently—and reasonably. He won't curl up like that on every lady's skirts, I assure you. Don't talk though, or I can't beat up this thing. Talk to Bingo; he's my friend."

This friendly, cool-tempered young man was, she thought, very odd to look at—long in the body and thin in the leg. He was quite new to her experience. Gentlefolk she knew, and other folk, her own, and all the infinite gradations between—county, clergy, professional, retired military, down to commercial and even lower. This was a gentleman certainly— and yet—well, there was Mr. Duplessis, for instance, with whom you were never to forget that he was a gentleman and you were village. Mr. Duplessis was very easy, until you were easy too—then he got stiff directly, and back you must go. But this strange gentleman didn't seem to notice such things; he seemed too full of what he was thinking about, or doing—and if he looked at you by chance, as often as not he didn't seem to see you; and when you looked at him, he never noticed it at all. She adjudged him "foreign," and to be sure, he had a narrow, foreign face, very swarthy, with a pair of piercing black eyes, a baffling smile, and quick, sudden ways of turning both against you, as if he had that moment found you out, and was amused. At other times, as she came to learn, those eyes of his could be fathomless and vacant, could stare through you as if you were a winter hedge. His hair was jet-black, and straight, and his moustache followed his mouth and curled up when he smiled. She had never seen a man so deft with his fingers or so light and springy on his feet. Those long, eager fingers— she could still feel them at her ankle and marvel at their strength and gentleness as they sought about and plucked free the biting wire. His dress too was extraordinary—a long white sweater with a rolling collar, a pair of flannel trousers; no socks, but sandals on his feet. Long and bony feet they were, beautifully made, she said. Whatever he was or was not, certainly he was kind and interesting; and perhaps the most baffling quality about him was his effect upon herself—that she was entirely at home in his company, and had no care to know what he thought about her.

He served her with omelette hot and poured her out a glass of pale wine, which smelt like flowers, and was stronger, she found, than it seemed. A picnic at midnight! It was great fun! She glanced at her host, and was answered by a gleam. He was enjoying it, too. "Do you know what I'm going to do next?" he asked her, breaking the first silence he had kept since the encounter. "I shall catch that absorbed ghost, which is really a horse, and take you your three miles in my cart. Before that I shall mend your puncture for you."

She wouldn't allow that. "Please, not. I can mend it quite well to-morrow, and won't have you spoil your supper. I have had mine, you must remember and if I am to have another, I insist upon your company." He laughed "All right," and fell to again.

Perhaps her wine made her talkative; but I think that she had leisure of mind to be interested. At any rate, she volleyed him a string of questions about himself, at all of which he laughed—but she found out mostly what she wanted to know. As thus—That cart contained his whole worldly property. "It's my house, or my bed, or both; it's my carriage and pair, my bank, studio, library, forcing-house, potting-shed, bath-room, bed-room, as I choose it. When it's wet I can be dry in there; when it's fine, I leave it alone. It's all I have, and it's more than enough. I've pared it down to the irreducible *minimum*, and yield now to one man only—the tramp. Him I believe to be the wisest son of man, for he has nothing at all. Now, you know, the less you have of your own, the more you have of everybody's. The whole world is the tramp's; but it can't be mine, because of that shell on wheels. I am as the snail to the hare—but what are you, pray, and the rest of your shackled generation? . . .

"There's a tent in that cart, which will go up in ten minutes—anywhere. And the materials of my trades are there—I've several. I scratch poetry— and paint in water-colours—and ain't bad at tinkering." At this she gazed with all her eyes; but he assured her, "I'll mend you a kettle as soon as your bike. I learnt sawdering from a drunken old Welshman under the shadow of Plinlimmon. He died in my arms presently, and left me his tools as well as his carcase. . . . You need not be shocked. I do it because I like it—I don't say that I should be ruined, mind you, if I gave it up . . . but one can't paint against the mood, still less write. . . .

"I've done this sort of thing—and gardening (I'm a bit of a gardener, too)—for nine years or more, and shall never do anything else. Why should I? I'm perfectly happy, quite harmless, and (I do believe) useful in my small way. I could maintain that, I think, before a judge and jury."

He had no need, certainly, to maintain it at length before his present hearer, who was very ready to believe him; but he seemed to feel in the vein to justify himself.

"You see, I'm self-sufficient. I renounced my patrimony on deliberation, and support myself and a little bit over. Tinkering don't go far, I own— sometimes I do it for love, too. But I sell a picture now and then to a confiding poor devil who only asks to buy 'em, and do very well. I destroy most of 'em, because they don't come off; if I had the nerve to sell those I should have more money for plants."

She stopped him here. "Plants!" she said, puzzled, "but——"

He quizzed her. "You look for my conservatory? My herbaceous border? I defy you. You'll never find them. If you could the game would be up. All the same, all my superfluous pence find their way to the nurserymen—nurserymen of sorts. . . ."

As she did not press him he resumed his monologue. "Mind you, I say that I have the best time of any man on this earth. But you're judging me, I know. The women are always the worst. They think it such shameful waste of time, when one might be dressing one's person, or looking at theirs."

She wasn't judging him at all; she was drinking him up—him and his wisdom. For the first time in her life she was really interested in something in a man which did not reside in his sex, or which, it is perhaps kinder to say, had no relation to her own. So absorbed was she that his cut at her kind did not affect her, if she heard it; but she noticed at once that he had stopped.

"Please go on—please tell me more about yourself—about your way of life, I mean. Oh, I think you are extraordinary!"

She had completely forgotten herself. Her eyes had not for a moment left searching his face; her hands cupped her cheeks, her knees supported her elbows; and all about her arms and shoulders her loose hair streamed and rippled. Her face was hot, her eyes like wet stars; she had never looked so pretty, perhaps because she neither knew nor cared anything about it, whether she looked well or whether he thought so. It was plain that he had other things to think of—and one thing is plainer, that if she had not, her hair would have been up long ago.

He laughed at her wonderment. "Oh, I don't know that I'm extraordinary at all—on the contrary, everybody else seems extraordinary to me. It's so simple. I don't doubt but I could make you see what a great life I lead—that's my business as an artist. But it would do you no sort of good—and I'm not a proselytizer. The thing is to get your fun out of what you're obliged to do—or, if you prefer it, to make it your business to do what you like. The Socialists say so, and so do I. After that we differ. We differ as to ways and means. They say that people can only be made happy by dynamite. Dynamite first, Act of Parliament afterwards. Mr. Wells tones down the dynamite; talks about a comet. It's dynamite he means. That's where he's wrong. You can shred people's morals by blowing their neighbours up—but not their characters. Their morals will go to pieces because character remains. You don't want that at all. Morals will always follow character, and that's what you must get at, but not by dynamite. Well, how are you going to develop character? I say by Poverty. Pride's Purge! There's my nostrum for the world-sickness—Pov-

erty, Poverty, Poverty! In fact, I'm a Franciscan—
by temperament and opinion, and not because I'm in
love with the Virgin Mary. I have nothing, and possess all things; I'm rich because I'm destitute; I'm
always filling myself because I'm always empty.
Do you see?"

She looked doubtfully, frowned a little, then took
her eyes from him. "No, I don't see. I don't understand you. I know that you are not laughing at me;
but I think you will now. Never mind; you've been
very nice to me."

"My dear young lady," he said, his glass in mid-
career, "I assure you that I'm not laughing at all.
I'm telling you what I believe to be literal truth.
Perhaps one of these days you will be really poor,
and then you'll agree with me. How can you fill
yourself if you're full already? and where do you
find any pleasure in life except in wanting a thing,
and getting it? Can't you distinguish between having and using? Can't you see that to possess this
Common, fenced and guarded by keepers and varlets
of sorts, would be exactly the same as to use it as I
do now, with all the hamper of the stake in the
county added on to it?"

She looked at her toes, frowned, tried to think—
then raised her eyes. "Yes, yes, perhaps I see that.
But you must know that I am quite poor. And
yet——"

"Ah," he said, "you're not poor enough. You
can't allow yourself to be. It isn't pence that you
must hoard, but opinion, my friend, the sound opin-

ion of your neighbours—and of yourself, too. Look here: apply what I've been saying about this Common to every blessed thing—from God to groundsel, from the Kingdom of Heaven to your villa at Putney —apply it to religion, to rank, to marriage, to murder, and blazes—and you'll see. But you shall work it out at home, for I'm going to take you to bed." He rose here and stretched himself, his hands deep in his pockets. Her eyes pleaded.

"Please, let me think of something first."

"Think away. We'll talk presently, but now I'm going to raise the ghost." He went lightly after his cropping horse, and Mary sat by the fire.

How all this tilted her balances! He little guessed what deeps he had stirred within her simple soul. Deeps! Why, what fisherman had ever yet dropped his hook below the pretty surface? What evidence had she, or any one, that deeps there were? Oh, the great views at his will and pleasure—this gentleman-tinker's, who made omelettes in the middle of the night, and talked like a ruler of men, putting down and setting up with unfaltering voice, altering respects, changing relationships like a lawgiver. Poverty—destitution—to go beggared of opinion as well as pence, and to be the richer for it? She might well pout her lips and wrinkle her little nose as she applied all this to her own concerns. Her heart sank to view her own belittling. Gossip, flirtation, little quarrels, and harsh judgments, a nod from Mrs. James, a smile from Miss de Speyne, dresses, a new blouse, young Perivale, Mr. Duplessis, Mr. ——. No, no, not

Mr. Germain! Even now there was a faint throb of the heart as she thought of the day after to-morrow, and hugged the comfort of an excitement to come.

"Ready, if you are," she heard, and rose to join her host. The gentleman-tinker was in the road with his horse and cart, passing the reins along. Bingo, snorting and stretching his hind legs, was very ready for the frolic.

"How's the ankle?"

"Much better. Too much better."

"Nonsense. That's one of the things we *must* have. I don't preach abstinence from limbs."

She laughed. "No, of course not. But I think that I should have liked to be kept in for a day—or two. And I know that I can't be."

"You're better out, I suspect."

"I'm not sure now—since you have been talking. You have made me think."

"You'll find it hard work. Meantime. you had better get up—it's gone midnight." That sent her up with a little shocked cry. He lifted in the bicycle, and mounted beside her. "Now—where are we going?"

She told him. Misperton Brand was the first village he came to.

"Oh, I know it," he said. "I had adventures there, ages ago. I encamped in a park—Lord Somebody's park—and they turned me out. But I met that lord afterwards, and he proved to be rather a good sort of man."

"He's Lord Cantacute. Do you know the Rector, Mr. Germain?"

"No. I don't get on with rectors. They seem to think that I should go to their churches, but I never do. I don't ask them to mine; why should they ask me to theirs? There's an obliquity about Christianity which beats me. What's his name? Germain? Any relation of Lord George's, I wonder? celebrated man, to whom the Americans ought to put up a statue. He gave them their country, I believe. Gave it away to them, you might put it."

She knew nothing of Lord George. "There's a Mr. John Germain," she said, not quite ingenuously, "who is head of the family."

He considered Mr. John Germain. "I believe I've come against him, too, somewhere. Germain—Germain—Shotaway—Shotover? That's it—Shotover House—big red and white place, with a pediment and a park. Near Reading. Yes, I was turned out of that, too. Solemn old boy, thin, with glasses."

She flushed up in the dark. "He's very nice. He's staying here. I know him. He's kind."

Her companion looked round. "Do you mean that he's kind to you, or kind all round? He wasn't very kind to me. He said that I fostered contempt for my class. I admitted it, and he got angry. Why shouldn't I, if I believe it contemptible?"

"He's very kind to me," she replied seriously. "He's a gentleman, you know, and——"

"And you're a lady. Well, that's not necessarily kind—to you."

"But," she said, "you don't let me finish. I am not a lady, you know—not of—well, not of his class. That's why I think him kind."

"I'm sure I hope you are right," her friend said. "How does his kindness show itself?" She made haste to justify Mr. Germain.

"Well, to begin with, in his being interested in me at all. He talks to me—he asks about my work."

"What is your work?" she was shortly asked.

Teaching, she told him; she was a governess.

He looked at her now, strange man, with real interest. "Are you, though? By Heaven, then there's a chance for you yet. You're above us all. He may well be kind, with the next generation depending entirely on you. Teachers and mothers—no parson can beat that. Is Germain a schoolmaster?"

She began in a shocked voice, "Oh, no! He's a gen—" but was drowned in laughter. He threw his head up and laughed to the sky.

"You're a wonder, I must say. I beg him ten thousand pardons—I forgot. Of course, he's a gentleman."

Mary was piqued. "That's not very kind of you," she said, with reproach in her tones, and he humbled himself at once.

"I'm very sorry, but I'll confess the whole. The fact is, you've jumped into a little pit which I had dug for you—headlong. Upon my word, I beg your pardon. But don't you know that these class-boxes into which you plump every mother's son of us, and are at such pains to keep guarded, lest one of us

should step out, are the very things I'm vowed to
destroy? Why, God be good to us, what are we to
do in our boxes—with all this going on?" He
stretched his arm out—"This dappled earth, sing-
ing, and spinning like a great dusty ball through
star-space! Oh, I must talk to you again about all
this—you, with children in your two hands to be
made into men and women! But not now—it's too
serious. When are you coming to report your ankle,
and tell me that I'm forgiven?"

She smiled upon him. "I've quite forgiven you.
It was I who was foolish. I am sure you must be
right. May I come on Sunday? That's my free
day. I should like to talk to you—about lots of
things."

"Delighted to see you," he said. "Come by daylight this time, and come by road. Here's your village opening."

He set her down at the top of the street, since she
would not allow him further. Prepared to thank
him with her prettiest, the words died on her tongue.
"Not a bit, not a bit," he cut them down. "I love
company. I've enjoyed myself immensely, orating
away. You're a rare listener; you seem as if you
had never heard it before. Good-night."

She held him up her hand—he touched it—turned
the horse, and was gone.

When she had lighted her candle the first thing
she did with it was to hold it up that she might look
in the glass. Her hot eyes and burning cheeks were
ignored for more serious disorders. "My hair!"

And then she laughed. "He would not know whether I had any hair!"

Late as it was, and tired as she was, sleep was long in coming.

IX

THE WELDING OF THE BOLT

POETRY, Lord Cantacute was saying at dinner, is
like a wind-egg—aberration in the producer, useless
for consumption. You don't attempt to eat a wind-
egg. It is remarkable, perhaps; but, once gaped at,
you had best leave it to the parent fowl that will be
glad of it. "You encourage cannibalism?" asked
the Rector, with a lifting eyebrow. Really, Lord
Cantacute saw nothing against it. Perhaps it was a
matter of taste—but so was poetry. And who else
could thrive upon the stuff? Since all this was
apropos of the absent Tristram, whose talents and
fluency were admitted while their trend was deplored,
Mrs. James could not fail to remember a thriving
consumer of his wares. Had she not caught him
administering wind-egg by spoonfuls to a hatless
young lady? The excursion was closed with a flash
by Miss Hertha de Speyne, who, from her golden
throne, said that poetry was very well if the mortal
poet did not practise what he sang. No other art,
she thought, had that grain of vice in it. Now, we
were not ready to practise poetry.

Mr. Germain contributed nothing to the game,

but ate his dinner, or gazed solemnly at one speaker after another. This was unusual; he was fond of abstract discussion, and had his ideas about poetry. He had his favourite practitioners, too—Virgil, Pope, Gray; poetry, for him, must be elegant above all things. Elegant, fastidious, deliberately designed. Dante he could not admire. Petrarch and Tasso were the Italians, their conceits not conceited, for him. He had even—but this was a profound secret— pitched a slender pipe of his own, and was now resuming the exercise. His vein was the courtly-pastoral. The nymph Mero, let us say, was sought by the God Sylvanus, who wooed her in a well-watered vale. Or a young shepherdess—call her Marina— was the dear desire of Cratylus the mature, who offered her with touching diffidence, the well-found hearth, the stored garners, the cellar, for whose ripe antiquity (alas!) he himself could vouch. The maid was not cold; it was himself who doubted whether he were not frigid. He besought her not to despise his silvering beard, the furrow on his brow. Boys, urged he, are hot and prone; but the wood-fire leaps and dies, while the steady glow of the well-pressed peats endures until the morning, and a little breath revives all its force. Thus Cratylus to Marina in his heart.

The inexpert poet is not content with numbers; as Miss de Speyne had said, he is apt to probe what he expounds. Also, by a merciful provision of our mother, no man is permitted to think himself ridiculous, nor indeed is necessarily so. The poets are

right there. The intentions of mature Cratylus may
be as honourable, his raptures as true, his sighs as
deeply fetched as any of beardless Corydon's. Only,
when desire fades in us, o' God's name let us die.
Our friend here cried in his heart that his had never
bloomed before. Spell-bound to a beautiful vision,
he walked enraptured in the light of it, travelling up
the path of its beam, sighing, not that it should be so
long, but that his steps should lag so short of his
urgency. And to the lips of his heart—as it were—
recurred and recurred the dear, familiar phrases,
true once and true now to who so love. The well-
found hearth, and One beside it: surely, happily
there! Denied him for so long; now in full sight!
The buffeting, windy world outside, the good door
barred, the ruddy fire, the welcoming arms, the low
glad voice! Happy, studious evenings—an arm
within an arm, a petition implied, and a promise—a
held-out hand, a little hand caught within it—a prayer,
an exchange of vows, a secret shared—a secret, a wonderful hope! Happy Cratylus, happy poet! Nay, it
was not too late for that—not too late, please God!

In his now exalted mood, every faculty shared the
high tension. His reasoning was exalted, and told
him that his deep distrust of his own class proceeded
from deep experience. The fierce, querulous, and
dead beauty of Lady Diana passed over the scene;
palely and feverishly she hunted her pleasures; and
Ægisthus stalked behind, attentive, to whisper in her
ear at the offered moment. No hopes could be justified under the white light of that torturing memory.

He knew very well, he told himself, that no woman of his daily acquaintance could give him what he longed for. In her degree each and every one must be for him a Diana Wymondesley—with her friend-ships, connexions, thousand calls this way, that way, every way, any way; with her flying, restless crowded life, winters in Cairo, summers in Cowes, Scottish autumns, Sicilian springs. When could she be at home? And he, with his longings for the hearth, that infinitely holy place, must stand, be courteous, play the great gentleman, flog himself to Cairo, Biarritz, Algiers, and feel behind the mask he wore the taloned bird rake at his vitals. Never, never more! Life is to be lived once, and to each his ap-pointed way; appointed if you must, chosen if you can. Ah, me, if choice were his at this late hour! His heart was beating high as he rose in his place for the ladies to leave the dining-room. Miss de Speyne, presuming on familiar use or her preroga-tive, sailed out first, a very Juno; Mrs. James lin-gered for a parting shot at her Rector.

"You may be right, James—it is not for me to contradict you. But Tristram is better at Pau than here; and I have good reasons for saying so." The Rector bowed to his wife, and for once approved Hertha's easy manners.

Returned to the Rectory, when the Rector had gone to smoke his cigar, Mr. Germain had a little conversation with Mrs. James. If he did not delib-erately seek, he deliberately provoked the turn it took. But it began innocently enough.

She asked him his time of departure on Monday, supposing that he must go, and tailed off into to-morrow's engagements. It was now that his face went a thought greyer, and that a shade more stiffening thrilled his spine. A visit to certain Manwarings was proposed for the afternoon. "Your morning you claim, I imagine?" she had said.

"No," he replied, "I gladly make it yours. To-morrow's, that is," and there he paused, and she waited.

He took up his tale greatly. "On Saturday my morning is arranged for. I have, as you know, taken upon myself to be interested in the concerns of your Miss Middleham"—he marked, but chose not to re-mark, the flash in the lady's eyes. *Her* Miss Middleham! "To-morrow I am to be allowed yet further into them; matters of moment, perhaps—I know not. That is for Saturday, at eleven."

"Oh," said Mrs. James—and the vowel held a volume, held it tightly. "Really she ought to be very much obliged to you."

"Not at all. The obligation, in my view, is quite the other way. At my time of life, my dear Constantia, we are apt to plume ourselves upon the confidences of the young. I should not venture——"

"The confidences of that particular young person," said Mrs. James with point—a dry point— "are likely to be modified on this occasion. But if she should happen to be unreserved, I could wish you would use your influence for her good."

"Doubtless," he agreed, "that is my sincere desire.

If you could suggest to me any direction in which my services——"

Mrs. James looked at him, and he, while meeting her gaze, must needs remark upon her hard-rimmed eyes. It was as if they had been set in metal. "We spoke of Tristram at dinner—I don't know whether you heard. I said that he was better even at Pau with poor Lord Bramleigh just now, than here. You may not have heard me."

Mr. Germain blinked. "I am not sure that I should have conceived you, had I overheard the remark. You paint Misperton in dark colours, if what I have heard of young Bramleigh be true. And—to resume the first subject of our conversation——"

"Unfortunately the subjects are connected," said Mrs. James, and saw him flinch. "Tristram is old enough to look after himself; but surely you will agree that his companionship is not the best for a girl in her position."

He had not for nothing worn a mask some twenty years of his life. Wearers of these defences become very expert by use, and can turn them against themselves at will. Mrs. James got no joy out of her revelation, and he little pain; he gave her a stately bow.

"I entirely agree," he said.

"Of course, of course." She accepted him, but went on; "we cannot but regret it, those of us who take an interest. Unfortunately I can hardly speak to her upon such a subject, since I have no authority over her—and James will not. He is pleased to be

diverted at what I have to tell him—you know his
way. I don't know how far your kindly inquiries——"

"We have hardly reached her matrimonial projects," said Mr. Germain, so simply that Mrs.
James lost her head.

"Matrimony! A nursery governess! My dear
John, pray don't misunderstand me." He continued to blink urbanely at her, master now of the
position.

"I wish to avoid precisely that. Little claim as I
have to discuss such matters with Miss Middleham,
I should certainly ask her to pause if I believed that
she could accept the addresses of a young man like
Tristram. Perhaps I am prejudiced—but——"

"Tristram," said Mrs. James tartly, "is as likely
to marry Mary Middleham as you are."

"Is he, though?" he said, with a little jocularity.
But he blinked again.

From the chamber of the beglamoured Cratylus
I may pass to that of his Mero—or Marina, if you
prefer it—who (with no Manwarings in prospect to
afford distraction) had a day of routine to go through
before the interview could be reached. There was
little in this to fix her mind or woo it back from stray-
ing into the vague. It is not surprising, therefore, to
find her on the morrow of her midnight adventure—
a note of apology and excuse despatched to The
Sanctuary—snug in her bed at an unwonted hour,
nursing her cheek and remembrances together, as
much alive to the fact that she had been interested

yesterday as to those which promised her that she
was to be absorbed to-morrow.

And then, as she lay wide-eyed, dreaming, wondering, softly-smiling, quick-breathing, her wide
horizons opened up to her by flashes, or were clouded
up suddenly, enfolded in the rosy mists of conscious
pursuit. To know, as she must, that her company
was desired, courted, deeply considered by a considerable gentleman could not but give a tinge of rose
to her dream-senses. The warm fleeces enwrapped
her, hugged her; they could be felt, they made her
cheeks tingle as her blood coursed free. Against this
passive ecstasy—this rapture of the chase—there rose
in strife a new feeling, a dawning sense of power to
judge and weigh, a discretion imparted, a dignity of
choice. And as this prevailed and her mind leapt
back to her friend of the night, see the mists thin and
part and grow pallid; see her caught breath and
brightening eyes as she strained to watch the far-
stretching plains of life, the distant seas, blue hills—
wonderful vistas, beholding which she seemed to lay
her hand upon the pivot of the world. The battle
raged over her form supine. Like a dormouse in her
nest she lay, but within her breast, within her mind,
the armies engaged swept forward and back.

A day of this must not be, and could not. She
must have stimulant, she must have excitants, must
do something or go mad. She recollected with a
thumping heart that she might see her friend again.
She was to report herself and her ankle; he had
asked her and she had promised to come. There was

an appointment. True, it had been for Sunday—
but what were Sundays to him? It might be to-day.
As she dressed she ·dallied with the temptation, and
before she had finished she knew that she had fallen.

Early in the afternoon she sprang into her saddle,
eager for the encounter. Her ankle was forgotten;
she felt strong and, exulting in her strength, cleared
the miles with that sense of delighted effort which a
bicycle only can give—because it replies so readily.
Her heart beat high as from Chidiocks, that suburb
of Misperton, she saw the white hill atop of which the
Common began. She walked it deliberately, holding
herself back that she might play with the pleasure
promised—a pleasure none the worse, mind you, for
being perfectly lawful. This man was her friend,
and she had never had a man for a friend before. She
felt good, and very strong.

There, then, was the white peak of the tent.
There, too, was the tilt-cart! So he was waiting for
her promise to be kept! There again was the back
of the prowling Ghost. Bingo ran on three legs across
the road—dear Bingo! And there was her friend!
Yes, but he was not alone. She was dismayed—had
not expected that. A horseman talked to him from
the road—a horseman? Ah, no, it was a horse-
woman; and her friend (if she might continue to think
him so) stood there in an animated discussion, and
declaimed upon a paper in his hand. Her heart fell
far, but she pressed on. Nothing in the world—
neither tact, nor delicacy, nor fear of detection-could
have stopped her. She must know more at any cost.

She went as far as she dared by the road, and then, dismounting, moved on to the turf and dropped her bicycle. Screened by furze-bushes she got to within fifty, thirty, twenty yards, and there stopped, knelt down, and watched with intensely bright eyes. The mounted lady was Miss de Speyne, the Honourable Hertha de Speyne, proud daughter of the Canta-cutes, a personage so far out of her reach that her least act was acceptable as a stroke of great Fate—a sunstroke or a thunderbolt. Alas, for her joys!

But her friend, no less easy by day than by night, in one company than another, held in his hand a drawing—as she guessed—and talked vehemently of it. She could hear his words—"It's not bad—it's not at all bad—I admit it; and thanks very much for allowing me. But if you say that of a drawing, you say the cruellest, worst—unless you call it clever. It wants breadth, it wants *maîtrise;* it wants, as all half-art wants, the disdainful ease of Nature, to pro-duce what Nature can never produce. There's a fine line in Baudelaire—well, never mind that. No—I've done better than this. I did some Savernake things which pleased me—trees and glades, evening things. We had some yellow skies, shot green—wonderful, wonderful! I got some poetry into them. But this"—he gave it a flick of the fingers—"this is rather smug, you know."

"I don't think it smug," said Miss de Speyne, with her great air of finality. "I like it."

"Glad of that, anyhow," was the artist's thanks-giving. "Your praise is worth having."

"I've worked very hard," the lady said; "but I'm afraid I can talk better than I paint."

"Ah, we all do that."

"Yes," she said, "that's the worst of it." They paused: she patted her horse, he looked with narrowed eyes into the weather. Presently she said, "I suppose you couldn't come and see my things—and bring some of your own—could you, do you think? My people would be delighted." He looked at her, considering.

"So should I be—charmed. Yes, I'll come if you mean it. When?"

"Of course I mean it," Miss de Speyne rejoined. "Could you come to luncheon, the day after to-morrow? That's Sunday."

"I know it is," he said with a laugh. "What a heathen you think me! Yes, I'll certainly come. But—where are you, exactly?"

"Misperton Brand—Misperton Park. You go through the village, and a little way beyond the Rectory you come to a lodge."

"Oh, I know it!" Then he laughed at his memories. "I'll tell you afterwards—after luncheon. Thanks, I'll come. But I must be back pretty early in the afternoon."

"Your own time, of course." She gathered up her reins. "Till Sunday," she said with a nod. He bowed—hatless as before. Miss de Speyne pushed homeward; and Mary Middleham, with hot splashes of colour in her cheeks, returned to her fallen bicycle, and never looked behind.

How much the grave benevolence of Mr. Germain may have gained by this little *contretemps* we may guess. Broad vistas, after all, are very well indeed for the robust; they are bracing and tonic. But ıı I am to be snug, give me rosy mists.

X

CRATYLUS WITH MARINA: THE INCREDIBLE WORD

UPON the day designed by highest Heaven—as we are led to suppose—they took the way of Misperton Park, the enamoured gentleman and the lady. They sat under the famous Royal Oak—a shade with which she was, we know, familiar—Cratylus talked, Marina sat modestly listening. If he saw her the spirit of the tree—the peering Dryad Mero caught and held to his words, it's all one. Her simple allure, her dainty reserves had ravished his senses; the tinge of sunburn in her ckeeks, the glint of conscious pride in her eyes, beat back like blown flame upon his blood. That fired his brain. In a word, he loved, therefore he believed.

He spoke of himself to-day, of his youth and marriage. Lady Diana was not named, but her knife under the cloak was implied. Sadly, yet without complaint, he related the ossifying of all his generous hopes. "This," he said, "was long ago, but the dead cannot all at once be hidden under the turf. I have been ten years long at a burying, and now have done. What remain to me of years, I know not truly; but they will be the more precious if they are to be few. I believe that I am very capable of happiness—perhaps even of bestowing it. My affairs are in good order; I have been fortunate, as you know, in worldly respects. A childless widower, I pick up my life again at fifty where I left it at five-and-twenty. And I tell myself—I have told myself but newly—that I may not be too late."

To this sort of soliloquy, to the grave voice that rehearsed it, she had nothing to say. He found that he must import her bodily into his conversation.

"For one thing," he continued, after a pause of exploration, "I now have leisure, as you have seen, to interest myself in my neighbours, and have derived so much pleasure from it that I am deeply grateful to those who have indulged me. You are one. I think that you must have remarked what happiness your society and your confidence have been to me." Her shamefastness, which tied her tongue, compelled him to probe. "Have you not seen that?"

She murmured that he had been very kind, that she was grateful. "Not so, my dear," said he, "but the persons must be transposed. The kindness is yours, the obligation upon me. Come! Can you not tell me that you have understood me? Can you not let me be satisfied that you realize your own benevolence? If you cannot, I must withhold what I was about to say to you. I should want for courage. I must ask for your assurance. You will not refuse it?"

Exciting, mystifying talk! She dared not look up

—but she asked him, What it was that she was to tell him?

He luxuriated in her bashfulness. "Why, my dearest child," he said, very near to her, "I want to know whether you believe me happy in your company?"

She would not look at him, but she said "I hope that you like me—I do hope that."

Then he took her hand and held it in both of his own. He gazed tenderly down upon her hanging head—not one meek beauty of her escaped him, neither of burning cheek, curved lashes, of heavy eyelids, rising breast. "Then, dear child, I will tell you plainly that I love you most sincerely; that you have my heart, such as it is, in your little hands— just as certainly as one of those hands is here in mine. I have told you the truth about myself—what I hoped to be, what I was, what I am become. And now, if you can repay that confidence with a confidence, I shall be satisfied indeed. But I must ask you again, Can you value the love of a man twice your age? Remember, I shall not be hurt if you tell me that you cannot. I shall respect your confidence, whatever it may be; and shall never trouble you again. . . . What do you tell me now, Mary?"

She had started visibly at the word "love," and had been revealed to him for a flash, which gave him the value of her wide eyes, and of the flying colour, which now left her very pale, then lapped her in flame again, and showed her like a red rose. A flash only; for immediately after she had bowed her head so deeply that her chin nearly touched her bosom, and she could have smelt the knot of carnations fastened there. Her hand was still his prisoner but she would have freed it if she could; for now she was startled indeed. Though she had been forewarned, her armour was not on. This word was a dart, and stabbed her deep. The incredible thing had come to pass.

She had been prepared for unbounded sentiment, for tenderness, for the captured hand; she had foreseen a breathless moment or so, a stoop, and a kiss. Such a string of episodes—just that string of them— would not have been strange to her by any means, and would have satisfied her anticipations perfectly. She would have been elated, would have made much of it in her mind, might possibly, after some interval, in some tender hour, have confided it to a bosom friend. On many dull days it would have shone like a lamp, assuring her of substantial things, of honour done, of a positive achievement of hers—to have won such condescension from a great gentleman. Here had been—you may say—a creditable triumph for the Middlehams. But a declaration in so many words—love offered and asked again; what could this mean but one astounding thing? She was frightened, and that's a fact; frightened out of her wits. The averting of her head, which so enchanted Mr. Germain, was of a piece with ostrich strategy. If she could have run and hidden underground she would have done it. For what can that word love from such a man mean but marriage? I beg the lady's pardon for leaving her hand in so embarrassing a case, her head so downcast, her breath so troublesome—but her difficulties must be faced.

Marriage, as she had been taught this world's economy, is the be-all and end-all for women here. It is almost a disgrace, and quite a disaster for a girl to slip into womanhood and not be wedded. The enormous seriousness, then, of the affair! All men talk to women of love, and a girl had need be quick to discern which kind is the staple, which kind is aimed at lip-service, which at life-service. There will be both to reckon with; the two rarely coincide. Many a young man will seek the flower of a girl's lips, sup of it at ease, and content himself—ah, and content her, too; whereas your serious wooer, with his eye upon comfort, a foothold, a mother for his children and a stay for himself, may well have other things to think of—a promotion, a partnership, a chance abroad, a legacy, a desirable corner house. Care will tighten his lips too hard for kissing. The future will be all that he reads after in your eyes. If he kisses, it will be by custom as likely as not; don't I say that he will have other things to think of? Now, Mr. Germain had not kissed Mary, though, to be sure, he had spoken of his love. And yet—and yet—yes, he wanted to marry her. Frightened? Yes, she was frightened; but she was full of thought, too.

She knew very well that her ways were not those of the world above her, the world of the upper air, where Honourable Mrs. Germains, Cantacutes, Duplessis, and the like talked familiarly together of parties and public affairs. There, as she saw the heights the women were so obviously desirable that there was nothing for them to do but pick up their happiness as they chose, and as their due. There could surely be no anxiety there, no whispered debates over what he meant, or had looked, or was thinking. Their lives were full to brimming point from girlhood up; everything fell into their laps, or could be had for money. Nothing surprised her more in the lives of her betters than the frequency with which they bought—except the case of the transaction. One even paid for work, if one happened to be in the mood to work—as when Miss de Speyne, desiring to paint, hired an artist to go about with her, open a white umbrella here and there, and paint beside her. Grey, grey and hard seemed her outlook beside theirs, when (as now) she was driven to compare them. And here—O wonderful fate!—was this brimming, crowded life opening to her; to her, Mary Middleham, who had worked for pence a year, and fended for herself, and had adventures from her seventeenth to this her twenty-fifth summer. Terrible, wonderful thing! She had neither a word to say, nor a connected thought. She wanted to hide her burning cheeks, felt that she must never look up again—and all this while Mr. Germain held her cold hand. It felt dead to her: and what must he be thinking of her?

He was very patient. "Well, my dear, well!" was the note he harped upon, and (how he could read you!) "Poor child! So I have terrified you." This

XI

COOL COMFORT

SATURDAY'S wonders, Sunday thrills—with her declared lover monumentally in the Rectory pew and his relatives all unconscious that they were soon to be hers (hers, Mary Middleham's: *O altitudo!*)—did not release her, in her own mind, from the promise of Sunday afternoon. Not only had she promised, not only had she something to tell him, a solid base for her feet from which to regard him, and a sanctuary in which to hide, from which to emerge at will, ready for any encounter; not only so, but she must put herself right with him. He had seen her, must have seen her, in a delicate situation—nothing to him, of course, but somehow everything to her. She could not, she said, afford that he should deem her a girl of the sort—to be kissed in a doorway by anybody, gentleman or no gentleman. There were reasons—special reasons for it; and since, as the fact was, these reasons did not now seem as cogent as they had yesterday, there was nothing for it but to cry them over and over to herself. "Engaged to be married—engaged to be married—to Mr. Germain—to Mr. Germain of Southover House. And he loves me dearly—and I love him." So she pedalled and sang.

Racing with her thoughts, the bicycle took her to the common of Mere that blazing Sunday afternoon. His eyes looked up from their work, twinkled and laughed at her. "So it's you, then! I thought you wouldn't come." He was mending the sole of a shoe, and resumed his cheerful tap-tapping directly he had greeted her.

She stood leaning on her bicycle, watching his work. Her new estate sat in full possession of her eyes.

"Yes, I've come. I couldn't come earlier."

He paused, hammer in air. "It was as well you didn't. I've been out lunching."

She knew that very well, and with any other man would have pretended that she did not. Some pretty fishing would have followed—with him out of the question.

"At the Park?" she said—turning up the statement into a question by habit.

"Precisely there," said he, and returned to his shoe. No fishing in such waters as his—but he looked up again presently with a laugh in his eyes. "I met your Mr. Germain," he told her—and she flamed.

"I wanted to tell you—I felt that I must. I am— I was with him when you——"

He nodded over his shoe leather. "So I supposed."

"That was Mr. Germain—you know——"

"I know. I recognized him. I had been to reconnoitre the Park——"

She could not, perhaps, have accounted to herself for her next question. "Do you like Miss de Speyne?"

He frankly considered it for a while, looking at the questioner without discomfort—to himself at least. "Yes. Yes, I think I do. She's a fine young woman and she's simple. She's herself. Yes, I like her very much. She can paint flowers—nothing else. But she paints flowers well." So much for the Honourable Hertha de Speyne.

"May I sit down?" Mary was quite at her ease again. He jumped up with apologies, and brought her cushions. Bingo came up, wagging his back, and, being caressed, sat up stiffly beneath her hand. She watched her friend fill his pipe and collected herself for her affair. Then she lowered her eyes, and began, hardening her voice.

"I came because I wanted your opinion, as I hoped—I mean as I thought I possibly might. You remember that I said I should like to talk to you? Well, I didn't know then—for certain—what I should have to say. But—" She stopped there.

"But now you do? Is that it?"

"Yes. Shall you think it strange of me?"

"I don't know—but it's very unlikely. If I do I'll tell you. Go on."

"It's about Mr. Germain. Do you remember that I told you—he'd been kind to me?"

His eyes were narrow, but upon her, critically upon her. He smoked slowly, as if he enjoyed every fibre of the weed on fire.

"Yes, I remember."

"He was so kind—he went so out of his way to be kind that I was puzzled. I could not help fancying——"

"Naturally. Well?"

She plunged. "He has asked me to marry him."

Her friend took his pipe out of his mouth, looked long at it, and put it back again.

"I saw that he had—yesterday." He might have seen pride shine in her eyes at that compliment. But, instead of looking for that, he asked, "And is he going to?"

"I don't know," she answered, pondering.

"But does he think he is?"

She fondled Bingo, who threw up his head, eyed her gratefully and accepted the compliment. Then she answered him.

"Yes—I believe he does." During the ensuing pause their eyes met for a moment.

"He's very much in love with the idea," said the gentleman-tinker. "He was highly uplifted to-day —anybody could have guessed." He added, as if to himself, "It may do. It sometimes does."

She considered this, then threw up her head and was eloquent. "It won't do—it can't. That makes me unhappy, instead of happy. I know that it is not right—whatever you may say of—of there being no classes. I feel that there *are* classes, more than enough, perhaps; but there they are and we can't help them. Whatever you may say about specimens in boxes, Mr. Germain is a gentleman, and my father is not; and his first wife was a lady—a Lady Diana Something—and his second, if it's me, won't be—but just a little ignorant person who has worked for her living since she was sixteen, and seen all sorts of people—and—and—done all sorts of things. No, no, it can't be right—for him, at any rate. How am I to satisfy him, try as I will? Why, there's Mrs. James at the Rectory—she terrifies me. I feel like a lump of earth beside her—and she likes me to— she looks and looks down at me until I do. And I fight against it—I try to meet her—I try to be myself, and to feel that I am as good as she is—and all the time I know I'm not. And yet—he's extremely kind—nobody could have spoken more gently than he did. He made me cry—he did, you know. I couldn't help it—and I had no answer for him and so—and so he thinks that I shall marry him. But I don't know whether I dare—I promise you I don't."

He watched her gravely, nodding his head from time to time; and at the end he smiled doubtfully.

"Well," he said, "and *I* don't know whether you dare. I don't know, you know, but I should say that you could dare most things you had set your heart on."

Her eyes quickened. "My heart is not set on it. I was very excited yesterday—any girl in my position would be—oh, most wonderful! But—if I could— if I dared, I should run away. I promise you."

He regarded her kindly. "Well, then," he said, "Run." She stared—their eyes met—hers fell first.

"No, no. I mustn't. He expects me now—besides, he has— No, I belong to him now—if he wants me."

The gentleman-tinker got up—appeared to be annoyed. He took a stride or two up and down the road. "This is against conscience—good God, it's against Nature. It's why I loathe marriage, why I would never marry. It's all feudal—it's the law of Real Property. You are in a market—he buys you with a kind word and a— Look here now—" and he faced her, frowning. "Will nothing teach you your value—will nothing give you respect for yourself?" He turned away abruptly. "I beg your pardon. I've no right to talk to you like this."

She forgot to be involved—forgot that she was involved—in his condemnation. "Please talk to me —please to make me understand," she said, but he wanted a good deal of persuasion. No, no. It has nothing to do with him; he should only make mischief—had made too much already; and, said he, finally, "I can't afford it. I am rather prone, I believe, to get interested in other people's affairs—and it interrupts my own confoundedly."

"I'm very sorry," she said, prettily contrite. He bit his cheek. "Not your fault, of course—all mine. I got interested in you when I found you in the wire —highly romantic that sort of thing. And—and— so it's gone on. Well—" He looked at her anxiously. "Well, I shall do harm, I'm certain; but I'll tell you what I think if you insist on it." She clapped her hands, glowed and sparkled like a diamond. She looked bewitchingly pretty.

"Please, please! I won't speak a word until you've done."

He sat, and began slowly.

"I stick to my opinion of classes, of course. You aren't in a position to judge; you've never had a ghost of a chance. As far as men go, there are only two classes—men who can behave and men who can't. My father taught me when I was a boy to call all men men, and all women ladies. There was the man who swept the crossing, and the man who sat on the Bench; but I remember that I got into a row for talking about the 'woman' who sold matches. 'All women are ladies unless you know to the contrary,' said my father. 'Don't you ever forget that!' And I never did. If you'll forgive me, there's nothing in what you say about your own unworthiness and Germain's magnanimity except one thing—and that is, that you, who have everything to gain, are the last person to admit what is so obviously true. And you are not quite honest. You don't fear yourself really—you are confident in your inmost heart that you can learn what you suppose to be solemn duties. But—" He collected himself for his But, while she hung her detected head.

"But he, mind you, is persuaded—and it's *you* who are helping him to believe—that he is a superior person doing you an enormous honour. He calls it kindness, of course, and so do you—oh, so do you! and that's what he's in love with mostly—the idea of exalting you, putting you on a pedestal, kneeling, making sacrifice, burning incense. He's full of it—

he was trembling with it to-day—and he'll do it, I'm certain, and then retire into his inner chamber and beat his breast and cry to his soul, 'How lovely she is—how sensitive to these wonderful honours! I put her there, O God! I did it—under Thee! Lord, I thank Thee for this glorious work which is mine.'   I suppose you think I'm a maniac.   I'm frightfully sane. . . ."

"He'll be as happy as a king, like his betters before him, Cophetua I., Cophetua II.—the whole dynasty.   That's his point of view, you know, and it's not a bad one.   It's very artistic.   Old Tennyson saw that.   But before you lend yourself to it—a girl like—well, any girl you please—I do think you should ask yourself where *you* come in.   How much worship can you stand?   How long can you be sensitive to benefits and honours?   How long before they become matters of course?   How long before you want the real thing?   Because I need not tell you that there *is* a real thing——"

Had he not broken off here she would not have met his eyes—nor he hers.   The saying would have been merged in the general drift of his harangue, which was serious enough.   But she caught at the break, caught at the words, caught at the sense, looked at him seriously, looked at him full.   His eyes, being upon her, met hers, and held them.   She was confounded.   That moment of interconsciousness was fully charged: it is much to his credit that he slipped out without abruptness.

He took a turn up and down the road before he went on.

"A man will go through life possessed with an idea, and be absolutely happy with it. Don't have any fears on his account. It is all that he wants: the woman's only business is to lend herself to it. But we're considering the woman—and there's this great difference. They don't like ideas at all. They like things—that they can touch, stroke, handle, nurse, wash and dress. If you find such things, you are all right. But if you don't——"

And then he stopped—in spite of her. She tried him with a "Well, what then?" but could get nothing more from him.

"Oh, I hope you will. Let's hope so," was all he would say.

She nursed her chin with her hand; he, at his length beside her, plucked at the turf. Too many confidences had passed for her to be reticent now. "You say you will never marry," she began.

"Never," he said. "The state's impossible, wrong from the beginning. It puts the woman hopelessly in the wrong. It's monstrous."

"Then you think— Yes, I believe you are right. At any rate, I mustn't let Mr. Germain——" .

He sat up. "Look here," he said. "Germain will make you a very good husband. He's a true man."

She was busy with Bingo, to Bingo's quiet satisfaction. "Yes, I'm sure of that. But——"

Her tongue was tied, and so now was his. The ensuing silence was not comfortable to either, and the instinct of a good girl made her end it at any price. Rising sedately, she held out her hand.

"Good-bye—and thank you very much. You have made me think."

He laughed as he shook hands. "You have made me think, too. Good-bye. All happiness."

She did not reply to that, but said, "We meet again, I hope."

"Sure to," he said. "This is an island." Then she must needs go.

Of the two of them the man was the more perturbed—but he had his remedy. After a frowning quarter-hour he was up and packing his tent. Within the hour he was on the road.

With her, no revolt against what was to be. There is no revolt visible under the sun for the poor. When Mr. Germain called the next morning to bid her farewell she received him with all the virginal airs of the consciously possessed. He measured her fourth finger. A pretty ceremony.

XII

ALARUMS

REVOLT is, as it always has been, within easy reach of the great; but a Rector's wife should attend upon her lord. The Hon. Mrs. Germain watched her James's eyebrow, waiting for the lift. It came, and her cry broke from her. "James, James, this cannot be possible!" She saw her fair realm in earthquake and eclipse.

The Rector, no less disturbed, could not for the life of him avoid his humour. "Alas, my dear"— one eyebrow made a hoop in his forehead—"all things are possible to amorous man."

"Amorous!" she whistled the word. "John— and that minx! You use horrible words."

"Hardly so, my dear. Not horrible in a man's regard for his wife. The state is sanctioned."

She was beyond his quibbles. "What are we to do? Heavens and earth, what can we do?"

He eyed his brother's letter ruefully. "Upon my word," he said, "this is a facer. I could have believed anything of any man sooner than this of him. Old John! Exactly double her age—and she a quiet little mouse of a girl out of a cottage. Woodbine

Cottage, eh? That's it, you know. Woodbine Cottage and white muslin have done it. Do you remember the valentines of our youth—gauffred edges, a pathway to a porch—the linked couple, and the little god in the air, pink as a shell? White muslin—fatal wear! He sees her so to all eternity; enskied and sainted, in muslin and a sash! Confound it, Constantia, I feel old."

She was beyond his whimsies. "You may be thankful that you do. This appears to me disgusting. Have we used him so ill that he should slap our faces?"

The Rector indulged his eyebrows again. "Diana!" he said.

She did not defend that dead lady, but even another Lady Diana seemed more tolerable to Mrs. James. *Pecca fortiter*, she could have said, had she had a head for tags. Lady Diana, sinning *de race*, would have been intelligible, say, to the Cantacutes. But here was no sin, but merely a squalid enchantment. A doting gentleman, a peering little nobody in muslin— How should this be put, say, to the Cantacutes? Aberration? Chivalry? Romance? Never Romance, precisely because that was just what it was —pitiful romance. James had hit it off exactly; it was the washy, facile romance of a sixpenny valentine, of a thing that housemaids drink with their eyes. Saponaceous—Heavens and earth! Mrs. James lifted her hands, and let them fall to her lap. "I simply cannot hold up my head in the village," she said. "James think of the Cantacutes."

"Why on earth should I think of the Cantacutes?"
He was testy under his trouble. "I have my brother
to think of. He's been hasty over this—which is
most unlike him—and secret as well. I had no notion any such thing was going on, not the least in the
world."

It was Mrs. James's duty to confess that some
notion ought to have been hers. And she did confess. "It so happens that I was speaking to him of
this girl the night we dined at the Park. He told me
that he was interesting himself in her and I asked
him to say something about Tristram."

"About Tristram?" says the Rector sharply.
"What about Tristram, pray?"

She could not but remember former warnings.
"I think you will do me the justice, James. You
have been told that Tristram has chosen to amuse
himself with her. Who has not? I remember telling you about it, when, as usual, you laughed at me.
I begged John to influence the girl—to induce her
to respect herself—and with this result!" The Rector pushed his chair away.

"You speak more truly than you know," he said,
rose and took a turn about the room. "Now I understand the haste. He had been hovering, poor,
foolish fellow—singeing his grey wings; but it was
you, Constantia, drove him to plunge. Take my
word for it. Dear, dear, dear, this is really a great
bore. I don't know what to do, upon my word I
don't."

"I shall speak to the girl, of course," said Mrs.

James, gathering up letters and keys. It is doubtful
if her husband heard her. He had stepped through
the window into the garden before she had risen.
"The Rector's Walk," a pleached alley of nut trees,
received him; for more than an hour he might have
been observed pacing it, with lowered head and
hands behind his back. But Mrs. Germain went
about her duties of the day with tight lips and eyes
aglitter. At intervals her anguish betrayed itself in
cries. "Monstrous! Monstrous!"

To her it was monstrous, for she saw the girl without glamour, standing amid the wreckage of a fair
realm—a little governess, wickedly demure. The
Germain banner was rent, the Germain character
blotted; that carefully contrived dual empire which
she shared with the Cantacutes was threatened; her
authority as a county lady, as Rector's wife, toppling,
her throne wanting a leg. She saw herself pitied,
her husband's family the object of lifted brows. And
she had been a loyal wife, and knew it, because she
had honestly admired the marks of race in the Germains. Herself a Telfer, she was of that famous
Norman house which lost first blood at Hastings;
and she never forgot it, least of all when she had
married into the Germains, who were county and
good blood, but not noble. She remembered, she
always remembered that—but she was a loyal wife.
Without and within, he and she were a strong contrast—he frosty, dry, and deliberate, she fiery, impulsive, storm-driven, not above the aid of tears; he
lean and pale, she a plump woman and a pink. His

instinct was to approve at first blush, hers to disapprove. They were good friends, and had never been more; there were no children. That had been a grievance of hers until she got into the way of saying that the Germains were a dwindling race, and—"look at poor John Germain!" I wish the reader to note the subtle change from complaint to complacency in Mrs. James's outlook. It marks her character. To be a barren wife through no fault of your own and to take comfort in saying that your husband comes of a dwindling stock shows that you have an eye for outline in a family. It is rather like excusing your Black Wyandottes, which give you no breakfast eggs—"Yes, but that's the mark of the breed." So here—"either I have children, or my husband is no Germain." Here was strong character exhibited; and all may be forgiven to strength. But weakness—mere dotage—mere desire; a landed gentleman of fifty and a girl in muslin—"Monstrous! Monstrous!" cried Mrs. James in her bitterness.

When Mary, home from The Sanctuary, heard the click of the wicket, and the swish of a silk petticoat over the flagstones, she knew what was coming upon her. Her colour fled, and returned redoubled, and a scare showed in her quick eyes. In a moment she called up her defences—her more than one letter—she had received a third that morning. "I shall see your father," that said, "an hour after you receive this, my Mary. If I know anything of his daughter he will not fail to confirm the signal trust which she has shown me." She had not been very sure what he meant by "signal trust"; it must certainly be something which any girl might be proud to have. And she had something more wonderful than a letter —a ring, the most splendid she had ever seen—a great sapphire set in a lake of brilliants. She glanced at it now as, hearing the lady at the door, she slipped it off and put it in her pocket. Mrs. James knocked, like a postman; and with a wild heart Mary went to meet her enemy in the gate.

"Ah, good-evening, Mary. May I come in? Thank you." She preceded her dependant into the little parlour, sat in the chair which had most the similitude of a throne, and began at once upon her subject.

"I have called to see you in consequence of a letter which the Rector received this morning from Mr. Germain. May I inquire if you guess—? No, indeed, I see that I need not." The girl's face told the tale; her eyes were cast down; inquiry of the sort was absurd. "I think, Mary, that you have strange ideas; I do, indeed; and am sorry to have to add that I know where you have obtained them." But Mary had spirit, it seemed.

"I obtained them from Mr. Germain," she said, with a certain defiance which may have been very natural, but had been better away. "I obtained them from him. They were not mine, I assure you."

Mrs. Germain opened her mouth and shut it with a snap. She opened it again a little way to say, "The thing is impossible," and another snap followed.

"So I told Mr. Germain," said Mary.

"My impression is very strong," continued Mrs. James, ignoring interruption, "that you have misunderstood Mr. Germain's kindness, and strangely so. That being the case——" Mary's eyes flashed.

"I beg pardon, Mrs. Germain, but that is not the case. Mr. Germain has gone to see my parents to-day. He writes me word——"

"You will kindly allow me to finish. I believe that you misunderstood something Mr. Germain may have said to you—some advice, or inquiry, or offer of help; that he may have seen your error and regretted it while he was too chivalrous to undeceive you. I consider that you may be preparing a great unhappiness for yourself and for him, and I am in a position to say——"

"I beg your pardon, Mrs. Germain," said Mary, "but nobody is in a position to say anything to me of this but Mr. Germain himself."

Now this was so obviously true that even Mrs. James accepted it. She had been too hasty, and while she was swallowing her chagrin Mary took her opportunity.

"I must tell you, please, that you cannot be more surprised than I was when Mr. Germain spoke to me as he did. I had never dreamed of such a thing; it is not likely that I should. He had been all that's kind to me ever since the school-treat—even now I can hardly believe that any one could be so kind; but when he—when he spoke to me—asked me if I could care for him—in that way—I vow to you I could not answer him. I was most stupid—I was

confused and could not collect my thoughts. And
I never did collect them," she cried with a sudden
burst of confession, "and never answered him at all
—except by crying, which any girl would have done,
I think; and then he—well, then he k——"

Mrs. James shut her eyes tight. "I know what
you are going to say. No! no! Be silent, I beg."

Mary put her hand to her throat, as if she was
being choked. Her eyes shone like jet. "I hope
that you will be just to me, Mrs. Germain, I do hope
so. I know that you put all the blame on me, but it
is unfair to do that. What could I do? If he spoke
to me kindly, must I not answer kindly? If he came
to see me, how could I refuse to see him? If he invited me to walk with him, what could I say, or do?
And then—when he asked me, Did I care for him—
and—and—oh, I must say it!—kissed——"

"Ah!" said Mrs. Germain, with a spasm. "Oh,
wicked, wicked!"

Mary flamed. "I am not wicked, Mrs. Germain,
and I must ask you not to call me so. Mr. Germain
would not like it at all. You cannot believe him to
be wicked; and if he did what he did he had good
reason. And now I will tell you that I never answered his question, and have not known how to
answer it."

"Answer it, girl! You prevaricate. Answer it—
in the face of his letter to my husband!"

"Mr. Germain has been more than kind," said
Mary, losing ground, "and—and——"

"And Mr. Duplessis has been more than kind, I

believe," said Mrs. James—and her words were knives. The girl quailed. "Pray, how much more kindness is my family to show you?"

Mary was now very cold. "One member of it," she said, "will show me none—will not show me even justice. Mr. Duplessis has no claim——"

"Claim!" cried the great lady, red as fire, "what claim should he wish to make? I think you have lost your senses." She may well have lost patience, courage, and a good sense. She stamped her foot.

"I wish you would leave me alone, Mrs. Germain. You are cruel to me, and unjust. I have done you no harm—no, but always my duty, and you know that very well. You drive me into corners—you make me say things—I am very unhappy—please leave me." She covered her eyes to hide the tears which pricked her.

Mrs. James was not to be melted by such a device. "If you are to be impertinent, I shall certainly leave you," she said. "This matter, however, cannot be left as it is. The Rector must see you about it. Good-evening."

But when the unaccountable Rector received the report from his wife he was pleased to show temper. "I think you have acted foolishly, Constantia, and more—I think you have acted with great want of consideration, I had almost said with want of respect for my brother. You have read his letter; you know how he stands towards Mary; and you rate her as if she were a servant caught in a fault. Really, that won't do. I must make amends. Preposterous!

That my brother's affianced wife should be treated
like a kitchenmaid! You have no right—no earthly
right—to say to her what you would not dream of
saying to my brother. Heavens! to John Germain!
head of one of the best families in England! Tst,
tst! I am very vexed."

He must have been, for he went early to the cottage
and asked for Mary. When she appeared before
him, flushed and with all her defences out, he held
out his hand to her, drew her towards him and kissed
her. "So we are to know you in a new capacity, my
dear," he said. "I shall be very ready for that."
Her tears gathered; one brimmed over and fell, but
did not scald.

"Oh, Mr. Germain—" she began—and ended
there with a choke.

"My dear, I'll tell you this—you have won a true
man. I know my brother better than you do, at
present, and you may take my word for that."

"Thank you, thank you," was all that she could
say.

"One thing more: you will be welcome at the
Rectory. You mustn't take anything that has been
said to you amiss. You know that when we are
taken aback sometimes we don't always—well, I'll
ask you. Has anybody ever made you jump? Eh?
Somebody has? Very well, weren't you rather cross
for a minute? Confess that you were. My dear, we
all are; but it don't mean anything."

"No, no, indeed. Oh, Mr. Germain, I don't
know what to do about all this!"

"Your duty, my dear, to God and man. It'll be before you every day: all you have to do is to take it up."

"Yes, yes, I know. But—Mr. Germain, I'm frightened—really. I'm ignorant and stupid—and of course I'm different from——"

"You've a pretty way of confessing it, at any rate," said the Rector. "It will all come right, I hope. You are very quick, I can tell—you'll learn your lesson in no time. I know you are a charming young lady, and believe a good one. There's not much more than that in any one that I've ever seen in these parts. Now don't be offended with me if I say that you are going to have a good husband, and ask you to deserve him."

"Oh, Mr. Germain!"—her tears fell freely—"I do want to be good—I do mean to try!"

"Bless you, my dear, I'm quite sure of that," said he, and gave her another kiss.

He told his wife that evening definitely that they must make the best of it, and gave her to understand that John's wife must be taken at John's valuation. If John chose to marry a kitchenmaid, that kitchenmaid was *ipso facto* on the Germain level; so also if John had selected an archduchess. A Germain could pick up or pull down, said the Rector in effect. But he also announced that he should go to town on the morrow—which weakened his decree.

So he did, and was away two days—an interval of time during which Mary went grimly about her duties and Mrs. Germain faced the problem of the

Cantacutes. This lady may be pitied, who felt her crown slipping and throne rocking on its degrees. Her loyalty to the family into which she had been married was sapped; she did not see how Germain character was to be admired if it betrayed a Germain into such a vagary. Her husband, her temperate, frosty James, was involved; for the first time in her life she was tempted to work against him. She could do that, mind you; she had the weapon to her hand, a double-edged tool—Tristram. A hint to Tristram at Pau and he would be here—and once here, should he look upon Mary as she believed he would, as the lion on a lamb printed by his paw, why, what chance had John Germain against him? That villainy she could practise if she chose; but she knew it was a villainy, and that she was no villain. Then there was another way, not villainous—nay, was it not a duty? She could tell John Germain what she knew of Tristram and hint at more than she knew. A Germain would shiver at such a tarnish on his ideal —she could see John shut his eyes as the spasm passed over him; but there was this difficulty about it, that she could not write to him without her husband's knowledge—nay, without his approbation— whereas, what more natural than that she should deplore with her cousin Laura Duplessis this miserable state of affairs? Mrs. James was no villain; she was merely a proud woman touched on a raw. Her security, her comfort, her authority, her self-esteem were all threatened by an act of dotage; what else was this infatuation of John Germain's, pray?

And there are sophistries to help the very best of us.
Had there been nothing between Tristram and
Mary, Mrs. Duplessis would have been invited to
sympathize; and there *was* nothing, after all. Tristram, with his high connexions, his talents, and his
superb air—and a little sly teacher! The thing was
absurd! Fully convinced of its absurdity, Mrs.
James marched down to the Cottage, and found her
cousin Duplessis arranged on a sofa with a white
lace mantilla over her head; her hand-bell in easy
call, and a smelling-bottle attached to her wrist by
a little chain.

Mrs. Duplessis had been handsome, and remembered it. Everything about her person reminded her
of that—her languor, her elegance, her thin hands,
her fine complexion, her tall son. "How I survived
the birth of that great boy passes my comprehension.
My nerves, you know! My dear Hector, all fire as
he was, had the tact of a woman. 'M'amie,' he said,
'never again; or I accuse myself of murder. Hence-
forward I am a monk.' He kept his word, but it
killed him. Do not men die for women? My poor,
brave Hector!" Apart from these tender reminiscences, she had her poverty to cherish, to tinge with
dignity, to show burnished—with a lovely *patina* like
old lacquer. "We live wretchedly, as you can see,
my dear soul; but we pay our way and hold our
heads up. We only owe to ourselves, and are indul-
gent creditors. Tristram, I suppose will marry:
il doit se ranger, vraiment. But he says that we can
afford leisure—our only luxury! The good Canta-

cutes are most kind, and Hertha a really charming
girl. . . . Why is it that young men cannot see
where their fortune lies? Cynicism? Arrogance?
Ingratitude? I ask myself these questions."

She was enormously interested in the news, and
gratified. "My poor soul, what a blow! John Germain, of all humdrum persons in the world—and the
girl not even pretty, you say. Clever, though. Have
you broken it to Emily Cantacute? I don't envy
you that task."

"It's not done yet," said Mrs. James grimly.

"Oh, my dear, but it is," her cousin replied acutely.
"John Germain is just the man to be in opposition.
Pride, you know. We all have that. He would call
it chivalry."

"Do you know how far Tristram might be concerned in this?" Mrs. James inquired shortly; Mrs.
Duplessis narrowed her eyes and slowly shut them.

"Tristram never gives confidences," she said, in
a carefully fatigued voice. "On such a matter I had
rather he did not."

Mrs. James would have none of this.

"My dear Laura, we are alone. I think I know
Tristram well enough to say that he has interested
himself in the girl. No doubt he has flattered her; I
think she has been grateful. It would not be surprising
if he were unprepared for such a change of affairs."

"On the contrary," said Mrs. Duplessis, "judging
by what you seem to think of her, I should imagine
that he might be prepared for anything. To be sure,
there is John Germain——"

" John Germain and Tristram are not good friends;
I happen to know."

"Ah," said Mrs. Duplessis, "that throws some
light."

"Perhaps it does," Mrs. James returned; "but
I should not like to say where it throws it." She had
a shrewd suspicion that she and her cousin might be
in the beam. There was a taint in all this.

The Rector came back that night greatly bothered. More than once in the course of the evening
he threw up his hands. "My poor, good brother!
Heaven help us all!"

"I found him inalterably fixed," he told his wife,
"and perfectly complacent. His serenity confounded
me, put me to shame. He sees his happiness as
clearly before him as you see his misery. He loves the
child for the very things which you dislike in her.
You say that she is common, and I cannot contradict
you. He says that simplicity can grace any station.
Ignorant we call her—he says, It shall be my privilege
to teach. You call her sly; he protests. But so is
the hunted hare. He says that the thought of a
young girl struggling single-handed with a world of
satyrs from her sixteenth year freezes his blood.
You class her with them: all satyrs together, you say.
Constantia, I tell you that his folly is more noble
than our wisdom. I boast myself a Christian, but
what am I in truth if not a very Pharisee? 'Lord,
I thank Thee that I am not as one of these'! Is
this Christian?"

"It seems to me common gratitude," said his wife.

"Pray, did you tell him that the girl was compromised?" The Rector frowned.

"Naturally, I did not, since I neither knew it, nor believed it. Compromised, Constantia! That is a dangerous word to use. That involves a good name."

"It does indeed, James. It involves ours. I tell you that the girl is stale." She might as well have shot him—she had never done herself more fatal mischief.

He seemed hardly able to look at her, nor did she know him when he did. "Do you dare speak so of any woman born? To the brother of this girl's—do you dare? You have shocked me beyond expression."

She was certainly frightened—but she had her duty to do. "I am sorry to have displeased you. I spoke advisedly. I hope that I always do that."

His pride was stinging him. He spoke now as if he were her enemy—coldly, as if he hardly knew the woman.

"If, as I am bound to believe, you are speaking with knowledge which I do not possess, I must ask you to let me share it. This is a very serious matter both to John and to Mary. With whom do you say she is compromised?"

Two and two make four, of course—but two shadows and two cannot make four plump facts. Mrs. James knew that she had gone too far. She had little but suspicion behind her. "I think that Tristram has made love to her," she said, and rehearsed the scene of the garden. As she put it now, the Rector made a wry face.

"This, at its worst, is discreditable to Tristram.

I see your point now. Mary, you suggest, has had experiences. All girls have them, I suppose, and certainly are not always the worse for them. You must have something worse than this to excuse your strong words."

Mrs. James had. She poured out all the garner of a year's eye-harvest, this young man and that young man—a moonlight encounter—God knows what not. And—"Mrs. Seacox told me," she said, "that Mary used to be a great deal in the company of young Rudd. She had seen them kissing." A sudden flood of disgust engulfed the Rector of Misperton Brand. He turned shortly on his heel and paced the carpet. Midway back he stopped.

"I can't tell you how I sicken at all this gossip— this traffic of nods and winks. It amounts to little at its worst. I will have no more of it. It is my duty to believe the best of my neighbours; I have not the eyes of Mrs. Seacox, nor, I hope, her understanding. I believe Mary to be a modest and virtuous young woman, and you have told me nothing to vary that opinion. Such matters—Matters! they are nothing but nasty surmises—are intensely distasteful to me; I will hear no more." He went into his study and shut the door. All the Germains were squeamish.

Rather hard on Mrs. James. And so was felt to be the result of her elaborate disclosure to the Cantacutes. This was that Hertha de Speyne went down in person and invited the girl to tea—and that Lady Cantacute called her "a nice little thing."

XIII

WHAT THEY SAID AT HOME

In obedience to one of those traditions before which the British parent lies prone, the moment that Mary Middleham was asked for and granted, the utmost care was taken that she should see as little as possible of the man with whom she was to spend her life. Spotless must she be brought out by the contractors, spotless be transferred to the purchaser. She was sent for from home, and home she went after a month of clearing up. There had been much to do; good-byes to say, some to avoid saying, if so it might be. Mr. Nunn, making her a presentation and a speech before his assembled seed-plots, also made her cry; but Mrs. James Germain, in the course of an icy tea-party, whereat the girl was present, unexplained, unaccounted for, and ignored, until the late entry of the Rector on the scene very nearly made her defiant. She had a spirit of her own —and there are ways of showing "persons their place" which spirited persons may not endure. At that tea-party—under Mrs. James's politeness and the chill insolence of Mrs. Duplessis—the prosperity of Mr. John Germain's love was like that of a bubble on a tobacco pipe—its iris globe throbbed towards inward collapse. His brother saved it to soar; he was charming—easy, homely, cool, and obviously glad to have her there. Touched profoundly, she became at once buoyant—as all young people must be if they are to live—and meek. When the company was gone he had her into his library, and discussed her affair as a settled, happily settled, thing—ending, rectorwise, with a little homily, in which he delicately but unmistakably showed her that she was going into a very new world and had better go in clean raiment. "Let there be no drawbacks to your future happiness, my dear, of your own providing. Marriage is the happiest of all states so long as it is a clear bargain. That is not always possible; with two people of an age much may be taken for granted. You are young, and your husband is not. He is wiser than you are and asks nothing better than to help you. Make him your friend before he makes you his wife; you will never regret it. And you may begin, I believe, by making a friend of his brother."

She replied brokenly, lamely, but she was deeply grateful—and he knew it. Atop of that came Miss de Speyne—the Honourable Hertha de Speyne—in a fast dog-cart to her cottage door, with an invitation to tea at the Park. She went—and had the sense to go in her simplest. Dress, manner, and looks appealed—Here am I, the girl as he found me, as I pleased him. Make what you please of me—if you please. Lady Cantacute could make no mistake in a matter of the sort—her manners were as fine as her

instincts. His lordship, even more finely, varied
nothing from his habits; and his daughter could not.
There was no company, and all went well; after tea,
better. Miss de Speyne invited her to walk; they sat
in the rose-garden. By-and-by came a question. "I
think you know a friend of mine—Mr. Senhouse?"
This had to be explained. Mr. Senhouse, it appeared, was the gentleman-tinker of Mere Common.
Mary sparkled as she admitted her acquaintance,
and after that all was well indeed. His acts and
opinions were debated. Miss de Speyne thought him
cynical, and hinted at some unhealed wound; Miss
Middleham could not admit that. She believed him
sound, if not spear-proof.

"He spoke to me of my engagement, but not as
anybody else would have done."

"Did he like it?"

Mary blushed. "I could hardly say. He spoke
very highly of Mr. Germain. He had met him here,
he told me."

"Yes. I wanted them to meet," Miss de Speyne
said—and Mary wondered.

"He told me, in the course of conversation, that
he should never marry"—she said, presently; but
Miss de Speyne, older than her new friend, held her
peace.

At parting, the tall, splendid young woman clasped
hands with her warmly. "Good-bye. It was nice of
you to come. I wish I had known you before—but
we're such fools in the country."

Mary said, "I hope you won't forget me after

I'm—" She felt delicate about this astounding marriage. But Miss Hertha reassured her. "When you've settled down, ask me and I shall come and see you. Of course, you'll be asked here—but you needn't come unless you like. This was bracing; she began to believe in herself, to say that she had nothing to fear, and to believe it. But she found out her mistake within a little, when, in mid-August, she left Misperton Brand, crossed London, and found her sister Jinny awaiting her on the Blackheath platform.

Jinny, the tall, the pert, the very fair, strikingly attired, despising all mankind and ignoring all womankind, sailed to meet her, intending to be patroness still. It was soon to be seen that her claim was not disputed. "Well, Molly, so here you are. Hand out your traps. And, for Heaven's sake, child, put your hat straight. Do you want all the world to know that you're engaged?"

Mary laughed, her hands to her hat. "It's all right, my dear," she said. "I've come down alone."

"If you'd come down with your Mr. Germain I should never have accused *him* of it, I assure you." Miss Jinny tossed her head. "Too much the gentleman by half. Is that all you have? The rest in the van, I suppose. Well, child, you look well enough, I must say. So he agrees with you?" They kissed each other on both cheeks.

In the fly, Jinny enlarged upon the recent visit of Mr. Germain. "My dear! he fairly scared poor father. It was, 'Yes, sir,' 'no, sir,' from him all the

time—and 'any arrangements you wish, sir.' I don't
see that sort of talk myself—but father was always
a worm. What he made of me I really can't say—
you know my way with gentlemen—take me or leave
me alone, is my rule. Well, he left me alone, and I
managed to get over that, as you see. I'm still the
same height in my stockings. So you mean to be
'an old man's darling,' Molly? Every one to her
taste, I suppose."

"Oh, Jinny, he's not old."

"He could be your father, my dear—easily."

"He's not going to be, I assure you."

"Well, we'll see. I should hope not, of course.
One thing's as plain as my nose; your people won't
see much of you when you're boxed up with that
old——".

"Jinny, please!"

"Oh, if you want me to tell falsehoods, my dear,
I'll do my best to oblige you. I'll call him young to
myself until it comes easy. Practice makes perfect,
they say. Why, here we are! This horse must have
the glanders or something. Perhaps he thought Mr.
Germain was after you. There's a lot of sense in
brute beasts." All this, which shows the rights of
elder, was meekly received.

Home-coming was nevertheless a sort of triumph.
The younger girls—all tidied up—allowed her to kiss
them as if she had become an aunt; father and
mother made much of her; she must see in their
faces a sort of anxious wonder—Can this be our
Mary then? Can I have begotten this young lady?

Can these breasts have nourished a Mrs. Germain?
She was to have tea in her hat, which Jinny refused
to do; but elaborately removed it and administered
the kettle, the muffins, the slices of bread, the jam-
pot. Blushing and successful as she showed, Mary
would have put an end to this splendid isolation if
she could. It was not possible until tea was over;
but then, when her father made her a kind of speech
—clearing his throat and frowning at one of the
girls, who was speaking the deaf and dumb language
to another under the table—then indeed Mary upset
all ceremonial, by jumping up, and knocking down
her chair, by throwing herself upon her mother's lap,
her arms around her mother's neck, by hiding her
face upon her mother's breast and anointing that
dear cradle with tears. Mr. Middleham's little
speech ended in a choking fit; the girls looked all
their misery; and Jinny sniffed and hardened her
heart. Mary had unbent, but she was made to see that
all her people knew that it was a condescension.

The sisters slept together as of old, and Jinny
must be wooed. For natural reasons Mary must
have Jinny's approbation, must coax and kiss and
strain for it. Jinny was not easily won, but after
a passionate while allowed the back of her mind to
be seen. She sat up in bed and asked a series of
questions. They were answered in low murmurs by
a hiding Molly.

"Molly, how did you get off from Misperton?"

"Quite well."

"H'm. Glad to hear it. No scenes?"

"Mrs. Germain was rather awful. She always hated me. The Rector was sweet to me. And oh! there was Miss de Speyne—I can't tell you how kind she was. Certainly, we had a friend in common . . . but——"

"That's not what I mean. You can manage *them*, I should hope. I know that *I* could. The Rectory, indeed—and you to go out before her! Molly, did you see *him* before you went?"

"Who do you mean?" said a suddenly sobered Molly.

"You know quite well who I mean."

"John Rudd, I suppose. There's nothing between us—now."

"John Rudd! John Germain! There's not only Johns in the world. There's an Ambrose—you know."

"Mr. Perivale! Oh, Jinny, that's ridiculous. Why, he only——"

"I know what he only—as you call it. I don't mean that at all—or him either. I asked you, Did you see *him* before you went?" There was no answer for a minute or more—and then a defiant answer.

"No, I didn't. He's away—abroad."

"Ah. Well, you'll have to, you know. Have you told old—Mr. Germain?"

"No—at least—I was going to. But that was when he—kissed me—and so I couldn't."

"That was when he kissed you? Do you mean to tell me——?"

"No, of course not. But he kisses my hand mostly."

"Well, I'm—" Miss Jinny did not say what she considered herself to be.

"Gentlemen are like that, Jinny—real gentlemen."

"Gentlemen! Do you mean to tell me that Tr— that *he* is not a gentleman?"

"That was quite different. He meant nothing but —it was all nonsense."

"I advise you to find out whether Mr. Germain thinks it nonsense."

"Of course, I shall tell him everything. I don't want ever to see Mr. Dup—him again. That was all foolishness." Mary sat up in bed and clasped her knees. Her eyes, staring at the bright light, were stored with knowledge—as if the soul within were shining through them at last. "I have a friend— a real, wise friend—who has told me this much— that there *is* a real thing. I believe that, I do indeed."

Jinny stared, then yawned. "I'm sleepy. That's real enough for me just now. What do you mean, child?"

"I mean that one might give up everything—risk everything—if one were sure, quite sure. But if one isn't—if one knows that one is a trifle, a plaything, to a—to a person, and that, to another person, one may be much more—then—oh, Jinny, Jinny, please!" Mary's arms were now about Jinny's neck, and Jinny allowed herself to be pulled down. Mary snuggled and put up her lips. After an instant she whispered, "Darling old Jinny, will you do something for me?"

"What is it?"

"Promise."

"What is it?"

"If Tr—if he comes here—will you see him for me? Oh, please, please——"

"Why can't you——?"

"No, no, I can't, you know I can't. Why, he looks at me as if I belonged to him—as if he had a right—! And when he does that, when he frowns and looks through you, and waits—and says nothing —I know what he means; and if he said one word, or moved towards me, or beckoned"— She shivered and hid her face. "I simply mustn't—I daren't. Oh, Jinny darling, please!"

After a time Jinny promised—but Mary's peace was broken up. A shadow haunted her outdoors and in.

Mr. Germain drove down to Blackheath to greet his bride. Her shy welcome, with gladness behind, to make it real, charmed him altogether. The family, after a respectful interval, left him the parlour, for which he was grateful. It would have, no doubt, to be explained that in marrying Mary he had no intention of taking charge of her people. Admittedly they were impossible, but it is very odd that he loved the girl of his selection the more for being simply and unaffectedly one of them. He respected her for it, but there was more than that. At the bottom of his heart he knew that if she were to lose sight of her origin, his love would suffer. It was absolutely nec-essary—he felt it—that she must masquerade for life, be a sweet little *bourgeoise* playing county lady; but playing it with sincerity, and obediently, doing her

best because she was told. The unvoiced conviction
lay behind what he now had to say to her. He told
her, for instance, that he hoped she would see as
much of her family as she pleased, after she was
married, though, of course, she would have the
duties of her new station to consider and to reconcile
with others. He did not suppose, he told her, that it
would be reasonable, or even true kindness, to ask
them often to Southover. "I esteem your father
highly, my dearest. He is in all respects what I
should have expected your father to be. Your
mother, too, is, I am sure, worthy of your love and
gratitude; your sisters seem to me happy and affectionate girls. I doubt, however, if they would be comfortable among our friends at Southover—" Mary
here said at once that she was sure they would not.

"They are different from you—quite different.
We are quite poor people—you would call us middle-
class people, wouldn't you?"

"I suppose that I should," he admitted; "but
would that hurt you, my love?"

"No, no, not at all. There is no harm in that;
and we can't help it—but——"

He leaned, put his arm round her waist and drew
her to him. "Well, my darling, well—? Tell me
of what you are thinking."

"I was wondering—if you can see that they
wouldn't do at Southover, what made you think that
I should do there, either." He held her closer.

"I'll tell you, my love. It was because I knew
what I should feel if you were ever to be there. It

was because my heart was full of you, so that I could never look on any scene that I loved without seeing you in it, and loving it the more for your presence there. When I thought of Southover, I saw you its little sovereign lady, and myself waiting upon you, showing you all the things about it which have been so dear to me in spite of—much unhappiness; and my heart beat high. I said to myself, You must be a miserable and lonely man, my friend, unless you can promise yourself this joy of service. Does my Mary understand me?" He stooped his head to hers, and asked her again, Did she understand? Yes, yes, she said, but she sighed, and turned her face away. Then he must needs kiss her.

Then she did try to speak, meaning, if possible, to lead herself up to a confession. She told him that she feared to disappoint him, that he rated her too highly. "I can tell you truthfully that your love has made me very proud and very happy; I must assure you that I shall do everything in my power to prove to you how proud I am. I will do my duty faithfully—you must tell me of the least thing which is not just as you like. I can't do more than that, can I?"

"Nobody in the world could do more than that," he told her.

"But there's something else. Mrs. Germain at Misperton doesn't like me at all——"

He nodded sadly. "I know, my dear, I know. She is a foolish, arrogant woman, but there are excuses——"

"Oh, of course there are!" She sat upon his knee. "I expect that she is right and that you are wrong—in a way." Then her eyes opened widely upon him: the hour had come. "But she thinks— she says that I am—bad." He turned grey. "Oh, no, my love, you misjudge her! Good Heavens— bad!"

She held her face back from him that she might look at him seriously. "She does, you know—but she makes no allowances. I have always tried to be a good girl—I assure you. Please believe that." He held her to his heart.

"My dearest, my dearest, you distress me. Good! Who is good if you are not? Purest of the pure— my Mary." But she shook herself free in a hurry.

"No, no, indeed, you mustn't say that. That's absurd. I am just an ordinary girl, who likes to be happy, and to be admired, and to have fun when I can——"

"Of course, of course. Oh, my beloved, do not reproach yourself." Then she turned in his arms, put her hands on his shoulders, and looked gravely and imploringly into his face.

"Promise me one thing," she said, "one thing only. I will ask you nothing more than that." She could not have been resisted by the Assessing Angel.

"Speak, my adored one."

"Whatever you hear of me—against me—ask me what I have to say before you condemn me. Prom- ise me that."

"My love and my life," he said fervently; and

she pouted her lips for a kiss. Thus she justified herself in this regard, and by a sophistry of her sex came in time to feel that she had made him a full confession. She told Jinny as much.

We were now in late August; the wedding was to be quietly at Blackheath at the end of September, and the exciting business of the trousseau must be undertaken. Mrs. James, it seems, had so far reconciled herself to the inevitable as to have consented to come to town and "see to things" which the child must have. Her own people being out of the question, Mary was to stay with her in Hill-street, which was one day to be her own house, and do her shopping. A liberal sum was in Mrs. James's hands for the purpose. There was to be no white satin; but Jinny was to be allowed to walk as bridesmaid. There was no way out of this. Her dress was to be chosen for her, and then she must come to London to be fitted; but she was not to be asked to Hill-street.

XIV

THE NEWS REACHES THE PYRENEES

PAU, in August, being what no man could be expected to stand, Duplessis and his friend Lord Bramleigh went into Spain, and lounged at San Sebastian. Here on a blazing noon of mid-September, as they were breakfasting at leisure, a budget of letters was delivered.

Lord Bramleigh, cheerful, wholesome, and round-faced, chirped over his, according to his wont. He read most of them aloud, with comments. "Old Gosperton's shoot—will I go? I'll see him damned. Why should I go and see old Gosperton shoot beaters? Not if I know it. Who's this? Mary St. Chad, by the Lord! Now what does *she* want? . . . 'I suppose you know that Bob Longford is . . .' I'll be shot if I know anything of the sort. I know he *wants to* all right; but you can't marry a chap's wife —at least I don't *think* you can. . . . Oh, sorry! Fellow's dead. . . . I say, Tristram, do you hear that? Old Bland-Mainways is dead, and Bob Longford's married his relic—married her in a week, my boy. What do you say to that? You marry a

man's remains almost as soon as he's remains himself. Pretty manners, what? . . ."

Duplessis took no heed; the babbler ran on. . . .
"This is my mater—wonder what she's got to say?
I rather funk the Dowager. . . . Hulloa! By Gad,
that's rum. I say, Duplessis, did you know a chap
called Senhouse at Cambridge? Pembroke, was he?
Or King's? King's, I think . . . it *was* King's.
Did you know him? Jack Senhouse—John Sen-
house—rum chap."

"Eh? Senhouse? Oh, yes, I knew him. Used
to see him about." Duplessis resumed his letters;
one, especially, made him frown—then stare out of
the window. He read others but returned to that.

Lord Bramleigh went on. "I want to tell you
about this chap Senhouse. Of course, I never knew
him at the Varsity—ages before me, he was. Good
footer—player—ran with the beagles—ran like the
devil; rowed a bit, painted a bit, sang a damned
good song: Jack Senhouse. Well, he's mad. Rich
chap—at least, his father was rich—alderman
somewhere, I b'lieve—say, Birmingham . . . one
of those sort of places. Well, Jack Senhouse chucked
all that—took to painting, scribbling, God knows
what. His governor gets cross—sends him round the
world on the chance he'll settle down by'n by. Not
he! Gets up to all sorts of unlawful games—cuts
the ship and starts off on his own across Morocco;
gets hung up at Fez—row with a Shereef about his
wife or wives. Foreign Office has to get to work—
makes it all right. Senhouse goes? Not he. Stays

there all the same—to learn the language, I'll ask you. Language and plants. He collects plants in the Atlas. So he goes on. Then he gets back home. 'Hope you'll settle down to the office, my boy,' says his governor. 'No, thank ye,' says Jack, and doesn't. He was off again on the tramp somewhere—turns up in Russia—if Warsaw's in Russia—anyhow he turns up where Warsaw is—talking to the Poles about Revolution. Still collects plants. They put him over the frontier. He goes to Siberia after plants and politics. More rows. Well, anyhow, he came back a year ago, and said he was a tinker. He'd learned tinkerin' somewhere round, sawderin' and all that—and I'm damned if he didn't set up a cart and horse and go about with a tent. He paints, he scribbles, he tinkers, he sawders—just as he dam' pleases. And he turns England into a garden, and plants his plants. He's got plants out all over the country. I tell you—the rummiest chap. Up in the Lakes somewhere he's got a lot—growin' wild, free and easy—says he don't want hedges round his things. 'Let 'em go as they please,' he says. So he turns the Land's End into a rockery and stuffs the cracks with things from the Alps. He's made me promise him things from the Pyrenees, confound him—you'll have to help me with 'em. And irises on Dartmoor—from the Caucasus! And peonies growin' wild in South Wales—oh, he's mad! You never saw such a chap. And so dam' reasonable about it. I like the chap. *He's* all right, you know. He's been turned out of every village in England pretty

well, 'cause he *will* talk and *will* camp out, and plant
his plants in other men's land. I met him once bein'
kicked out of Dicky Clavering's place—regular
procession—and old Jack sittin' up in his cart talkin'
to the policeman like an old friend. Admirin' crowd,
of course—the gels all love him, he's so devilish
agreeable, is Jack. I tell you, he learnt more than
one sort of sawderin'. And as for his flowers—well,
you know there's a language of 'em. Well, now,
what do you think? I've heard from the Dowager,
and I'll be shot if she hasn't just turned old Jack out
of my place! Found him campin' in the park, with
one of the maids boilin' his kettle, and another cut-
tin' bread and butter for him. Plantin' peonies he
was—in my park! Dam' funny business; but the
end's funnier still. The Dowager, out driving, comes
home—sees Master Jack waiting for his tea. Stops
the carriage—sends the footman to order him off.
Jack says he'll go after tea. This won't suit the
Dowager by any means—so there's a row. Jack
comes up to explain; makes himself so infernally
agreeable that I'll be jiggered if the Dowager don't
ask him to dinner, and up he turns in evenin' togs,
just like you or me. After dinner—'Good-night, my
lady,' says Jack. 'I must be off early, as I've some
saucepan bottoms waiting for me—and I've promised 'em for to-morrow sharp'—says Jack. Now—
I say, I don't believe you've heard a word of all this."

Duplessis, I think, had not. He had been frowning at the glare outside, biting his cheek; in his
hand was a crumpled-up letter.

"Look here, Bramleigh, I must get out of this," he said. "I want to go home." Lord Bramleigh, never to be surprised, emptied his tumbler.

Then he asked, "What's up? No trouble, I hope?"

He had a gloomy stare for his first answer, and for second—"No, I don't say that. I don't know. That's why I am off—to see."

A man's pleasure is a matter of course to your Bramleighs: the moral and social order must accommodate itself to that.

"That's all right," said Lord Bramleigh, therefore. "When do you go? To-morrow?"

"I go this evening." The effect of this was to raise Lord Bramleigh's scalp a shade higher.

"We swore we'd go to Madame Sop's to-night, you know." Madame Sop was a Madame Sopwith, a lady of uncertain age and Oriental appearance, who gave card-parties.

Duplessis said, "You must make my excuses—if she wants 'em. I'm going."

"A woman, of course," said Bramleigh, tapping a cigarette—but had no answer. Duplessis caught the Sun express, and, travelling straight through, reached Misperton Brand in less than two days.

On the afternoon of the third day he was at the door of the little house, Heath View, in Blackheath. The door was open, and within the frame of it stood a tall young woman with hair elaborately puffed over the ears and a complexion heightened by excitement.

"Good-afternoon," says Duplessis. "Miss Middleham at home?"

"Yes," says Jinny, "she is. Will you come in?"

He followed her into the parlour and was offered a chair. "Thanks very much," he said, but did not take it. He stood by the window, and Jinny Middleham stood by the door.

Presently Jinny said, "I am Miss Middleham, you know. Or perhaps you didn't know it." Duplessis stared, then recovered.

"I beg your pardon. No, I didn't grasp that. But you're not my Miss Middleham."

"I didn't know that you had one," said Jinny. "It's the first I've heard of it."

He laughed. "You'll think me very rude in a minute; but I'll explain to you. It was your sister I wanted to see. She is—a friend of mine. My name is Duplessis. She may have told you." Jinny was as stiff as a poker.

"I have heard my sister speak of you, certainly. I understood that you were—an acquaintance."

Duplessis nodded easily. "Put it at that. I suppose I may see her?"

"She's away," said Jinny. "She's staying in London—with the Honourable Mrs. Germain."

He began to bite his cheek. "Can you give me Mrs. Germain's address? It's not Hill-street, I suppose?"

Jinny was very happy just now. "I suppose that a letter to Mrs. Germain at Misperton would find her. You are related to her, I believe?"

"My dear Miss Middleham," said Duplessis candidly, "let's keep to the point. It seems to me that you don't want me to see your sister."

"Oh," says Jinny, "it don't matter at all to me." He knit his brows.

"Then you mean——?"

"I mean," said Jinny, "that my sister is going to be married to Mr. Germain. That's what it comes to."

Duplessis bowed. "I see. Thank you very much. Then I think, if you'll allow me—" He bowed again and went towards the door. The scene was to be over. Jinny put her hand upon the latch. "Where are you going?" she said, very short of breath. There was a thrill yet to be got out of this.

What was sport to her mortified him to death. "Really, I don't know that I need trouble you any more," he said. "You will give my kind regards to your sister, I hope." But Jinny kept the door-handle in possession.

"Mr. Duplessis," she said, "I ought to tell you that my sister would rather be excused from seeing you. At least, she says so. She said so to me. You best know why that may be."

He ill concealed his mortification. "We won't talk of your sister's affairs, I think. I am happy to have made your acquaintance——"

Jinny tossed her head up. "My acquaintance, as you call it, is for them that want it. My sister's is her own business. I tell you fairly, Mr. Duplessis, that she may be very unhappy."

He flashed her a savage look. "Good Heavens,
I believe that. Why, the thing's monstrous! You
might as well marry her to a nunnery. The fellow's
frozen—stark cold." Jinny steadfastly regarded
him.

"You know very well that you never meant to
marry her," she said. He grew cold instantly.

"Once for all, I must tell you that I decline to discuss your sister's affairs with any one but herself.
And since you tell me that I am not to see her, I will
ask you to let me bid you good-afternoon. I am
very sorry to have given you so much trouble."

It was over; there was but one treatment for such
a cavalier in Jinny's code of manners. She opened
the door wide. "Good-afternoon," she said. He
bowed and went out with no more ceremony.

He felt spotted, and was furious that such a
squalid drama should have engaged him. A fluffed
shop-girl—and Tristram Duplessis! Filthy, filthy
business! But he went directly to Hill-street—
whither a telegram had preceded him, terse and sig-
nificant according to Jinny's sense of the theatre.
"Look out," it said.

That sent the colour flying from Mary's lips, and
lighted panic in her eyes. She crushed it into a ball
and dropped it; then she went directly to Mrs.
James and asked leave to go home for a few days.
She shook as she spoke. She said she was feeling
very tired and unlike herself; she wanted her mother,
she said simply, and as her lip quivered at the pathetic sound of that, her eyes also filled. Mrs. James,

not an unkind woman by any means, was really sympathetic. "My dear child, I quite understand. Go home, of course, and get strong and well. Although you may hardly believe me, I care very much for your happiness—and John would wish it. If he could have been here I know he would have taken you. You shall have the carriage. Now, when would you like to——?"

"At once, please, Mrs. Germain—at once." Mrs. Germain rang the bell and ordered the carriage. Mary could hardly wait for it; she spent the lagging moments pacing her room, and before it was fairly at the door she was on the doorstep. She took no luggage. Crouched in one corner of the hatefully dawdling thing, she stared quivering out of the window. At the corner of the square by Lansdowne House she gasped and cowered. A cab passed her, in which sat, scowling and great, Tristram Duplessis, his arms folded over the apron. Did he—? No, no, thank God, he had not seen her. She was safe in the ladies' waiting-room; but the traverse of the platform was full of peril. Not until the train moved did she feel herself safe. She hungered for Jinny's arms as never in her life before. The brave, the capable, the dauntless Jinny—Mercy of Heaven, to have given her such a sister in whom to confide!

But Mrs. James—the sweeping eye having lighted upon the ball of paper—Mrs. James wrote to her brother-in-law that night:—

"My dear John,—In case you may be hurrying back to town, I think I should tell you that Mary

has gone to her people for a few days; she will write me the day and hour of her return.   There is nothing serious; but she complained of being overtired— not to be wondered at.   Even young ladies may find the pleasures of shopping a tax.   It is possible, I think, that family matters, of which I know nothing —as I am not in her confidence—may have called her home.   She left this telegram here. 'Blackheath' is on the stamp, you will notice.   Mary spoke of her mother to me when she said that she must go, and seemed unhappy.   I put this down to her being over-wrought—and no doubt you will hear from her by the post which brings you this.   Most of my work is done here, I am happy to say.   I hope you will be pleased with Mary's things.   I must say that she looks charming in her wedding gown.   But Ninon may be trusted *for style*.   James is getting restive without me.   Soames is no doubt at his tricks again. I shall be glad to be at my post.   Your affecte. sister,
                                 "Constantia Germain."

"P.S.—Tristram is back from San Sebastian. I had a visit from him this afternoon, some three minutes after Mary left.   He asked after her.   You know that they were old acquaintances.   Lord Bramleigh remains in Spain.   He seems in no hurry to greet his bride.   She is staying with the Gospertons at Brenchmore.   They expect him there from day to day."

Next day Mr. Germain presented himself in Hill-street, nothing varied in his deliberate urbanity.   He had not heard from Mary, he said, in reply to a question; there had been no time for a letter to reach Southover, and the absence of a telegram was reassuring. He intended to go to Blackheath in the course of the afternoon. No doubt she had over-tired herself. He applied himself to other topics and said nothing of Duplessis nor of the Blackheath message until luncheon was over. Then, as Mrs. James went by him through the door which he held open for her, he said, "I had forgotten: you have Tristram back? If he should happen to call, pray tell him that I should be glad to see him if he could spare me a moment."

Mrs. James stopped in her rustling career. "But I don't think it at all likely he will call—again," she said.

"No? Very well. Perhaps I shall encounter him somewhere. Or I could write."

"Quite so," said Mrs. James. "It is easy to write." Then she shimmered away up the stairs. He went into the library, and, after some pacing of the floor, sat down to his desk, wrote, signed, and sealed a paper. He rang the bell.

"I wish you and Gutteridge to witness a paper for me, Jennings," he said to the man. "Fetch him in here, please." The two functionaries signed the sheet as he directed them. "Sign there, if you please, Jennings. And Gutteridge below your name. . . . That will do. Thank you." He put the paper and a crumpled telegram together in a long envelope, sealed it, and wrote shortly on the outside. He locked it in his desk, then resumed his pacing of the room.

As he walked his lips moved to frame words—"Impossible! Purity's self. . . Her eyes ray innocence. . . ."

But he knew Tristram, and could not get his leisurely image away. And Tristram had been much at Misperton; and had a way of—his lips moved again—"My darling from the lions! From the power of the dog!" He went back to his desk, took out the envelope he had sealed, and would have torn it across—but did not. Instead, he put it in his breast-pocket, and left the house.

In the little parlour of Heath View he stood presently awaiting her. Jinny had seemed relieved to see him when she opened the door. Mary had been lying down, she said, and would come when she was tidy. He smiled and said he would wait. He was noticeably white and lined in the face.

She came into the room presently, flushed and very bright-eyed. He thought that she stood there like a mouse sensing the air for alarms, prompt to dart at a pinfall. His heart beat to see the youth and charm of her; his pain was swallowed up in longing for his treasured bliss. He almost sobbed as he held out his arms. "Mary—my child—my love;—" and when she ran in and clung to him with all her force, he clasped her in a frenzy. Whatever darksome fears his honest mind may have harboured, whatever beasts he may have fought, there were none after such a greeting as this. He poured out his love like water upon her, kissed her wet cheeks and shining eyes, and with, "There, my little lamb, there, my pretty one, be at rest, be at peace with me," he soothed her, and felt the panic of her heart to die down. Then, sitting, he drew her to his knees and let her lie awhile with her head on his shoulder.

She whispered in his ear, "Oh, it was sweet of you to come! I wanted you dreadfully—you don't know."

"No, my precious one, I don't indeed. But I am well content that you should have needed me. I pray that you always will, and that I may never fail you."

She lifted her head back to look at him; she smiled like an April day. "*You* fail me! Oh, no, you'll never do that." And of her own accord she kissed him. The good man simply adored her.

"Now will you tell me what upset you so much?" he asked her, but she shook her head roguishly and said that she didn't know. "It was my stupidity— I was frightened—suddenly frightened of all the grandeur—the great rooms, the butler and footmen —the people in carriages who called—" She stopped here, her large eyes full upon his own. She breathed very fast. Then she said, "That's partly the truth—but there's more."

He could not bear it. He could not face what she had to say. He knew that he was a coward, but he could not; despised himself, but could not.

He clasped her close. "Tell me nothing more, darling child. You will reproach yourself, and I cannot bear it."

She struggled to be free. "Oh, listen, listen to me, please!"

He kissed her with passion. "My life is yours; would you rob me of it? I cannot listen to you——"

She gave over, and lay with hidden face until she dared to look up again. Then, when both were calmer, she showed her serious face. Playing with his eyeglasses, she did relieve her mind of one of her fears. "Do you know," she said, "unless you are with me—always—I am sure that I shall do something mad, or bad. Run away from it all—hide myself." She nodded her head sadly. "Yes, I'm quite sure." He could afford to look at the future, not the past.

"Why, then, my love, I shall be with you always—night and day. Do you hear me? Night and day! How will you like that?" She hung her head, peered up at him for a second, and hung her head again. He could do nothing but kiss her after that.

He stayed to tea, which she prepared with her own quick hands. She and Jinny entertained him, and he had never liked that pronounced young woman so well. It was her birthday, Jinny's birthday, he was told. "A few days only from mine," he said, with a fine smile to Mary, which made her understand him, and blush. "Twenty-nine to-day," said Jinny candidly, cutting cake. "This is my cake, Mr. Germain. I suppose you'll give Mary a better one."

"I shall give her the best I can, Miss Jinny, you may be sure," he said heartily, and she nodded to him her confidence in his love. He treated her with grave politeness, which lost all its distance by the evident interest he took in her affairs. She gave herself no airs or graces, was neither pert nor sniffing for offence, nor airy, nor merely odious. Germain's own manners were so fine, so based upon candour and honesty that one could not fail to respond. Even Jinny Middleham forgot herself; and as for Mary, she sat quietly on the watch, really happy, really at ease about the dread future—and whatever terrors she may have owed to Tristram she had none now. Yet she was to have one more chance. At parting she clung to him again, and begged him not to leave her for long. "I'm safe with you—I feel that. Oh, how did you make me like you?"

"By liking you myself, I expect, little witch."

"I'm not a witch. I'm a dunce, and you know that I am. But listen——"

"I listen, dearest."

"I am going to be the best girl in the world. I'm going to do everything that you tell me—always."

"Beloved, I am sure."

"Wait. You haven't forgotten what you promised me?"

"What was that?"

"You have forgotten! Oh, but you must never forget it. It is important—to me."

"Tell me again."

"It was—always to ask me before you believe anything against me. That was it—and you promised." He took her face between his hands and looked long into her eyes.

"My dearest heart," he said, "I'll promise you

better. Not only shall I never believe anything against you—but I shall never even ask you of the fact. Never, never."

She searched his face—her eyes wandered over it, doubting, judging, considering.

"I had rather you asked me," she told him; but his answer was to kiss her lips.

She went with him to the garden gate, seemed most unwilling that he should go. Farewells spoken, her ring-hand kissed, she stood watching him down the terrace, and then, as he never looked back, walked slowly into the house and shut the door. Had she stayed a moment longer she would have seen an encounter he had at the corner where you turn up for the station. Perhaps it was better as it was; I don't know. He had paused there to hail a fly with his umbrella, and having faced round towards his way, saw Duplessis advancing towards him. He felt himself turn cold and sick. The fly drew up. "Wait for me where you are," he said, and went to meet the young man. Duplessis saw him on a sudden; his eyes, blue by nature, grew steely and intensely narrow.

"Good-evening, Tristram," said Germain. "Constantia told me of your return." Duplessis dug the pavement with his stick.

"Did she? Well, it is true, you see."

"I do see. You are going to pay Mary a visit, I suppose. She's not very well, I'm sorry to say—a little overtired. Otherwise, I am sure she would have been delighted."

Duplessis made no reply, and the other continued: "I told Constantia that I hoped to see you—to tell you a small piece of news. I am about to be married again. Mary has been so kind as to confide her future happiness into my hands. Perhaps you won't misunderstand me if I say that some little fraction of that happiness depends upon her not seeing you for the moment. When she is rested, we may hope— The wedding will naturally be a very quiet one. Her people wish it, and my taste agrees with theirs. Otherwise we should have liked to have you among our guests. We promise ourselves the pleasure of seeing you at Southover in the near future. I think the place will please you. You must give an account of my pheasants in December."

"That's very good of you, Germain," said Duplessis, looking him full in the face.

Mr. Germain turned to his waiting fly. "Have you other engagements in Blackheath?"

"None," said Duplessis.

"No? Then perhaps I can offer you a seat in my carriage."

"Thanks," said Duplessis, "I'm walking;" nodded, and went forward, the way of the heath.

"The station," said Mr. Germain.

He could thank God, at least, that she had not meant to deceive him; he could thank God, at least, that she had done with the past. But he had received a mortal wound, and after his manner concealed it. His lovely image was soiled; the glass of his life to come dimmed already. He saw nothing more of Mary until the wedding day, though he wrote to her in his usual fashion and on his usual days. "My dear child," and "Yours with sincere affection." She did not guess that anything was amiss, could not know what they had cost him to write them twice a week. His brother and sister-in-law noticed his depression. Mrs. James indeed was tempted to believe that, at the eleventh hour—but the Rector knew him better. All his forces were now to put heart in the bridegroom. He spoke much of Mary.

XV

A PHILOSOPHER EMBALES

THAT young man with the look of a faun, at once sleepy and arch, the habit of a philosopher and the taste for gardening at large, whom we have seen very much at his ease in society quite various, was by name Senhouse—patronym, Senhouse, in the faith John, to the world of his familiars Jack Senhouse, and to many Mad Jack. But madness is a term of convenience to express relations, and to him, it may well be, the world was mad. He thought, for instance, that Lord Bramleigh was mad, to whom we are now to hear him talking, as much at his length and as much at his ease as of late we saw him in the company of Miss Mary Middleham, or of Miss Hertha de Speyne of the Cantacute stem.

Perhaps he was more at his ease. He lay, at any rate, before his tent, full length upon his stomach, his crook'd elbows supported his face, which was wrinkled between his hands. His pipe, grown cold by delay, lay on the sward before him. One leg, from the knee, made frequent excursions towards the sky, and when it did, discovered itself lean and sinewy, bare of sock. His sweater was now blue, and his trousers were grey; it was probable he had no more clothing upon him. Upon a camp-stool near by sat Lord Bramleigh of the round face, corded and gaitered, high-collared and astare. To express bewilderment, he whistled; concerned, he smiled.

"Well," he said presently, "I think you might. We're short of a gun—I've told you so."

"My dear man," said the other, "I shoot no birds. I'd as soon shoot my sister."

"That's rot, you know, Jack."

"To me it's plain sense. God save you, Bramleigh, have you ever seen a bird fly? It's the most marvellous—no, it's not, because we're all marvels together; but I'll tell you this—boys frisking after a full meal, girls at knucklebones, a leopard stalking from a bough, horses in a windy pasture—whatever you like of the sort has been done, and well done— but a bird in flight, never! There's no greater sight —and you'll flare into it with your filthy explosives and shatter a miracle into blood and feathers. Beastly work, my boy, butchers' work."

"Rot," said Bramleigh—"but of course you're mad. Why are my cartridges filthier than your pots of paint? Hey?"

"Well, I make something, you see—or try to, and you blow it to smithereens— However, we won't wrangle, Bramleigh. You're a nice little man, after all. Those Ramondias—it was really decent of you."

"Much obliged," said the young lord; and then— "I say, talking of the Pyrenees, you knew Duplessis?

He's our man short. He's chucked, you know. He's awfully sick." Senhouse was but faintly interested.

"Yes, I knew him—Cleverish—conceited ass. What's he sick about?"

"Gel. Gel goin' to be married—to-day or something—end of September, I know. Tristram's mad about it. He was at San Sebastian with me when he heard about it—and bolted off like a rabbit—mad rabbit."

Senhouse yawned. "We're all mad according to you, you know. So I take something off. I can understand his sort of madness, anyhow. Who's the lady?"

"Oh, I don't know her myself. Gel down at his place—in a poor sort of way, I b'lieve. Companion or something—he played about—and now she's been picked up by a swell connexion of his—old Germain of Southover. Be shot, if he's not going to marry her."

The lengthy philosopher smiled to himself, but gave no other sign of recognition until he said, "I know that lady. Brown-eyed, sharp-eyed, quick, sleek, mouse of a girl."

"Dessay," said Lord Bramleigh. "They know their way about." The philosopher threw himself upon his back and gazed into the sky.

"Yes, and what a way, good Lord! Idol-hunting —panting after idols. Maims herself and expects Heaven as a reward. I don't suppose that she has been herself since she left her mother's lap. And now, with an alternative of being sucked dry and pitched away, she is to be slowly starved to death. I only saw her once—no, twice. She had what struck me as unusual capacities for happiness—zest, curiosity, health—but no chances of it whatsoever. Ignorant—oh, Lord! They make me weep, that sort. So pretty and so foolish. But there, if I once began to cry, I should dissolve in mist."

"Oh, come," said Lord Bramleigh, "I don't think she's doin' badly for herself. She was nobody, you know, and old Germain—well, he's a somebody. He's a connexion of mine, through his sister-in-law —she was Constantia Telfer—so I know he's all right."

"I'll do her the justice to say," Senhouse reflected aloud, "that she didn't sell herself—she's not a prostitute. She's a baby—pure baby. She was dazzled, and misunderstood the sensation. She thought she was touched. She's positively grateful to the man—didn't see how she was to refuse. She's a donkey, no doubt—but she had pretty ways. She could have been inordinately happy—but she's not going to be. She's in for troubles, and I'm sorry. I liked her."

"She'd better look out for Tristram, I can tell you," said Bramleigh. "He's an ugly customer, if he don't have his rights. Not that there were any rights, so far as I know—but that makes no difference to Tristram."

"Is she worth his while? I doubt it."

"She will be. Germain's rich. Besides, Tristram sticks up for his rights—tenacious beggar."

"Should have been kicked young," quoth the philosopher, and sped Lord Bramleigh on his way.

"Mary Middleham, O Mary of the brown eyes and pretty mouth, I should like to see you married!" he thought, as he packed his tent. "There's a woman inside you, my friend; you weren't given her form for nothing. You are not going to be married yet awhile, you know. It'll take more than a going to church to do that. You've got to be a woman first—and you're not yet born!"

He lifted a shallow box of earth, and fingered some plants in it. "Ramondias—beauties! One of these springs there'll be a cloud of your mauve flushing a black cliff over the green water. There's a palette to have given old England! Mauve, wet black, and sea-green. I have the very place for you, out of reach of any save God and the sea-mews and me. But even with them you won't have a bad 'assistance.' That's a clever word, for how is the artist going to make a masterpiece unless the public makes half of it? Black, mauve, and green—all wet together! We'll make a masterpiece in England yet. . . .

"That girl's great eyes haunt me. Lakes of brown wonder—they were the colour of moorland water—a dainty piece! I could see love in her—she was made for it. A dark hot night in summer, and she in your arms. . . . ! Good Lord, when the beast in a man gets informed by the mind of a god—there's no ecstasy beyond the sun to compare with it. . . .

"Two things worth the world—: Power, and
Giving. When a girl gives you her soul in her body,
and you pour it all back into her lap, you are spend-
ing like a king. Why do women mourn Christ on
His cross? Where else would He choose to be? A
royal giver! To have the thing to give—and to give
it all! He was to be envied, not mourned. . . .

"Old Germain—what's he doing but playing the
King on the Cross. He feels it—we all feel it—but
has he got anything to give? It's an infernal shame.
He's bought the child. She'll never forgive him;
she'll harden, she'll be pitiless—have no mercy when
the hour strikes. There'll be horrors—it ought to
be stopped. I've half a mind——

"Damn it, no! She must go to school. If there's
woman in her, after travail she'll be born. . . .

"To school? To Duplessis? Is he to school her,
poor wretch? What are his 'rights?' Squatter's
rights, you may suppose. So she's to be a doll for
Germain to dandle, or an orange for Duplessis to
suck, and betwixt the feeding and the draining a
woman's to be born! Wife, who's no wife, mistress
for an hour—and a pretty flower with the fruit un-
formed. . . .

"If I bedeck the bosom of England and star it with
flowers, do I do better than Germain with his money,
or Duplessis with his rights? And if I were to court
her bosom . . . Oh, my brown-eyed venturer in
deep waters, I could serve you well! Go to school,
go to school, missy—and when you are tired, there's
Halfway House!"

That evening under the hunter's moon he struck his camp. He had told young Bramleigh that he was soon for the West, where he preferred to winter. "I shall be in Cornwall by November," he had said, "and that's time enough;" and this being late September, it is clear that he projected a leisurely progress from Northamptonshire, where he now was, to the Cornish Sea. He had indeed no reason for hurry, but many for delay. That fairest of all seasons to the poet's mind—that "close bosom-friend of the maturing sun" was to him foster-mother, whether her drowsy splendours fed him or he felt the tonic of her chill after-breath. He worked out, he said, in winter what he had dreamed in the autumn, and he could afford to lose no hours from her lap.

Loafer deliberately, incurably a tramp, he was never idle—whether mending kettles or painting masterpieces (for he had a knack of colour which now and then warranted that word), his real interest was in watching life and in establishing a base broad enough or simple enough to uphold it all. He was not too proud to learn from the beasts, nor enough of a prig to ignore his two-legged neighbours: but for the life of him he could not see wherein a Lord Bramleigh differed from a ploughboy, or a Mary Middleham from a hen partridge—and it was a snare laid for him that he was constantly to be tempted to overlook the fact that they differed at least in this, that they had the chance of differing considerably. He would have been greatly shocked to be told that he was a cynic, and yet intellectually he was nothing more. He did himself the honour of believing most people to be donkeys: if they were not, why under the sun did they not do as he was doing?

The answer to that was that if they did, he would immediately do something else, and find plenty reasons to support him. He had not worked that out—but it's true.

It was also true—as he had told Mary Middleham —that he lived from hand to mouth. His father, Alderman Senhouse, J.P., of Dingeley, in the Northern Midlands, was proprietor of the famous Dingeley Main Colliery, and extremely rich. His mother had been a Battersby, well connected, therefore. He had been to Rugby and to Cambridge, just as Duplessis had been, and at the same times; like Duplessis he idled, but unlike him, he cost no man anything. For his needs, which were very simple, he could make enough by his water-colours, a portrait here and there, an essay, a poem. Then—and that was true, too—he had the art and mystery of tinkering at his disposition. He had earned his place in the guild of tinkers—a very real body—by more than one battle. He was accepted as an eccentric whose whim was to be taken seriously—and as such he made his way. He had never asked his father for a sixpence since he left Cambridge and was on very friendly terms with him. His brothers took the world more strenuously; one was partner at the colliery, another in Parliament, a third—the first born—was Recorder of Towcester.

So much for his talents—now for his accomplishments. He was an expert woodman, a friend to every furred and feathered thing, could handle adders without fear, and was said to know more about pole-cats, where they could still be found, and when, than any man in England. He had seen more badgers at ease than most people, and was infallible at finding a fox. All herbs he loved, and knew their virtues; a very good gardener in the West said that the gentleman-tinker could *make* a plant grow. There's no doubt he had a knack, as the rock-faces between Land's End and St. Ives could testify—and may yet. He had a garden out there, which he was now on the way to inspect. But he had many gardens— that was his passion. He was but newly come from one in Cumberland.

He said of himself that he was a pagan suckled in a creed outworn, and that he was safely weaned. There was a touch of the faun about him; he had no self-consciousness and occasionally more frankness than was convenient. The number of his acquaintance was extraordinary, and, in a sense, so was that of his friends—for he had none at all. Accessible as he was up to a point, beyond that point I know nobody who could say he had ever explored Senhouse. That was where the secretiveness of the wild creature peeped out. Nobody had ever said of him that he had loved, either because nobody knew—or because nobody told. Yet his way with women was most effective; it was to ignore their sex. "I liked her," he would say meditatively of a woman—and add, "She was a donkey, of course." You could make little of a phrase of the sort—yet one would be glad to know the woman's opinion. We have seen that he could be a sympathetic listener, we know that he could be more, in moments of difficulty—and there we stop.

Lastly, I am not aware that he had any shame. He seems always to have done exactly as he pleased —until he was stopped by some guardian of custom or privilege. This frequently happened; but so far as I can learn the only effect upon Senhouse was to set him sauntering elsewhere—to do exactly as he pleased. He never lost his temper, was never out of spirits, drank wine when he could get it, but found water quite palatable. He was perfectly sincere in his professions, and owned nothing in the world but his horse and cart, Bingo, the materials of his trade, and some clothes which had not been renewed for five years. We leave him at present, pushing to the West.

XVI

THE WEDDING DAY

SAINT SAVIOUR'S CHURCH was by many sizes too large for the party—a modern edifice in the Gothic taste, carried out in pink brick with white facings. It was large and smelt of damp. The bridegroom wore his overcoat throughout the ceremony. It was distinctly high, and Mrs. James's hands were many times up, and her eyes all about for witness of the "frippery" they beheld. Stations of the Cross were affixed to the pillars of the nave, lamps twinkled in the sanctuary; dimly in an aisle she made out the plaster effigy of a beardless young man in the Capuchin habit, pink cheeks, and a fringe, who carried lilies in a sheaf. "The hermaphrodite," Mrs. James did not scruple to call him for his pains. "Can we not have some of these things taken out?" she had asked her lord; but the Rector was precise that they must have a faculty, and that they were ten minutes late as it was. He was to officiate, that was one comfort; but it diminished the bridegroom's party by one.

That occupied, barely, the front pew on the right; the bride's company that of the left. Mrs. James,

Lady Barbara Rewish, an old friend, Miss Germain, a pale sister, Mr. Gradeley, Q.C., who was best man, and smiled at his own thoughts, and the Right Hon. Constantine Jess, like a large comfortable cat, who had been President of the Board of Trade and hoped to be again; that was all—but it was too much for the Middleham connexion, which shrank into a row of ciphers as the rite proceeded.

Jinny Middleham, whose shyness was taken for impudence, would have made a very handsome appearance if she had not been so painfully aware of it; the bride, shorter by a head, looked like a child. She wore pale grey cloth and feathers, and had a black hat. All that art could do for her had been done; her slight figure was enhanced, her little feet seemed smaller, her gloves were perfect—and yet, as Mrs. James recognized with lead in the heart, if John had picked her up in her poppies and white muslin, and married her then and there one could have understood it. A man might love a milkmaid —but a little doll in a smart frock, a suburban miss in masquerade—ah, the pity of it! And yet the girl's eyes were like stars, and her face, if it was pale, was serious enough. "It won't do—it will not do," said Mrs. James to herself—"I despair." She despaired from the moment of the bride's entry upon the arm of her little anxious whiskered father—when she saw old Lady Barbara raise her lorgnette upon the group for one minute—and drop it again, and snuggle into her lace. "There's nothing in it—not even romance," that look told Mrs. James. "It's ridiculous

—it's rather low—but here I am. And Germain's an old friend." Lady Barbara Rewish, alone among his equals, sometimes called Mr. Germain Jack.

That anything possibly low could be set beside Mr. Germain seemed incredible—but, if credible, then tragic. He wore race in every span of his tall, thin figure, in every line of his fastidious, patient face. His simplicity was manifest, his courtesy never at fault. The slight stoop towards her which he gave his bride as she drew level with him—the humble appeal, the hope and the asking—should have struck the word from his old friend's mind. Thus a man defers to a queen, she might have said—and yet in that she did not she was wiser, perhaps, in her generation than the children of light. Germain was really, now and throughout the ceremony, revelling in the æsthetic. The position, in its pathos and its triviality at once, appealed to the sensual in him. How lovely her humility, how exquisite, how pure his pride! Benevolence! Behold, I stoop and pick for my breast this hedgerow thing! See it for what it is in all this state—see it trembling here upon the edge of a new world! Is not this to be loved indeed —where I only give, and she must look to me alone? To be sought as a mother by a frightened child, to be source and fountain of all, to give—this is to be happy. And, incapable of expressing it by a sign, he was at this moment supremely happy, and, though he would have been aghast at the thought, supremely luxurious. He was, in fact, indulging appetite in the only way possible to him.

The Rector of Misperton, safe behind his panoply of shrugging eyebrows, hardened, too, by use and wont, administered the rite with calm precision. The words were said:—"I, John, take thee, Mary Susan," "I, Mary Susan, take thee, John"—how she murmured them and how he loved her!—the book was signed—but Mr. Gradeley, Q.C., had no pleasantries at his command, and Mr. Constantine Jess had never had any. Old Lady Barbara kissed the cold bride, and hoped she would be happy. "I'm sure he's in love with you," she said, "and you must be good to him. I've been in love with him myself any time these ten years. But he wouldn't look at me—and I don't wonder. I'm such a wicked old woman." She told the tale on the way to the Wheatsheaf Hotel, where the bride was to be sped, of how poor old Lord Morfiter had married his cook—"She was a Viennese—and, of course, they are wonderful —such tact! Or is it the stays? There's a place in Wigmore-street. At any rate, it worked very well, and really there was nothing else to be done. No one understood him so well as she had—no one! She always cooked for him when they were alone—or had one or two people dining. Perhaps it'll be all right here."

Mr. Jess bowed. "I sincerely hope so. But— forgive me—do I understand—? Was Mrs. Germain——."

"Lord bless us, no!" cried Lady Barbara. "I don't suppose she ever saw a cutlet, off a dish. A Bath bun and a cup of coffee is *her* standard, you may be sure. Of course, she'll be different in a year, you know. She'll drop her people and all that."

"Quite so, quite so," said Mr. Jess. "And get what you call 'tact'——."

"Oh, she's dressed herself beautifully—or Ninon's done it for her. She'll pay for dressing. I call it a pretty figure. Charming. And she's got fine eyes," Lady Barbara replied. "That's what did it, no doubt. Constantia tells me that Tristram Duplessis—." Mr. Jess grew animated.

"A clever young fellow, Duplessis. I have had him under observation lately. My secretary is leaving me, and there has been talk—I hear, by the way, that the Cabinet is hopelessly divided: breaking up,—really, you know, on the rocks."

"So poor Lord Quantock was telling me last night, with tears in his eyes. Then *you* come in, it seems."

"Well, well," said Mr. Jess soothingly, "we shall see what we shall see."

"No doubt," said Lady Barbara, bored with Mr. Jess.

The reception was rather ghastly. Lady Barbara supposed "we ought to mingle," and gallantly tried it upon Mrs. Middleham, who had her daughter Mary's fine eyes crystallized, as it were, in her head, stiffened into glass and intensely polished! Mr. Germain, seconding his friend's effort while rigidly ignoring that an effort was to be made, performed the introduction—"Ah—do you know Lady Barbara Rewish? Mrs. Middleham," and departed, not without hearing Mrs. Middleham say that she did *not* know her ladyship.

"Such a pretty wedding," said Lady Barbara; "she looked delicious."

Mrs. Middleham, who was not without character, said that Mary was a very good girl. She had her "back up," as her daughter Jinny said, and neither gave nor took any odds. Lady Barbara replied that we were *all* good at that age—and then found herself stranded. To see Jinny with Mr. Gradeley, Q.C., had been a cure for the spleen. She ignored him, till he perspired in her service.

Mary was cutting the cake while Mr. Germain was engaged in the very unpleasant task of watching his sister-in-law "put things on a proper footing" before Mr. Middleham. He could tell by the quivering eyelids of the poor man that things were being put there with vigour. "No, madam, no," Mr. Middleham was heard to say. "I don't know that we could fairly expect more than that."

"Nor do I," said Mrs. James, with the air of one who adds, "I should think not."

"Mr. Germain has been more than kind," he ventured to proceed; "princely, indeed—and we should not presume——."

"Of course not," said Mrs. James, and was echoed, somewhat to her discomfiture, by Mrs. Middleham, who had escaped from Lady Barbara by the simple means of walking away.

"I think that Mrs. Germain may take for granted that nobody from our house will intrude where he is not wanted," said Mrs. Middleham with dignity. "Whenever Mary comes to see us she will be welcome. That she knows. We shall go where we are welcome—and nowhere else."

"Then we quite understand each other, I see," said Mrs. James.

"I hope we do," said the other. "It shan't be my fault if we do not."

Mr. Germain was very uncomfortable, but there was now none too much time for the train, according to his calculations. While Mary was "changing her hat"—as it was put—the wedding party, rigidly segregated, stood astare, each at its window, upon the gusty vagaries of a late autumn day.

Mary was at the glass, flushed and on the edge of tears. Her hands were at her hat, while her eyes searched Jinny's stony pair for a sign of melting. But Jinny was immovable. In vain did the pretty bride turn this way and that, invite criticism, invoke it: Jinny's disapproval persisted. This was not to be borne—with a little whimper the victim turned, clasped Medusa round the waist; with one hand to her chin she coaxed for kindness. She stroked Jinny's cheek, tiptoed for a kiss. Presently she fairly sobbed on Jinny's bosom.

"Oh, you are unkind to me—you hurt me dreadfully! What have I done, that you won't love me?"

"Done!" cried Jinny. "Hear her!" Then with blazing wrath she scorned her sister. "I'll tell you what you've done, my dear. You've married a gravestone. Sacred to the Memory of John Germain, Esquire—that's what you've sold yourself to—take your joy of that. The price of a kissed hand! You'll find out before morning, my beauty. If I marry a crossing-sweeper, he shall be a man."

"You liked him, you know you liked him——."

"Yes, for a grandfather, my dear; but for a husband, if you please, I'll have a man. And so might you—over and over. You've been as good as promised half-a-dozen times——."

"Jinny, you know that's not true." She was ruthlessly put away to arm's length.

"But it *is* true. There was Rudd—what do you say of him?"

Rudd must be owned to. So far off he showed so dim a speck in the distance, there seemed nothing in it.

"Young Stainer—you forget him, too, I suppose——."

"Stainer?" said poor Mary. "He was a boy, Jinny."

"He had a pair of arms, I believe. And I should like to hear your opinion of Fred Wimple. You were never at Folkestone in your life, I suppose? You never talked to Sandgate by moonlight? Never met any one in your life by moonlight?"

The remembrance of a meeting by moonlight, more recent than any at Folkestone, enabled Mary to consider Mr. Wimple's case.

"I don't think you need drag up flirtations against

Jinny was seen to blush. Riceless, slipperless they went their way—and the party dissolved like smoke.

It was afterwards agreed at Blackheath that Mr. Germain and the Rector were gentlemen.

XVII

THE WEDDING NIGHT

TORQUAY was the place for the honeymoon; but Exeter was to be the end of that day's stage. Mr. Germain's valet put them into the train, handed his master the tickets, Mary her jewelcase, took off his hat and retired to an adjoining compartment. Everything was very easy, done with an absence of enthusiasm which might have chilled a more resolute heart than this bride's. It was done, she reflected, as if a wedding was a matter of every day. Why, a budget of evening papers, *Punch*, *Truth*, and other things had been laid in order upon the opposite seat. Was he going to read all these? It was almost incredible—but after the events of the afternoon she could have believed anything. She felt her ring to make sure, and then her eye caught sight of the paper on the window—Reserved to Exeter—J. Germain, Esquire. Perhaps great people always reserved carriages when they travelled—perhaps a carriage would always be reserved for her when she went about alone. There would have been a maid if she had chosen; it had been proposed to her. She had laughed and said, "Of course not!" But he had taken his man-servant—and how could he? On his wedding journey! Had he taken him before—? This was his second wedding, she remembered.

Anxiety as to whether the train could be caught might account for the bridegroom's silence during the carriage journey. His watch was open in his hand. For some time, too, after the train moved, he kept silence. She found herself looking soberly at the little pointed toe of her shoe when her thoughts were broken in upon by the capture of her hand. The sudden attack made her heart beat; she blushed hotly, lost her command of experience. As if it had been the first advance he had ever made, she dared not raise her eyes. She must be wooed from the beginning if she was to be won.

This was the way to charm him; he was charmed. He called her his Mary, and asked, of what she was thinking? She didn't know, couldn't say. Was she thinking of their coming life together? No, not then. "I think constantly of that," he told her and put his arm about her. She let him draw her closer as he developed his plans for their joint happiness. "Calm spaces for work together, my love—there is so much in which your help will be a pride to me— and something I do believe, in which I can be useful to you. We must keep up our languages—French, Italian, even Spanish (quite worth your while for Cervantes' sake): I do think I can help you there. Then your music—I could not bear you to abandon that. I have a little surprise for you when I bring you to Southover—you shall see. Then riding.

I think you don't ride? You shall be under Musters's care. Musters is an admirable fellow—you will like him. We ride together daily, I hope. Will you like that?"

"Yes, yes, I shall like everything. It will all be very wonderful to me—all quite new."

He smiled, as if tolerant of a simplicity which could find daily horse-exercise wonderful—and she felt it. In her present state of acute sensibility she needed anything but this treatment. He should have taken her as an adorable dunce and laughed at her outright between his kisses, or he should have whirled her off her balance in the torrent of his ecstasy. But Mr. Germain never laughed—it was not a Germain's habit—and ecstasy at four in the afternoon was not possible to him. He liked his cup of tea at a quarter past, and when that hour came proposed to Mary that she should give it him from her tea basket—Lady Barbara's present.

She was thankful for the relief, and almost herself again in the bustle of preparation; she forgot her dumps, and when he burnt his fingers and said "Tut-tut!" she fairly laughed at him and took, and even returned, his kisses. Things were better; but he very nearly imperilled the position thus hardly won, by wiping his mouth with a silk pocket hand-kerchief. True, she had been eating bread and butter—but was this a time—?

They chatted after tea—first of Berkshire where her home was to be. He spoke of his "riverine property." She could almost see the edge of his

estate as they slipped away from the ragged fringe
of Reading. Then, by natural stages, he was led
to reflect upon the society she would meet about
Southover. The Chaveneys—he thought she would
like the Chaveneys; they were her nearest neighbours, five miles off. Sir George was asthmatic—a
sufferer; but Lady Chaveney was a charming
woman, a woman of the world. She had been a
Scrope of Harfleet. The girls were quite pleasant
young women; and there was a son—rather wild—
an anxiety occasionally. Then there were—but her
eyes were wide. Five miles off! Were those the
nearest people? She had thought there was a town
—was not Farlingbridge the post town? He considered Farlingbridge. Yes, Farlingbridge was a
mile and a half from the Park gates—a market town
of 2,000 souls. There was a Vicar, a worthy man,
of the name of Burgess. He met Burgess, of course
—on the Board of Guardians, for instance. There
was a Colonel Dermott, too; yes, he had forgotten
Dermott. Nobody else. Her "Oh, I see," was his
reproof; he was ashamed of himself. "Two thousand other people, of course! Everybody will be
delighted to see you, my dearest. Don't misunderstand me. They won't call, probably—Foolish old
customs die hard with us. But there won't be a
door in Farlingbridge which won't be open to you.
I shall go with you, if you will allow me. I have
long wished to know more of my neighbours—but
you know how sadly I have lived." He drew her
closely to him—"How I have lived so long without

my Mary passes my comprehension! Do you remember that last July was not the first time I saw
you?"

She was pleased, and showed that she was. She
questioned him shyly. Had he seen her before this
year? What had he thought? What made him
notice her this time? His answers were in the right
vein. He was allowed to be the lover—and so the
moments passed, and Swindon with them. The
train swung slowly by a crowded platform. He
released her.

Silence succeeding, she relapsed at once into her
desponding mood. She was embarked indeed—but
on what a cruise! The Chaveneys—five miles away
—Sir George and Lady Chaveney— She knew
what that meant; how the County reckoned, from
one great house to another. Why, if a Colonel Dermott, a Reverend Burgess were as nothing—from
what a depth of blackness had *she* been dragged up!
. . . A toy, an old man's plaything, Jinny had
called her . . . picked out of a village and put in
a great house . . . five miles from anybody. . . .

During this time of long silence, of reverie, in the
which, though his arm embraced her and his hand
was against her side, his eyes were placidly shut,
while hers gazed out of window, fixed and sombre,
at the flying country, she suddenly started and became alert. Misgivings faded, a wash of warm colour—as of setting suns—stole comfortably about
her. For a moment, it may be, she was conscious
again of wide horizons. The train was rolling

smoothly—so smoothly that its swiftness had to be felt for—over an open common backed by a green down. Furze-bushes dotted it, clumps of bramble; there was a pond, a dusty road, geese on the pond, a cottage by the road, with a woman taking linen from the hedge. Along the road, pushing to the West, went a cart, drawn by a white horse; the driver sat on the tilt, smoking, his elbows on his knees; a grey dog ran diligently beside. Could this be—? Could it be other? Oh, the great, free life! Oh, the beating heart! Oh, the long, long look! Mary strained against the arm of her husband; his hand felt her heart beat. He opened his eyes, looked at her, and smiled to see her eager gazing. But what mystery of change in women! The next moment she had turned to him, her eyes filled with wet. She turned, she looked wistfully upon him; her lip quivered. "My darling?"—and then she flung herself upon his breast. "Oh, take me, take me, keep me safe!" she cried. "I will be good to you, I will, I will! But you must love me always——"

"My sweet wife, can you doubt it? What has frightened my pet?" She hid her face on his shoulder. "Nothing—nothing—only thoughts. I'm not good, you know. I told you so—often."

He pressed her closely to him. "Who is good? Who dares to ask for love? We ask for mercy—not love. But we can always give it. It is our blessed privilege. You have the whole of mine." He kissed her hair—all that he could reach of her, and she lay with hidden face for a long time. The unknown

resumed its chilly grip —the horizon narrowed again,
the fog hung about the hedgerows which hemmed it
in. But the outlook was not quite the same—or the
out-looker was changed. The tilt-cart was jour-
neying to the West, and so was the train. . . . But
Mr. Germain exulted in every mile which he could
watch out with that dear head upon his shoulder.
The tired child slept!

"Exeter, my love!" he awoke her with a kiss; she
blushed, looked dazed, and snuggled to him in an
adorable way. But for that unlucky servant of his
it is possible that the day might have been saved yet.
But inexorable order resumed its hold, and she
chilled fatally between station and hotel. A carriage
and pair was waiting for them, a cockaded coachman touched his hat; the porters touched theirs;
the luggage followed with Villiers; up the stairs of
the hotel there was quite a stately procession. . . .
They were shown their rooms; sitting-room, dining-room, two bed-rooms, all *en suite*. Mr. Germain disappeared with anxious Villiers; a gigantic
chambermaid, old, stately, with a bosom fit for
triplets, superintended the unpacking of Madam's
trunk, which was plundered by two smart under-
lings with velvet bows very far back upon their
sleek heads. Would Madam require a dresser?
Madam said, Oh, no, thank you—and then had to
ring in confusion for somebody to fasten her bodice.
Madam looked charming, when all was done, in a
gown of dangerous simplicity, and Madam knew it
—but there beat a wild little heart under the tulle,

and a cry had to be stifled, a cry to a friend on the open road—for good fellowship, sage counsel, and trust to float between eyes and eyes. Her treadings had wellnigh slipped; she felt herself to be drowning—as it were, in three feet of water.

She sat at his table, and ravished his delicate fancies with her pretty embarrassments, her assumed dignity, her guarded eyes and lips. King Cophetua lived again in this honest man, who had no need to protest to Heaven that he would cherish his elected bride. He was now perfectly happy, wallowing in sentiment, bathing every sense. The exquisite antithesis he had made! From nothing she was become this! Sweet before, and now all dainty sweet; rare unknown, now known to be the rarest. Her white neck with a jewel upon it, her scented hair with a star, rings glittering on her fingers, her gown as dainty as her untried soul—and through the clouded windows of her eyes that shrinking soul looking out —wistful, appealing, crying for help. Ah, what loyal help should be hers! Complacent, benevolent gentleman.

She sipped his champagne, she watched everything, missed nothing, gave no chances, knew herself on her trial. She was strung up to the last pitch, and staked all her future upon the hazard of this night. If she was cold in her responses, slow to take up, quick to abandon positions in the talk, she may be excused. She could be bright enough when she was at ease—but who is at ease with his honour at proof? Great honour had been done her, she knew;

and it required all her honour in return. That
prompted her to a curious requital. She burned to
cry out to this courteous gentleman in black and fair
white, and to these noiseless, prompt attendants—
"Look at me well—I am nothing, a shred from the
wilderness. He has chosen me for his breast,
decked me out—I am a slave-girl—my ignorance is
hired. How dare you wait upon me, you who would
pass me in the street, and nudge, and tell each other
with a wink what I was, and how you found my
looks? Was I so low that I must be thus lower?
Can you not spare me this?" She burned with
shame, was dangerously near to panic. More than
once she must bite her lip to hold back these words—
and as she bit, he looked at her and adored her splendid colour and lovely frugality of glance and speech.
. . . She left him to his port, and sat alone in the
drawing-room, a prey to all the misgivings.

When he took her in his arms and struggled with
himself to tell her all he had found in her of excel-
lence and beauty, she could only hide her face. But
she clung to him at last, sobbing out her protest that
she would serve him utterly. "Oh, you are good to
me, you are good! Oh, help me to be what you
wish. I am so ignorant—I cannot tell you—" She
broke off here, and, holding herself stiffly in his
arms, looked strangely in his face. "Do you know
—have you thought—that—that—I cannot be what
you think me?" she said; and when she saw that
he was taken aback, "Listen," she said, "let me sit
by you." He took her on his knee and held her

swinging hand. Her eyes were veiled as she tried to speak to him. "I have been—I began to work, you know, when I was sixteen. I went away from home——"

She caught him unawares, or she hit by some fatal telepathy the centre of his thought. He flinched at the blow, but she could not know that, being too full of her own affair. She must discharge her heart at all costs—and at this eleventh hour, if so must be. Now let him be generous if he is to be accounted wise!

Once too often he was tried. This time, at the crisis, he did not respond. Generosity, which is Love's flag of victory, was not at command. The hand that shaded his eyes made a deeper shadow. His voice was small and still. "Yes, my dear, yes?"

She lifted her head and looked up, not at him, but over the room. She went on as if she was reading her story off the wall. But she was reading it from Jinny's eyes of scorn.

"You must know me as I really am before you— before to-morrow. I was engaged—once—before I knew you. He was a farmer's son—Mr. Rudd. He thought—I thought—he gave me a ring. That was soon after I had gone to Misperton. I was twenty-two."

He sat very still, hiding his face. It looked as if he were crouching from a storm. "Yes, yes, my child. Why not?" She was pitiless.

"Oh, but— . . . I have more to tell you."

He seemed to shrivel. "You wish to speak of

these things? You were very young." And yet his voice said, Tell me all—all.

"At sixteen? Yes. Of course I was very foolish."

"There had been— Before you went to Mr. Nunn's—before you went to Misperton?"

She left his knee, and sat opposite to him upon a straight chair. She folded her hands in her lap and began her tale. As if she had been in the dock she rehearsed her poor tale. He neither stirred nor spoke.

She made no excuses, did not justify herself, nor accuse herself. She did not say—it never entered her head to say—You, too, have made mistakes. There was a Lady Diana for your bitterness. But she knew what she was doing only too well; and a force within her said, "Go on—spare nothing—go on. Whatever it cost you, be done with it. No peace for you else." . . . "I must tell you that there was a gentleman—you will not ask me his name. I think that you know it. He gave me a book—and—other things. I have not seen him since—since you spoke to me at the school-feast."

He stirred, but did not look up. "I will ask you not to see him."

"I will never see him. I have refused——"

"He has tried to see you?"

"I took care that he should not."

"I don't wish to seem unreasonable," he said slowly; "I cannot bear to seem so to you. But—it would be for our happiness."

"I assure you that I have no intention. I hope

you will believe me." His lips moved, but he did not look up. She rose. "I am very tired," she said; "I think I will go now." He got up immediately; the fog seemed in the room. She came and stood before him.

"Be patient with me," she said. "Be kind to me. I shall try to do everything you wish."

He made as if he would take her, but she drew back quickly.

"I should have told you all this before if I could have thought you would care—would allow it. Indeed, I have tried more than once, but you— Now, I am glad that you know me—but I am very tired."

"Mary," he said, and held out his hands to her. She looked into his face, then shut her eyes.

"I am very tired. Please let me go. Good-night." He held open the door for her.

BOOK II

I

IN WHICH WE PAY A FIRST VISIT TO SOUTHOVER

THE house—Southover House, Farlingbridge, Berks—stands terraced above formal gardens in the Italian taste; ribbony borders, edged with white stone, form a maze of pattern. Urns on pedestals, statues of nymphs and fauns, stone seats, stone cisterns, gleam among the carpeted flowers. Beyond these is the great park, with a wall (they tell me) six miles round. The herd of fallow deer is praised by Cotton in his famous book. Mr. Germain used to show you the passage.

The mansion, built by Wyatt, is classical; an exact rectangle of pink brick faced with Bath stone. It has a pediment and a balustrade, with white statues at intervals along the garden front. Within, it is extremely proper, having narthex and atrium, or, if you please, vestibule and hall. The reception rooms open out of this last, and above it a gallery gives on to the chambers, about whose doors the valets are to be seen collected at seven-thirty or so of an evening. They wait for their masters, while they observe and comment in monosyllabic undertones upon the doings of their betters below. Surprising how much a man-servant can get into how little. From April to June, from September to November, the hall is used for tea and after-dinner lounging. It is the core and heart of the house. During the summer months tea should be, on the terrace unless Nature is willing to see Mr. Germain vexed; in wintertime it is always in the little library where the Murillo hangs.

I choose the time of tulips for our visit, when Southover has had a new mistress for two years come the fall of the leaf. The family, as they say down here, has been abroad this year; has not long returned. It went to the Riviera directly after Christmas, to Mentone; was in Rome in February, and studying churches in the Rhone valley in March. It Eastered in Seville, going thither by Barcelona and Granada, and came home by Madrid and Paris. Now it is mid-May, and the Italian gardens glitter with tulips. Tea is served, according to custom, in the hall at a quarter before five. The footman on duty—his service passed by the butler—has retired, but the statelier functionary stands at his post, tapping his teeth with a corkscrew. The hour is now five—gone five. Silver chimes have proclaimed it to an empty hall. There he stands, a solemn, florid personage, full of cares, regarding in an abstracted manner the glittering array of covered dishes, cups, and covered jugs. Now and again he adjusts a teaspoon, now and again humours a spirit-flame. At a quarter past five Mr. Germain enters the hall from the library, his secretary, young Mr. Wilbraham, at his heels.

The butler, with a careful hand, placed a rack containing three triangles of toast upon a little table. He poured a cup of chocolate from a porcelain jug, and added that to the feast. The afternoon's post, upon a salver, was held for Mr. Wilbraham. These things done, he waited until Mr. Germain was in his deep-seated chair. "The ladies are not returned, Sir," he said, and went his noiseless way.

Mr. Germain, who looked white and had faded eyes, munched his toast in silence. Young Mr. Wilbraham, quick, gentlemanly, pleasantly alert, demolished envelopes and their contents while he ate muffin. Three or four letters he handed to his patron.

"Those look to me personal," he said. Mr. Germain, having adjusted his *pince-nez*, inspected the envelopes and put them unopened into his pocket. Toast-munching was resumed, and silence. Once or twice Mr. Germain looked at his watch, once compared it with the hall-clock, but made no other sign.

Wilbraham poured more tea, spread himself honeycomb on bread and butter, and went on with his letters. He broke the silence. "The Association has written again to know whether you have decided. They hope you will come forward. Sir Gregory has gone to Madeira. They say, he's quite made up his mind."

Mr. Germain blinked solemnly at space, without reply.

"And I've a note here from Mr. Jess—rather, from his secretary. There was a meeting at the

Reform on Monday. Your name was mentioned.
Mr. Jess hopes that he hasn't been indiscreet. He
referred to the possibility."

Mr. Germain, without turning his head or ceasing
to munch, asked here, Who was Mr. Jess's private
secretary.

"Duplessis," said brisk Mr. Wilbraham, adding,
as if to himself,

"Clever beggar." After a pause Mr. Germain
got up.

"I shall rest for a little, Wilbraham. We will
consider these things before dinner. Meantime I
will ask you to remember that they are between you
and me. Strictly so."

"Oh, of course! Quite understood," the friendly
young man nodded.

The master of the house had his hand on the
library door when a step on the flags of the vestibule
caused him to look quickly round. There was a
moment during which he could have been observed
to hold his breath in suspense. A tall and sumptu-
ously fair lady, free-moving, deep-bosomed, robed
in white—all her dresses robed her—came into the
hall. She wore a broad-brimmed Tuscan hat, which
set about her like a halo, and carried flowers. This
was the Honourable Hertha de Speyne, the last of
the Cantacutes.

Mr. Germain turned away from his refuge and
stood attentive; Wilbraham jumped to the upright.

"Shall I have in some more tea?" he asked at
large. "This has been here since five."

"Not for me," said Miss de Speyne. "I hate it. But the others are coming. I saw them in the bottom. They've been on the lake, I think."

"And you?" This was from Mr. Germain, with a courtly inclination.

"Oh, I've been painting, of course."

"Happily, I hope."

"Miserably. Deplorably. I've scraped out everything, and come away at least with a clean canvas. Few painter's can say as much of a day's work."

"Few would confess it."

"Ah, I've been taught the blessing of an uncharged heart. Mr. Senhouse taught me that last year. What I was trying to do was perfectly impossible. One knows too much; one has botany, flower-shows, catalogues behind one. Fields of asphodel! But suppose you had been shown how asphodel grows?"

"Have I fields of asphodel here?" Mr. Germain looked his polite misgivings.

"You have a glade of Poets' narcissus—like a Swiss valley. Mr. Senhouse could have done it—an Impressionist. It's not for me. I see them stiff in vases; I know that they have stalks."

"So, surely, does Mr. Senhouse."

"Indeed he does. He knows that they have souls. But he's ruthless with his brushes; he·forgets their souls, and his own science."

"And you——?"

"I'm so proud of mine that I could never forget it." She looked out into the vestibule, to the sunlight

beyond. "Here comes Mary. Do get some tea for
them," she urged Wilbraham—who flew to the bell.

Mr. Germain remained where he was—long
enough to see his wife's eyes dilate at the sight of
him there, long enough to hear the laugh falter upon
her lips; and then he turned and slowly gained the
library. He shut the door behind him. Mrs. Germain, with a high colour and gleam of light in her
fine eyes, came quickly to the tea-table. She was
followed by two young men in flannels—self-possessed, assured, curt-spoken young men with very
smooth heads.

"Oh, we're dreadfully late!" she cried. "Hertha,
have you been in long? Have you had everything?"
In a much lower key she asked, "Has—was—he
here when you——?"

Miss de Speyne looked kindly at her friend.
"He was just going when I came in; but he stayed
and entertained me. It was awfully kind of him.
I know he's very tired."

Mary stood by the tea-table, fidgeting a cup by
the handle. She looked uncomfortable. "I'm
frightfully sorry. Hertha, I meant to be in by a
quarter to five."

"It's all right, you know," said one of the young
men—the youngest of them—lengthily at ease in a
chair. "You're only an hour slow. I call that
good."

She made no answer, but went on fidgeting the
teacup. The entry of butler and footman with supplies did not move her.

Young Lord Gunner stood to his muffin, and confidently explained:

"It's my fault, you must know. I was diving after half-crowns—and getting 'em, too."

"He was though," said Mr. Chaveney from his chair. "I ought to know. They were my half-crowns."

"Well then, of course, I had to change. I'm not a mermaid, as it happens."

"Not yet, my boy," said the loser of half-crowns.

"So I sent a chap up for my chap with some things, and changed in the châlet. That's why we're late, if you must know."

Miss de Speyne was pouring out tea. "I see. And the others reckoned up their losses——"

"Words to that effect," said Mr. Chaveney.

Lord Gunner put down his cup. "Don't know what they did. But I've brought them safe to port. Wilbraham, I'll play you squash rackets before dinner. It'll do you good. You're overdoing it, you know, and you're not used to it. You'll get a hemorrhage or a nervous breakdown, and we shall have to give you a rest-cure. Chaveney shall score."

"Can't," said Mr. Chaveney. "Ordered my trap. My people are going to take me out to dinner. They won't be denied."

"England hath need of him," said Wilbraham. "Come along, Gunner. My things are in the court. I'm due at the desk at seven."

Mr. Chaveney—very young, very fair, and very

flushed, with long and light eyelashes—was now at the piano. He swayed as he played.

"Do you like that?" he said, looking at Mrs. Germain, who was still pensive. "It's 'Carmen.'"

"Beg pardon," said Lord Gunner. "It sounded like Chaveney." The youth ran up a scale.

"Go and play rackets, Gunner, and leave me to my art. I'm going."

"He'll stay to dine—you see if he don't," was Lord Gunner's passing shot. He was answered by a crashing chord.

Miss de Speyne, regarding the pianist's back, said in a gentle voice, "He's in the library. You'd better go to him for a minute."

Mrs. Germain had the knack of making her eyes wide and round so that you got the full-orbed splendour of their brown light. "I expect he's asleep. I'll see him before dinner." Her friend shook her head.

"He's walking up and down. He'll rest after you have been."

"Do you think so—really?"

"I'm sure. You had better go." Mrs. Germain stayed no longer, but went quickly, holding her head stiff.

She stood in the doorway of the library, inside the closed door, a charming figure for all her anxious eyes. She was in blue linen, with a wide straw hat; was sunburnt and fresh, looked ridiculously young. Mr. Germain paused in his pacing of the long carpet and waited for her to speak—which presently she did, rather breathlessly.

"Oh," she said, "I was afraid you might be resting, or I should have come——"

He shut his eyes for a moment. "No. It is not possible just now,—nor desirable. I have much to think of."

She went quickly to him and held out her hand a little way. "Aren't you well? May I stay with you? I meant to have been in early, but——"

"But it was not convenient, you would say?"

"No, not that. I couldn't get them to leave the water. They were absurd—like children. One was throwing money in for the other to dive after. I did try—but they went on just the same. Did you expect—did you want me? I promise you that I tried to come. I tried hard."

Something of the sort had been what his self-esteem exacted of her; something of the sort must have been tendered him or he had been really ill. He was now softened, he smiled, took up her offered hand. "My little love," he said, drew her near and kissed her forehead. For a moment she urged towards him, but then, having glanced timidly up and seen his averted eyes, she sighed and looked to the floor, her hand still held.

He led her to his escritoire, put a chair for her beside it, and sat in his own. "Constantia writes to me, Mary, that she and James would like us to pay them a visit—in July, as usual. What do you say?"

She considered this for some moments. Her head was bent towards her hands in her lap; she looked at her weaving fingers—a habit of hers. "That would be to the Rectory, I suppose?"

"Obviously," said Mr. Germain. "You will remember that it was a yearly custom of mine." She had every reason to remember it; but he must hear her say so. "You will not have forgotten that, Mary?"

"No! Oh, no! Of course I haven't." She looked at him for a moment—trouble in her eyes and flame in her cheeks.

"Last year," he resumed, "I had Southover to show you—and there were reasons why I should not take you back so soon. This year there could be no such reason. I think that you might be pleased to see Misperton again; more particularly since you and Hertha de Speyne have struck up such a happy friendship. She is a noble young creature in every way; nothing could have pleased me more. Constantia will, of course, write to you; but, being my sister-in-law and happening to have other matters of which to speak, she mentioned it to me in the first event. I can assure you that there has been no want of respect——"

She flashed him another reproachful look—reproachful, not that he should think her offended, but that he should pretend to think her so. "Oh, of course not! How could you imagine such a thing? It is absurd—really absurd."

He made no reply, was evidently waiting for her decision. She gave it reluctantly. "We will go, if you wish it," she said.

He was immediately piqued. "That is hardly

cordial, is it? I am not sure that I should, or could, wish it, on those terms."

She had reasons of her own for disliking it extremely; but she kept her counsels in these days. "I will tell you exactly how I feel, if you will be patient with me," she said. "I am sure that the Rector would be glad to have me there with you; and of course Hertha would like it. If there was nobody else I should love to go. I shall remember Misperton as long as I live. Wonderful things happened to me there; don't think that I can forget them for an hour. But Mrs. James—Constantia, I mean—doesn't like me at all. Why should we disguise it? She disapproves of me, doesn't trust me, thinks me a nobody —which I am, of course——"

"I beg your pardon, my love—" he would have stopped her; but she saw what in particular had offended him, and ran on.

"I am your wife, I know. But I am a person, too; and I own that I would rather be with people who— who respect me for what I am in myself, as well as for what you have made me. Forgive me for saying so; it is rather natural, I think. And it happens that I should like to see my parents again, and my sisters. It is six months since I was at Blackheath. So that would be an opportunity, and a reason—while you were at the Rectory."

"You wish me to go there alone?" She could guess at the scalding spot beneath his armour-plate.

"I should love to go with you," she said, "if—if it could be managed."

"I may mention to you," he said coldly, "that you will not find an old acquaintance there. Since his mother's death my young relative, Tristram Duplessis, has bestirred himself. He has sold the cottage."

She had not been prepared for an attack in flank, and blenched before it. Then she told her fib. "My reason against going with you had nothing to do with Mr. Duplessis," she said; and, watching her, he did not believe her.

He turned to his papers. "It shall be as you wish, my love," he said. "I will write to Constantia. It may well be that I shall not care to resume a broken habit. Are you going up to dress? If so, and if you should happen to see Wilbraham, would you tell him that I am ready?"

She hovered about his studious back, as if on the brink of speech; but thought better of it and went slowly out of the room. Intensely conscious of her going, he cowered at his desk, looking sideways— until he heard the door close. Then he began to read, with lips pressed close together.

In the hall Mrs. Germain almost ran into the arms of Wilbraham, who, scarlet in the face and wet as with rain, was racing to his room.

"By jove, I beg your pardon, Mrs. Germain!"

"You only made me jump," she laughed. "Have you been playing all this time?"

"I know, I know! It was Gunner's fault, upon my honour."

"It always is Lord Gunner's fault. Mr. Germain asked me to tell you that he was ready."

"Good Lord!" cried the unhappy youth. "And I'm sw—as hot as anything."

"Go and change," she said kindly. "I'll go back to him."

He was fervent. "You are an angel! But I've told you that before." Their eyes met; they laughed together. He pelted upstairs.

"Mr. Wilbraham will be with you in a second," she said, entering the library again. Had she seen him spring round as she came in? No doubt of it. "I left my book down by the lake—and I know you don't like that. Do you?"

"No, dearest, no. I confess the foible." His eyes invited her nearer. She advanced to his table and stood by him, her hand touched his shoulder. He was inordinately happy, though he made no immediate sign. But presently his arm went about her waist, and then she bent down and leaned her cheek for his kiss. They remained together, saying nothing, until she heard Wilbraham coming down, three stairs at a time. Then she slipped away and just caught him outside the door.

"I had to tell a fib," she told him. "I said that I had left my book by the lake."

"Well!" He looked at her. "I'll bet that's not a fib."

"No," she laughed. "But it was meant to be. Now I'm going to get it myself."

"You are an angel!" he said. "Don't. I'll go presently. I should love to."

"No. I shall go myself. I deserve it."

"You deserve—!" He stopped himself. "Look here," he said, "send Gunner. No, he's changing. Send young Chaveney."

She opened her eyes—fatal use! "Is Mr. Chaveney here? I thought he said——"

Wilbraham chuckled. "Did you suppose he'd go when it came to the point? Not he! Why, before we'd played half a set he came to borrow some clothes off me."

He glided smoothly into the library. Mrs. Germain fetched her book.

II

REFLECTIONS ON HONEYMOONS AND SUCHLIKE

THE years fly, we know, and come not again, and there's balm in that for the wounds they leave. For we forget a good deal, and Hope is a faithful lover, and never quits us for long together; and then there's honest Use-and-Wont, surely our friend. Because you were a fool yesterday, you're wise to-day; and if you're a fool to-morrow—why, the alternation is established. There's a progression; it is like the rotation of crops.

There's a mort of healing in a brace of longish years. The county, which had found little Mrs. Germain stiff when she came home from her honeymoon, now looked to her for stiffness when it felt relaxed. Her idiosyncrasy was accepted, you see; once admitted to be a person, she became a personage. And, discovered by the county, she discovered herself. She found out that she had a character; she had never known that before, nor had any others who had had to do with her: Mrs. James, to wit, Miss de Speyne, her husband. The process of these discoveries ought to entertain us for a chapter, and its resolution shall be attempted. But the county learned it first, when it came to rely upon her stiff-

ness. The Chaveneys, the Gerald Swetebredes, the
Trevor-Waynes, the Perceforest people, before the
two years were over, forgot that they had ever eyed
each other, with brows inquiring "Colonial?" or
spelling "Hopeless, my dear!" Such looks had
passed, but now, on the contrary, they leaned—
some heavily. Lady Chaveney was one. "She is
charming with Guy," she said more than once,
"quite charming. An influence—in the nicest way."
She added, once, as if the news was sacred, "I believe he's told her everything." Guy was the Chaveney heir, the florid, assured youth whom we met
just now on our visit; he had been pronounced
"wild" by Mr. Germain; and he *had* told her everything. She took herself quite seriously with Guy, in
the elder-sister fashion, Mr. Germain, at first approving, as, at first, he had approved every sign of
her making way. He came, before the end of two
years, to feel differently, lost touch with the sense of
his benevolence, felt to be losing grip of many things.
But in the early days he had approved, there's no
doubt—in those days of stress and taut nerves when,
returning from a honeymoon by much too long, she
had found Mrs. James pervading the great, orderly
house, and had, without knowing it, braced herself
for a tussle, and unawares found herself in it, and
amazingly the winner. Her husband had backed her
up there, in his quiet way. Short, quick, breathless
work it had been—a fight in spasms. She had been
crossing the hall when the great lady came out of the
Little Library.

"Ah, Mary—A Mrs. Burgess has called, I see—
wife of some one in Farlingbridge. She called while
you were out. A politeness very natural under the
circumstances—but not the custom here, I think.
Lady Diana, I happen to know, never—I suppose
you will send cards by the carriage. That would answer the purpose very well. We have never known
the townspeople, you know—in that sort of way.
There is a tenants' party in the summer. They
come to that."

Mary had listened. She was pale, but her eyes
smouldered.

"I can't do that, Mrs. Germain. I mean, I must
return the call."

"Ah? It will be against my recommendation."

"I am very sorry. I asked Mrs. Burgess to call
when I met her the other day at Waysford."

"Really? Waysford? One would meet her
there, I suppose. A Sale of Work?"

"Yes. But I asked her to call upon me. It was
kind of her to come so soon."

Mrs. James pressed her lips together. So soon!
Why, the woman would fly! "Does my brother
know of this, may I ask?"

"I don't know," said Mary, out of breath. She
was scared, but meant to go on.

"It will be better that he should be told."

"If you think it will interest him—yes," Mary
said, and went upstairs—to stare out of window,
clench and unclench her hands. Mrs. James reported the case to her brother-in-law, and Mary

drove, the next day, to Farlingbridge—her husband
with her—and returned the call. Nothing more was
said; nor, when the visit of a Colonel Dermott, V.C.,
and his lady, townspeople, too, had to be witnessed,
was a word of warning uttered. But Mrs. James left
within a fortnight of her rout, staying only for the
first dinner-party at Southover. That was how she
learned that Mary Middleham had character. It
shocked her; and it was annoying, too, that she
could expect no sympathy from James.

The house-parties for the winter shooting, and
those dinner-parties for the county had to be gone
through with somehow. She set herself squarely to
the task, and was glad enough to believe towards the
end of her two years that she was learning the business. There was little to do, indeed, but be agreeable, but she found that more than enough. Agreeable she could be when she felt happy; her nature
was as sweet as an apple. But if she felt hurt she
must show it, and she discovered that that was a
cardinal sin. Then there was the language to master,
the queer, impertinent, leisurely laconics of these
people—expensive, perfectly complacent, incredibly
idle young men, old men without reticence, airy,
free-spoken women, and girls who unaffectedly ignored her. To cope with such as these she must be
even as they were, or seem so. The quickness of
their give-and-take in conversation, the ripple and
flow, the ease of the thing, asked an alertness of her
which excited while it tried her to death. Perpet-
ually flagging at the game, she spurred herself per-

petually; for she discovered that there is no more
deadly sin in the code than an awkward pause, that
being all of a piece with the end and aim of living—
which is smooth running. A woman should die
sooner than drop a conversation, or murder it.

She was at her best with the men, as perhaps she
might expect. She could run, she could walk all
day, chatter, laugh outright, seem to be herself;
they paid her the compliment of approving looks.
But among the women she knew that she *must* be
herself, a very different thing. She felt infinitely
small, ill-dressed, ill-mannered, clumsy, and a dunce.
It was from them, however, that she gained her
reputation of being stiff; she had them to thank for
that. It had come to her in a flash of spirit one day
in the summer of her first year, that if ignoring was
in the wind, she could ignore with the best. She
chose to ignore Mrs. Chilmarke, Mrs. Ralph Chilmarke, a beauty, a dainty *blonde* and a wit. She did
it steadily for three days, at what a cost she could
never have guessed when she began it, and her
reward was great. Mrs. Chilmarke respected her for
it, and the Duchess—a duchess was in the house—
was frankly delighted, and said so. She had watched
out the match, and had backed the *brune*.

Under such exertions as these character will out,
while it may slumber through years of pedagogy.
But she worked hard at her lessons directly she
had found out what she wanted, and was tolerably
equipped for her tour in France and Italy when the
time came. She made no way with Latin—Mr. Ger-

main had to give that up; and English literature made her yawn. She insisted on botany, for reasons unknown to the good gentleman, and became great friends with the head gardener, a Scotchman, who made the initial mistake of supposing her a little fool, and was ever afterwards her obedient servant. Shall we do wrong in putting this study down to Senhouse's credit? I think not. Quietly and methodically, after a method all her own, Mary Germain began to find herself, as they say. But before she did that her husband had to find her; and *he*, poor gentleman, who had had to begin upon their wedding day, was at the end of his discoveries before he was at the end of his honeymoon. So far he struggled, but after that he suffered—dumbly and in secret, within his plate armour. The fact is, there had been too much honeymoon. His evident discomfort had made her self-conscious, killed her ease, threatened her gratitude—upon which he had proposed to subsist—and turned him from an improbable mate into a rather unsuccessful father of his wife.

October is a bad time for honeymoons; the evenings are so long. Nevertheless, at Torquay, her mind had been fairly easy about him. He had liked the hotel. At Saltcombe he had been pretty miserable, much on her conscience. He had taught her chess, it seems, and if she had known what she was about, chess might have done pretty well. But unfortunately she took to chess, and began to beat him at it by audacious combinations and desperate sallies

quite unwarranted by science. That vexed him
sadly. He abandoned the game, telling her frankly
that he could not help being irritated to see skill out-
vailed by temerity. "One plays, you see, my love,
for the pleasure of playing, not to win. That is the
first condition of a pastime." She told him she was
very sorry, and he kissed her. But after that Villiers
used to lay newspapers and reviews on the sitting-
room table while they were dining. She consoled
herself with the remembrance of that kiss on the lips;
it was nearly the last of them. He selected her forehead, from Saltcombe onwards, or her cheek. From
Saltcombe they went down into Cornwall—Truro,
Penzance, Sennen, St. Ives. There it was that she
learned to be happy in her own company. She spent
hours alone, scrambling among the rocks, watching
the sea.

Her life was filling, her vistas opening. This was
great gain, to feel the triumph of discovery. She
had never been so far afield before, and the wild
splendours of rocks and seas made her at times like
a thing inspired. She was amazed at herself—at the
stinging blood in her which made her heart beat.
She used to get up early at Sennen, steal, hatless, out
of the sleeping inn, and fleet over turf to the edge of
the cliffs. There she stood motionless, with unwinking eyes and parted lips, while the wind enfolded her.
All was pure ecstasy; she was like a nymph—bare-
bosomed, ungirdled, unfilletted, in the close arms of
the Country God. From such hasty blisses she returned drowsy-eyed, glossed with rose-colour, with

a sleek bloom upon her, and ministered to her husband's needs, dressed with care, with the neatness which he loved. She sat queitly by him, hearing but not heeding his measured tones, dreaming of she knew not what, save that the dreams were lyric, and sang of freedom in her ears.

They took more tangible shape as they waxed bolder in outline and scope. There was a tumbledown white cottage on the cliff beyond the coast-guard station; two rooms and a wash-house below green eaves. It faced the open sea, but lay otherwise snugly below a jutting boulder, and was so much of a piece with rock and turf that the sea-pinks had seeded in the roof and encrusted it with emerald tufts. Her fancy adorned this tenement; she saw herself there in a cotton gown, alone with wind and sea. What a life! The freedom of it, the space, the promise! Not a speck could she descry upon the fair blue field of such a life. Childlike she built upon the airy fabric, added to it, assured herself of it. Some day, some day she would be there—free! The thought made her perfectly happy; she felt her blood glow.

Mr. Germain complained of the damp Cornish air and took her to St. Ives and Newquay on the way to Southover. Once on the homeward path, he had no eyes for her in Cornwall; all his hopes were now set upon the feast he should have of her, queening it there in his hall—queen by his coronation. She, for her part, was all for lingering good-byes to her glimpses of the wild. She went obediently, but car-

ried with her the assurance that she should see her
cottage again; and by some juggling of the mind, in
the picture of it which floated up before her at call,
she came to see always near it the tilt-cart and its
occupant, her friend of the open Common. A com-
munity down there! The tilt-cart stood in a hollow
of the rocks within sound and sight of the sea; the
Ghost cropped the thyme above it; Bingo ran bark-
ing out of the tent, and, seeing her, lowered his head
and came wriggling for a caress. Above them all,
dominant, stood her friend, bareheaded to the buffeting gale, so clearly at times that she could see the
wind bellying his white trousers or flacking the
points of his rolling collar. His face unfortunately
was not always to be seen; a mist over it baffled her,
but egged her on. For a flash, for a passing second,
his bright, quizzing eyes might be upon her; she
could hear the greeting of the dawn laugh from them,
and feel her bosom swell as she answered it, and
knew the long day before them—and every long
day to come. What a comradeship that might be—
what a comradeship! She came to thank God daily
that she had such a friend, and to declare stoutly to
herself that she had no need to see him. Friendship was independent of such needs; the necessities
of touching, eyeing, speaking—what were these but
fetters? Lovers might hug such chains and call
them leading-strings. Poor lovers could not walk
without them. But friends had their pride in each
other and themselves. Each stood foursquare in
the faith of his friend; the independence of each

was the pride of the other. So far was she from loving Mr. Senhouse that she learned without a pang of
his visit to the Cantacutes in the following summer,
of his painting days with Hertha de Speyne, and
was surprised at herself. It drew the two girls closer
together; it gave zest to letter-writing, and brought
Miss Hertha more than once to Southover. Senhouse was the presiding genius of their fireside talks;
between Hertha and Senhouse Mary began to find
herself—a person, with a reasonable soul in human
flesh.

Her wedding-day, and the days that followed it,
had dismayed the flesh; she could not be one to
whom marriage was a sacred mystery, to be unveiled
to piercing music. She had cried herself to sleep—
once; but she cried no more. If she had been in
love with her husband, even if she had ever been in
love with anybody, she might have been won over
by pity or by passion; but poor Mr. Germain was
incapable of the second, and somewhat to her surprise she found herself unpersuaded, though she was
touched, by the first. She did pity him, she pitied
him deeply, but she could not help him. Esteem
she gave him, gratitude, obedience, meekness,
respect. But herself—after that once—never, never!
For that discharging of her conscience of its poor
little trivial, human load had been forced upon her by
pure generosity on her part (she knew it), and had
cost her an agony of shame. And it had chilled him
to the bone—she had seen his passion fade before her
eyes, such passion as he had. Her generosity had

stultified her, played the traitor. She never taxed him with want of magnanimity, didn't know the word—but she found herself resolute, and was as much surprised as he was. What dismay she had, as the honeymoon wore on, was brought her by her own position, not by her husband's; that a girl such as she, with undeniable proofs to hand of her attractiveness of face and person, with experience of men and their ways, should find herself daughter to her husband! An indulged, courted, only daughter, if you please—but certainly a daughter. Here was an anti-climax, to say the least of it; and her dismay endured through the honeymoon—until Cornish cliffs gave her happier things to dream of. It disappeared as the great red flank of Southover House filled up the scene. Tussles with Mrs. James, the sweets and perils of victory, ordeals of shooting-parties, dinner-parties, household cares, and, above all, routine—such drugs as these sent her heart to sleep. By the time she had been eighteen months a wife she had forgotten that she had never been other than a maiden.

Now, what of Cratylus, poor Cratylus the mature, who, clasping his simple Mero (or Marina) to his heart, found that he had to reckon with her character first? Good, honest man, he had never supposed her to have one; and the bitter thing was that the finding of her character woke up his own. He saw himself again in full plate-armour, cowering behind it, hiding from himself as well as from the world a terrible deformity—an open sore in his self-esteem which could never be healed again, which, at every chance of her daily life, must bleed and ache. Oh, the pity of it, on how light a spring all this had depended—a hair, a gossamer! Exeter—fatal day of Exeter! He had believed himself young again. As she clung to him, half-sobbing, after dinner, he had pressed her to his bosom, called her his bride, his wife. She had not dared to look at him, had bowed her head, hidden her face in his shoulder, let him feel the trembling, the wild beating of her heart. Then her broken confessions; pitiful, pitiful! What did they amount to, when all was told? But they, and what followed upon them—his own conduct, his own curse; and her conduct, and her curse—were his nightmare. He had found out that he could not live if he must remember them. He fought, literally, for life; and after a six months' toil had succeeded in living. He spent himself in benevolence and care, gave her everything she could want, before she asked, taught her, prayed for her, watched over her. She was never out of his thoughts—and, poor girl, without knowing it, she stabbed him deeply every day.

He had his benevolence to fall back upon. He could be King of Southover, of the Cophetua dynasty; he could dazzle her, take her breath away, and have the delight, which he had promised himself, of seeing her misty eyes and cheeks flushed with wonder. Yes, yes; but the æsthetic nerve, you see, dulls with use, and the worst of a king's homage to a beggar maid is that the more obsequious the hom-

age the less beggar is the maid. If you set a coronet
in her hair she will blush deliciously for a week; but
in two years' time it will be there as a matter of course,
put there nightly by her woman—and bang goes
your joy of that. So with all the other enrichments
of society, travel, book-learning. The more she had
of them, the more she was able to take for herself.
He who put her in the way of knowledge could not
grumble if she acted upon what he had taught her.
Such gifts as his destroy themselves. It had filled
his eyes with tears to see his wilding in the great terraced house, to watch the little airs of dignity of
matronhood, wifehood (alas, poor gentleman!) flutter
about her, and, like birds, take assurance, and alight.
Her cares were charming, too. It was pretty to see
her knit her brows over some tough nugget of Dante's,
exquisite when she came faltering to him, coaxing
for help. But then, naturally, the more help she had
the less she came. It grew to be her pride to get
through alone—her pride and his disaster. No.
Tristram Duplessis had been wiser in his generation
than he. If you love to fill a thing you must take
care to keep it pretty empty. Thus it was that King
Cophetua kneeled in vain. He had kneeled too low.

But there's a balm in the passing years for Cratylus as well as for Marina. The musical clockwork
of Southover, which he had promised himself, became his. He went about his duties as landlord,
county magnate, patron of reasonable things, tolerably sure of a welcome home from a pair of kind
brown eyes. Kisses might be his if he chose to call

for them, clinging arms, a warm and grateful heart.
Such things had to be his solace; and sometimes
they were. And he still fought for his treasure,
against all the odds, with his teeth set hard. If he
had lost grip it was because her muscles were more
practised. He must try another, and another, if he
would whirl her in the air. He must impress her
anew, prove to her that he was a man, honour-
worthy and loveworthy. His ambitions were re-
kindled: that was the result of his musings. In the
spring of the year, when the tulips blazed in the
Italian gardens, and Mary Middleham had been
Mary Germain for a good eighteen months, we heard
him speak with young Mr. Wilbraham of Sir Gregory and the Farlingbridge division of the county.
There was a chance of lighting up the wonder again
in a pair of brown eyes. He hoarded the thought for
the month, and by June had made up his mind.
Then he broke it to his Mary. "I will gladly put my
experience at the service of the country," he told her,
"and convince you, if I can, that I am not too old for
a public career." She had told him that he wasn't
old at all, and had kissed his forehead. They happened to be alone for a few days just then; so that
he could draw her down to his knee and talk to her
about himself, and the part she would have to play
for him in London. The house in Hill-street must
be reopened.

III

MATTERS OF ELECTION

THE country showed the periodic symptoms the moment Parliament was dissolved; the market-place of Farlingbridge hummed with rumour. Farmers in gigs pulled up to discuss the affairs of the nation with farmers on horseback, with hedgers, ditchers, tinkers, anybody. Class flowed over class, and The Reverend Stephen Burgess, Vicar of the town, exchanged evening papers with Reverend Samuel Rock, Congregational minister. Blue and red were in the air; Mr. Germain had long sittings with young Mr. Wilbraham. Presently a deputation attended, by leave, at Southover and was received in the library. The seat was to be contested, it seemed; the Honourable Leopold Levitt intended to fight. Now would Mr. Germain fight him? In a weighed speech of twenty minutes Mr. Germain declared his loins to be girded. "Pompous old boy," said Mr. Tom Blyth, the Liberal harness-maker, to Mr. Peake, the Liberal agent; "but he's good enough for the Honourable Levitt." Mr. Peake thought he was just good enough. It was to be a narrow thing, a close-run thing. The addresses of the candidates showed as much. "Those great institutions to which this country of ours—" cried the Honourable Mr. Levitt in ink. "Those institutions to which this great country of ours—" was the peroration of Mr. Germain. There was to be very little in it. Mr. Peake, the agent, said that the ladies would do the trick. The Honourable Mrs. Levitt was stout, and twenty years older than her Leopold.

The writs were out in August, the election was to be in October. Mary, who had begun to lose colour during the summer heats, grew animated again at the prospect of the bustle. She had been getting introspective, too, had been sometimes fretful, sometimes glum. She thought more than was good for her about things which could not be helped. But for a flying Sunday visit, she had not seen her own people since her wedding day; for Mr. Germain had given up Misperton once more, and seemed to dislike the notion of her leaving him at such a time as this. Here, then, was a chance for her to be useful. She told her husband that she felt sure of Farlingbridge, and when he shook his head despondent she told him why. "They like me there, you know," she said, blushing and laughing. "I know they do; besides Mrs. Blyth told me so. Oh, and Colonel Dermott stopped me yesterday and said that you might be easy. He'll speak for you wherever you want him." Colonel Dermott was an introduction of hers to the penetralia of Southover; a fiery Irishman with a turn for sarcasm. What he had really said to her was that he'd go to the stake for her, but that it wouldn't be necessary. He admired her unaffectedly.

As the campaign progressed on its roaring way Mr. Germain became conscious that greater efforts than his own were necessary. The Honourable Mr. Levitt was untiring. He drove his own drag, and seemed to have a speech on the tip of his tongue for every village green. To Mr. Germain speeches were matters of enormous preparation, literary and economic. He balanced his periods as carefully as his convictions; he polished them, gave them form; but he could not fire them, because he had no fire. "We must give it 'em hot, Mr. Germain, we must indeed," said Peake, the agent. Mr. Germain knew very well that he gave it them cold. The charming spectacle of his young wife, in red cloth, driving her ponies in red harness, a red bow on her whip and red roses in her bosom, far from kindling him, whitened the ashes of his hearth. She was pretty, she was gay, she went again and again to the attack, and coaxed for votes as a child for sweets. One great sensation was when Guy Chaveney ratted, and wore red; another when Levitt publicly alluded to her as his "fair enemy," and was drowned in the cheers of his own party. Colonel Dermott swept her into debate with his hand. "Here's the lady we follow and serve, gentlemen," and he turned to her where she sat glowing on the platform. "By the powers, gentlemen, I'd run her up to Westminster by myself," he went on; "but we'll share in the enterprise, if you please." A little more of that and we were in, said Mr. Peake.

Help from on high was promised, of an exciting

kind. The Right Honourable Constantine Jess, President once of the Board of Trade, now Secretary of State apparent, offered to come down and help his old friend. He offered, I assume, in such a way that he could not be refused; for his approach was announced to Mary one morning over the breakfast table, and received by her with the calmness proper to county ladies. But there had been more. "He brings Tristram, his private secretary. You remember Tristram Duplessis, Mary?"

She managed it. "Yes," she said. "I remember him very well."

Mrs. Hartley—Mrs. Leonard Hartley, I mean—said that she had heard him speak. He reminded her of Mirabeau. Sir James Plash had asked, "Which Mirabeau?" and driven Mrs. Leonard into a corner.

"Oh, Carlyle's, of course!" she answered—and the talk flowed over Tristram Duplessis.

But behind her fortification of silver urns and coffee-cups, she did remember him. Her eyes wide, sombre, and brooding, made no sign. It is the prerogative of county eyes to be still, and of married eyes to be indifferent. She did not smile at her thoughts, nor betray that they were not of a smiling kind. But she felt her heart quicken its beat, knew that she was to be put to the proof, and that her husband had chosen it to be so. To the racing rhythm in her head ran the refrain, "I knew he must come. He never forgets."

Notes must be written and answers received. His was very short:—

"Dear Mrs. Germain,—I am very glad to come and help you. Certainly, we must bring him in. Yrs. sincerely, Tr. Duplessis." It required sharp scrutiny to read between the lines of such a letter, and sharp scrutiny was applied—more than once. She pinched her lip over it as she sat alone, and carried it with her as she walked the park—but when she found herself doing that she tore it up. "I am very glad to come and help you"; that "you" was an after-thought. "Certainly, we must bring him in"; that "we" proved it. She knew, better than most, how Tristram could imply himself in a note. He had forgotten nothing, never would forget anything. No! No more had she forgotten.

Of all her former lovers this was the one man who could cause her any disquiet, or have evoked any sensation. She could never have recalled herself as she had been, two years ago, by any other aid than his. John Rudd? Ambrose Perivale? It is doubtful if she would have known them again. Sharper memories, a sharper fragrance clung about Tristram. Of all of them, it was with him that her relations had been the least explicit; but it had been he, also, who had thereby implied the most. He was master of implication—that delicate art which leaves it to the imagination of the object to read what precisely is implied. Had Tristram implied love? She never knew: that made Tristram's dealing so exciting. Of course he had admired her; his savage looks, as if she stung and vexed him, had assured her of that. Her presence—her near presence—seemed always

to make him angry; her absence angrier still, since he
always came after her, and never forgot to let her
see how angry he had been. Yes, he admired her;
but admired other things more, much more: his
books, his scholarship, the power he had, and, vastly
more, himself. He was endlessly interested in himself, only "liked" her as showing him himself in new
aspects; but she accepted that as a part of him, like
the cut of his clothes; and there was no doubt as to
her own feeling; she had admired Tristram on this
side adolatry, just on this side. Tristram intended to
be Somebody: he used to tell her so, in a way which
made her understand that he knew her to be a little
Nobody. All the same, he couldn't keep his eyes off
her, or his steps from turning to where she was, or
was like to be. In a sense, then, she had drawn Tristram Duplessis; and that's an exciting thing for a
little nobody to do.

If he had been her lover as well, it had been in a
way of his own. He had told her often and often that
he disapproved of her—of her too speaking eyes, for
instance (which could and did speak in those days),
of her little affairs with Dick or Tom, as to which he
had given himself the trouble to be exactly informed;
of her lack of ambition; and because she was a dunce.
And she had laughed or blushed, or been offended—
she had never been hurt; and had allowed herself to
be put under the rod of his tongue, or the gibe of his
eyes again and again. She thought now—with hot
cheeks—that she ought to have felt herself insulted,
and, with hotter cheeks, that it was doubtful even

now whether she would feel herself so. To have a book thrown into her lap, with the inference that she couldn't read it; to be kissed without leave asked, or to kiss again without notice taken—these should have insulted Mary Middleham: but would they insult Mary Germain? Tingling cheeks were no answer.

Tristram had indeed been very exciting; he had been unaccountable, arbitrary, splendid; to have attracted his scowling looks had been one of her triumphs. It had been a triumph, even, that Misperton Brand knew all about it, and that part of it had been scandalized. Yet—and for all that—thinking over it now, with his coming again so close at hand, she knew perfectly well that she had not been in love with him, and was not in love with him now. He had treated her in too lordly a fashion altogether. Dimly she could guess that love was another affair. It might be possible for a girl to worship a man as a god—but that was never love. She knew better than that now. But certainly she must confess, even now, to a tenderness for her reminiscences of Tristram, who had singled her out of a herd, watched, followed, engrossed her, and in his own morose and grudging way had seemed to be in love with her. He had known how to kiss, anyhow. As she inhaled the sharp fragrance of those days she was again excited. There had been glamour. She recalled, with a thrill, the Sunday afternoon when Mrs. James had caught him reading Shelley to her under the apple tree, and blushed anew as she had blushed then.

And the continuous alarm of the affair! The moments snatched in pauses of the chase! Yes, there
had been glamour, and it had been sweet—perilous
and sweet. It was a thing to remember, but not to
fear. She didn't think she need fear anything, especially as she had told Mr. Germain all about it—
or as good as told him.

But it's always ticklish work, meeting an old
heart's acquaintance on new terms. Neither party
to the business can face it quite unmoved. For him,
there's the painful, curious inquiry:—"This, this is
she with whom I had fondly hoped—! Now, look,
there is knowledge stored within those limpid eyes—
and I might have put it there! She and I share experiences, which He—that interloper—can never
share. With this I must dress my wounded side."
All that his handshake, or his bow, may convey to
her. Upon her side—the sedately conscious of two
men's regard—veiled within her eyes there's this for
the ousted lover: "You may spare me the rod. I am
another's, who might have been yours. You loved
me once, you told me; be charitable now!" And all
that she will express in the flutter of her greeting.

Tristram Duplessis, loose-limbed, flushed, frowning as of old, may have implied it, or she, who played
him hostess of Southover, may have appealed in that
fashion. "How d'you do?" was what he said in
words, when he took her hand, which she held out,
in a nerveless clasp. He had arrived late in the
afternoon, when the hall was fully occupied; stock-
inged young men, in from shooting, short-kirtled

ladies, in from getting in their way; a dowager or two reading evening papers, and a whiskered professor in slippers. One must imply skilfully in such a company.

And then, to be sure, there was Mr. Constantine Jess, ponderous, benevolent, all for domesticity, to be reckoned with. All women liked Mr. Jess because, although he was prodigiously learned, he owned to a weakness for small talk and soft voices. It was he, then, who had the triumph of the entry. "Ah, Mrs. Germain, this is a welcome indeed. And doth not a meeting like this make amends?" His quick, full-cushioned eyes swept the corners of the room—"My dear Lady Barbara—! Lady Wentrode, your servant—How d'ye do? How d'ye do?" These things accomplished, he turned to his hostess, cup in hand, and sank into the cushions by her side. "We have not met, I think, since that auspicious day—two years ago? Is it that? Dear me, how Time makes sport with us! One should hear the Titans laugh. I had promised myself an earlier contemplation of your felicity, but—business! business!" He sighed, drained his teacup, and asked for more. "It must have been within a week of your marriage that my young friend and I took a fancy for each other. A marriage of minds! Tristram, my dear fellow, when was it?" He had taught his secretary the duty of playing chorus. That was very necessary to Mr. Jess.

Tristram, leisurely, as of old, sipped his tea before answering, got up and waited for another cup while

he collected his reply. "It's a long time—I know
that. Thanks, no sugar."

"Oh, I'm so sorry—I forgot." She looked up at
him hazardously. "You always took it, I thought?"

"I know. But I've dropped all that. Better
without it." He spoke lightly.

The campaign was broached by Mr. Jess. "Well,
and how does my friend in the field? Gallantly, I
am sure; happily, I hope."

Mrs. Germain thought that he would win. "He
works very hard. He's speaking now, somewhere—
out of the carriage, at a harvest home. I ought to
have been with him, but——"

"You stayed to be hospitable to us. We are
grateful. At least, I speak for myself. Tristram
there takes kindness for granted."

"Not Mrs. Germain's," said Tristram, and
startled her.

However, she laughed. "I don't think it was very
kind of me; I was glad to be let off. I'm sure everything will go right now. Did you know that you
must begin to-night, Mr. Jess? Do you mind?
There's a meeting at the Corn Exchange at eight.
We are dining early."

Mr. Jess laid his comfortable hand upon his
heart. "I follow my leader. Where she calls me I
am ever to be found."

And then she raised her eyes to Tristram. "Will
you speak for us, Mr. Duplessis?" He started, as
out of a stare.

"Who? I? Oh, I'll do as I'm bid, of course."

"Enlist him, my dear lady, enrol him," cried Mr. Jess, twinkling, "but if you love me, let him follow me. He has a note like a trumpet."

"Really?" She opened her eyes upon Tristram.

"I can make a row," he admitted. "But perhaps Germain won't like that."

"I am sure he will like whatever you do," said she. Duplessis made no answer, but did not shirk the reflection that, if he did, it would indicate a striking change in the gentleman's views.

At this moment a fair-haired young lady in a riding-habit—Miss Nina Swetebrede of Copestake —came in, craving tea. She distributed her nods and smiles on either hand as she advanced to the table. "Dear Mary, I'm *so* tired," she pleaded. "Do feed me, and make a fuss of me, and I shall love you." The newly arrived gentlemen were made known to her, and Mr. Jess courtly and tenderly jocular, ministered to her needs. She annexed him without scruple. This left Duplessis in possession of the tea-table. But the attack was Mary's.

"So you have taken to politics in earnest?"

He shrugged. "I don't know that I'm in earnest. That's putting politics rather high. The game is as good as another."

She might have known that he would never admit earnestness—to her. But she felt snubbed.

"The fact is," he went on, "that either every side in politics is partly right, in which case it's only common honesty to say so—or that all sides are entirely wrong, which means that only rascals can succeed at it. So that, in any event, one must be more or less of a rogue."

She ventured a little laugh. "I know what you mean—or think I do. I know more about politics than I did—once."

He parried that. "One gets to know something, of course. You talk of nothing else here, I suppose?"

There seemed to be a sting in this. Loyalty must meet it. "But indeed we do—" she began, and he saved the position for her by saying that he wished he could say the same for himself. "But there'll be no chance of rational conversation," he told her, "until that fellow's safely in the Home Office."

Mr. Jess was placidly contemplating Miss Nina Swetebrede's candid blue eyes, and knew nothing of what may have tickled his hostess. Tristram, in a few minutes, asked to be shown his room. "I've got a heap of letters to write, and some to read. May I ring?"

In the pauses of the party strife, when the champions were out in the lists, Mrs. Germain played lightly upon her heart-strings, plucking chiefly that chord of glamour as she remembered it to have been. Duplessis, who noticed everything about her down to the smallest detail—her clothes, her neatly cut shoes, her manner with servants, with Germain, with the roaring public of the hustings—thought that she carried off the thing very well. Better, no doubt, in his absence; but still, very well. She was shy of

him, and that was charming, because it gave her
colour and sparkle; she was quickly on her dignity
—and that was touching. She seemed to court his
good opinion, to dress her little window wistfully.
She made him think of a pullet with its first egg;
still more touching, by Jove! because there was no
egg, and little likelihood of one. And how careful
she was! And how she appealed! "Here I am,"
she seemed to be saying, with every look, "trusted
and responsible, but oh, so safe! Be generous!"
He began to judge her again. A girl of her sort, she
could no more help using her eyes than avoid breathing through her nose. With every darted look, with
every droop of the lids she put herself at his discretion. Well, she needn't be afraid, poor little soul.
He could afford to be generous to one who amused
and touched him at once.

Pity is a heady wine. In a man of this sort—your
conqueror-by-instinct—it inspires magnanimity; and
the worst of that virtue is—you can't be truly mag-
nanimous until you have reduced the object of your
charity to destitution and misery. Before you can
lift her out of the mire you must see her in it. He
may have been tempted, but her appealing look
tempered his rage. Even his grudge against Germain was less sharp than it had been. Germain!
Germain, and this love-lorn little creature with her
peering eyes! Good Heavens, let her take her joy
where she could.

They were rarely alone together, and when they
were she was extraordinarily circumspect. But he

was master of inuendo, and knew her a good scholar.
There was no need for him to say Heigho! to hear
it echo from her breast. And the less he said the
more she would have him say, he fancied. But he
was wrong there.

He said to her once before he left Southover—"I
must ask you this. You are happy?"

She stiffened instantly, and looked steadily in front
of her—at the south front of Southover, it so happened. "I am very happy."

"That's good. I had to ask, you know."

"Had you?" she said naïvely—and then, "I wonder why?"

"You would say I have no business to care?"

She faced him. "No, I shouldn't. You are free
to do as you like."

"And you—?" He frowned. "Aren't you free,
too?"

She touched the flowers in her breast, looking at
them. "Yes, of course, I am. It was nice of you
to ask me. I am very happy."

A *cul de sac*, that way. Damn it.

Once, at dinner, the person of Jack Senhouse
came up for debate. Several persons present had
some hand in the game. Mr. Jess and Tristram
tossed the name about, across and across. Lady
Barbara Rewish flicked it as it passed; Mr. Germain gave it a sedate lift into the air. When it came
to Mary, she let it drop. Mr. Senhouse belonged to
her innermost self; nobody present knew that she
had had anything to do with him. But two things

nearly lost her her self-possession. One was to hear her friend in public discussion—and here she exulted in her secret. The other was Duplessis's scorn of him. That made her hot.

"I was at school with that idiot," he had said, "and at Cambridge. He was always a waster—but he used to comb his hair in those days." He looked down the table at Mary; the shuttlecock was with her, and she let it drop. He saw her do it.

Mr. Germain was now under way, and gave it a lift. "I remember that Mr. Senhouse proposed on one occasion to sleep near my coverts—too near to suit the views of Cradock, however. I regretted what followed."

"What did follow?" somebody asked.

"Well—I regretted it," said Mr. Germain, closing his eyes for a moment. "Mr. Senhouse accepted my explanation in the kindest way. I must confess that I took no particular notice of his hair, save to observe that he wore it uncovered."

"He wears it long," said Tristram, and glanced at Mary Germain.

"If he wears it uncovered," said Mr. Jess, "he'll wear it longer than you, my young friend."

"He may wear it to his heels," Tristram replied; "but not in my company." Here Mrs. Germain gave the signal, and the gentlemen were left to politics.

"That idiot" robbed Tristram of some chance of magnanimity. In the drawing-room he found it out.

"You know Senhouse?" he asked her. She had
no fear of him now.

"Quite well. He is a friend of mine."

"Has he been here?"

"I think not. He doesn't like big houses."

"Oh, he'd come, you know. He's mighty affable."

"I should be very pleased to see him. I like him
extremely."

He laughed. "He's a great talker. Always was."

"He talks very well," said she, "and listens very
well."

"Personally, he leaves me speechless." Here Duplessis rose, and added with fatigue, "But I see we
are not going to agree about Senhouse."

She looked blankly before her. "No—obviously."
Mr. Germain asked her to sing, and she obeyed with
alacrity. She sang prettily, but not well. Ordinarily
she failed in attack; but under Duplessis's watching
brows it seemed that some new spirit had entered
into her. She had never sung better.

The election came and was made, and John
Germain, Esquire, of Southover House, triumphed
over Mr. Leopold Levitt. The very next day the
new Secretary of State (for all had gone well with the
party) made his farewells, and took his private secretary with him. Tristram, wanting scope for magnanimity, had been morose since the Senhouse discussion.

She thanked him lightly "for helping us." "Us!"
to Duplessis.

But he gulped it. "I am glad to have been

of any use. You'll be in town for the session, of course."

"I suppose so. We shall hope to see you."

"Many thanks. You are not supposed to see through Secretaries of State—but Jess should be a good medium. So it's *a rivederci.*"

She gave him her hand. "Good-bye—." But he held it for a minute.

"We are friends again—after this?"

She withdrew. "Yes, indeed. Good-bye."

Friends! It was the result of some very careful balancing, and an odd result, that if Senhouse lost nothing in her regard, Duplessis lost nothing either. His arrogance, you see, was so entirely in character; and it is satisfactory to a woman to find a man come out true to type; it's assurance of strength in him. He had been very odious, and his judgment of a better man was laughable; but he had been superb, all the same. So that it seemed she could be friendly with the pair of them.

There was still a third friend to reckon with. On the day of the departure of the election guests Mr. Germain was very talkative at dinner, and drank more wine than usual; two glasses of port, for instance. He was full of his projects, high in hope; you could detect the cheer under his voice. "Does my Mary see—?" or "I hope my dear one can follow that line of thought," or "I think my child may be satisfied with such a position of trust"—it might be. He thanked her for the "loyal help" she had given him; made her sit with him after dinner, instead of sending her to the drawing-room; held her hand, patted or stroked it, and presently fell asleep, holding it still. Finally, when it was bedtime, he took her in his arms.

She submitted to his embrace, and gave him the kisses he sought; but no more. Presently she looked kindly at him, with a certain power unknown to him before. It spelled gentle negation—pronounced with extreme gentleness, but not to be mistaken. Then she kissed him of her own accord, disengaged herself, and went away. He sat, with shaded eyes, for a long time motionless, but not asleep. His eye-brows were arched to their highest; once or twice his lips moved; he seemed to be crying out upon himself. When they met in the morning it was as usual, or seemed to be so. But his dream was over for good and all; and he had muffled himself against the cold.

IV

WE are to see her now spread her wings for London, and butterfly flights about the flowers and sweets there. Hill-street affords a standard by which to measure her growth. That decorous house in Hill-street which had cowed her when she went to it on trousseau-business, and had driven her once, fairly crying, upon the mercies of Mrs. James, she could now find small and dark. She thought it a stuffy little house, and wondered how many the table would dine, how many must be shut out of the drawing-rooms. There's a famous anecdote of Mrs. James's, often and impressively told by her, which comes to mind here.

It concerns Gerald Gunner, "Laura Gunner's second boy," a famous gentleman-jockey, and, though his years were few, remarkably a rip. "Charming manners, like all that family, but most high-spirited, wild, they say. Bad influences were at work, no doubt. His friends were loyalty itself; everything was hushed up, and more than once. But—" and Mrs. James used to lower her voice— "there was a *fracas* at Sandown. Lord Windle-

sham's horse—they say, my dear, that he 'pulled' it.
You will know what that means, I dare say. I believe there was no room for doubt. Lord Gunner—"
that was, of course, the old lord, father of our recent
acquaintance—"allowed him fifty pounds a year, so
long as he remained in Canada, cutting logs or build-
ing railways—or whatever they do in the wilds; and
the poor boy went out—*in the steerage*. The Heskeths,
during their tour, went to see him some years ago,
and, my dear, it was deplorable! Miles and miles
into desert-swamps. No neighbours, and, of course,
no church privileges. A hovel, literally a hovel,
built by his own hands; barely weather-proof—not
quite that, I am told, in one corner. They arrived
in the evening, rather late, and found him shelling
peas into an old biscuit-tin. His Eton birch and a
portrait of the Queen were absolutely the only orna-
ments; but this, to my mind, is deeply pathetic.
Would you believe it? That poor young man
dressed for dinner every night, directly he had cooked
it. It got cold, and his jacket was *in holes*—but he
never omitted it. Mrs. Hesketh assured me that
she wept. And fifty pounds a year! Think of it.
Of course, he made nothing. What could he make,
with *his* training?"

It is a sad story. Mrs. John Germain's polite education had begun later than Gerald Gunner's; but
to find a house in Hill-street stuffy is symptomatic of
broadening views.

On the other hand, she showed the *bourgeoise*
undismayed when she permitted herself to be ex-

cited. She was all agog for town delights. Lady
Carhawk, a Berkshire dame, was to present her, and
photographs of her little person, stiff, feathered and
bejewelled, making her look, as some wit said, like
a Spanish Madonna strayed into a fair, went down
to Blackheath with promises of a speedy visit in full
dress. Cards fluttered daily upon the hall-table.
Mr. Germain engaged a second secretary: Mrs.
Germain began to think of one, too.

She attacked her pleasures, as once her task-work,
with zest and spirit; she made scores of acquaintances.
Lady Carhawk must have liked her—herself a lik-
able, florid lady; the Duchess of Lanark showed that
she did; Lady Barbara Rewish and others of the
sort found their old hearts touched by the grateful,
graceful girl, who never took a favour without showing that she was much obliged, never refused one
(and that's a rare abnegation), and if she asked you
to do anything for her, coaxed for it with bright eyes
and wooing lips. The Duchess called her a nice little
thing, a pretty soul, a good girl; and the Duchess's
third son, Lord Vernon, did his best to prove how
good she was—and succeeded. She got nothing but
good out of that, for his weaknesses were well known.

Much of this little success she owed to her Southover drilling, which had taught her how little she had
to fear, how little was expected of her in a world
where chatter is the staple, and high spirits a matter
of good taste. Practically, she only had to listen and
to smile. Now she looked her best when she smiled
—her teeth were really perfect. As for listening,

excitement gave her colour and glitter, her gowns were as good as they could be—and what more do you want but the wish to please? That she had. She courted your good opinion, was anxious to be approved. Besides, she could be patronized, and liked it.

There had never been any question of her success with the men, so little, indeed, that it was curious to see how well she stood with the women. Her early years, it has been hinted, did not want of experience: she proved her femininity before she was sixteen. And betwixt the cubs of the village and the young lions of politics is no difference in kind. You vary the allure; but brown eyes are still brown, and ginger is always hot in the mouth. Of these splendid youths Palmer Lovell must perhaps be reckoned with first, he who, for her sake (or so it is said), forsook a young and handsome Viscountess. After a stormy sowing in one field he was now complacently reaping in another. Mr. Germain's party owned him an acquisition, and the same feeling was to be expected of Mr. Germain's wife. Lovell constituted himself her Mentor, waited about great stairways for her, attached himself to her side, and sat out all and sundry. He explained himself unaffectedly as a Hope of the Party, and she was very willing to believe him. But somehow the information did not thrill her as it had when she received it from Tristram Duplessis; with the rising of whose light above the firmament sank the orb of Mr. Lovell.

Horace Wing—romantic to the waist, thence

downwards dancing master, approved himself in her
eyes. He was handsome, affable, an artist in his way.
She had an instinct for style; and he had that. He
knew where to depart from the tailor's ideal, which
is tightness; he knew where to be loose. He could
unbutton a coat to better purpose than any man living—or a phrase, when he saw his way. He always
coloured his phrases. You were thought to hear
birds in the brake, to see cowslips adrift in a pasture
—happy country things—when he discoursed. Some
considered his flowers forced, things of the hot-bed.
But he was discreet, because really he was timid.
The Byron of the Boudoir, Lovell called him, scorn-
ing Mr. Wing. But Mrs. Germain, who knew little
to Byron's discredit, and understood boudoirs to be
made for two, was much taken with this fine gentleman. On his part, he found her attractive because
his world did. He was acutely sensitive to opinion,
with the feelers of a woman for it. I don't mean that
he knew what was in fashion—of course he did; but
that he could detect what was going to be. There he
was almost infallible.

There were others about her—it was quite a little
triumph in its way,—whom to name would be tedious.
But one was a very great man indeed. Robert John
Bernard, Marquis and Earl of Kesteven, a Knight
of the Garter, and an Ambassador. Lord Kesteven
was no less than sixty-odd years old, had a Mar-
chioness somewhere and three mature children, and
a reputation for incisive gallantry second to no
man's. He managed his affairs of the kind deliber-

ately; he had method. When he died it was said that not one single note in a woman's hand was to be found among his papers. That was not for want of hunting for them: and yet—well, if old Kesteven looked at you twice you were worth looking at. That was said. Now, he looked at Mrs. Germain more than twice.

With these tributes at her feet, with such heady incense in her nostrils, it isn't wonderful if she attended the coming of Duplessis with assurance of amusement, wondering what offerings he would bring. Real goddesses, we may suppose, take their worship as of right, but a make-believe goddess discovers an appetite for it the more she gets. She felt perfectly ready for Tristram, and more than ready by the time she had him. It seems that he had thought her out—she might have inferred it had she not been piqued by delay—and decided that he must give himself value. At any rate, he did not present himself at Hill-street until the card for her first evening party made it a matter of duty. Then he came, and was received with airy smiles—as if he had been an old crony! He found her to be extremely at ease in his company, was disconcerted, and showed it. He had come as one prepared to be fatigued; he departed with frowns as one who fears that he has been fatiguing. "Good God!" he said to himself, "she'll be calling me Tristram in a day or two." He reflected that, if she did that, he was done for; that would show that he had ceased to strike her imagination, had become so much furniture, a sort of house-dog. Deeply mortified, brooding over it, he began to need her. His self-esteem sickened; she only could restore its tone. He became really alarmed about himself, couldn't work, failed of audacity, missed his spring. He saw her again—he was in a black mood. She rallied him upon it, and sent him away to entertain Lady Barbara, whose rights no man dared dispute.

Lady Barbara accepted him as a target for some of her archery. "I saw that young lady married to our friend"—and she nodded towards their hostess. "You, I fancy, did not. A most hopeless business I thought. I remember a sister with fluffy hair. Hopeless it would have been if she had been clever— but, thank goodness, she's not. She has just sense enough to be herself; no airs, no smirks nothing to hide. She told old Kesteven all about herself, I hear, at a dinner-party; father, mother, sister Jinny. Kesteven was charmed. That's a sensible girl, you know, not a clever one, who'd spend herself in scheming how to let bygones be bygones. On the contrary, this girl hoards them, for a relish."

Tristram looked very glum. Was she hoarding *him?* For a relish? The old archer went on with her practice.

"Look at her now with Horace Wing. Horace is weaving his gossamers; he thinks she's enmeshed. She's not, you know; she's only pleased. I tell you, she's exactly what she always was. Once upon a time Tom Styles 'took notice' of her, as she would say, hung about the church-door, Sundays. That

was a triumph in its way. Now it's Lovell, or Jocelyn Gunner, or old Kesteven. I don't suppose she
has ever been in love in her life—but I fancy that you
can correct me if I am wrong."

Duplessis faced about. "I? I'm afraid I can't
help you. She knew my people in the country. We
were rather friendly; we liked her. I'm glad to
think that you do, too."

"She amuses me," said Lady Barbara, "and I
certainly admire her honesty. Horace Wing won't,
I think. She'll puzzle him with her gratitude. Horace wants dearer tributes. All you young men do."

Mr. Germain came up to bow over his friend's
hand. "I'm talking of your speech, Germain," she
told him.

"Kindly, I know," said he.

"You were rather magisterial, I thought; but at
least you knew what you were talking about. Tristram here says that's not necessary."

Mr. Germain blinked. He never looked at Tristram, and did not know. "Fortunate, if true," he
said coldly; "but I cannot myself afford to believe
it."

"Ah, Germain, you're too rich, you see," Tristram
said, as lightly as he could, and withdrew to a doorway, whence he could see Mary. Lady Barbara inquired, with eyes and eyebrows, to no purpose. Mr.
Germain was blandly obtuse.

"She's charming," said the old gentlewoman, and
caught him unawares. He started, coloured.

"Yes, yes, I find her so—hourly."

"Who dresses her?" Mr. Germain raised his head.

"Really—. I believe there are consultations—. She looks well to-night. A happy nature, my friend."

"Charming, charming," Lady Barbara murmured; and then—with a look from the door to her friend. "What is he doing now?" Mr. Germain grew alert.

"Tristram? He goes his way, I believe. He was bickering with poor Jess the other day. Jess is the soul of good-nature; but there are limits."

"Plenty!" cried the lady. "There should be more. He'll be in the House by-and-by—a thorn in all your flesh."

Mr. Germain repressed himself. "If he could get a seat. Want of means would restrict his chances. I fear he is arrogant."

"He's able."

"He believes it. That is his only capital sum, I fancy. But I am not in his confidence."

"He has the run of your house?"

Mr. Germain again lifted his head. "He is Constantia's first cousin. My wife is interested in him. She has known him for some years; but she shares my anxieties."

Lady Barbara was touched by his gallantry, but not put off. "An old friend?" she persisted.

"She is willing to believe him so."

Lady Barbara nodded her head. She was a stoic herself.

V

LORD GUNNER ASCERTAINS WHERE WE ARE

GEORGE LORD BRAMLEIGH, roundest and youngest
of men of six-and-twenty, overtaking Jocelyn Lord
Gunner in St. James's-street, tipped him on the
shoulder with his stick-handle. Gunner turned, red
in the face.

"Damn you, Bramleigh, shut up," he said.

"Couldn't shut up to save my life, old chap," his
friend replied. "I'm so fit I don't know what to do
with myself. Come back into the Fencing Club and
make passes at me."

Gunner growled, "See you shot first," and walked
on. Bramleigh joined him, humming an air.

"Look here," said Gunner, after a time. "D'you
know a man called Duplessis?"

"Rather," says Lord Bramleigh. "Go on."

"That's what *he's* doing," Lord Gunner mused.
"His goings-on are awful. He'll make the lady
talked about—and she don't deserve it."

The lady must be named, and Lord Bramleigh
whistled at her name. Reminiscences of a morning
at San Sebastian came upon him, but were withheld.
Lord Gunner poured out his grievances.

"I don't mind a chap hanging round—not one bit. If I wasn't hanging round myself a good lot I shouldn't see it, and shouldn't much care if I did. There's nothing in that. Besides, there are plenty of us. But he messes about; that's what I can't stand. He messes about. And he seems to think she belongs to him."

"That's the way to make her," said the sapient youth. "That's his little plan."

"No, it's not, my boy," he was corrected. "You're off the line. That's what he really thinks—and, by God, he shows it. He's like a dog with a bone. He snarls and turns up his lip the moment you come into the place. Or if he comes late and finds any one there—as he mostly does—he sulks. 'Pon my soul, I hate the brute." The young man tilted back his hat, and looked up at the sky—a pale blue sky, irradiated by the sun and by the burnished copper wires of our affairs. "Where are we now—end of April?—beginning of May? She came to town in February—and here we are in May. I believe he's only been away from the house for three days on end—and that's just now when he's in Paris."

"You ought to know," said Bramleigh: the other snorted.

"I do know. He's up to no good, that chap, I'll bet you he's not. He's not a good sort with women. I happen to know. Now—"

"May a man ask," Lord Bramleigh interjected, "what *you* are up to?"

Lord Gunner looked down at him in surprise.

"Oh, *you* may, Bramleigh. I can stand it from you. I'm all right, you know; I wouldn't hurt her. She'd have a pretty stiff time of it with old Fowls-of-the-air Germain* if it wasn't for some of us, who go and amuse her. She's a jolly girl, you know, and she deserves something."

"Dash it all," cried Bramleigh, "she got something when she married old Germain. She had nothing at all. I'm told he picked her up in a nursery." Lord Gunner jerked an angry head.

"Yes, I know, I know. That wasn't the game, I'll be shot. Why, any one could have done it! He played the God in the Machine; came bouncing out of the sky, and sent the servant in for her. 'Beg pardon, miss, but here's the Archangel Michael come for you. Best clothes, please, shut your eyes, and you'll be married to-morrow.' That was the way it was sprung upon her. What was a girl to do but bless her stars, and say she'd be with him directly? Well, and what I say is, If old Fowls-of-the-air finds he ain't up to the part, he can't drop it and leave her in the lurch. If he can't make himself entertaining, he must be helped."

"That's what Duplessis says," Lord Bramleigh supposed. But Gunner could not allow it.

"I beg your pardon. He says, 'My bread, I believe.' He's a grabber. The mischief of it is that I can't say anything."

---

*The poor gentleman must have been more than usually on stilts when he made the speech (on poultry farming) which earned him this *sobriquet*.

"I think not," said Bramleigh tersely. "But I know a man who could. Just left him."

"Who's your friend, Bramleigh?"

Lord Bramleigh would not be drawn. "Oh—man you wouldn't know. Not your sort. But the lady knows him."

"Couldn't you give him a hint?"

"I could," said Bramleigh with deliberation. "I could, but"—he looked up at his tall friend—"but if I did, I shouldn't leave *you* out, old chap."

Lord Gunner halted and faced him. "You may say what you please about me. I don't care what you say." He looked over to Bond-street. "That's my road," he said.

"The way to Hill-street?" asked Bramleigh.

"The way to Hill-street," he was told.

Lord Bramleigh remained upon the Piccadilly pavement for some minutes, lost in what must be described as thought. His lips were framed for whistling, but no sound came. His eyes stared at nothing in particular. Then he was heard to say, "I'll do it, by Gad," and seen to turn on his heel. He walked down the hill again, the way he had come up.

Her life was such a whirl, it may well be that she had no time to wonder whither she was flying. At any rate, she marked neither time nor direction, nor was aware that her friends were remarking on both. If you had checked her suddenly with the question, Was she happy? she would have stared before she answered you, Of course!

From day to day she hardly saw her husband alone. He breakfasted, as of old, in his room; his secretary came at ten, and stayed to luncheon. He had a nap after that, and went down to the House at four. He might return to dinner, he might join her at a party in time to take her home; but by then he would be so tired that he would drop asleep in the carriage. She may have known, or she may not, that his eyes were often upon her, intensely observant of her gaiety and appreciative of her good manners; she can hardly have known that she was seldom out of his thoughts. It must be confessed that he was not more than a perfunctory guest in hers: she wore his name in her prayers as she wore it abroad—in that world of his to which he had enlarged her, where she now fluttered her happy wings. She paid him, in fact, the service of lip and eye which we pay to God in church. He was, no doubt, the Author of her being. "My husband says"—"My husband thinks—": she never used such a phrase without the little reverential hush in her voice, or without à momentary curtsey of the eyelids. When he showed himself in a room she went instantly to his side; when he was present at a dinner-table her tones were lower, her laughter less infectious. He was Disposer Supreme: he was secure of that dignified but remote office. It was one which he was well qualified to fill; and it was, unfortunately for him, the only one about her person which was then at his service. Nobody knew this better than the poor Stoic himself, nobody knew it less than the engrossed little lady.

It was not until the end of April, or, as Lord Gunner had ascertained it, the beginning of May that she became aware of the fact that she had been seeing Duplessis every day since the short Easter recess. It was forced upon her notice by this other, that for those days he was absent, and that she missed the homage of his knit brows. They were more to her, she found, than Horace Wing's postures or Palmer Lovell's placid contemplation of her charms. Yet each of these rising statesmen was much more her servant than Tristram could care to be. Lovell used to advise her about her gowns: it had got to that. His aunt, Lady Paynswick, had a shop—so that it was reasonable. Mr. Wing took each new apparition of her as an occasion for poetry—surface poetry, so to speak, which a more experienced subject might have found pert; but it sounded very well at the time. Duplessis did none of these things, neither saw, nor admired: he simply frowned. But she liked to be frowned at in that sort of way—she had always liked it. It meant, "You sting me. I have no rest. You could cure my scowls, but you won't. I detest you, because I love you." It was a tribute, implied power—and how could she help liking that? One of the great joys of power is that you can sit back at your ease, twiddle your thumbs and say to yourself, "An I would, I could—!" You must needs feel charitable to him who puts you in the way of that.

After his three days' truantry, when he returned to her side, she showed him that she was glad to see

him. Generous, but mistaken: it made him crosser
than ever. He could be abominably rude when he
chose—and he chose to be so now. She was at the
Opera, alone in her box. He came in after the first
act, nodded and sat down. This she forgave, even
to the extent of offering her hand. "You've been away
—it is nice of you to come. I'm all alone, you see."

He said, one must go somewhere. She laughed
that off. What had been the favoured country? He
named Paris, as if it hurt him horribly. Paris! She
had been there once—on her way home from Madrid. Some day she must be taken there again. It
had been extraordinary—had seemed like walking
on light. Duplessis said that it hadn't been like that
at all, but like walking in smells among a leering
populace. All this was far from gay; but she was
very good-tempered.

It would seem that he had come there to quarrel
with her; for that is what he did. After an act and
an interval of monosyllabic answers, spells of brooding, moustache-gnawing, and other symptoms of the
devil, she roundly asked him what ailed him. He
affected blank astonishment. Ailed him? Ailed?
What on earth should ail him?

"Then," said she, with colour, "I think you
might be civil." He stared, and met a pair of
stormy eyes.

"Am I to understand—?" he began.

"You are to understand," she told him, "that you
are making me very uncomfortable. I have done
you no harm."

Her ancestry, you see, must peep out. She was
preparing a scene—and what can one do then?

"Is that a hint?" he asked her. She turned to
the stage.

"You drive me to it," she said. "You have been
very rude." He rose.

"I can spare you that, at any rate," he said,
opened his hat with a clatter, bowed and left her.
Her bosom rose and fell fast, and faster, as the
clouds gathered and swept across her eyes. Hateful
man—but what had she done? A tyrant: he bullied
women. She felt very lonely; the great house seemed
to grow dark, the great music to howl and bray.
Palmer Lovell came in presently, after him came
Gunner; but she could get no joy out of them, and
waited on miserably for her husband. She found
herself praying for him, who at least would be gentle
with her. He was late, however, and she could bear
no more. She left after the third act.

In her brougham she had a vision—it could have
been nothing else. At the corner of Endell-street,
under a gas-lamp and in the full light of it, she saw
a tall man standing. He was reading a newspaper,
and had no hat on his head. Her heart jumped—
oh, that could be but one person in the world! Her
friend! Senhouse in London!

The detestable Tristram was forgotten; Palmer
Lovell, the mellifluous Wing went down, soused in
Cornish seas. Cornish seas, sluiced rocks, green
downs, birds adrift in the wind, opened out across
the yellow flare of a London night. She went wide-

awake to bed, and lay sleeplessly there. The very next afternoon, as she was coming out of a great shop in Regent-street, crossing the pavement to get into her carriage, she almost ran into his arms.

VI

SENHOUSE ON THE MORAL LAW

SHE could have jumped into them. "You!" she cried. "Then it wasn't a dream at all. I saw you last night—near the Opera."

He teased her with his wry smile. "And I saw you last night at the Opera."

"You were there! Oh——"

"I was in the gallery. I left because, much as I love Wagner, I love air more. I suffocated."

"Oh, but you might have come to see me," she said, with a pout not at all provocative—a pout of sincere regret. "It was quite cool down there. In fact"—she laughed at a memory—"it was very cool indeed. Too cool."

"I don't follow you," said Senhouse.

"You needn't. Perhaps I'll tell you"—she looked doubtfully at him, pondering. "I should like to tell you lots of things. Oh, heaps! Everything—from the beginning. I'm married, you know." He nodded gravely.

"I can see that you are. All well?"

This made her think. "Rather well. But we must talk—it's obvious. Will you——?" She looked at the carriage and the footman at the door of it.

"If that's your carriage—no, I won't, thanks. Have you walked five yards to-day? No? Then we'll walk somewhere and have it out. You might send that sepulchre away. I'll see you home." Her eyes shone.

"I should love it. It shall go." She told the footman her intentions, and sailed happily away in convoy with that tall, loosely clad young man who, to the footman's concern, carried his hat in his hand. "Blooming Italian feller—airing his 'ead of 'air," he told the preoccupied Musters, who said, "Tlk! Tlk!" to his horses.

She, too, remarked it. "Why, you have got a hat!" He held it up.

"Yes, indeed—and I'll wear it if you insist upon it."

"But I don't," she told him. "I shouldn't know you if you did."

He led her at a brisk pace—to meet his long strides she had to break into a run now and again. But she was prouder of his company than of any she had had yet, and caught herself humming airs by the way. There was indeed heaps to say. She plunged into her stored reminiscences as a boy into a pool—went in deep and rose shaking her head, breasting the flood.

"I must tell you—I believe I saw you on my wedding day! From the train—just a glimpse. I saw the Ghost plodding along—Bingo running in the grass—you were sitting on the tilt, smoking, of course. You were in white. Were you there? It

must have been you. We had passed Swindon, I
know—it was before we got to Bath. You were
going West, and so was I—so were we, I mean. I
wondered if we should meet out there—Exeter?
Were you there? Oh—and I mustn't forget. It is
the most important of all. He—my husband—took
me to the Land's End."

He looked down quickly at her. "When were
you there?"

"In October. It was about the middle of October.
Do you mean to say——?"

"I was there in November," said Senhouse, "and
stayed till February—there or thereabouts. I am
always there for the winter. I have business there."

She had put her hand to her side. Her eyes
spelled ecstatic conviction. "I *knew* it—I *felt* it.
How wonderful!"

"What's your wonder, my friend?"

"Why, that I should have seen you there!"

"But you didn't."

"Ah, but I did. That's just it. I was certain you
were there—I expected to find you in every hollow
of the rocks. The place told me of you—it seemed
to bear your mark. If I were an animal I should say
that I could smell you there."

He was amused. "You're not far wrong. I was
thereabouts. You might have smelt some of my
deeds—Flowers—I grow 'em on those cliffs. You
might have seen 'em."

Her eyes were roundly open now—wonderfully—
but she shook her head.

"No, no. I saw nothing of the sort. Do you mean—gardens?"

"Sort of gardens. I work those rocks. I plant things—they are natural rock gardens, those boulders. I started it some six or seven years ago—naturalizing alpines. I've got some good saxifrages to do there—androsaces of sorts—drabas, campanulas, columbines. Then I began on hybridizing—that last infirmity. There's a scarlet thrift I'm trying—fine colour. It don't always come true yet, but it's a pretty thing—*Armeria Senhusiana*, if you please."

Now she was inclined to be serious, with a confession to make. Hertha de Speyne had told her something of all this, and given her an interest in it. Mischief prevailed; she sparkled as she probed him.

"I don't quite understand. You have a rock garden—*you!* I have remembered your scorn of property—of owning anything—and—! Really, I am rather shocked. A garden of yours!"

He looked blandly interested. "Mine? Bless you, no. I haven't got a garden for these things. I grow 'em out there on the rocks. They're anybody's—yours, Tom's, Harry's. I'm only the gardener. And you prove to me that I know my business, because you must have been through my nursery half a dozen times—and saw nothing of it."

"Nothing at all, I promise you." Her share in his little triumph was manifest, she was intensely pleased. "That's lovely," she said—and then, "You know, if I had caught you out—I should have been awfully disappointed."

"I hope I shall never disappoint you, ma'am," he told her. "No. If I owned all that I don't think I should care for it. I esteem those things down there for taking their chance. Tourists hardly ever hurt them. It's the wet that does most harm; the winter wet—sluicing mists, rotting rains—" She touched his arm—nearly stopped the walk.

"I can't keep it up," she said. "I have tried, but it's not to be done. I knew, afterwards, that you did these things. Hertha de Speyne told me. Are you angry?"

He looked closely at her—not at all angrily.

"You talked me over with her, did you?" She blushed.

"Among other people. I know that you were with the Cantacutes the summer before last." Then, with a sudden memory, she stopped again, almost took his arm.

"Did you see—do you know a white cottage— right up on the cliff? A green roof?"

His eyes twinkled. "Rats' Castle! Rather. It has sheltered me more nights than one."

Her lips pressed together as she nodded her head. "I might have known that. I beg your pardon." Thinking of what she was to speak, presently she told him in a grave voice that she intended to live in that cottage—"before I die."

He took that calmly. "You might do worse."

He had come to London, he said, to supply his needs—to sell some pictures in Cranbourne-street, and to see some books. His library was in Blooms-

bury; she gathered, the British Museum. He
wanted "Aristophanes," the "Arabian Nights." He
had nearly everything else. Narrow inquiry revealed
his tastes. He owned two books. "Don Quixote"
was one, "Mangnall's Questions" the other. No—
Bible? No. "Don Quixote" was better than the
Bible, because it was our own. We were not Orien-
tals—at least not now. Everything that a man
could need for his moral and spiritual supplies was
in "Don Quixote"—religion, poetry, gorgeous laughter, good store of courage, wisdom, fortitude. Mangnall was enough for the rest. Old-fashioned, perhaps: but then he, Senhouse, was old-fashioned.
"I always read "Don Quixote" before I say my
prayers."

They were by now in Hyde Park, beyond the
carriage road, nearly alone with the trees and grass
and certain sooty sheep which cropped there. He
found her a chair, but himself sat on the ground and
clasped his knees. She must hear his views upon the
Bible; but she had to press for them. No, no, he
told her at first—it wasn't his business to preach.
Presently, however, he broke out. "You're just a
counter in a game at this hour—put up between the
dressmaker and the policeman. You are property—
and that's the Bible's doing. Why—why—look at
the Ten Commandments—'His wife, servant, maid,
ox, ass—everything that is his!' You come after his
house, if you remember; you come with the flocks
and herds—there you are, even now—and there you
must be until the system breaks down. Your jealous

God, your jealous husband—don't you see that
they're one and the same? The policeman and the
dressmaker; the dueña and the eunuch of the door.
Oh, good Lord! That's Oriental, you know, Turk's
delight. You won't find that in 'Don Quixote'—a
sane, Latin book; but it's in half of the New Testa-
ment. Saint Paul! Women must cover their heads
in church. Why? I'll tell you: the *yashmak!* The
harem is not to be seen—shameful. . . .

"The Catholics are right. They keep the Bible
for the learned. They *know* it won't do. If the Italians, for instance, the most practical, clear-headed
people in Europe, were to get familiar with the
Bible, the Pope might have his throat cut. There'd
be a revolution. . . .

"That's only one point out of a thousand, but it's
a good one. It concerns the welfare of more than
half mankind, and its relation with the other fraction.
If men are to buy and hoard women, it's quite clear
that women mayn't have souls of their own. . . . The
whole social system depends upon their having none.
You are property my friend—marketed by the
dressmaker, safeguarded by the policeman. It is
really too degrading. It degrades the man more
than the woman; makes him a kind of stock-keeper,
the most atrocious form of capitalist there can be.
The Bible, of course, did not establish that—the
system's as old as Hell; no, but it sanctioned it once
and for all. Ever since that Levantine sophist saw
'big business' in Christianity, and ran it in Europe,
the only hope of religion has been in what lurked of

paganism—lurked in the uplands of Tuscany, in the
German forests and Irish swamps. . . .

"Religion is a habit of mind—not a taught thing.
We are all religious in a thunderstorm. But we don't
get it out of the Decalogue. We are all religious when
we are in love; laws of property are forgotten—men
and women are themselves. The accursed part of
the system is this, that they can't be themselves from
the beginning. You must learn the rules before you
can break them. Now if there were no rules at all
there would be no rebels. I hope that's clear."

She listened with head gently inclined and pondering eyes, partly amused, partly disturbed by his
vehemence, but not scandalized, because it was so
like him, and because he was he. Womanlike, however, she must reduce his theories to practice, apply
his rules, bring them home, or near home. Women,
he had said, were property—well, was she her husband's property? Bought? Marketed by the dressmaker? What did that mean, exactly? When, with
a grunt, he stopped his harangue, she tried to formu-
late her speculations.

"I believe that I see what you mean about rules—
keeping and breaking. It's all very puzzling.
Women are put wrong with men from the very beginning—I see that now. What did you mean
about 'being themselves?' Have I ever been myself?"

He laughed, staring at the ground. "Never."

"Well, but—how am I to begin?"

"Go your own way. Defy the dressmaker."

She leaned forward, her elbows on her knees. "Do tell me what you mean about the dressmaker."

He stared at the ground again. "I don't know that I can get much nearer. She teaches you to—to set snares—to lead the eyes—I don't think we can talk about it."

"What am I to do?" She asked him that in a tone so serious that he knew she must be answered.

"Ah," he said, "I can't help you, you know. You must fudge it out as best you can. I'm dreadfully sorry—but that's the truth. You might come to a pass where I could be of use—I hope you won't —there's no reason to suppose it. Meantime——"

"He's kindness itself," she said, looking beyond him. "He was kind from the very beginning—but —I know that I ought not to have married him."

"Perhaps," said Senhouse, "he ought not to have asked you."

Her eyes fell. "No," she said, "perhaps not."

After a pause of some intensity on her part, she broke out. "What you tell me of yourself fills me— makes me excited. It's glorious. You stand on your feet—you are free as the air—owe nothing— while I—what am I? Not even myself. The dressmaker made me—the policeman guards me. My husband—but if I had no husband, what could I do? Belong to somebody else? If I broke a rule——"

He stopped her with a gesture—a quick jerk of the head. She met his eyes.

"The pity will be if you break a rule without getting full value for the escapade. Don't do that."

"I wasn't thinking—I didn't mean you to think—"
He had frightened her; she was quite breathless.

"You must understand," he said, "that, in my
view, you are no wiser to put your body in a cage
than your mind. Both must be free. Don't make
the mistake of thinking that a woman who breaks
our law of property in one way is worse than the
shop thief who breaks it in another. To wound the
feelings of a good and generous man is a serious thing
—but not to take bread when you are starving. At
least, that is how I look at it. But—you must be
very sure you *are* starving. Sincerity is the supreme
virtue, and insincerity the only deadly sin."

She nursed her cheek, while dreams showed themselves in her grave eyes. Whether she was pondering what he said or no, there's no doubt she was giving
it personal application again. Tristram was in her
mind—her morose, exclusive lover. Was her friend
giving a benediction to Tristram's plain desires?
What was she to do then? Was she to be possessed
by Tristram—at last? Sincerity, he said, was all.
Was she sincere? Could she ask—dared she? She
knew that what he told her she should believe—Yes;
and she juggled. She did not want to know what
he would say—because she knew it already. Blame
her as you will—that's the fact.

Very woman that she was, she went about and
about the thing she dared not—peering for the
assurance of her fears. She looked softly at him as
he sat there, plucking the grass by handfuls or making mounts of torn plantains—she looked wistfully.

"You are my friend then—whatever happens to me?"

He met her melting eyes candidly. "Depend upon me."

"Ah," she said, "but I do! Well, then, I must do what seems to me best—I must be brave." He smiled.

"Have your adventures, of course. Don't be afraid of them. Be true to yourself, though—at every cost."

"Yes, yes, I promise you that. . . . When shall I see you again?"

He gazed blankly at the sky. "I don't know, really. I'm a wanderer, you know. But the Land's End finds me from November to February mostly. I begin to work West about October. I am due in the North now—in the Lakes. Wastwater will find me—somewhere thereabouts. I shall be there till September. I leave London to-night—no, to-mor-row—" Their eyes met again, without embarrass-ment. He was the only man she could have com-merce with in this way. "I shall see you at Land's End some day or other," she told him. "When I'm wounded——"

"Caught in a wire by the foot," he laughed. "All right—I'll set you free."

"But suppose you were in Berkshire when I was there—How should I know that you were there? Would you call at Southover?"

He laughed. "No, indeed I shouldn't. I'm a hedgerow chap. I move by night mostly."

"Well, but—you might be within a mile of me, and I should never know it."

"Yes, you would, of course," he said, simply. "You'd know by the trail."

"What trail?"

"Don't you know that? I'll show you. Old Borrow calls it the *patteran*, and swears he got it from a gipsy girl called Ursula. You needn't believe him; I don't. But the trail is certain. A woman who lived in a cave at Granada showed it to me. Look here." He plucked up a handful of grass. "Here's a four-went way"—he marked it with his finger in the dust. "Now watch"—he scattered the grass, which took, roughly, the form of a curved pointer. "You see that on a road—it means the way I am gone. But I do mine with leaves, when leaves there are—with leaves from the sunny side of a hedgerow. You can always tell them." Her brows inquired—she was intensely interested. "Dunce, they are bigger of course, and darker. I use them because the gipsies, who are everywhere, use leaves, too, but never take the trouble to select them. Now you'll always know *my* trail by that. Do you see?"

She clasped her hands together—her eyes danced. "How splendid! How glorious! Then we have a language. I can find you whenever I want you. For if I wanted you very badly, I could set a *patteran* for you, couldn't I?" He nodded. She said in a low voice, "You don't know how strong you have made me—you can never know. Thank you a thousand times."

"Not a bit," he said, lightly. "If we're friends, you are entitled to know my little games."

"And may I speak to you like that—when I go anywhere?"

"Do. We share."

She sighed. "How can I ever thank you!"

The sun was low when she got up, saying that she must go home. It was discovered to be seven o'clock. Why, she cried, they had forgotten to have any tea!"

"Poor girl! Will you have some now?"

"No, no. I don't want it. But I must go. Will you come with me? Or are you engaged?"

"You know I'm never engaged. I shall come with you, of course. Will you drive?"

She shook her head. "No, that's too quick. Let's walk over the grass. It's no distance."

She talked to him of her friends—of all her friends but Duplessis. This he observed. Did he know Mr. Horace Wing? By repute only, it seemed. He could be seen in photograph shops—a very "pretty fellow"; too pretty, Palmer Lovell? Unlicked, he judged. Then he tried her. "I know young Bramleigh," he said with one of his straight looks into the deep of you. "I met him yesterday."

She received the shock unfaltering. "Lord Bramleigh? I hardly know him." He had failed. Lord Kesteven—for she went on blandly with her list—he had never heard of. He asked "What he did?" and made her open her eyes. "Do!" she said, with a comical air of being shocked. "He's a Marquis." This made Senhouse perfectly happy, but he apologized for laughing. "I've nothing against him, you know. I believe it's an honest calling. Does he do nothing else but be a kind marquis to you?"

She affected scorn. "He's an Ambassador—in Paris. I hope that's honest enough for you."

"I hope so, too," said Senhouse, "but I'd rather be a marquis. Is he your friend?"

"He says so. I think he means to be." All of a sudden she leaned towards him; he felt her urgency. "You are my friend. I have no others. You have promised me your friendship."

"You have it, my dear," said Senhouse. They walked the rest of the way in silence; but he stopped once, and interested her again. It was in Mount-street—of all places. He stopped short, as if he was listening; his head high, eyes closed. He was sensing the air, listening to it, smelling it. Narrow Mount-street took the semblance of a forest path, brambled, dusty, hemmed with bracken fronds and silvered roots. "There's rain—there's rain," he said—"I can hear it coming. May be a day off, but it's on the way." She watched him incredulous. "Are you a magician? What are you?" He laughed. "I've got feelers, that's all."

At the door in Hill-street he left her. She was inclined to be tremulous, tender—but he was completely cheerful. He would have gone with a wave of the hand had she not held out her own. As it was, she had prepared a little formal speech—"I cannot tell you how glad I am that we met—I——"

"Don't try to tell me," he said. "I know it. One

takes that for granted—among friends, you know.
That's the privilege of the estate."

"Yes, yes—of course. Well, I won't thank you
for doing what pleases you. I am sure that it *has*
pleased you." She fished for an answer.

"Take it for granted," he repeated.

That braced her. "I will. I do. Good-bye."
This time he did wave his hand.

"Mr. Duplessis have called, Madame," said Greatorex at the door. "He have left a parcel. Lord
Kesteven have called—and Mr. Wing."

The parcel—discreetly phrased—proved to be
most palpably a truss of roses. She unfastened it
herself, and found a slip of paper pinned to the stalk
of one. "Forgive," was written on it. Smiling
wisely, she went upstairs to dress, her bouquet in her
hand.

VII

HAD Duplessis, flowers in hand, sued his forgiveness at any time, she was not the woman to be stern. That was not in her; she was at once too sensitive to the flattery of the prayer, and too generous to refuse it. But at this particular time she felt very strong; fresh from communion with her friend, secure in him, she felt equal to judging a dozen Tristrams —and to judging them leniently. "They know not what they do." That was why she had smiled so wisely to herself on her way upstairs; and it may have been why she wore some of his flowers in the waistband of her gown that night. It was one of her most charming gowns, too; mouse-coloured tulle. In the belt of this she set crimson roses, of Tristram's offering.

She dined out, and went on to a party. Duplessis was waiting for her at the foot of the stairs; they went up together. He had never yet taken possession of her in that manner, and cannot be excused of brutality. But he was quick to presume; was not at all a good object for generosity. Her eyes had answered his inquiry—"Forgiven?" before he touched

her hand; she had said "Of course," and the rest
followed as a matter of course. He assumed from it
his right to be offensive, and her privilege to be un-
offended. She went upstairs by his side, so far as he
was concerned, possessed to all intents and purposes
—under his protection. She did not know it then or
even feel it; her lightness of heart buoyed her up.
Had she not been encouraged in adventure?

By the time they were well past their hostess at the
door Tristram had resumed this air of the vaguely
irritated lion. He looked grandly about him over
heads—his height gave him pretence.

"What are we to do here—? All these people—a
wilderness of monkeys—" When a young man,
sure of welcome, had come up on toe-tips to shake
hands with Mrs. Germain—had bowed, prattled,
bowed and gone, Duplessis showed more than fatigue. He had seen his crimson flowers at her belt,
and they bretrayed him. "I want to talk to you.
Let's go and sit down somewhere. It can't be here."
He spoke shortly, as if he meant it.

She took his arm without question, and he pushed
a way through a couple of full rooms. Beyond these
was a little boudoir, beyond that a library, empty.
She sat, and he stood fidgeting with reviews on the
table, taking up and throwing aside like a child sick
of toys. And she sat softly there with cast-down eyes,
waiting until he chose to remember her.

She was very conscious of his mood, and not un-
satisfied with it. The whole thing was a game, an
adventure, say, and this a recognized move in it.

"Have your adventures—don't shirk them. Sincerity is the great matter. Be yourself whatever happens." He had been plucking up the grass at her feet as he told her that, and she had not been able to see his face, though she had tried. He spoke deliberately, as if he was screwing the words out one by one —as if they ought to be said, cost him what they might to say. Had they cost him anything? Ah, if she could have known that!

But—"Be yourself whatever happens!" Had she a self? What was it? Was it that of a young woman who—of one of those women who like to be coveted, are ready to be owned, who indeed always are owned by one or another? "His servant or his maid, his ox or his ass—" Must she be property, personal property? Ah, but let her never forget that, such as she was, Jack Senhouse was to be her friend—always— at the call of her need. Then she remembered the *patteran*, and smiled to herself.

Presently she looked up at Tristram, scowling over the *Deux Mondes*. "What are you going to do with me, now I am here?" she asked him lightly; whereupon he turned short, and sat down near her.

"What *can* I do with you? What's possible? What am I allowed to say? I feel like a caged cat. Am I to pay you compliments, ask you if all's well? Has it come to that? I know what you would say if I did. You are not happy. It's evident."

It was only in this man's company that she failed of self-possession. With men far greater than he, such as Kesteven; with men defter than he, men of the Wing vein, she could, as it were, hold the reins, and feel the mouth. With Duplessis she was always liable to strike back upon former days. At any moment, had he but known it, he could have put her, so to speak, into a white muslin frock, turned her into the fluttered village coquette. Oddly enough, with all his wits, he had never known it until this moment; he had always read her new position into her old ways. But now it was too plain to mistake; he had but to lift his hand and—! The discovery ran through his veins like a strong wind—to make him shiver.

She was looking down at her hands in her lap, picking up her fan plumes one by one, and running them between her fingers. A latent trembling possessed her, which he felt rather than saw. The same fever caught him.

"Where's Germain?" He spoke masterfully.

Her reply was studiously simple. "He'll come for me by-and-by. He's at the Speaker's dinner."

"He's always somewhere else." Mischief prompted her to ask if he complained of that; but he was not to be drawn.

"If you were my wife," he told her, "I should never leave your side. If you were my wife, I should be your lover always."

Here was a lie, obvious even to her; but the devout imagination in it was enough to thrill her. Watching her closely, he saw that she was thrilled.

"You're not happy," he said, "and I'm not happy. You made a frightful mistake—but mine was worse."

It was hardly the moment to assure him that he was quite wrong. If a gentleman does you the honour to discern misery, even where none exists, it proves attention, at least, to your circumstances. It's an oblique compliment.

She said gravely, "I don't think we ought to talk about such things. I have never given you any reason to think me dissatisfied with——"

"Oh," he broke in, "we're not considering the creature comforts, I imagine. You came here in a carriage from your big house—and you'll go back to a big house in your carriage. I can understand that these are pleasant arrangements; and after two years of them, for what they are worth, you may well confuse them with the real thing. But that—! A full cup, nodding at the brim! Life together! No world, nobody in the world but two souls—ours! And work: work together! Good God, it's ghastly to think of."

He looked haggard, and there was a hollow ring in his voice, the hoarseness of a consumptive. Her heart went out to him in pity, and her hand was laid for a moment on his sleeve. "You are not well—you work too hard. Please don't."

"Work!" he said, "I have none. I wish I had. I've quarrelled with Jess."

"I know. I'm very sorry. I wish that we—that I——"

He suddenly and squarely faced her. "Look here, Molly," he said, and made her heart beat and her eyes quail. He, and he only, had called her Molly.

"You know what's the matter. There has hardly been a day since you've been in town that I haven't seen you—I've found out where you were to be—and I've been, too. You possess my mind; I think of nothing else, can't sleep for thinking. I believed that I should get over it, and perhaps I should if I hadn't seen you again last autumn. There was the mischief. I vow to you I didn't want to come, shouldn't have come if Jess hadn't insisted. A confounded ass—! It all began again then—and now, I tell you fairly I shan't get over it. I'm not going to try. It's stronger than I. . . . And I believe that you care, too. I do believe that, I know you do. You wouldn't sit there so still if you didn't—you wouldn't hide your eyes if you didn't. You dare not show me how bright they are. Ah, but I know how bright they can be, and what makes them shine! No, no, you and I be-long——"

"Oh, don't, don't—please don't!" The cry was wrung from her, and the courage to look at him came. But then, as she turned her head away, she said faintly, "You mustn't," and made things ten times worse.

His next words beat her back. "I love you, do you hear? I adore you—I care for nobody, no rights or claims in the world; I can't live without you. If you won't listen to me, if you drive me too hard, I shall— No, no, that's wicked. Molly, I'll do you no harm, I swear to that. But you and I have got to be together, or I shall go mad. Now you know it all."

She rose, and he with her. Both were shaking; but she spoke first.

"Let me go now, please—take me back. I mustn't be found here." He was ready.

"I'll take you away, now. I'm glad I've had it out with you. Now you know the facts at least."

She put her face in her hands. "It's dreadful. I ought not to have listened to you. It was very wrong. What are we to do?"

"Love each other dearly," said Tristram, and took her in his arms and kissed her. She shuddered and shut her eyes, but did not try to move. Her lips were parted; there came a long sigh. "My darling, my darling girl," he said, and kissed her again. They heard steps, and sprang apart. Her terror was manifest. "Come," he said, "we must get out of this."

She took his arm—she looked as sleek as a stroked dove. They went into the rooms without another word. She was almost at once confronted with people whom she knew, and Duplessis left her with the first group she encountered. She saw him shoulder his way through, nodding to right and left in his grand, careless way; she saw him go out and knew that he would not come back. Engaged in the chatter usual to such times, she talked at random, laughed without knowing what amused her. When she was told that Mr. Germain had been seen—was here looking for her, she gathered her wits at once and went to find him.

He was talking in his calm, superior way to a great

lady. His Court dress suited him—he looked like
his ancestor, Sir William, pictured in the dining-
room at Southover.

The great lady put up her glasses and smiled at
Mary. "Here comes that pretty person you've
given us. How d'ye do, my dear. What's the
secret of your bright eyes? Late hours agree with
you, it's plain; but this poor man of yours wants
care."

"Yes, indeed," said she, thankful of the turn-off.

Mr. Germain made her a bow. "If you have
come to take me away, my dear, I shall not deny
you the pleasure. The whole duty of a wife in the
season is to take her husband from parties. Am I
not right, Duchess?"

"My dear man," said she, "I don't pretend to
such privileges. My husband has been in bed these
two hours. Good-night, you happy pair. Now, my
dear, when will you come to me? The 20th, of
course—my ball. I trust you for that. But do come
in to luncheon—positively any day except to-morrow
and Thursday—oh, and Saturday. Saturday is
hopeless." She tapped Mary's cheek with her fan—
"What a dawn colour!"—and smiled herself onwards, fat, satiny, and benevolent. The Germains
gained their carriage, and he was asleep before they
were in Carlos-place. She sat absorbed, gazing out
of the window, still under the spell of Tristram's
love-making. She went to bed—lay wide-eyed in the
dark for a while; then sighed deeply, and smiled,
and slept. Her last waking thought was sophis-

tical. "He told me to have adventures—and to be myself. And he's my friend, whatever happens." Entrenched behind her philosopher, she had no dreams.

VIII

ADVENTURE CROWDS ADVENTURE

ODD thing! The rain nosed out by the man of weather came to pass. But it delayed for a week or more, which was time enough for many other prophecies to be fulfilled. When, however, it did come it struck her imagination. She awoke late from a night of deep sleep to hear it thudding on roof and balcony and to see, when she looked out, the heavy trees of Berkeley-square streaming like waterweed under a sluice. Here and there a cruising hansom thrashed a way through, now and again a milk-cart. The butcher-boys wore their baskets on their heads. Her first conscious thought was of Senhouse, bare-crested to the wild weather. It would be wild in the open, and, of course, he was in the open. On some wide common, perhaps, facing the gale, with the rolling collar of his jersey flacking like ship's cordage. Ah, to be there with him, sharing the joy of battle!

It was with a sense of suddenly leaving the wholesome, great air for that of a hot-house that she turned to her breakfast tray and pile of letters. She picked up the first of them; the hand was Tristram's. A

letter from him, and a visit, were now daily events.
A letter to him, also, must be written daily, and
somehow delivered.

This one was cavalier in tone. "Sweetheart,—
I must see you, if only to arrange how best we may
meet. What a storm last night! But what a clear
blue promise before us! I shall be in the Burlington
Arcade—Gardens end—at noon. Come. "Tr."

Even she, never yet free from her early subjection
to him, felt that this was not how lovers write to their
sovereign ladies. An assignation—and in such a
place—proposed to Mrs. Germain! She coloured
high and clear. He had done what she could never
have believed possible; he had really offended her.
Nothing in the whole world could have persuaded
her to go.

But by-and-by that sophistry which is ever at
hand to clinch a woman's argument the way she
wants it to travel, modified her view, suggested a
duty. Insolent, arrogant, exorbitant lover that he
was, he must be taught his place. He should see her
inaccessible; he should see her cold profile as she
drove by him without so much as a turn of the head.
Perhaps then he would know that she was not a village girl at his disposal. Perhaps. Thus, at least,
she reasoned—and thus she did. The brougham was
ordered for a quarter to twelve—she kept it fifteen
minutes, and then gave the order, "Bank." Her
bank was that of England, and stands in Burlington
Gardens.

She had no real errand there, but she feigned one.

A cheque was to be cashed. The footman was to take it—and even as she gave it him she saw Tristram at the mouth of the Arcade—in an overcoat to his ankles, his wet umbrella in his hand.

She sat rigid in her place, wide-eyed for events. While looking at Musters's careful back it was perfectly possible to see her lover at his post. He was watching her intently, she knew; but he did not move. He did not intend to go a step out of his way to meet her. True, he had walked to the Arcade—he, who lived in the Albany! A most cavalier lover, this.

The game went on . . . the minutes passed. The footman came back with her money and waited for orders. She named a shop—a jeweller's close by, in Vigo-street. Jinny Middleham was to be married, to a Mr. Podmore, a clergyman, and must have a present. How happily things turned out; the cheque would serve. The touch of Musters's whip caused the hoofs to clatter on the asphalt; the brougham lunged forward and swept her by the shameful trysting-place. She peered sideways as she passed; Duplessis, looking full upon her, did not even lift his hat. Nor, during the hour she spent, fingering enamels, rivières, and rings, did he appear at the shop-door. When she went by the Arcade on her return he was not there. She felt strongly the sensation of escape, and was surprised to be so free from disappointment. Senhouse came back to his own place in her thoughts—he and the wind on the heath. Both good things.

But in the afternoon, at about six o'clock, her cavalier was ushered into her drawing-room, where she sat alone, and stood by the door looking at her until the man had gone out. Then he crossed the room quickly, came straight to her, knelt, took both her hands and kissed them.

He humbled himself. She hardly knew him for the same man. And he did the thing handsomely, too, named himself grievous things, exalted her, wouldn't hear of any excuse. Her generosity, easily moved, was all on his side in a few minutes. She could not hear him accuse himself. Perhaps he had been thoughtless; but she had had no right, she said, to be so angry.

Finally, she wouldn't listen. "If you go on talking so wildly," she told him, "I shall begin to think you don't mean it." And then he did explain.

It appeared that there had been reason in what he had proposed. A certain delicacy taught him that he could not continue calling at the house after what had happened. That could hardly fail to appease her. His seeming insult, then, had really been intensely prompted by his fear of insulting her. She considered this with hanging head.

"Mind you, Molly," he went on, being master of her hand, "I can't withdraw one word of what was forced out of me that night; I can't wish undone one single act. I adore you, and I must tell you so; I love you, and must show my love." Here he kissed her. "The question is, how and when am I to see you. See you I must and will. I wanted to talk to you about that—and how was I to do it? Would you have had me ask you to my rooms?"

It did occur to her here that a better place could have been found, since they met most nights in the week in somebody's house; but she put the cavil by as unworthy. Since he was in her husband's house, however, not disturbed unduly by the delicacy which had troubled him overnight, it would be as well to hear what he suggested.

"I'm not going to be unreasonable," he told her; "I shall settle down presently, and things will jog along, no doubt, for a bit. But at this moment, when I have just won you—after two years, Molly, after two years—I must have you more or less alone for a few days. Upon my soul, I think you owe me that."

He made her feel that she really did; but he frightened her, too. She looked quickly into his face, where he knelt gazing at hers. "You must tell me what you mean," she said. "I don't understand. Alone? For a few days? That is surely impossible."

He explained with eagerness. "Of course, of course! Don't, for God's sake, misunderstand. I would not ask you to do anything which would cause you discomfort. Heaven forbid. I said, 'more or less alone.' Isn't that plain enough? If I can't see you here, it can only be at some of these infernal crowds we all flock to—and how can we be sure of a moment there? Look here, my dearest, think of this plan. I should like you to go and stay with your people for a bit."

That did sound feasible. Her quick mind jumped after his instantly. "My people?" she said, wondering. "Yes, I should love to see them all again. Jinny, my sister, is going to be married. I should have gone for that in any event. Yes, of course, I could go there if——"

He poured out his plans. She should go to Blackheath at once, and he would take her down, leave her at the door. He should take rooms in Greenwich: there was an hotel there, not bad at all. You looked over the river; the shipping was magnificent. Every day he would meet her somewhere—they would both be unknown. Every day they would spend together: Greenwich Park, the river; they could sail to the Nore, round the Mouse. It would be Heaven, he said. And then he pleaded—his love, his misery, his longing. "Without you I'm a lost soul, Mary; if I'm worth saving, come and save me. In the sight of Heaven you were mine on the day I kissed you first. Do you remember when that was? How long ago? Do you think I have forgotten it? Never, never. That kiss sealed you mine—mine for ever. And what am I asking of you now? A few days' human companionship—a sop which you are to throw to a starving man. Haven't you charity enough for that? Ah, but I see that you have—you can't hide it from me." She could not.

He went on from strength to strength. "I save the proprieties by this plan; I secure you absolutely from prying eyes and profane tongues. You will have your people, your mother, to fall back upon if

I could be—if you could fear me scoundrel enough—
My beloved! I wrong you to name such a thought.
You may disapprove of me—you may be hurt—God
forgive me! by things that I say, do, look. They are
things wrung from me by this throttling passion—for
three years I have been gripped by the throat. Ah,
and it must end, or be the end of me! Well—Molly,
look at me. What will you tell me?"

She did look at him then—for one dewy moment.
Pity, kindness, infinite wistfulness, pride—mingled
in the fire, melted, and lay gleaming in her eyes. Won-
deringly she searched his face, ready to quail before
the savagery she expected to read there; but he was
wise—she could find nothing there but honesty,
frank and manly desire; for he saw to it that she
should not. Before she turned her head she had
given him her hand. He stooped and kissed it softly;
then went away.

Before dinner she went to her husband in the library where he sat, with his reading-lamp, blue-
books, and spectacles. "Come in," he had called in
answer to her knock, but did not turn when she entered. As she approached his desk, approached his
studious back, she felt like a school-girl, coming to ask
if she might leave early—with a fibbing reason for the
teacher, which disguised the secret, fearful joy of the
real reason. The school-girl showed in every halting
word, in every flicker of the covering eyelids. . . .

"I was going to ask you—Would you mind if I
were to go to my people for a few days—soon?
Would you be able to spare me, do you think?"

He turned quickly, hurt by her meekness. "My love! Of course! Can you ask me such things?"

She could not afford tenderness from him just now. She took a business-like tone.

"My sister is to be married shortly, as you know. There is a good deal to do. I could help mother, you know. Jinny is staying with Mr. Podmore's family."

He nodded approvingly. "Quite so, quite so. It would be only kind. You have engagements, no doubt—but nothing pressing, I suppose. Have we not people here, by the way?"

"Not until the 26th. This is the 11th."

"Yes, yes, my dear. Make whatever arrangements suit you. When do you think of going?"

"I thought, the day after to-morrow. But——"

"Well, my love?"

"I should not care to go, if I thought—that you might want me."

He turned to his desk. "Want you!" he said under his breath. "Want you!" So careful was he that she could never have guessed the bitterness of that soft cry.

But she lingered yet. "Of course—it is quite close to town. You could write—or telegraph—I could come in a moment."

"Yes, my dear one, yes," he said, his face averted. "It would be easy enough. But I am not likely to disturb you in your happiness."

This would never do. "It would be my duty to come."

He groaned. "Oh, my dearest, spare me!"

She must misconstrue that, or she must fail; she must gulp it down, and she did—but it turned her sick.

"Thank you," she said staidly. "Then I will write to mother." Her fingers were within an inch of his shoulder; they hovered over, almost touched it. Then she went. He covered his face with his hands. I think he prayed.

IX

THE PATTERAN

As she lay watchful in her bed the night before her escapade, she vowed that she had no love for Tristram, none whatever. At the same moment she protested with a cry that she had none for her husband either; indeed, it was rather the other way. Surely, surely, she was entitled to resentment against that poor gentleman. For what reason under Heaven had he broken in upon her laborious days if, now that he had her, she was to be no more to him than a figure at his table? Was this the whole duty of wives? She knew better than that. Nay, then, had wives no rights? Was she bought to be a nun? She declared to herself that she would be willing, should that enable her to help him in his work. But she knew that nothing would enable her; she had insight enough into character to read what manner of man he was. "He can tell me nothing—nothing. And the more he needs me the less he can say so. If I went to him on my knees and begged him to be open with me, he would shrivel before my face. No, no, he must be for ever bestowing favours—he loves to be the benefactor—and that's all he loves.

If he could pity me he would love me again—in his way. But—" and she clenched her little hands and stiffened her arms—"he shall never pity me— never." And then she blushed all over to feel how she had crept to him to ask his leave of absence, and how she had cowered there, with drooping eyelids too heavy to be raised. Alas! and how she had fibbed.

A thought of Tristram here, of his kisses and strong arms about her, made her heart beat. The wild joy of being possessed by so fine a creature was not to be denied, once you blinked the truth that in the very act of taking possession he would despise you for suffering it. That had to be blinked, though. Whatever she might have become by right of marriage, by intercourse with Tristram's own world, by familiarity with its ways—to Tristram she was still a little governess, sent into this world to be kissed and fondled—but no possible companion for a gentleman, or man of parts. Formerly, if she had felt this, she had accepted it; but now—well, it had to be blinked. Mary was no fool. She knew quite well that she had learned the ways of the great. She knew that she was a success. She had been clever enough from the beginning to see that safety lay only in being absolutely herself. While she had gone in and out of Misperton Brand, from school-house to church and back, she had turned her eyes and ears —all her senses—upon these lords of the earth who were lords without effort. Her Cantacutes, James Germains, and their friends—every gesture of theirs had been a study to her. By instinct she had bored into the very marrow of these people. They alone in the world could afford to be themselves. And directly she could afford it she put that into practice—with success, as she knew very well. Tristram Duplessis, however, would have none of that, ignored it. He was entirely himself, too, and never allowed her to forget that she was his inferior. Every look he gave her was, in its way, an insult, implied "You are mine, my dear, for the picking up." She knew that she ought to be offended—but she was *not* offended. She knew that such a homage as his was not flattering—and yet she *was* flattered by it. Then why should she run away from what pleased her? As she asked herself this question, to which the answer had been so easy a little while before, she found herself now echoing more faintly her "Why, indeed?" Was not love a necessity to women? Was she to have none of it? Was she to be an unwedded wife for ever, and unloved? What had her friend told her, that wonderful day in the Park when, it had seemed, the scales fell from her eyes and she saw men and women where before she had seen herds, dressed by the milliner and marshalled by the police? Love, he had said, is a real thing—one of the few real things we have; and it has been turned by the lawyers into a means of securing real property. "It's bad enough that women should lend themselves to that; but worse things are done in love's name, I believe." Well then, if Tristram loved her, in his way, was she not justified in giving him what she had left to give? At that moment she felt his arms about her, his breath upon her cheeks. Yes, yes, he loved her—he had always loved her. Let come what might of that.

She turned on the light and left her bed; she sat at her writing-table and scribbled a few words on a sheet—"I am going to Blackheath to-morrow—by train. I shall leave Charing-cross at 4.15." She put that in an envelope, wrote his name and address, stamped it. Now, what was the time? Two o'clock? It could still be posted so that he would get it at eight. Dressing gown, slippers, a hasty twist to her hair, a cloak and hood—she opened her door noiselessly and crept downstairs.

She was some time unfastening the front door— time enough to cool; time enough to decide with a leaden heart that she had no love for Tristram. The keen pale air tempered her still further. "Be your-self," she had been told; and "Sincerity is the whole matter." Insincerity! There lay the sin. She had to go to the corner of the Square to the pillar-box; but not a soul was in sight: it could be done. Gath-ering her cloak about her, she ventured out, and walked tiptoe forward, with eyes all astare for a po-liceman or late cab. . . .

The houses seemed made of eyes; there was not a blind window but had a witness in it. Mocking, leering, incredulous, curious, heavily reproving she dragged before them her load of shame. Oh, that it should have come to this, that she was a spectacle for all London's reproach! But she sped onwards on light feet, her letter in her hand.

Where Hill-street broadens into the Square stands a great lamp, the centre, as it were, of a pool of light. There had been a storm of wind and rain in the early part of that night, and the surface of the road was fretted with gleaming reflections where mud and water had been blown up into billows. As she stood for a second or two by the pillar-box, her letter not yet posted, her eyes, painfully acute, fell upon this wide, dimpled and cresseted bay, and, although her mind was disturbed, took some sort of interest in the effect. Following the light inwards, she found her looks arrested by something else—a torn spray of a tree, blown, no doubt, from one of the planes in the Square garden—which lay by the pillar-box, almost at her feet. It was about eighteen inches long, bent in the midst, and pointed to the north. Strictly, it pointed north-west.

Immediately she remembered the *patteran* which Senhouse had explained to her. Wonderful thing— if he had passed this way while she was contending with her sin, and had laid this sure sign in the road to show her where he was to be found! It pointed to the north—no! to the north-west. That seemed to make a certainty of it. Her heart beat high, and the flood of happiness rose within her until she seemed to be bathed in it to the chin. She stood alone in that great glaring emptiness, unconscious of everything but her triumphant release from bondage. To the north—safety was in the north, comradeship, health, freedom to breathe and move her limbs! Smiling to herself, she dropped her letter into the pillar-box,

picked up the *patteran* and returned swiftly to the
house, to bed and to happy sleep. Absolved! She
was absolved.

In the morning she arose with the feeling of elation
one has at the opening of an honest adventure; the
day is before you, the world lies mapped out; you
are not to fail—you cannot. She dressed, breakfasted
and read her letters. There was one from Tristram,
which she had not even the curiosity to open. She
lit the corner of it at the spirit-lamp and held it daintily
out while it curled and blackened under the flame
and dropped in charred flakes into the slop basin.
Ghosts of words in silver characters flickered as they
perished—she saw "homage," "heart's queen,"
"kiss," and "my arms." She wrote to her mother at
Blackheath that she was unexpectedly delayed but
hoped to come soon. She would write again, she
said, or send a telegram. Meantime a trunk would
arrive and might wait for her. At eleven she asked
if Mr. Germain was up, and being told that he was,
went in to see him.

If he had been in the mood to notice anything but
his own troubles, he must have remarked upon her
altered habit. She was radiantly well, self-possessed,
and cool. She kissed his forehead lightly, asked how
he had slept, and then told him that she was lunching
out and should have her luggage sent down to Blackheath. She had given orders to her maid, and
should not want the carriage.

Mr. Germain listened heavily, fingering a blue-
book and a pencil. He made no inquiries, had no

suggestions to offer. She anticipated what he might
have had to say as to an approaching visit of the
James Germains by telling him that all arrangements
had been made—and then she said, "I won't disturb
you again. I know that you are very busy."

"Yes, yes," he said. "My work presses upon
me." He sighed, and then asked with studied politeness, "You go to-day?"

She laughed. "I've just been telling you about it."
She stooped and kissed his forehead again. "Good-
bye," she said, "I'll write, of course—if you'll promise to read what I send you."

He caught his breath, and shut his eyes tightly as
if something hurt him; but he did not move from his
chair. Nor did he once seek to meet her eyes. She
could see that he was deeply depressed, but felt no
pity for him just then. Her youth was too strong
within her, her adventure too near, and her freedom
too certain. Yet she hovered above him looking
down at him drooped in his chair, quivering over
him, as it were, like some gossamer insect new-dawn-
ing to the sun. A word, a sigh, a look would have
netted her in; but nothing came. He sat stonily
astare, his face hidden by his hand—the other keeping his page in the blue-book. Looking down, as
from the battlements of heaven an archangel might
survey the earth, she touched his shoulder with her
finger-tips, and was gone.

In reasoning it all out, or rather in flashing her
instinct upon events—for that was her way—she
knew that Senhouse could not himself have laid the

patteran for her guidance. None the less, she was
sure it was intended for her, and that it pointed truly
to where he was. It was June; he would be in Cumberland. Wastwater would find him, he had said.
Her plan, as she worked it out, was to take train to
Kendal and inquire.

This she did. While her trunk and dressing-case
were being delivered at Heath View, and while Duplessis was biting his nails under the clock at Charing
Cross Station, she was being carried smoothly to the
north, snugly in a corner of a third-class carriage,
her cheek to the window-pane, and her bright unwinking eyes watching the landscape as it rushed up
to meet her. The villa gardens and hedgerows of
Herts, the broad Leicestershire cornfields, Bletchley
with its spire, Rugby, Crewe, then the dark over all;
but scarcely for a moment did her eyes leave the
nearing north. She arrived at Kendal at midnight,
and had some tea. Then she found the ladies'
waiting-room, lay on the sofa, and slept.

X

THE BROTHERS TOUCH BOTTOM

The James Germains paid a visit to Hill-street in
June. It was most unfortunate that it was so wet,
but the time was otherwise convenient, since Mary
was away on a visit to her people. This was how
Mrs. James put it—she was never remarkable for
tact. Nor did she care to be. Surely, she would
say, openness is best. Mary once departed, then,
Mrs. James was installed the very next day. The
Rector followed her.

From the first he did not like his brother's looks.
John, he thought, was ailing—ailing and ageing.
He showed an unwholesome white in the cheeks, a
flabby quality in the flesh, poor appetite, low spirits.
Vitality was low; he was feeble. He ate hardly anything, and betrayed a tendency to fall asleep in
pauses of the conversation. Yet he talked, in flashes,
during dinner of his projects, with something of the
old hopefulness. He had lately been asking a series
of questions, agricultural questions, "somewhat
carefully framed"; he had pressed the Minister in
charge of such matter. He was "not without hope"
that some good might result. Then a deputation of

tenant-farmers had been talked of; he "should not be unwilling" to introduce that. It was very characteristic of him to talk negatively; the Rector used to trace it to a Scots ancestress—a Forbes of Lochgour. But he owned to being weary—alas, that a legislator should admit that in June! and said that he looked forward to the recess "like any school-boy." Mrs. James, who loved "plans," asked him his. He had none, it seemed. "Time has pressed upon us both of late; my work and her dissipations! But I must talk it over with Mary so soon as she returns. Her wishes must carry weight with me. I should delight in showing her Switzerland—or Norway——"

"You would not, perhaps, delight in the thousands of people doing the same thing?" Here was Mrs. James, with her challenging note. The Rector marked with concern that John let it go.

She inquired whether he would resume his visits to Misperton Brand. "The Cantacutes often speak of you," she told him, and then remembered that of course he saw the Cantacutes here in town. He bowed his head.

"Then you know, of course, that Tristram's affair —if it ever was an affair—with Hertha is quite at an end?"

No—Mr. Germain had not known that. "I see very little of Tristram," he told her, and resumed the question of holiday-making.

Mary had great leanings to Cornwall. She had been attracted to it upon her first visit, had often talked of it, and lately had seemed to prefer it to Switzerland. She would like to be there later in the year; spoke of November as a good month. "I cannot say that it agrees with me," he added. "A languid, relaxing air—and in November! To my mind a visit to the Land's End in November would be the act of a suicide. But Mary is young and strong; and her wishes are naturally mine—and her pleasures also . . . her pleasures also." If he sighed he was not aware of it. A silence fell upon the table, which became painful to two of the three, though not to be broken. The Rector plunged back into politics. "They tell me at the clubs that Lord Craye leaves India. . . ." But it would not do. Mrs. James had the good taste to rise. The carriage was ordered at 10 to take her to a party.

When she had gone the brothers sat without speaking for some minutes. The Rector drank his claret; John Germain was in a brooding stare. The younger broke the silence.

"Dear old boy, I wish that we could have stopped up a few more days—but the Diocesan Inspector can't be put off. I tried him with my silkiest—he's inexorable—adamant. And then there's Constantia, with a bazaar on her conscience. A bazaar—in July!"

John Germain did not lift his head from the hand that propped it. "My dear fellow, I understand you perfectly. We all have our duties. We must all face them . . . whatever it cost . . . whatever it cost us."

The Rector looked keenly at him. "You are not

yourself, John—that's as clear as day. I do wish that Mary had not left you. It was not like her. She should have known—" His goaded brother sat up sharply—like one who lifts his gory head from the press of battle, descrying fresh foes.

"Mary wished to go. I could not deny her. Indeed, I wished it also. Her parents are alone, and she is useful to them. I believe, nay, I am sure that she is happy there."

"Your belief," said the Rector, "is as pious as the fact, and as rare. The fashion of the day is for children to tolerate their parents. The cry is, 'You brought us into the world, Monsieur et Dame; yes, and thank you for nothing!' Thank God, Mary hasn't caught that trick. But I do think that, if she is needed here, a hint from you——"

"But I will give her no such hints," Germain said fiercely. "I am not so self-engrossed. I am inured to a solitary life, and she is not. I remember her youth, I remember her activity."

"One would have thought that London in June—" the Rector began, and was checked at once. Germain said shortly that the activity excited by London in June was not wholesome. "She is better there than here," he added, and snapped his lips together.

James Germain, having raised his eyebrows at this oracle, immediately lowered them again, and his eyes with them. After a pause he spoke more intimately, feeling his way along a dark, surmised passage.

"I believe you to mean that all this whirl is very new to her, and over-exciting. Must you not be patient, must you not lead? Accustom her to it by degrees? You know what I think of Mary, and that I have followed her steps with interest. You have told me how bravely she held her own in the country; and you aren't likely to forget that she had two years in which to do it. You speak of our duties —meaning, I take it, your own among others? Well, where do these lie, these duties? Where we find ourselves, or where we may choose to put ourselves? You may tell me that public life is, in a sense, your sphere—and so it is, I grant you. But when you entered Mary's little sphere—as you did, something of the suddenest—had you not then to inquire whether that could be made elastic enough to include your own? Surely you had. This Parliamentary career of yours, now. Nobody is more naturally at Westminster than yourself: that's of course. I wish there were more like you, men of sober judgment, weighted with their private responsibilities. Upon my conscience, Parliament seems a place for buccaneering now-a-days—a high sea. I rejoiced, I say, when you stood up. But whether you could fairly ask a girl of Mary's training to take over such work with you—by your side—" Here John Germain held up his hand.

"One moment. You are right, James. I could not. I acted for the best, so far as I could see my way. I listened to my hopes. It was important that I should do something to interest her in—in our life together. There were reasons, serious reasons, into which I cannot now enter. Her life at Southover. . . . She was not happy, she was not contented. She could not be."

James had now nothing to say. He frowned, to conceal his pain. John spoke on slowly, as if labouring both words and breath.

"I have failed her—I have failed her. And since that—I have held out my hands, tried to speak. I am dumb before her youth and eager life. I love her dearly, I need her—but she cannot know it, will never know it. Experience is what she cries for, not of the mouth, but of the heart and blood. I have no blood to give her, and my heart is in a cage." He spoke calmly, with the icy breath of despair upon his mouth; but it was to be seen that his thin frame trembled. . . . "A barrier grew up between us, not made with hands. Fate made her speak when I was at my lowest; it called me to listen when she was made strong by need. Since then she has respected me through fear; loved me by duty. I should have charmed her fears away, made love her food. Alas! You know that I have failed—from the very first."

What could the other say? What could he do but bow his head?

". . . I have endeavoured not to be selfish in this serious matter. It would have been easy for me to have kept her in the country; a plausible thing—it was implied when I took her. But I was not able to do that. The idea of the sacrifice of one so salient and strong, so well-disposed, with so much charm, was abhorrent to me. Deliberately, knowing full well what risks I ran, I chose for this Parliamentary work; and now I have, under my eyes, the result which I feared—the snares are all about her; she cannot walk without danger. And I must watch, and be dumb."

He sat bitterly silent for a while. Then his eyes flamed, and he struck the table with his closed hand.

"Nobody shall take her from me. There is a point beyond which I cannot go. She is mine in all duty and conscience. I am vowed to protect her, and I will do it—both now and hereafter. Where she is now she is safe from the dastardly designs which beset her here. Her father will protect her, her father's house. When she returns, I must take some steps—I must consider my plans—I have time enough. On this I am utterly resolved, that I will rescue her soul from destruction . . . my darling from the lions . . . from the power of the dog."

His voice broke; he could say no more; but his face was white and stern. James Germain had no help for him.

XI

OF MARY IN THE NORTH

She had followed out Senhouse's precepts as nearly to the letter as might be; neither staff nor scrip had she—no luggage at all, and very little money. In her exalted mood of resolve it had seemed a flouting of Providence to palter with the ideal. To follow the *patteran* unerringly—a bird's flight to the north—one could only fail by hesitation. Time, and the pressure of that alone, had insisted on the railway. The road, no doubt, had been the letter of the law.

Perhaps, too, a map was another compromise; but she found one in the station where, having made full use of its water, hair-brushes, and looking-glass, she dallied in the gay morning light—hovering tremulous on the brink of the unknown. It showed her Wastwater—where he had told her he was always to be found; and it showed her Kendal, too, dim leagues of mountain and moor apart. A loitering lampman entered into conversation with her. He was a Langdaler, he told her; used to walk over once a week to see the old folks; and there was another call he had thither, it seems. There was a lady—his "young lady," who took it hard if he missed his day.

He spoke profoundly of Rossett Gill and Green Tongue, of Angle Tarn and Great End, and of the shelter under Esk Hause, which many a man had been thankful of before to-day. He advised the train to Windermere, the coach to Ambleside; thence, said he, you would get another coach to the Langdales, and there the road stops and you must take to Shanks's mare. Here he looked her up and down, not disapprovingly. "Yon's a rough road for you," he considered, "and the track none so sure where the ground is soft. But you'll do it yet," said he; "and I'm thinking there'll be looking for ye out of Wastwater." She blushed, and denied. "Then he's a fule," said the lampman. His final warning was that she should inquire at the hotel before she started off to walk. She promised, and went into the town for a breakfast.

Fold within fold, height above height, wood and rock and water, the hill-country opened to her and took her in. When she changed coaches at Ambleside she was driven into the arms of the west wind, and could feel that every mile brought her nearer to her friend. Before the end of this sunlit day she would be face to face with the one being in all this world who might know, if he would, every secret of her heart. As she thought this, she pondered it. Every secret of her heart? Might he then know all? Yes—and she could tell herself so without a blush—even to that which she dared not confess to herself; even to that,

he might know them all. She was in great spirits,
and there were those in her company upon the coach
who could have commerced with her, by way of exchange or barter. But though her eyes sparkled,
and her parted lips were dewy, she had no looks for
gallant youth. She faced the north-west, and never
turned her face.

The horses drew up, and stretched their necks for
water and the nose-bag; the passengers tumbled
into the inn for luncheon. Mary, faltering no more,
struck out along the valley, up Mickleden, for the
sheep-fold and Rossett Gill. The coachman had
told her that this road could not be mistook; her
trouble would begin from the Gill. "Follow the
beck," he said, "to Angle Tarn—that on your left
hand—and over the pass. Make you then for the
gap betwixt Great End and Hanging Knott. Esk
Hause we call it—a lonesome place. You shall not
turn to right or left, if you mind me. Due nor'-west
lies your road, down and up again to the Sprinkling
Tarn. Maybe you'll find a shepherd there. 'Tis
a place to want company in, they tell me. You
should strike the Styhead pass near by—if you're
in luck's way."

At starting, she felt that she was; springs in her
heels, music in her heart. Up the broad valley, over
rocks and tufted fern, beside clear-running water
she sped her way, until under the frowning steep of
the Pikes she began to climb. Here she had needed
both patience and breath; but being alone with all
this mountain glory, she must frolic and spend her-

self. She took off boots and stockings and cooled
her feet in water and moss; she crossed the beck, and
re-crossed it, picked a knot of harebells for her belt,
stooped to drink out of clear fountains, rested supine
in deep heather, fanned herself with fronded fern,
watched the clouds, the birds, bared her arms to the
shoulder and plunged them after trout. She played
with her prospect, and had never been so happy in
her life. At five o'clock, biscuits and chocolate; and
instead of being by Sprinkling Tarn she was not yet
at Esk Hause.

It was here that she misgave herself, and for a
moment knew the wild horror of the solitude. Man
is not made for the fells; Pan haunts them, and the
fear of him gripes the heart suddenly and turns man
to stone. The sun, sloping, had hidden himself beyond Great End. The world looked dun and sinister
—estranged from her and her little joys and hopes.
She stood on a trackless moorland encompassed by
mighty hills. The black earth oozed black water
where she trod; right over against her stood a mass
of tumbled rock, spiked at the top as with knives.
She was to go neither right nor left, she had been
told; but which was right and which left by now,
when she had roamed broadcast and at random a
few times?

The knowledge that she was intensely alone
braced her against her nerves. She beat back panic
and considered what had best be done. Here stood
the shelter, a rude circle of stones breast-high. Within was a seat half hidden in tall fern and foxgloves.

Until she knew her road more certainly, she would not leave that refuge from the night wind; but at the thought of night coming down and finding her here, alone with bat and crying bird, made her shiver. With the shelter, then, always in her eye, she explored the tableland where now she was on all sides. The walking was rough and boggy; she was near being mired more than once. Fatigue settled down upon her as her spirits fell dead; despair rose up in their place and drove her to frantic efforts. She climbed heights which could give her no helping prospect—since all was alike to her, one intricate puzzle of darkening purple valleys and clouded peaks. And here the darkness came down like a fog and found her still. She huddled closely into her cloak and sat in the shelter, while fear, reproach, and doubts of which she would never have dreamed drove howling over the field—like the warring women of the Rheinfels scenting havoc from afar off, who, or whose likes, we suppose, people the uplands in the night-time while men and women in the valleys sleep with their children about them.

At nine o'clock it was dusk, but not dark; she heard quite suddenly and with distinctness a child crying. "Boohoo! Boohoo!"—a merry note. There was no doubt that it was silver music to her. A child crying, and not far away; she left the shelter immediately, her heart clamative for this blessed solace.

It led her further than she had expected, directly away from the shelter to the edge of the moorland

and down hill among rocks and boulders. She knew that she could not find her way back, knew that she had risked everything. Stopping, with her heart beating fast, she listened for the sobbing wail; caught it again, more clearly than before, and went down after it. The descent became steep, and she very hot; but now the scent also was hot, and she in full cry. Presently it struck upon her close at hand. "Boohoo! Boohoo!"

"Don't cry," she called out clearly. "I'm coming —don't cry."

The wailing stopped, but not the snivelling, by whose sound she was led. She peeped round a great buttress of rock and saw a barefoot boy, his face in his arm, crying pitifully. She ran forward and knelt by him—"What is it? Tell me what the matter is." He showed neither surprise nor alarm—he was beyond that stage—but as she continued to coax him, put her arm round his neck and tried to draw him to her, he turned up presently his bedabbled face and gave her to understand that he was lost and hungry. Mary laughed for joy. Here was one in worse case than she. "But so am I, my dear!" she told him; "we're lost together. It's not half so bad when there are two of us, you know. And I've still got some food left. Now dry your eyes and come and sit by me—and we'll see what we shall see."

He had a pinched, pale face, freckled, and a shock of sandy hair which tumbled about his eyes. So far as could be seen he had no shirt; but he was company, and more—he was poorer-hearted than herself. The mother in all women awoke in her; here was a child to be nursed.

He came to her without preface and sat by her side. She did not scruple to wipe his eyes and mouth with her handkerchief; she embraced him with her arms, snuggled him to her, and fed him with chocolate and biscuits. He seemed hungry, but more frightened than hungry, and more tired than either; for when he had finished what she first gave him he lay still within her arm for some time, with his head against her bosom. Presently she found that he was simply asleep. Happier than she had been for some hours, she let him lie as he was, until presently she also felt drowsy. Then she laid him gently down in the brake, took off her hat, and lay beside the lad. The cloak covered them both; in two minutes she was asleep.

He awoke her in the small grey hours by stretching in his sleep, and then, by a sudden movement, flinging his arm over her and drawing himself close. She took him in her arms and held him fast. He was still deeply asleep. She could hear his regular breath, and feel it too. "Poor dear," she whispered, "sleep soundly while you can." Then she kissed him, and herself slept again.

A sense of the full light, of the warmth of the sun upon her, added to the drowsy comfort of the hours between sleep and waking. The boy was still fast, and she hardly conscious, when some shadow between her and the comfort in which she lay basking caused her to open her eyes. Above her, looking

down upon her, quietly amused, stood Senhouse,
holding his horse by the bridle. The long white
sweater, the loose flannel trousers, bare feet, bare
head—but he might have been an angel robed in light.

She sat up, blushing and misty-eyed. "It is you!
You have come in my sleep. I have been two days
looking for you." The extraordinary comfort she
had always felt in the man's presence was upon her
immediately. Nothing to explain, nothing to exten-
uate, nothing to hide—what a priceless possession,
such a friend!

"Two days!" he said. "You might easily have
been two months—or two years for that matter.
But you have made a mighty good shot. My camp
is not six hundred yards away. I'll show you. But
who's your sleeping friend?"

She looked down at the lad, whose face was buried
deep in bracken. She put her hand on his hair.

"I don't know—some poor boy. I heard him
crying last night when I had completely lost myself,
and followed the sound. We comforted each other.
He gave me a good night, anyhow. We kept each
other warm. But I know no more of him than that.
We'll find out where he belongs to when he wakes.
He wants food mostly, I think." And then she
laughed in his face—"and so do I, I believe."

"Of course you do," said Senhouse. "Come along,
and we'll breakfast. I've just been out capturing the
Ghost. He had wandered far, the old beggar."

Mary jumped up. "What are we to do with the
boy?"

"Oh, he'll sleep for an hour yet. We'll fetch him when his grub's ready. You must help me, you know, now you're here."

"Of course," she said, and walked by him, carrying her hat in her hand. "Are you surprised to see me?" she must needs ask him.

Senhouse raised his eyebrows. "No—I won't say that. I should like to know why you came, though. No trouble, I hope?"

She looked at him, radiant. "No trouble now. I saw your trail—your *patteran*—in London."

He started. "No, indeed, you did not. I haven't been near London since I saw you there. I came straight here by train. But I'll tell you a curious thing. Three nights ago I dreamed of you."

Her eyes shone. "Tell me your dream." But he would not, and she could not make him.

Past Sprinkling Tarn, and by the pass which hangs round about the Great Gable, he led her to a green plateau, high above the track, where she could see the tent. Bingo stood up and barked a welcome short and sharp. Then he came scrambling down the scree to meet her, knew her again immediately, and was profusely happy to see her. It was all like coming home for the holidays. She turned her glowing face to Senhouse, and her brimming eyes.

"Oh, why are you so good to me, you two?" she asked him, with Bingo's head and fore-quarters in her lap.

"Why not?" said Senhouse.

XII

COLLOQUY IN THE HILLS

By the time the coffee was made, and the porridge, and Mary had emerged from the tent, washed and brushed and sparkling, she bethought her of the boy. "I'll fetch him," she told Senhouse. "He must be fed." Senhouse nodded, so she went back to her *gîte* of the night. The boy had disappeared, and with him her cloak.

Senhouse chuckled when he heard her faltered tale. "Nature all over—bless her free way," he said. "She'll lap you like a mother—and stare you down for a trespasser within the hour. She takes her profit where she finds it, and if she can't find it will cry herself to sleep. Don't you see that you were so much to the good for our friend? Well, what have you to regret? You warmed him, cuddled him, fed him—and he's gone, warmed, cuddled, and fed. You've been the Bona Dea—and he's not a bit obliged to you; very likely he thinks you were a fool. Perhaps you were, my dear; but I tell you, fools are the salt of the earth."

"Yes, I know," Mary said. "Of course I don't mind the cloak. He wanted it more than I did.

But what will become of him—poor little pinched boy?"

Senhouse picked up a bleached leaf of rowan— a gossamer leaf—and showed it to her. "What will become of that, think you? It all goes back again. Nothing is lost." He threw it up, and watched it drift away on the light morning wind. Then, "Come and have your breakfast," he bade her.

As they ate and drank she found herself talking to him of matters which London might have shrieked to hear. But it seemed not at all strange that Senhouse should listen calmly, or she candidly discuss them. He had not shown the least curiosity either to find her here or to know why she had come; in fact, after his question of "No trouble, I hope?" and her reply, he had become absorbed in what he had to do that day—the meal to be prepared, and the plantation of Mariposa lilies which he was to show her. "The work of three years—just in flower for the first time. You're lucky in the time of your visit—another week and you would have missed them." But her need to speak was imperious, and so she gave him to understand.

She told him, therefore, everything which had been implied in former colloquies—and found him prepared to believe her. Indeed, he told her fairly that when he had first heard from her that she was to marry John Germain he recognized that she would not be married at all. "Mind you," he went on, "that need not have mattered a bit if the good man had had any other career to open to you. It was a question of that. You might have been his secretary, or his confidante, or his conscience, or his house-keeper. But he's so damned self-contained—if you'll forgive me for saying that—that he and the likes of him start in life filled up with everything except nature. There was really nothing for you to be to him except an object of charity. Nor did he want you to be anything else. He actually bought you, don't you see, so that he might do his benevo-lence comfortably at home. You were to be bene-ficiary and admiring bystander at once. And you must have made him extremely happy until you began to make use of his bounties, and learn by what you had to do without them. Where was he then? It's like a mother with a sucking child. She makes it strong, makes a man of it; and then, when it leaves her lap and goes to forage for itself, she resents it. What else could she expect? What else could Ger-main expect? He gives you the uses of the world; you find out that you are a woman with parts; you proceed to exercise yourself—and affront him mor-tally. I'll warrant that man quivering all over with mortification—but I am sure he will die sooner than let you know it."

Her eyes shone bright. "Yes, that's true. He is like that. Well, but——"

Senhouse went on, speaking between pulls at his pipe. He did not look at her; he looked at his san-dalled feet.

"I may be wrong, but I do not see what you owe him that has not been at his disposal any day these two years and a half. I suppose, indeed, that the blessed Law would relieve you—but by process so abominable and disgusting that a person who would seek that way of escape would be hardly fit to be let loose on the world. That being so, what are you to do? The fact is, Germain's not sane. One who misreads himself so fatally, so much at another's expense, is not sane. Then, I say, the world's before you, if you have courage enough to face the policeman. He can't touch you, you know, but he can stare you up and down and make you feel mean." Then he looked at her, kindly but coolly—as if to ask, Well, what do you make of that? And if he saw what was behind her hot cheeks and lit eyes he did not betray the knowledge.

She could herself hardly see him for the mist, and hardly trust herself to speak for the trembling which possessed her. "Oh, I would dare any scorn in the world, and face any hardships if—" but she bit her lip at that point, and looked away; he saw tears hover at her eyes' brink.

Presently he asked her, "What brought you up here to see me?" and she almost betrayed herself.

"Do you ask me that?" Her heart was like to choke her.

"Well," said he, "yes, I do." She schooled herself—looked down and smoothed out the creases in her skirt.

"There's some one—who wants me."

"I can't doubt it. Well?"

She spoke fast. "He has—wanted me for a long

time—since before I was married. Perhaps I have given him reason—I didn't mean to do that—but certainly he used to think that I belonged to him. I was very ignorant in those days, and very stupid—and he took notice of me, and I was pleased—so he did have some reason, I think. Well, it all began again last year—imperceptibly; I couldn't tell you how. And now he thinks that I still belong to him—and when I am with him I feel that I do. But not when I am away from him, or alone. I am sure that he does not love me; I know that I don't love him. I feel humiliated by such a courtship; really, he insults me by his very look; and so he always did, only I couldn't see it formerly. But now I do. I desire never to see him again—indeed, I dare not see him; because, if I do, I know what must happen. He is stronger than I, he is very strong. I know, I know very well that he could make me love him if I let him. You have no conception—how could you have? You don't know what a woman feels when she is—when such a man as that—makes her love him. Despair. But I must not—no, no, I would sooner die. I could never lift up my head again. Slavery." She shuddered, and shut her eyes; then turned quickly to Senhouse. "Oh, dear friend, I came to you because I was nearly lost one night. I had all but promised. I saw your sign in the road —or thought that I did—just in time, just in the nick of time. And when I saw it, though I had my letter to him in my hand, telling him where to find me the next day— Do you know, I felt so strong

and splendidly free that I posted the letter to him—
and came straight here without any check—and
found you. Ah!" she said, straining her two hands
together at the full stretch of her arms, "Ah! I did
well that time. Because that very night when I was
fighting for my life you were dreaming of me." If
Senhouse had looked at her now he would have seen
what was the matter with her. But he was sunk in
his thoughts. "This fellow," he said, broodingly,
"this fellow—Duplessis, I suppose?"

"Yes."

"I used to know Duplessis—at Cambridge. And
I've seen him since. He's not much good, you
know."

She was looking now at her hands in her lap,
twisting her fingers about, suddenly bashful.

"But I think," Senhouse went on, in a level voice,
"I think you had better go back and face him."

She started, she looked at him full of alarm.
"Oh, don't tell me to do that—I implore you. Let
me stay here a little while, until I'm stronger." He
smiled, but shook his head.

"No, no. Too unconventional altogether. Really
I mean what I say. If you are to be free you must
fight yourself free. There's no other way. Fight
Germain, if it is worth your while; but fight Duplessis at all events. That is essential. Bless you,
you have only to tell him the truth, and the thing's
done."

She was very serious. "I assure you, it is not. He
won't care for the truth; he won't care what I tell

him— No, don't ask me to do that. It's not—kind of you."

Senhouse got up. "Let's go and look at my lilies," he said. "We'll talk about your troubles again presently." She jumped to her feet and followed him down the mountain.

He led her by a scrambling path round the face of Great Gable, and so past Kirkfell foot into Mosedale, bright as emerald. As they neared the mountains, he showed her by name the Pillar, Steeple and Red Pike, Windy Gap and Black Sail. High on the southern face of the Pillar there was, he said, a plateau which none knew of but he. To reach it was a half-hour's walk for her; but he encouraged her with voice and hand. There! he could tell her, at last; now she was to look before her. They stood on a shelf which sloped gently to the south. Mary caught her breath in wonder, and gave a little shriek of delight. "Oh, how exquisite! Oh, how gloriously beautiful!" A cloud of pale flowers—violet, rose, white, golden yellow—swayed and danced in the breeze, each open-hearted to the sun on stalks so slender that each bell seemed afloat in air—a bubble of colour; she thought she had never seen so lovely a thing. Senhouse, peacefully absorbing her wonder and their beauty, presently began to explain to her what he had done. "I had seen these perfect things in California, growing in just such a place; so when I lit on this plateau I never rested till I got what it was plainly made for. Full south, you see; sheltered on the east and north; good drainage, and a peaty bottom. I had a hundred bulbs sent out, and put them in three years ago. No flowers until this year; but they've grown well—there are nearly two hundred of them out now. I've had to work at it though. I covered them with bracken every autumn, and kept the ground clean—and here they are! With luck, the tourists won't light on them until there are enough and to spare. They are the worst. I don't mind the Natural History Societies a bit; they take two or three, and publish the find—but I can stand that, because nobody reads their publications. The trippers take everything—or do worse. They'll cut the lot to the ground—flowers and leaves alike; and, you know, you kill a bulb if you take its leaves. It can't eat, poor thing—can't breathe. Now just look into one of those things—look at that white one." She was kneeling before the bevy, and cupped the chosen in her two hands. "Just look at those rings of colour—flame, purple, black, pale green. Can such a scheme as that be matched anywhere? It's beyond talk, beyond dreams. Now tell me, have I done a good thing or not?"

She turned him a glowing face. "You ought to be very happy."

He laughed. "I *am* happy. And so may you be when you please."

"Ah!" she looked ruefully askance. "I don't know—I'm not sure. But if I am ever to be happy it will be by what you teach me."

"My child," said Senhouse, and put his hand on her shoulder, "look at these things well—and then ask yourself, Is it worth while troubling about a chap like Duplessis, while God and the Earth are making miracles of this sort every day somewhere?" Thoughtful, serious, sobered, she knelt on under his hand.

"Love between a man and a woman is just such a miracle—just as lovely and fragile a thing. But there's no doubt about it, when it comes—and it ought not to be denied, even if it can be. When there's a doubt, on either side—the thing's not to be thought of. Love's not appetite—Love is nature, and appetite is not nature, but a cursed sophistication produced by all sorts of things, which we may classify for convenience as over-eating. 'Fed horses in the morning!' Well, one of these days the real thing will open to you—and then you'll have no doubt, and no fears either. You'll go about glorifying God." He felt her tremble, and instantly removed his touch from her shoulder. He sat on the edge of the plateau with his feet dangling. "Let's talk of real things," he continued after a time, "not of feelings and symptoms. This is one of my gardens—but I can show you some more. Above this plateau is another—just such another. I filled it with Xiphion iris—what we call the English iris, although the fact is that it grows in Spain. It's done well—but is nearly over now. I just came in for the last week of it. And of course I've got hepaticas and auriculas and those sort of things all over the place—this mountain's an old haunt of mine. But my biggest job in Cumberland was a glade of larkspurs in a moraine of Scawfell Pike. I surpassed myself there. Last year they were a sight to thank God for—nine feet high some of them, lifting up great four-foot blue torches off a patch of emerald and gold. I lay a whole morning in the sun, looking at them—and then I got up and worked like the devil till it was dark. . . .

"Some brutal beanfeasters from Manchester fell foul of them soon after—fell upon them tooth and claw, trampled them out of sight—and gave me three weeks' hard work this spring. But they have recovered wonderfully, and if I have luck this year I sha'n't fear even a Glasgow holiday let loose on them."

She was caressing the flowers, half kneeling, half lying by them. "Go on, please," she said when Senhouse stopped. "Tell me of some more gardens of yours."

He needed no pressing, being full of his subject, and crowded upon her his exploits, with all England for a garden-plot. To her inexperience it seemed like a fairy tale, but to her kindling inclination all such wonders were fuel, and he could tell her of nothing which did not go to enhancing the magic in himself. Peonies, he told her of, in a Cornish cove opening to the sea—a five years' task; and a niche on a Dartmoor tor where he had coaxed Caucasian irises to grow like wholesome weeds. Tamarisks, like bushes afire, in a sandy bight near Bristol—"I made the cuttings myself from slips I got in the Landes"— Wistaria in a curtain on the outskirts of an oak wood in the New Forest. That had been his first essay—

ten years ago. "You never saw such a sight—the trees look as if they were alight—wrapped in mauve flames. And never touched yet—and been there ten years!

"I've got the little Tuscan tulip—clusiana is its name, a pointed, curving bud it has, striped red and white—growing well on a wooded shore in Cornwall; I've got hepaticas on a Welsh mountain, a pink cloud of them—and Pyrennean auriculas dropping like rosy wells from a crag on the Pillar Rock. Ain't these things worth doing? They are worth all Chatsworth to me!"

She caught his enthusiasm; her burning face, her throbbing heart were but flowers of his planting. Once more she was splendidly conscious of discovery, of unsuspected distances seen from a height and once more exulted in the strength which such knowledge gave her. No education could have bettered this—an interest in life itself, in work itself. All that day she laboured by his side—digging, weeding, fetching and carrying in that sunny hollow of the hills. She cooked his meals and waited upon him; she grimed her hands, scratched and blistered them, tore her gown, blowsed herself, was tired, but too happy to rest. This, this was life, indeed.

Towards dusk, after dinner, she was so tired that she could hardly keep her eyes open; and Senhouse who had been watching her with shrewd amusement, bade her to bed. The tent was at her disposal, while she remained. Slowly she obeyed him, unwillingly but without question. The day was fading to a lovely close; night, as it were, was drawing violet curtains over the dome of the sky. The great hills were intensely dark, and the valley between them and below lay shrouded in a light veil of mist. It was so quiet that they could hear the Lingmell beck crisping over the pebbles or swishing between the great boulders; and once a fish leapt in a pool, and the splash he made was like a smack on the cheek.

Mary obeyed slowly. She stood behind him where he sat watching all the still wonder of the dusk, hoping he would speak, afraid herself to break the spell of her own thoughts. She was excited, she felt the exquisite luxury of ease after toil; if she had dared she would have indulged her quivering senses. She could deceive herself no more; she had no need in the world which Senhouse could not satisfy, and no chance of happiness unless he did. But she respected him more than she loved him; it never entered her head for a moment that it would be possible for her to draw such a man on. Still she stayed, as if unable to leave him; his mere neighbourhood was balm to her fever.

So they remained for some unmeasured time, while the silence became crushing and the dark blotted out hill and hollow. She could not hear her heart beating, and the pulses in her temples. In a manner she was rapt in an ecstasy: she thought no more; she was possessed; her happiness was at the point of bliss.

Senhouse sat on, motionless, he, too, absorbed in contemplation—like a priest before his altar-miracles.

He may not have known that she was so close to him;
or he may have known it very well. If he did, he
showed no sign of it. His thoughts, whatever they
were, held him, as he sat, his chin between his clasped
knees, rigid as a dead Viking, crouched so in his
tomb of stones. His black, glazed eyes were fixed
sombrely towards the shrouded valley—across it, to
the mountains beyond. So at last, when her pleasure
became a pain so piercing that, had it endured much
longer, she must have cried aloud, she shivered as she
clasped her hands together over her breast—and
then lightly let one fall to touch his shoulder.

She must needs speak to him now. "Do you wish
me to go?"

He answered shortly. "It will be better. Yes,
you had better go."

"Very well—I will. But to-morrow? Am I to go
home to-morrow? I shall do exactly what you tell
me. You know that."

He did not move, nor answer her immediately.
She hung upon his silence.

Then he said, "I'm a man, you know—and you're
a woman. There's no getting away from that."

"And you wish me——?"

"I'm a compromise—by my own act. This is
Halfway House. You may rest here, you see—and
go on—or go back."

She could school her voice, but not her hand which
touched his shoulder. She had to move it away before she spoke. "And if I decide—to go on?"

"You must not—until you know what it means.

Some day—possibly—when you see—not feel—your
way, it may be— Look here," he said abruptly,
"we won't talk about all this.   I told you—in cold
blood—what I thought you ought to do.   Go back
and see Duplessis.   Don't ask me to reconsider that
—in hot blood.   I'm not myself at this time of night.
I saw straight enough when you put it to me.   I
value your friendship—I'm proud of it.   More I
must not say.   It is something to have made a woman
like you trust me.   That's too good a thing to lose,
do you see?   And I'll tell you this, too—that you *may*
trust me.   If you do as I tell you, it will work out all
right."

"Yes, yes—I believe that.   But you told me this
morning to follow—my heart."

"I did, my dear, and I meant it.   But not what
your heart calls out at midnight."

She stood where she was a little longer; presently
she sighed.

"I will do as you bid me—because you bid me;"
and he laughed.

"Reason most womanish."

"Don't laugh at me just now," she said.

He folded his arms tightly, and stooped his head
towards them.   "I daren't do anything else," he told
her; "and I will not."

In the dark she stretched out her hands to him;
but soon she gave over, and gloried in the strength
he had.

"Good-night," she said; and he answered her
without moving, "Good-night."

She stole away to his tent; but he sat on where he was, far into the night.

In the morning light they met as if nothing had happened; and after breakfast he took her by Wast-water to Seascale—to the train for the south. He was the old informal, chatty companion, full of queer knowledge and outspoken reflections. He told her his plans, so far as he could foresee them. He should be going to Cornwall in November.

Then he put her in the train, and touched her hand lightly, as his way was. He looked into her face, and smiled half ruefully. "Don't forget Half-way House," he told her. She could only sob, "Oh, no! Oh, never, never!" He turned away—waited for the train to move—then waved his hand. As the train carried her under the arch, and bent on its course, she had her last glimpse. He stood, white and slim, against the grey buildings. She waved her hand, and was carried onwards to the south.

XIII

THE SUMMONS

SHE knew now that she loved Senhouse, and that knowledge filled her with indescribable triumph, and gave her unimagined strength. At the same time, the quietude of her new joy really amazed her. She could lie back in her corner seat of the train and watch her flight to the south, be conscious that every thresh of the great driving wheels was taking her from her beloved, reflect that she could neither write to him nor hear from him—wanderer that he was, and sojourner in tents—and regret nothing, and long for nothing more tangible than she possessed already. He had her heart; she had made her surrender on that night of intense colloquy. That had been her true bridal night—by that mysterious intercourse she had become his irrevocably. A great security possessed her, a conviction, which it would have been blasphemous to question, that all was well. If one had told her, you and he may never meet again, she would have laughed in his face at the absurdity. Such a thing was not worth argument, spelt its own refutation.

An immense content possessed her, a security

which excused her from looking back, and made the
future indifferent. She thought neither of her husband with remorse nor of Duplessis with apprehension. She was not appalled by the flatness of her
immediate prospect: of a return to town and its
round of flurry, chatter, and dress; of Southover and
its autumn rites. These things were shadows of life:
the real life was hidden in her heart. She would send
her tricked-out body to dinner-parties and other
assemblies of dolls, while she herself would be
elsewhere, in some blue immensity of air, breasting some great hill, breathing the breath—which
was food—of her mother the Earth—*her* mother!
Their mother! She and her beloved were brother
and sister. Entertainment here, for the flying miles,
to which the threshing wheels lent processional
music.

If she hardly knew herself it is no wonder. She
crossed London by rote, reached Blackheath, walked
sedately to her father's little house, entered the little
dull door, and kissed her parents, whom she found
at tea—all in a dream. They made much of her, the
great lady she was become; found it not amiss that
she appeared in tumbled gown, with soiled blouse,
and hat remarkable for its unremarkableness. Great
ladies could do as they pleased, being a law unto
themselves. Nor were they confused by her replies
to the proper inquiries. "Mr. Germain?" she said,
"I think he's very well. I haven't seen him since I
left London. We don't see much of each other, you
know, Mother." A stack of forwarded letters was

indicated, telegrams among them. She nodded her head, and passed her cup for some more tea.

She heard of the girls' progress—all out in good boarding schools of her providing; next of Jinny's triumphs in the Lincolnshire home of the Pod-mores. "Jinny has a bold way with her, as you know, Mary. They were not inclined towards her at first. There was a question whether she should not pack up her box again the day after she got there —but Mr. Podmore—her Mr. Podmore—went on his knees, *on his knees*, Mary—and she consented to stay. Very bold of Jinny, considering that old Mr. Podmore is a Rural Dean——"

Mary smiled. The simple talk went on. By-and-by it came out that a visitor had called to see Mary several times—a Mr. Duplessis, a very tall young man. "He came here the evening we had expected you, and I thought the chimney was afire when I heard his knock. Exactly like the fire brigade. I opened the door in a twitter—and there he was—six feet-two of him, and a tall hat atop of that. "Is Mrs. Germain at home?" he asks me, and I say, "She may be, for she's not here." Then he says, "You are Mrs. Middleham, I take it." I tell him he takes me rightly. "Don't you expect your——Mrs. Germain?" I told him the truth. "I'll call to-morrow," he says—and he did, Mary, and to-day, too. A handsome, upstanding young man—very much at home with the likes of me. I suppose—but you know your own business best, of course."

Mary stroked her mother's cheek. "Dear little

old Mother," she said, "I know you're afraid for me. Mr. Duplessis is quite harmless. I'll see him, if he comes to-morrow."

In the intervals of housework—for she insisted upon being useful—she wrote to her husband from day to day, telling him in her first letter that she had been unable to write before as she had been travelling. On this particular information he made no comment whatsoever; indeed, he confined himself to such generalities as the state of the weather, his cold, "which, under medical advice, I am nursing at home," and the proceedings of Mrs. James. "Constantia is a great comfort to me. You will be pleased to hear that I am not without hope of inducing her to prolong her visit. She speaks very kindly of you. My brother, I regret to say, has been called home by parochial cares. . . . The Cantacutes dined here last evening. I regretted that I could not be down to receive them. However, Constantia. . . ." She replied pleasantly to all this, feeling not one grain of discomfort out of anything which Mrs. James could or could not do. She begged to be kept informed of his cold. "You know that I will come to you the moment you care to have me." In answer to that, by return of post, he wrote that "on no account" must she alter her plans. "Believe me, I am fully contented that you should be with your parents. It is, I understand, reckoned a failing of the past generation that children should admit any claim in them who bore and nurtured them. Personally, I do not pretend to be abreast of the times in this particular;

nor should I wish you to be so. I am assured that there is no cause for uneasiness on my account, and will most certainly see that you are kept supplied with bulletins. I beg my sincere respects to your father and mother."

After that she heard nothing more from him.

Duplessis had called two days after her arrival, but she had been out, and he had not waited. He came again after three days' interval—having written to announce his intention—at 11 o'clock in the morning. She was on her knees, in pinned-up skirt and apron, her arms bare to the elbows, scrubbing the kitchen floor, when his knock resounded through the house. The quick blood leapt into her cheeks, but she held to her task. Her mother came fluttering in. "That's your visitor, Mary. What am I to do? —and you in such a state!"

"Show him in here, Mother," says Mary.

"Never, child. He'll think you demented."

Mary was inflexible; her eyes glittered. "I shall see him nowhere else," she said.

Upon his second attack, a scared and serious Mrs. Middleham opened the door. Mary, pausing in her scrubbing, heard the dialogue.

"Oh, good-morning. Mrs. Germain?"

"My daughter is here, Sir."

"Oh, she's come, has she? Do you think she would see me?"

"She says so, Sir. I have asked her. But she hopes you will excuse her untidiness——"

"Oh, of course——"

"She has been kind enough to help us here—she
is at work now. You will please to overlook——"

"My dear Mrs. Middleham——"

"If you will follow me I will show you where she is."

Mary rose from her knees to receive him, having
wiped her hands and arms on her apron. Her
cheeks were burning and her eyes alight—but she
looked none the worse, assuredly, for that.

When Duplessis, stooping his fair head, entered
the kitchen, she came forward lightly to receive him.
"Good-morning," she said. "You will take me as
I am?"

"I'll take you how I can," said Tristram, shaking
hands. "Your mother prepared me for this attack
of industry. You might let me help you."

Mary laughed. "Don't destroy my mother's illu-
sions. She is convinced of the complete idleness of
the upper classes. If she lost that she would have to
alter all her ideas of society."

"I don't know anything about the upper classes;
but Mrs. Middleham can have no notion how hard
I can work," Duplessis said. "I was at it all last
night. Dancing till Heaven knows when."

"I'll warrant Heaven does," said Mrs. Middleham to herself. She was not able to find anything
to say to this magnificent visitor.

Duplessis and Mary made a fairer show, for she
had learned to dread, with the high world, a single
second of awkwardness. She was even able to continue her work on her knees and chat with Tristram,
who, for his part, sat calmly on the kitchen table and

talked nineteen to the dozen. It is difficult to say
which side of this simple performance scandalized
Mrs. Middleham the more—that Mary should be
on her knees with a scrubbing brush, or that Duplessis should not be. The good blunt woman sat it
out as long as her endurance would last, growing
more and more stiff in the back, primming her lips
in and in until she showed none at all. Finally she
rose with a "You will excuse me," and stalked out of
her own kitchen. She sat in the empty parlour and
looked at a photograph album as a protest. Mean-
while Mary's hour had come. It had been on the
edge of her tongue to ask her mother to stay—but she
had dismissed the thought as unworthy. She fixed
her mind upon the plateau of Mariposa lilies, and
her eyes on her work, and scrubbed for life.

"Molly," said Duplessis, "why did you run away
from me?"

She elbowed her brush stoutly. "Because I was
afraid of you," she said—then stopped and looked
up at him. "But I'm not now—not in the least
afraid."

"You need not be. You wrote to me that you
were coming on the 13th."

"I know."

"And this is the 20th, and you are only just
here."

"No. I have been here four or five days."

"Where were you—when you were not here?"

"I was travelling."

"Travelling!"

"Yes. But I decline to be questioned."

"You mean, I suppose, that you will decline to answer."

Her colour rose. "You always correct my language, I know. My exact meaning is that I deny your right to question me about my own affairs."

"But if they are my affairs, too? May I not know what you are doing with them?"

She thought. "Yes—I suppose you may do that."

"Very well. Then I will ask you why you sent me word that you were to come here on the 13th ' by train,' and then did nothing of the sort?"

On her knees still, she faced him with her answer. "Yes, I will answer that. When I wrote, I intended to come—and expected that you would meet me. But when I posted the letter I had changed my mind. I did *not* intend to come."

He stared, with very cold, bright eyes. "You did *not* intend to come when you posted the letter? Pray, did you intend me to expect you at the station?"

She answered him, "Yes, I did expect it."

He raised his eyebrows. "Really, my dear friend, you interest me extremely. Did you think that six hours or more at Charing Cross Station would be good for my nerves, morals, or constitution?"

"I will tell you what I thought," she said. "I thought that waiting at Charing Cross would be no worse—to say the least—for a man than an appointment in Burlington Arcade could be for a woman."

Duplessis bit his cheek. "That was your gentle reproof, then, for my blunder?"

"Yours was only a blunder because I saw what it really was. It had never entered your head that I could be other than honoured to meet you anywhere. You presumed that I should run there."

"You ran very near to it, my friend," he said. "That is, you had yourself driven."

She bowed her head. "I admit it. I was a fool—but I am not a fool now."

"No," said Duplessis, "you are not. You are, as a matter of truth, extraordinarily beautiful just now, and I am more ridiculously in love with you than ever. But—" She rose from her knees and stood before him.

"Let me finish what I have to say to you, please," she said. "That was not my only reason for deceiving you. I wished you to wait for me in vain, because I wished you to understand that I could not see you any more. I wished you to believe that our intercourse must be over. I chose the harshest means I could think of. I might have written it, no doubt, but you would have answered the letter, and I am no match for you in writing. I might have seen you and told you—but I couldn't do that."

"Molly," said Duplessis, folding his arms, "why couldn't you see me?"

She looked down. "Because I couldn't."

"It was because you dared not," said Duplessis.

She did not answer; she was trembling a little now, and he saw it. But presently she looked him straight in the face.

"Yes," she said, "that is true. I did not dare."

He laughed gaily and started forward to take her;
but she put her hand up.

"No," she said, "you are mistaken. I dared not
then, but now I dare. I can meet you now whenever you please, and have no fear at all."

Duplessis, red in the face, scowled and watched
her from under savage brows. "Am I to understand by that that you have ceased to care?"

"You must understand that I do not love you."

He left the table where he had been sitting and
took a turn about the room. Presently he stopped in
front of her. His height gave him great advantage.

"I decline to take that answer. I cannot believe
that you mean it seriously. I think that you loved
me two, nearly three years ago, and that you have
loved me of late since last October—some nine
months. I know that I have never for a moment
ceased to love you. Through your engagement—
horrible entanglement as it was—through your years
of married life—miserable eclipse—my love has
gone on, my need has increased. You know that;
you cannot doubt me. It was not my doing that you
were false to our love; I couldn't interfere; it was
begun without my suspicion, and all the mischief
done before I could get home. After that I did my
honest best to get on without you—and then your
fool of a husband must drag me in. What next?
The inevitable, the undoubted. We two were drawn
together: it had to be. And now you ask me to believe that—for no reason at all—it must stop. My
dear girl, you can't swap horses crossing the stream,

you know. I decline to be switched off like so much electric current. Who's the other man?"

This surprising turn to his speech nearly threw her off her pedestal. But she could answer him truthfully.

"There is no question of caprice or of other people at all. The real truth is that I have grown wiser. I know now that I was losing my self-respect by permitting you to love me as you did—in the manner you saw fit to use. It was not love at all—you had got into the habit of considering me as your property, and you could not bear that anybody else should claim a right to me. Directly I saw that, I knew that I couldn't allow myself to think of you, to be with you —if I was to be—if I could hope to hold up my head."

He was very angry. "May I know what, or who, enabled you to see this unfortunate aspect of my affairs?"

"I can't tell you that," she said. "It came to me suddenly. I think your asking me to meet you in such an extraordinary place had something to do with it."

"I beg your pardon for that," he said at once. "Honestly and sincerely I am ashamed of that. Only it is fair to say that I meant no possible disrespect to you. I couldn't well meet you in your own house. The weather was beastly—I thought we could discuss our plans—and might as well do it under a glass cover as under umbrellas. We might have been there five minutes. Really, I can't admit that the base is broad enough to hold all the superstructure."

"It was nothing," she admitted; "I was only offended for a moment—and of course if I had still been nursery governess I should have gone, without a question. I should have been flattered, I am sure. But—ah, surely you can be honest with yourself, surely you know what it is you want of me. Why, if I could bring myself—would it be worthy of you to—?" She broke off, impatient at the hopelessness of convincing him. "Mr. Duplessis," she said, and he frowned at the style, "I have been wicked, I think—at least, I have been so foolish that I can hardly believe it was I. I am sure you won't be so ungenerous as to pin me down to a mistake. I beg you to take what I say now—as I mean it."

Looking up at him, she saw that she had made no way. The more she said, she could see, the greater the fire in the man. He stooped right over her, and she could hear the fever in his voice.

"My love, my adorable love—I shall never give you up—never—never——"

She cowered. "Ah, be merciful——"

He said, "My mercy shall be my love and service"—and took her hands.

She strained away—she turned her head—"No, no," she murmured, "I implore you." But he drew her in—"My beloved—my darling——"

The street knocker clamoured—a double call—and as he started she sprang back to the wall, and gained the door. She went down the passage and met her mother with a telegram in her hand. "For you, Mary. No bad news, I hope."

Mary read. "Think it would be well if you could come to-day.—Constantia Germain."

She had not heard from Hill-street for three days. Yes, certainly she must go.

"Mother, I must go home immediately. Mr. Duplessis will take me. I'll tell him to wait."

She returned to the kitchen; Duplessis was biting his cheek leaning against the table with folded arms. His breath was still quick.

"Mr. Duplessis," said she, "I have had a telegram from home—from Mrs. James. My husband is ill and I must go to him. Will you take me, please?"

He jumped forward. "Of course. I'm very sorry. I'll do everything. Go and get ready—I'll find a cab."

XIV

VIGIL

A SHADOW, not hers, which moved, kept Mary silently employed. She was watching it. She was not conscious of having spoken a single word from the moment of farewell to her mother until her arrival at Hill-street. Duplessis had accompanied her from door to door. She cannot have been aware of it, or she would have dismissed him at Victoria.

Not that he had been obtrusive—far otherwise. He saw to everything, and what conversation there had been, he had made it. She might have been grateful to him for all this, had she observed it. Once only had a cry escaped her. "He is dying. He will die thinking me wicked. What shall I do?"

He had answered her. "No. He is a just man. You have nothing you need fear to tell him."

"He is dying," she repeated, her eyes fixed upon the dun waste of houses and chimney-stacks. Duplessis could not doubt this. It seemed as certain to him as to her. He, too, discerned the moving shadow.

As he helped her out of the cab in Hill-street the carriage came quickly up and the Rector of Misperton in it. He and she met on the pavement. Duplessis lifted his hat, re-entered the cab and departed —seen, therefore, by the Rector, by Musters, and the carriage-groom, and by the stately butler and his familiar at the open door. She and James Germain went up the steps without greeting. As she went straightforward to the stairs she heard the Rector's inquiry, "Well, Greatorex?" and Greatorex's reply, "The doctors are there, Sir. There is no change."

She went lightly up the stair, to the door of her husband's room; she knocked lightly. A nurse opened. "Who is it, please! I don't think——"

"I am Mrs. Germain. I must come in."

Mrs. James, the doctrine of the Soul's immortality lambent upon her features, stood by the window talking in whispers to a great physician. Another, equally imposing, was by the bed, his hand on the sick man's pulse. At Mary's entry the lady broke away and came towards her. The light of conflict was in her eyes, tight upon her lips; she was prepared for reproof in any form—but none came. Mary did not see her. She walked past her on tip-toe, to the edge of the bed, and sat herself in a chair which stood there, and looked at the shadow which was not her own. It hovered, now, moved no more. Sir Lambton Tweedale, his investigation ended, joined his colleague by the window.

Mary thought that he was dead. He lay on his back with nearly closed eyes, and she could discern no movement for breath. His face was colourless, and so frail, so diaphanous did he look, she thought that

she could see the colour of his eyes through the lids,
a haunting thought. He seemed to be watching her
through them, as if they were a thin veil—to be reading her, whether guilty or not. Of pity for him lying
there so noble, so patient, and so fordone; of awe
before his remoteness from her lot, his immortal
indifference; of remorse for what had been, or a shud-
der for what might have been—she had none. But
her eyes watched him intently, with a new power in
them, a fierce and feverish light—as if she had the
will and the means to draw the dead back to life.
For one half-hour only, to fulfil one need. He must
hear her tell him her story; and then he might die
in peace.

One of the great pair came to where she sat on the
watch, and bowed. "Mrs. Germain, I think?"

She nodded sharply, without turning her eyes.

"I could—we could—have wished that you had
received earlier notice of this serious turn. It seems
to have been Mr. Germain's express desire that you
should not be needlessly alarmed. He was perfectly
conscious and master of himself twenty-four hours
ago. But a great change took place yesterday afternoon, it appears. Neither Sir Lambton nor myself
can be held answerable for——"

She stopped him by an impatient movement of
her head. "Do you think he is—in danger?"

"Undoubtedly. It is right that you should know
that it is serious."

"He will die?"

"Ah, we must not say that."

She looked him through and through. "Then he is not dead?"

"No, no."

"Thank you. That is all I want to know."

The learned pair went out together and Mrs. James with them. The nurse remained—to drink her tea and hover. She was very ready with whispers; but Mary sat, with fixed, intense eyes, willing her husband to live, and asked for no details. By-and-by the Rector came in on noiseless feet and stood by her. Between these two there had always been sympathy; generosity on his part repaid with gratitude on hers. But now she would not turn her head. Nor even, when she felt his hand touch gently on her shoulder and stay there, could she bring herself to acknowledge the kindly act.

He remained by her so for a long time. Then, "My child," he said, "have you had any tea?"

She shook her head. "No, thank you. I don't want any."

"It could be brought you here."

"No, thank you."

"You must be brave, Mary."

Ah, she knew that! "I must, indeed," she said.

"Remember, please, that I knew of this no sooner than you did."

She started, she flushed. What did this mean, then? Was it possible that Mrs. James—for reasons —Ah, and if it was, did it matter? Did anything matter? Only one thing—and that was of her provision. She resumed her hungry, patient watch.

The Rector still stood by her, his hand on her shoulder.

"Be patient, my dear. Trust the future to the good God."

She said, "I do. But he will not die yet. I am sure."

"Ah, my dear—" he began, in his despair. But she spoke on vehemently.

"He cannot—he will not. He will know me again presently—and speak to me. That is necessary for us both. We have things to talk about. Then he will die."

The Rector shrank. "You talk strangely. What do we know? My dear old brother! . . . Will you not come and rest—after your—?" He stopped there, and she understood his reason.

"I'm not at all tired," she told him. "I shall sit here until he wakes, and knows me. I can rest here quite well. I don't want any food or anything." The Rector urged her no more, and presently left her.

She sat on through the dinner-hour, the change of nurses, motionless and absorbed. Once the patient stirred, sighed, muttered with his lips. Listening to him, breathless herself, she could now hear his breath —so short and light it was that she must have over-looked it all these hours. From this time onwards through the ministrations of the night-nurse, through visits of the Rector, through ominous absence of visits from the Rector's wife, through the bustling entry of Dr. Goodlake and his voluble explanations—double pneumonia—absence of will-effort—and the like—

she was in a fever of hope and anticipation, waiting, like one tense at the starting-post, for the signal.

At midnight Mr. Germain stirred and began to moan, regularly, hopelessly, in a way to break your heart. This, too, her certainty gave her the heart to endure. Such nourishment as he could be given set him wandering. He spoke ramblingly—often of her —cited scripture—"My darling from the lions," she caught; and "the lion and the dragon shalt thou tread under thy feet." Once he cried aloud, "Ha! Tell Wilbraham I will not see him—" and again, moaning, "No, no, it is untrue—it cannot be true." There followed a time of broken sleep—at three o'clock, with a grey line of light between the curtains, she saw his open eyes fixed earnestly upon her.

She was on her knees by the bed in a moment. "I am here," she said. "Do you know me?"

His lips moved, "Yes."

"I was at home when I heard of your illness—but I did not go home when I left you. I went to the north to consult a friend—about myself. Do you hear me? Can you hear me?"

Again he sighed "Yes." His eyes were fixed upon hers—with interest, she thought—but without any judgment. The night-nurse discreetly left the room.

She asked his patience, and plunged into her story—her story and his own, with Tristram's part interwoven. "There was one who used to see me," was her way of bringing in Duplessis, and after that Tristram was "he" throughout. She would not use his name; felt she could not, and knew that she need not. Full understanding lay behind those unwinking, charged eyes, terribly watchful and indifferent to anything but curiosity. She saw them as the patient eyes of an investigator, expectant of a final experiment. "I have studied this case for three years—now, at last, I am to have it." He knew everything—had known everything from the beginning: she had no news for him; "how she would put it," was what he was waiting for—for that only she had drawn him back to life.

This knowledge, this realization drove her to candour past belief. She felt as if she was stripping herself for public exhibition—found herself talking in a dry voice of lovers' intimacies and of still more secret things—of things which women feel but do not even think. She had to examine herself unflinchingly during this confession, which reduced itself, for lack of matter, to one of motives. In the course of it she had to face a fact never faced before only felt. She could not love Tristram, she did not love Germain— whom, then, did she love? The fine colour flushed her cheeks, the true light flamed in her eyes as she told herself—and then told her husband.

"I know myself now. There is one man who could do with me as he pleased. But he will do nothing with me. I trust him utterly; he has changed me. He has given me a soul, I think. He has taught me the worth of things which I never valued before; and what life is, and happiness, and truth. It is through him that I went home and faced what I was afraid of —left him and all the wonderful things he could make

me see. I might never see him again—but I left him.
I am doing what he would wish now in telling you
all this. Untruth is impossible to him, and must never
be possible to me again. That is why I have waited
here to tell you. I had to tell you—I had to tell myself. Now I have told you everything——"

She stopped there because she felt that if she were
to go on she would have to be insincere. Contrition
for what she had done and allowed to be done in the
days of her blank ignorance, prayers for forgiveness,
promises of amendment—such things, proper for bedside confession—what would they imply, what involve? That she loved this poor watcher? Alas!
Pity might have urged her to deceive him so; but
she dared not deceive him—and, moreover, she was
certain that he could not now be deceived. The light
of another world shone upon him, shone through him,
and enabled him to read hearts. She did not shrink
from this supernatural power of his—if it had been
profitable she would have given him her life-blood.
It seemed to her as clear as daylight that the utmost
she could do for him had now been done—when she
had discharged her conscience before him, and
cleared her honour. She believed that he would feel
himself honoured by that act; and as she stooped
over him to kiss him she told him as much.

"It is kind of you to have listened to me. You
have done me so much honour, so much kindness—
but this is the greatest you have ever done me. Do
you understand that I feel it so?" For a moment
his terrible intelligence pored upon her as she hung

over his bed. It searched her, explored her, wondered, judged. A flicker of a smile—a momentary relaxation of his rigid lips—a faint wavering of his attention; then he sighed, and closed his eyelids down. The strain was over, she had been heard, assessed, acquitted. When the night-nurse came in she found the patient at peace, and Mary Germain crouched on the floor asleep, her head upon the edge of the bed.

XV

THE DEAD HAND

HER calmness, which was not the stupor of grief, from this point onwards shocked her friend and disturbed her enemy in the house. The Rector could not but feel it a slight upon his dead brother and an attitude most unbecoming to so young a widow; but Mrs. James was made uncomfortable by an attitude for which she had not been prepared. Whatever the girl's faults may have been, she had never been brazen. Why, then, was she brazen now? Why almost—yes, indecent in her indifference? Mary proposed nothing, objected to nothing; took no part in the funeral arrangements, answered no letters, read none, allowed her sister-in-law entire control, sank back, with evident contentment, to be the cipher in her own house, which, of course, she ought to have been from the first. There was something behind all this; Mrs. James was far too intelligent to misread it. This did not mean that Mary was overwhelmed—by grief, or shame, either; it did not mean that she felt herself in disgrace. No. This was impudence—colossal.

The Rector, to whom this reading of the girl was

propounded, could not deny it colour. "She's very young to have such troubles upon her, and of course she's still very ignorant. She can't express herself. I don't at all agree with you, Constantia; but I own I should have preferred to see her in tears."

"Why should she cry, pray? She has all that she wants—a sure income and her liberty. At least, that is what she supposes; but we shall see."

"You paint your devils so impossibly black, my dear," said the Rector, "that really they refute themselves. I am sorry to have to say it, but you are incapable of being just to this poor girl. However, as I own, tears had been a sign of grace."

Certainly she shed no tears, that any one could see. She was frequently in her room alone, and may have cried there. The Rector made advances, by look, by gesture, even by words. He was not an effusive man; would sooner have died than have invited anybody to pray with him—but for all that he did put himself in her way, heart in hand, so to speak—and when she gently disregarded him he felt chilly.

She did not attend the funeral, nor did she choose, though she was urged, to be present at the reading of the will. She told the Rector, who pressed this duty upon her, that she couldn't oblige him. "Please don't ask me to do that. I have nothing to expect— and if he had left me anything I should have to think about it very seriously. He took me from nothing; I brought him nothing; he has done more for me, and allowed me to do more for my parents than I could ever have asked—even of him. I make no claims at all, and have no expectations. I have never thought about such things——"

"Naturally, my child, naturally not. But—after such a shock as this—after the first pang of loss—it is wise to think of the future. You had no settlement, you know."

"How could I?" she asked simply. He smiled at the question.

"Well, my dear, well. Your parents might reasonably have looked—my dear brother was very impulsive in some ways—I can't doubt but that he intended to make proper provision. But he kept his affairs very much to himself—too much. However, at such a time—to judge the beloved dead—! No, no. For the same reason I can't press you——"

"No—please do not," she said, and turned to the window. He left her.

The will, then, was read before the Rector and Mrs. James, Miss Germain, and Miss Hester Germain, and produced its effect. It bore the date of a month before the testator's second marriage and was expressed to be made in view of that coming ceremony, and to take the place of any settlement. It left her Porchfield House in Farlingbridge, "otherwise known as the Dowry House," with all its furniture and household gear, and three thousand pounds a year charged upon his Southover estate "so long as she remain chaste and unmarried." Mr. Dockwra, solicitor, slurred his phrase, excusing it. Mrs. James liked it extremely. In the case of remarriage, Mary was to have five hundred pounds.

That was all, said Mr. Dockwra, so far as Mrs. Germain was concerned; and he only said this much because he was asked by Mrs. James Germain if there was no further reference to her. For the rest the deceased gave handsome legacies to his sisters, though they were otherwise provided for, and liberal remembrances to his servants—annuities calculated upon their years of service; and referred to the fact that the Southover property and the London property alike were in strict settlement upon his own children, should he have any, and, failing them, upon his brother James.

Mr. Dockwra then produced a small bundle of papers. "There was a codicil," he said, "which bore date the 26th of August—a week before Mr. Germain's wedding. By this document he left five hundred a year to "my cousin Tristram Duplessis," so long as he remained unmarried. Thus tersely expressed, the Rector started as if he had been shot, and his wife compressed her lips.

"I think that I should explain," said Mr. Dockwra, "that this codicil was not drawn by me, and that I had no knowledge of its existence until the day after Mr. Germain's death. Mr. James Germain, however, as executor, handed me then the sealed envelope containing it. That envelope contained one other paper—a telegram, which (as it has no obvious reference to the disposition) may have been put there by oversight. I shall hand it now to Mr. Germain."

The Rector took it, opened it, looked at it, and raised his eyebrows. Presently he put it quietly on the table before him. Mrs. James, without turning her head, read it. It was very short—*Middleham, Hill-street, Berkeley-square—Look out.* Mrs. James smiled at her thoughts—and presently left the room.

Mary must now be told what she had not cared to hear. The Rector broke her the contents of the will but said nothing of the codicil. He had not asked his wife the meaning of that second document, and did not mean to. It pointed to a domestic mystery. Without being a prude, all such matters were distasteful to him.

He was very kind, as he had always been. "You will be very comfortably left, you see, Mary," he said, "at any rate, let us say, while you are looking about you."

Mary had shown no more than a polite interest in his report. Three thousand a year? Porchfield? She may have been dazed, but she certainly was not dazzled. James Germain reflected to himself on the ease with which one gets acclimatized. Little more than two years ago this child was working hard for sixty pounds a year; now she hears that she is secured three thousand—without moving a muscle.

"I need not tell you," he went on, "that your home is here or at Southover for any length of time convenient to you. Indeed, I am sure I might include the Rectory in my general invitation. We have been so nearly related; I could not bear to think the tie severed by my dear brother's death. Apart from that, we have learned to love each other, I hope. I shall always look upon you as one of us—if you will let me; and your settlement at Porchfield will be a reason the more to keep me at Southover."

"That is very kind of you, Mr. Germain," Mary said—but without enthusiasm. After a few more efforts, the worthy man left her alone.

It was then Mrs. James's turn. She came in, after knocking, with the telegram in her hand.

"This, I think, belongs to you," she said.

Mary took it, read it, and remembered. A quick flush of colour showed that she did.

"Yes," she said, "but it is of no importance now." And she tore it across.

But Mrs. James was not to be balked. "You must allow me to explain its importance. It was found in the envelope containing the codicil to my dear brother's will—a codicil which he made within two days of your receiving it."

Mary, still looking out of the window, commented idly. A codicil? Was there a codicil? That meant that you changed your mind, didn't it?

"In this case," said Mrs. James, "it means, I think, that my dear brother explained his mind. I thought that the Rector might have informed you."

"No," said Mary. Mrs. James cleared her throat and began to enjoy herself.

"By that he left five hundred a year to my cousin Tristram Duplessis—so long as he remained unmarried."

Mary was puzzled at first. She knew by the speaker's tone that she was in disgrace—and connected it with Duplessis at the mention of his name.

She stared at the bitterly incisive lady. "Mr. Du‑
plessis—five hundred—if he doesn't marry? What
has that to do with—?" She stopped—her eyes
widened and deepened—showed fathomless. "Ah!"
she said, and picked up the torn paper. She read the
date, August 24th. "What did you say was the
date of the will?"

"It was a codicil," said Mrs. James.

"The date, please, the date," Mary asked her,
fretfully.

"It was dated the 26th of August."

Jinny's birthday! Mary remembered it perfectly.
He had had tea with the two of them, and she had
clung to him afterwards, with a confession on the tip
of her tongue. He had never been more loving to
her than on that afternoon—and he had Jinny's
telegram in his pocket—in his breast pocket—while
she had clung sobbing to his breast! And he had
left her that evening, full of love, as he had seemed
to be, and gone home and tied Tristram by the leg.
Ah—so he had known everything—always! Before
that night at Exeter—he had known it from the be‑
ginning.

She sat very still—the telegram in her lap—and
her eyes cast down, as she played idly with the
pieces, lifting them up and letting them fall. The
triumphant foe could see nothing but her heavy eye‑
lids, and the fringe of her lashes curving upwards as
they brushed her cheeks. If she expected victory she
was to be disappointed.

"I am glad you sent him my telegram," she

said. "I am glad he knew about Mr. Duplessis and me."

Mrs. James lifted her head. "It was certainly advisable that he should be told. Personally, I could not interfere. I told him nothing that may have presented itself to me——"

"No," said Mary, "of course not. It was no business of yours." Mrs. James jumped.

"It seems to me that it was very much a business of *yours*, if you will forgive me."

"It was," Mary said. "And I told him all about it."

Mrs. James started. "I told him," Mary said, "on the night he died. He quite understood."

"It is horrible to me," cried Mrs. James, "that he was kept in the dark so long."

"He wasn't at all in the dark," Mary said. "That is plain now. I wish that I had known it before."

"You may well say so. Apart from candour, apart from sincerity, surely it is the sacred duty of a married woman to have no secrets from her husband."

Mary looked up. She had the eyes of a woman acquainted with grief. "I am not a married woman," she said. "I fancy that you must know it."

XVI

THE tale of Germain's posthumous disposition of his chattels ran, as such tales will, all about town, and lost nothing in the running. Women took it complacently, after their kind. Of course it was odd; and yet, in its way, was it not a tribute? One or two pretty young wives told each other that it was touching; a Miss Lavender shed tears. In the clubs they said plainly that Duplessis had been bought off. Palmer Lovell, with his back to the fireplace, cried out in his strident boy's voice, "If that's not compounding a felony, it's compounding a felon. But what the devil of a right has old Germain, alive or dead, to whip his wife in public?" No clubman had an answer to this. The best thing of all was said by Lord Kesteven in Paris: "God be good to us, what Turks we all are! Here's old Germain taking the harem-key into the grave with him."

That keen-faced old lord came to London and called on Mary in Hill-street. He observed her pale in her black weeds, but with a haunted kind of beauty upon her which she had never had before. Her eyes were enormous, he said. She was very

quiet in her manner, seemed dazed, but not cowed—
apprehensive, you might think. She looked up at
him in a mutely expectant way, as if she expected
him momentarily to hit her, and was too tired even
to flinch at the impending blow. He felt deeply for
her—all sorts of things, and after his manner, therefore, was more bluff and direct than usual. "Well,
my young friend, and what are you going to do with
yourself? I should advise you to get out of this.
No woman can be expected to stand it."

She flushed at the bold attack, but did not avoid
it. "I hear nothing of what is being said. I am
sure he did not mean to be unkind. That is not like
him. I was to blame."

"I won't talk about it, or I shall get angry. Cant
—in a man's will—to disguise something worse, and
nastier—pouf! Look here, my dear, try France—
try Paris. My sister Margaret de Guiche would like
you to pay her a visit. She said so. She's alone, and
you need see nobody. De Guiche is in Petersburg.
You couldn't have a better dueña than Margaret.
It will be a kindness to her—and a kindness to me.
I wish you'd think of it."

She listened with hanging head, and veiled eyes.
Her eyelids, always heavy, seemed now as if they
were of intolerable weight. She watched her twisting fingers as she thanked him for the proposal.
She would think of it, she told him—she had everything to think of.

"I know that very well," Kesteven said; "but
there are some things which I hope you need not

consider. One of them is the great regard I have for you."

Oh, yes, she was sure of that. He had shown her so much kindness.

"I'm glad to hear it," he continued; "and I'll go as far as this. If you decide to renounce your legacy —on reflection—I should claim the privilege of helping you to do it. I can hardly go further—but so far I am ready to go. Remember that. Remember that I am allowed to call myself your friend. Remember, if you choose, that I am five-and-sixty, and take heart—if you need heart."

It was clear what was implied in this speech; but she did not feel equal to quieting the anxiety which underlay it. She made no remark.

"At any rate," said his lordship, "I tell you that you may command the Hôtel de Guiche. Margaret may be trusted—and perhaps I need not add that you may trust me, too." But he couldn't get her to say more than she would think of it, so took his leave. He kissed her hand.

So far she had not seen Duplessis, nor heard from him; but the sense that an interview with him was impending, was, as it were, swinging like a sword over her head, fretted her nerves so badly that she was incapable of thinking what she could say to him when he came to her—as of course he would—with an offer of instant marriage. That would be, in his view, the only possible answer to the public affront he had received. But as the days went on and he made no sign she began to wonder dimly whether, after all, she might not escape—and from such faint sighings thrown out into the vague she came by degrees to hopes—and from hopes to plans and shifts.

Everything in town conspired together to make her position impossible. The chill reserve of Mrs. James—whose frozen civility was worse than any rebuke; the letters of her parents from Blackheath, kind, repining, half-informed letters which said in effect, We don't know what is being cried against you, but be sure that we are on your side; and the terrible letters of Jinny (almost Mrs. Podmore by now, and vigorously on the side of decorum)—"the disgrace which has been cast upon our family . . . your unfortunate *liaison*. . . . One can only hope that you will let them be a warning, child. . . . Let us be thankful that things are no worse . . ."—all this made the poor girl so self-conscious that she could hardly lift her head. She thought that the very servants were judging her—as, no doubt, they were; she felt beaten to the earth; and the fund of commonsense, the fund of charity, which she had at her call —through mere panic—suspended payment.

If she had been left to herself she would have borne her husband no grudge for seeking to tie her publicly to his name. She would have pitied, not blamed him, for supposing that three thousand or thirty thousand a year could have held her. And certainly that midnight confession absolved her in her own conscience. If she had looked back upon her dealings with Duplessis it would have been to see what a little fool she had been—to blush at her ignorance, not at her shame. But now her world insisted on her disgrace; she was made to stand in a sheet like a Jane Shore; the straight, clinging, disgraceful robe imprisoned her body and soul. She felt that she must die if she stayed where she was, a public mock; but until Duplessis delayed so obviously his coming she had felt bound in honour to see him.

To be just to Duplessis, he kept himself away by violence, obeying an instinct—which was a true one. He had no doubt but that she would marry him now —he could not for the life of him see how any two people could otherwise reply to posthumous impudence of the sort. Indeed, he felt in his heart of hearts that she owed him that. But his instinct told him that that could not be put to her for the present, and that to be seen in her society, to visit her, even to write to her, would make her burden heavier to bear. He contented himself by renouncing his legacy in the most precise terms—in a letter to Dockwra the lawyer, and in another to James Germain. If this act came to Mary's ears, as he hoped it would, no harm would be done to his affair. Rather, she would see in it a plain declaration of his feelings. But, unfortunately for him, it did not. James Germain was at Misperton by this time, and Dockwra communicated directly with him, not through his wife. James Germain, true to his fastidious sense, thought it no business of Mary's—and was thankful it was none of his.

The delay of a week, ten days, a fortnight, gave

her courage. Her feverish dreams, hopes of a release, left her. She knew now that she was to be free,
and, once resolved, schemes began to gather in her
brain, to develop; her mind went to work, and she
became happy. There was no doubt at all where she
would go. All her ideas of freedom were centred in
one place—Land's End. The sea, the rocks, the
birds—and the low white cottage facing them all—
open-doored to them all. Her dream of nearly three
years; now to come true! If Senhouse was at the
back of her mind, he was kept rigorously there. She
felt virginal now when she thought of Senhouse,
found herself blushing, and put the image away as
not lawful. Freedom from the intolerable eyes about
her—the butler's—her maid's—Mrs. James's—this
ghastly mummery of clothes and ceremony—she
agonized to be quit of it all; but now she intended to
be, and could not afford time to agonize. She turned
all her quick wits to the work, applied method and
deliberation to it, and could almost fix a day, so
plain did everything seem.

Method cautioned her to go slowly to work; the
first thing to do was to accustom Mrs. James to her
walks abroad. She devoted a week to this—went
alone, deeply veiled, into the park every day, and
spent gradually increasing hours there, doing nothing more.

Then, one morning, she went circuitously to the
Bank in Burlington-gardens, and asked for her pass-
book. There was some £300 to her credit—the remains of her pin-money allowance. Two days later

she presented a cheque for £300—which left her a balance of £27 10s.—and asked for the money in gold. The porter took the sack to her cab, and she gave the direction "Hill-street"—but once out of hearing she put her hand through the window at the top and gave another order—the Army and Navy Stores.

Leaving her sack of money in the cab, she bought herself a Gladstone bag. Perhaps it is evidence at once of the folly and fortune of women that she was not robbed; she may well have deserved to be, for, being full of her ingenious schemes, she had given no thought to the matter—had neither taken the man's number, nor told him what she was entrusting to him. She had not so much as troubled to shut the cab door after her. The man himself, with a "Well, I'm damned!" had done that, and it may be that the very magnitude of his opportunities had bereft him of the means of using them; for she found him smiling on the rank when she came out. The bag was handed in to her—uncovered—she gave the new direction "Paddington," and *en route* deposited her sack of sovereigns and locked it in the bag.

At Paddington she dismissed the cab, not extravagantly, and disappeared with a porter and the bag. She put it in the cloak-room, took a ticket for it, then went back to Hill-street.

Two things must be done, two letters be written— one to her mother, one to James Germain. He had always been her friend; she was really fond of him, and liked to think that he would regret her loss, while she was bound to guard against his trying to recover her. To her mother she wrote very simply that she was suddenly called away on affairs connected with her husband's death, and might have to go abroad. It would be difficult to write—but she would send an address as soon as she had one of any permanence. She added, "Darling Mother, be as sure of my love for you and father and all of you, as I am of yours. I promise to tell you how I succeed in my business, or if I fail in it. You will never be out of my thoughts, as you are never out of my prayers. Love me always, in spite of anything that you may hear against me. I have been foolish, very ignorant, and very blind—but no worse, Mother, upon my honour. I am wiser now, and intend to be a good woman. Trust your Mary; who loves you and kisses this paper."

She wrote in the same strain to the Rector of Misperton. "I am not able to bear the strain of London for the present, and intend to travel for some time before making my plans. I feel the need of quiet, and shall trust in you to do all you can to ensure it to me. After the comforting words you gave me I am sure that you may rely upon my doing nothing which should make me unworthy of them. I am resolved not to see Mr. Duplessis again. I could never be happy with him, nor make him happy after what has passed. If he should inquire for me, pray tell him that this is my sincere conviction, and ask him not to attempt to dissuade me from it. I can never thank you enough for your invariable kindness to me; that must always be one of my happy recollections of the life that I have ended. If I have to begin again without it, it is because I cannot ask you to continue it until I have proved myself more worthy to have it. I am going away now by myself, to work and to learn, and to forget much, but never to forget your kindness. I beg you to remember sometimes with charity your affectionate friend, MARY S. GERMAIN."

It was on the tip of her pen to write to Tristram; as she sat hesitating the phrases printed themselves one after another in her head, and she wrote them down. "You never loved me—but I was proud to be even in your notice. I am greatly to blame for the renewal of what was idle on your part and foolish vanity on mine in the beginning. I can only be glad that my husband, though he knew everything, heard it all again from my own lips—I told him the night he died. I hope that you will be happy and famous. I know that both are in your power. Do not try to find me, I beg of you. Forget me, and love a woman who is more suited to you by birth and education. I know that if you try you can succeed in this. If you have any feeling of regard for me you will do as I ask you now.—MARY S. GERMAIN."

Two of these letters she posted with her own hand that night. Tristram's she reserved.

Then she made her last preparations. She packed her jewel-case carefully, tied and sealed it, and addressed it to the bank. She dined in her boudoir and spent the rest of the evening with Bradshaw, planning out her route. Love of secrecy, love of intricacy, which were both characteristic of her, decided her against so simple a course as a journey from Paddington to Penzance. She worked out a way more to her taste: Waterloo to Basingstoke, thence to Swindon, and thence by the Great Western to Exeter, where she would stay for a while. This necessitated an early start in the morning, for she must go to Paddington and recover her three hundred pounds. She would take no luggage whatever, would buy what she wanted in Exeter. Loyalty to Senhusian ethics decided her to this.

Meantime, it was necessary to be rid of her maid for an hour. That she effected by the simple means of sending her with the note to Duplessis, and with her jewel-box, to be taken to the bank, and a receipt obtained. The moment she was alone she dressed herself as she intended to appear—in black jacket and skirt and a grey silk blouse—in hat and veil studiously plain. Then she left the house in Hill-street on foot, got a cab in Davies-street, and was free.

All went well with her as far as Basingstoke; but there she was imprudent. She asked at the office whether she could book through to Penzance, and break her journey for a week, and being told, after some delay, that she could not—"Then Exeter, please," she said. "Second single to Exeter," and receiving it, holding it in her mouth, she half turned to get a better light into her purse, and caught sight of Horace Wing—the courtly Horace—who must have heard her. In the shock, as he hastened forward, cap in one hand, golf-clubs dragging by the other, she left her change on the counter, bowed and fairly ran. This was very indiscreet; but she escaped, and the porter came after her with her bag. Horace Wing, after gaping, had a shuddering fit. He did not follow her, and was not able to smile at the encounter for some weeks.

Her carriage was empty: she was alone now, with all her life, like an open sea, in front of her. She sat, looking out towards the West, her hands quiet in her lap; she had no sense of high adventure, no bosom full of hope—peace possessed her altogether. She felt that she could lie her length upon some green bank, sheltered from the wind, and sleep herself to death. Such a feeling as this was so foreign to her nature that she was surprised at herself, asked herself whether some chord in her had not been broken. She was sanguine by temperament and always lived in the future; if on any morning of any week she could not wake up with the sense of an excitement to come, to be waited for, to be felt nearer—that day was so much dead weight, so much space of drab, to be got through, in order that she might live to-morrow. She told herself that she was mortally tired—that her present reward was to be able to live unwatched and unjudged. That was enough for any girl surely— let the morrow's outlook provide for the morrow.

Even while she was thinking these thoughts she caught herself unawares. She found herself watching the flying landscape anxiously, and smiling as she watched. The open common, the duck-pond, and the white road—yes, and the tilt-cart drawn by a white horse—plodding to the West! Three years ago, almost to a day—she and the tilt-cart had taken that road. And then she had been a bride of an hour —and now she was a widow of an hour. She caught herself blushing, was confused, felt eyes upon her: the carriage seemed full of eyes. For a while she continued to watch, to watch through the mist in her own eyes—and then she turned suddenly in her place, opened her novel and read diligently in it until the train, stopping at Taunton, showed her that the place of dangerous memories was past.

She would not allow her thoughts to recur to that curious little drama of the mind: in fact, she worked hard to avoid the temptation. She abandoned her novel, opened her purse, and did her accounts. She made lists of necessary purchases, and began to post up the diary with which she had provided herself.

When she reached Exeter she stepped out—Miss Mary Middleham. Her bag bore a label to that effect.

XVII

FIRST FLIGHT

Mrs. Merritt who had been housekeeper to the late Canon Blackrod and now let lodgings in a house of her own, was amiable, and by the possession of that quality was able to keep her curiosity within bounds: but it was her daughter Polly, a Devon maid of apple cheeks and sloe-black eyes, who taught her enthusiasm for her lodger. Polly Merritt adored the quiet and pretty young lady who, though she wore such beautiful clothes, gave herself none of the airs which were clearly within her rights; who would wash her own blouses, trim her own hats, or sit below-stairs chatting affably, while she trimmed one for Polly herself. In such familiar intercourse all the necessary safeguards of landladies were proved to be secure. Miss Middleham, it seemed, was an orphan, by profession a teacher of languages, who had found it necessary to leave her London employment to escape a gentleman's attentions. Most reasonable, most proper. The gentleman was one indeed, highly connected, in fact, cousin of an Honourable; but impecunious and not very steady. Girls who are orphans must look after themselves: there had been nothing for it but flight. Admirable forethought! Nothing, certainly, but praise could be given to Miss Middleham for conduct so discreet.

"It'll bring him round, Miss, depend upon it," Mrs. Merritt had considered. "It'll make him look nine ways. As good as a slap in the face, any day."

"Better, I hope," Mary said.

"Some of 'em wants one thing, some another, Miss. Let him know that you're in earnest, whatever you do."

"I am quite in earnest, Mrs. Merritt," Mary told her; "and I think I have made that plain."

"Did you tell him so, or write it, Miss?" Polly must ask. "Writing's better—but it's dull work."

"I have done both, Polly. He doesn't know where I am. I made it quite clear to him that he could not."

Mrs. Merritt, having observed her guest, passed the back of her hand rapidly across her nose. "To be sure you could, Miss. It's easy to be seen that God Almighty never gave you that pair of eyes for nothing. To call a man, or send him about his business—ah, I'll warrant you."

"Poor fellow," mused the tender Polly. "I pity him."

In private conversation afterwards Mrs. Merritt assured her daughter that she need not. We should have the young gentleman here before the swallows were away: let Polly mark her words. Our young lady was a snug young lady—that was a certainty. She was not a girl who would go without letters of

a morning for long together. Letters! That sort
live on 'em, as a man on his eleven o'clock beer.
No, no. She was used to company, any one could
see. She was meant to be somebody's darling. How
else did she get her pretty ways—and why to goodness wear her pretty frocks, but for that? Meantime, she had been used to the best, you could see;
and she should have it here.

What Mrs. Merritt, however, did not know, and
Polly did know, was that another gentleman stood
in the background. Here lay the root of Polly's passionate interest in her friend: a constant appeal to
her imagination and judgment and wonder. A gentleman was to be expected; there was always a gentleman. But two gentlemen! One more gentleman,
and Polly might have felt the responsibilities of Paris.
In fact, she did feel them as things were.

Mary had come to Exeter, meaning no more than
a passage-bird's rest there—a night or two, and
away. Her cottage at the Land's End, solitary vigil
face to face with the sea and the rocks, tending of
the hidden garden there, a waiting and watching—
and a great reward: that had been her fixed intent.
Nothing seemed to be in the way. She was free as
air: why should she wait?

It is very odd, though, how you cannot carry
through these hot-blood thoughts in the cold blood.
That momentary shyness which had come upon her
in the train, when she had caught herself looking
out for a remembered village-green and had been
abashed, came upon her the moment she began to

think of Cornwall with a view to going there. She
found herself trembling, found herself delaying,
drawing back. Had she been her old self, never
sought and never mated, in this tremulous plight she
had remained; but she had learned to face such
difficulties, and did not shirk it. The more she
thought of it the plainer it became that she could not
have the cottage, could not sit down there and wait
for Senhouse. Virgin as she was, and virginal as she
was now become again, the picture of herself in such
an attitude, and in such an act, filled her with shame.
And if to picture it was dreadful, what would the
day-long reality be but unendurable? But where,
then, was her sense of comradeship, of perfect amity
between him and her? She did not know. It was
gone. And what would he—wondrous, clear-seeing
friend—say to her for this prudery? That she did
know: she could see him appeal for laughter to the
skies. Alas, it could not be helped. She was a
maiden, therefore might be wooed. She was a
maiden, therefore could not go a-wooing. So he and
she might never meet again! Better so—oh, infinitely better—than that they should meet by her act.

Thus it was that Polly Merritt came to learn about
the other gentleman. Mary's perplexities had been
stated, and Polly was thrilled.

"Oh, Miss! And he's never spoken?"

"No," said Mary. "At least—not about that."

"What was the nearest he ever got to?"

Mary looked wise. "He told me to go away,
once."

"He did! Why were you to go then?"

"Because—oh, because he could see, I suppose, that I didn't want to; and——"

"Well?"

"Because—I sometimes fancy—he didn't want me to. At least, I think he didn't. He said, 'You had better go home. I'm a man, you know.'"

Polly opened her eyes wide. "That's as plain as my nose. I should think so! So, of course——"

"Yes, of course I had to go." She looked down at her toes, just as if Senhouse had been standing above her, bidding her go.

"I dream sometimes," she said, "that he comes to me in the night, and looks at me—never speaks, but just looks. Not at me, you know, but through me—right through to the pillow. That's enough. Then he turns and goes away, and I follow him out of door, into the warm dark—and he turns sharply upon me and is dreadfully angry. I've never known him angry; but dreams are like that. I see his face quite changed—wild and cold at once, and terribly stern. And I run away into the empty house, and wish that I were dead. No, no. I could never bear that—to seek him and be spurned. I would sooner never see him again."

Polly was deeply moved, but practical. A girl must look ahead—far beyond dreams. "You had best not, Miss," she said, "if that's likely to be the way of it. Is he that sort—your hot-and-cold?"

"Oh, I don't know—how can I tell? That has never been between us, save that once, when he told

me to go away. He's a wonderful talker about all
sorts of things; he can make them all extraordinary.
I feel, after listening to him, that I understand all
life, all experience. Everything seems reasonable.
But when it comes to—us—he won't speak. I believe he can't. And I understand him better when
he doesn't."

"So would any one, I should think," said Polly
Merritt. "But how's he going to look at you if he
never sees you, and don't know where you are?"

"Ah," said Mary with far-sighted eyes, "I don't
know."

"You might write to him, I suppose—and slip in
your address, by accident like."

Mary shook her head. "I couldn't. Besides, he
has no address. He just comes and goes—like the
wind."

"Has he no house of his own?"

"No. He lives in a tent—in a cart."

"What! Like a gipsy? Oh, Miss!" This
would never, never do.

But Mary admitted it, thoughtfully. "Yes. I
think he might be a sort of gipsy."

This, to Polly, was final. "I do think you're better
here, Miss Middleham, if you'll excuse me."

"Perhaps I am," said Mary.

Polly had veered. "I'll warrant the other gentleman would have a house to offer you."

"Oh, yes, I suppose so. But——"

"Ah, that's just it—that's just it."

Mary admitted it. "I suppose it is. But he says

that he will never marry. He doesn't believe in
marriage."

"Ho, indeed!" cried Polly. "Then pray what
does he believe in?"

"I don't know. I'm not sure."

Polly tossed her young head. "It wouldn't take
long for me to be sure."

Then Mary showed her face, and her eyes shone
clear. "I am sure of this, that if he called me I
should follow him over the world, however he chose
me to be. But I know he never will. He is unlike
anybody else—he comes and goes like the wind."

"Let him, for me," said Polly. "'specially when
he's going."

The summer waned and fainted; autumn mists
crept about, and found her still in Exeter. Pupils
came slowly, but she got one or two, and there was
promise of more. The Vicar of the parish helped
her. She taught in his Sunday school, did him some
visiting, danced with his boys and sang with his girls.
Through him she got an engagement in September,
in a young ladies' academy—to teach Italian two
days a week. She got to know a few people. There
was a gentlemanly young man called Bloxam, who
escorted her home from choral evenings; then there
was a curate—*quod semper, quod ubique*—who lent
her books and professed himself ready to discuss
them afterwards, by correspondence or otherwise.

These things faintly amused her; the simplicity
of such devices, for instance, the little buildings-up
of the little architects! She felt herself, ruefully,

slipping back into the parochial, losing touch with her wide horizons. The tonic properties of freedom, which at first had been as delightful as the mere ease of it, were now staling by use. She began to find herself grow dull. The one fact upon which she could build was that she was again earning her living.

"You should let other people judge of that. If you would like my opinion of your clothes, for instance——"

She shook her head, without speaking. He tried a more direct attack.

"You forgive me for coming?"

She suspected a tenderness. "Oh, it is very kind of you. I don't have many visitors. I am glad to see you."

"That's good. May I see you again, then, while I can?"

She inquired: "Are you likely to be here long?"

A light hand was necessary now. "Oh, dear no—unfortunately. A day or two at the outside; time to buy cartridges. You remember the Ogmores? I am due at Wraybrook on the seventh. Pheasants. But until then——"

This was the fourth, you see. He would be horribly in the way. "I am occupied a good part of the day," she told him. "I have pupils."

He raised his eyebrows. "Really! Have you—" he flushed, and leaned forward. "Have you renounced your——?"

"Not in so many words," she said. "I have simply dropped it. Nobody knows where I am."

"You knew that I had formally renounced mine?"

She had not known that. There was an implication in it—which she had run here to avoid; and here it was. "Did you?" she said shortly. "I'm not surprised."

"Of course not," he agreed. "You could not

expect me to do anything else. And you have done precisely the same. That, also, I took leave to expect." He saw concern gather in her eyes, broke off abruptly, and plunged into gossip. "Does your late world interest you still? Do you want to hear the news? Palmer Lovell's engagement, for instance? A princess of Italy, I give you my word—a Donna Teresa Scalchi, rather a beauty, and a great shrew. Palmer can bite a bit, too. That will end in tears. And Hertha de Speyne marries abroad. Morosov, an anarchist of sort. They can collect plants in Siberia—" he broke off again, remembering that others had collected plants in Siberia. Watching her, he saw that she remembered it, too. "Oh, and old Constantine and I have kissed; we are fast friends. Once more I write speeches, which he mangles. He's to be at Wraybrook, waiting for me. He can't bear me out of his sight—he's like an elderly wife. Frightful nuisance, of course—but I hope you are pleased."

She looked at him for a moment. "Of course I am pleased. I always wanted you to succeed."

He rattled on. She had never seen him in such good spirits or manners. When he left her after an hour she was quite at her ease. He said that, if he might, he would come in the evening, and take her for a walk. It would do her good; and as for him she might have pity upon a fellow at a loose end, with nothing on earth to do but buy cartridges.

When he had gone she sat still, looking at her hands in her lap. Could she maintain herself for three days? Already she felt the fences closing in—

she had felt them, as they moved, though never once had she been able to hold up her hand or say, Stop: that you may not assume. Tristram was master of implication, and her master there. Throughout his airy monologue he had taken her for granted—her and her origin, her humility, her subservience to his nod, her false position with Germain, her false position now. Why, his very amiability, his deference to her opinion, his tentative approach—what were these but implications of his passion for her, a passion so strong that it could bend his arrogant back, and show a Tristram Duplessis at the feet of a Mary Middleham? She writhed, she burned to feel these things, and to be powerless against such attack. And he was to come again this evening, and every day for three days he was to come—and no help for her, she must fall without a cry. Yes, without a cry; for she was cut off from her friend, by the very need she had of him. What was she to do? What could she do—but fall?

She struggled. At three o'clock in the afternoon she told Polly Merritt that if the gentleman called again he was to be told that Miss Middleham was not well and had gone to bed. Polly wondered, but obeyed. "Lovers' tricks!" quoth Mrs. Merritt. "That'll bring him to the scratch." It did. He received the news at the door, with an impassive face —all but for his eyes, which, keen and coldly blue, pierced Polly's sloe-blacks to the brain, and extracted what might be useful to him. "Many thanks, Miss Polly," he had said presently. "You're a good friend,

I see. Look here, I'll tell you what to do. I'll bring
some flowers round presently, and you shall put 'em
in her room, and say nothing about it. Do you see?"
Polly saw.

The next day was a busy one for her, and she saw
nothing of Tristram until the evening. Then, to her
dismay, she found him waiting for her outside the
gates of Rosemount Academy, where her Italian
lesson had been given. If she bit her lip, she blushed
also; and if he remarked but one of these signals it
was not her fault. Cavaliers had attended at those
gates before—not for her only, but for her among
others. Such a cavalier, however, so evidently of the
great world, had never yet been looked upon by the
young ladies of Rosemount.

"Oh," cried Mary, startled, "who told you——?"

"Your amiable friend, Miss Polly, betrayed you.
I hope you'll forgive her."

"I suppose I must. Probably you frightened her
out of her wits." But he swore that they were very
good friends indeed. He thought that Miss Polly
liked him, upon his word; and Mary could not deny
that. Polly undoubtedly did.

His admirable behaviour inspired confidence;
inquiries after her health, no reference to ambiguous
exotics, no assumptions, no plans for evening walks.
He went with her to her door, and left her there with
a salute. But before she could get in, while she
stood with her hand on the knocker, as if by an after-
thought he came back to her from the gate. Jess
had summoned him to Wraybrook, he said. He

knew that there was something to tell her. Positively
he must go the day after to-morrow. Now, was she
free to-morrow?

She was; but she hesitated to say so. Well, then,
would she give him a great pleasure? Would she
come with him to Powderham—explore the park
and the shore, have a picnic luncheon and all that
sort of thing? Would she? As he stood down there
below her, with flushed face and smiling, obsequious
eyes, she thought that she really might trust herself,
if not him. Polly, opening the door, was nodded to,
and told that she need not wait. Polly needed no
telling.

"Come, Mrs. Mary," he urged her, "what do you
say? Will you let me look after you for this once?
Will you please to remember that never once since
we have known each other—how many years?—
have we had a whole day together? Extraordinary
fact."

"It's quite true," she reflected, "we never have.
Once we very nearly did, though."

"Twice," he corrected her; but she could not
admit that. Well, which was her instance?

It was long ago, when she had been at Misperton
—had been some six months there. One Midsum-
mer Day—surely he remembered! He had promised
to take her to Glastonbury; the dog-cart was to meet
them at Clewgate station——

"Ah, yes," he cried—"And I called for you—and
you were ready—in a brown holland frock——"

"Had I a brown holland? I remember that I was

quite ready. And then a note came down from Mrs. James——"

"Beloved Mrs. James——"

"And you pretended to be angry——"

"Pretended! Oh, my dearest friend—I swore."

"I know you did. And I——"

"You pretended to cry——"

"No, no, there was no pretence. I did cry."

"Mary," he said, "why did you cry?"

She recovered herself. "Because I was very young, and very stupid."

"Now for *my* instance," he said. "Not so very long ago, you were to go to Blackheath—by train; and I went to Charing Cross station." But, with a flaming face, and real trouble in her eyes, she stopped him.

"Please, don't—you hurt me. I think that you forget."

He begged her pardon so sincerely that she could not refuse the morrow's appointment.

They met at the station—she in a straw hat and linen frock—for the weather was wonderful; he in flannels. The perils of adventure glittered in her eyes; he played the courtier, sure now of his game. She begged for third-class tickets, but he compromised for second—and flagrantly bribed the guard to keep the carriage. It was impossible that she should avoid the knowledge that she was practically in possession—impossible that she should not see the approving smiles of the bystanders. "A pretty girl and her sweetheart"; simple comedy, of never-

ending charm. Abhorrent to the Senhouses of this
world, but not to be extirpated until Birnam come to
Dunsinane.

Softly the knowledge brooded upon her, softly
virginal she sat, very much aware. The epicure
returned to Master Tristram, who by a whisper
could have had her, but refrained. He sat by her,
but respectfully—he discoursed at large. Powderham Castle—he spoke of that. It was a pity that the
fine place could not be seen; but the Courteneys had
let it, and he didn't know the people. It was full, he
happened to have heard. He believed that Bramleigh was staying there. He forgot if she knew
Bramleigh; a quaint little man. But probably she
wouldn't want to be bothered with a lot of people;
so they must be contented with the park. Thus
Tristram discoursed; and at his discretion sat she,
saying little, looking at him never, heeding every
shade of inflection, and every hair's breadth of
movement of his. They reached the station; he
helped her to descend.

All seemed well with Tristram's wooing. His
lady was in a pensive mood, softly receptive of his
implications. The temptation to paint in bolder
masses was not resisted, nor that more subtle form
of art—the silent art. Speechless they loitered together; and sometimes their hands touched, and
sometimes he hovered over her, as if protecting her
with wings. Her eyes were veiled; she appeared
sleek as a dove under his hand. Once he breathed
her name—"Mary, oh, Mary—"; but he saw her

shiver and stiffen, and knew that she was still to be won. So be it! But he could not give over the delicious chase. To have her thus wide-eyed, quivering, straining beside him—like a greyhound taut at his leash; he was beside himself with longing, and like a fool gave way.

"My dearest—" he began, but she checked him with a fierce cry—"No, no!—Not that—" and though he could see nothing but the sharp outline of her cheek and chin he knew that she was watching something. He looked about him vaguely. What on earth—? The sea—a narrow strip of blue tumbling water, spuming where it touched the yellow sands—the flecked, pale sky—the gorse—larks above it—in a far corner a gipsy's tent, and a white horse foraging—. What on earth—?

He drew back. She seemed to start forwards as if to escape from him—but then she turned suddenly, and he saw that she was pale, that she trembled, and that there was real trouble in her eyes.

"I am tired," she said, "very tired. May we go home now?"

"Of course—what a brute I am. But I thought that you— Won't you tell me what has tired you all at once?"

"I don't know—it came over me—suddenly. But I do want to go home, please—immediately." Her eyes were full—brimming. He was touched.

"Come then, we'll go to the station. It's no great distance. Unless you would rather sit——"

"Oh, no, I couldn't possibly! No, no, indeed,

I must go home. My head aches dreadfully. I think a sunstroke—perhaps. I can hardly stand up——"

He saw that that was true. "Come," he said, "take my arm. We'll go at once."

When they had turned back she seemed to recover. She walked, at any rate, as fast as he did—set the pace. But she would not talk any more. In the train she sat apart, looking out of the window—and after a time he let her alone.

At Exeter when he put her in the fly and would have followed her, she put her hand on his arm. "Please don't come with me. I shall be myself directly. I beg you not to come. And don't think me ungrateful—indeed, you have been kindness itself. I'm very much ashamed of myself——"

"I'll see you to-morrow—to say good-bye. You will let me do that? I must know how you are, you see."

"Yes—come to-morrow if you will. Good-bye. I am much better. I shall be quite well. But come, of course, if you had rather."

"Of course I shall come." He lifted his hat, bowed, and turned away. She watched him walk towards his hotel. Then, with a face of flame, she turned to her own affair.

This was to be her last bid for freedom; her last chance. If she was to be the crying shame of her sex, it must be so. Come what might, she must call for help.

She stayed the fly at the door, paid the man, and watched him turn and go galloping down the hill.

Then she turned to her affair—across Exeter it took her, to the Honiton road.

She walked the whole way, some two miles out of the city, beyond the suburbs to where the open country began. And here she laid her *patteran*, with branches of crimson maple, torn from the sunny side of the hedge. At the corners of two by-roads she laid them—one to the South, one to the North. Not satisfied with that, she went North herself to the Cullompton road, and laid two *patterans* more. Her cheeks burned like fire, and in her heart was a bitter pain; she felt that she had unsexed herself, was bedraggled and bemired. But her need had racked her —you can't blame the wretch writhing there if he call upon his God.

when his friend joined him and, sighing his content at a good dinner ahead of him, produced and lighted a cigar. Senhouse found himself reading for a second time a paragraph of a leading article which began thus:—

"Ever since the by-election in Farlingbridge, caused by the death of Mr. Germain, the Government has been losing seats with a steadiness as reasonable as reason can require." Midway through his second reading he stiffened and sat up.

"Excuse me, Löffner," he said, "but I must leave you for an hour or so."

Herr Löffner beamed and bowed. "I am sorry, but submit. Only—you must promise me to come back, or I lose you, *du wilder Mann.*"

Senhouse was not vague; on the contrary, he was remarkably collected. "Yes, I'll come back. But this is a matter of losing myself—or the reverse, as the case may be." He nodded, and walked straight out of the hotel into the street. Bingo, stepping delicately, with ears set back and muzzle to earth, followed close to his right heel. He shared his master's contempt of London, but added fear.

The hour was late for callers, since it was now half-past seven, but he knew nothing of hours. He went directly to Hill-street and rang the bell. After a long interval a caretaker released many a bolt and peered round the edge of the door. A respectable, grey-haired lady, very anxious.

"Mrs. Germain?" said Senhouse. He almost heard her sigh.

"Out of town, sir."

"So I see. But where is she?" Bingo lifted his head high, snuffed the air, misliked it, and yawned.

The elderly lady had no more doubts. "She would be at Southover House, Sir. The family is expected on the 15th for a few days, on their way abroad."

Senhouse jerked away all this surplusage. "The family? What family? It is Mrs. John Germain, I mean."

Whatever caution may have lingered in the caretaker now disappeared, in the occasion of a treasured wonder to be revealed. "Oh, Sir, we don't know anything about her. It's all a mystery, Sir, and has been since Mr. John—passed away."

"What do you mean by that?" she was asked.

Her cue! "She's not been seen or heard of, Sir—not by her own family nor by ours. She went away by herself in July—after the event, Sir—and here's October come round, and never heard of yet."

Senhouse betrayed nothing; but his mind moved like lightning. "Tell me exactly what you mean," he bade her; and she did, omitting nothing. He listened, made no comments, and gave no chances.

Then he asked her, "Do you know Mr. Duplessis's address?"

She did not.

"His club?" She said she would call her husband.

The husband in his shirt-sleeves was all for speculation upon the affair—speculation at large, illustrated by reminiscences. Duplessis was a good gambit;

but the moment he had opened by saying that many a time had he stood behind Mr. Duplessis's chair at the Reform he found himself rehearsing to his wife things that she had heard but an hour ago. Senhouse had snapped out his "Reform! Thanks," and gone his way.

At the Reform—Bingo coiled on the steps, with one eye wary for peril—he learned that Duplessis was in Devonshire. "Wraybrook Park, near Honiton," was his address. He returned to the hotel and found Herr Löffner immovable in his place, and still with a cigar. But he was deplorably hungry, and leapt to his feet the moment he saw Senhouse.

"Thank God for you," he warmly said. "Come and dine."

"I can't dine, Löffner. You must hoard your thanksgiving. I'm going down to Devonshire." The *savant* gazed at him.

"To Devonshire—without dinner! That is not possible, my friend. To begin, it is bad for you—secondly, it is late."

"Oh," said Senhouse, "I'm a night-bird, you know. I don't want you to come with me—in fact, I'd rather you didn't. You've got lots to do at Kew, and can meet me there. But I must be off in half an hour. I shall catch the 9.25."

Herr Löffner looked at his watch, then at his friend's dog, then at his friend. Smiles played about his face and eyes. "What mischief do you meditate? What dark work?" he said; and you could hear the enthusiasm gurgling beneath, like flood

water in a drain. But Senhouse was unfathomable,
and for once not smiling.

"It's serious work I'm after. Life-and-death
work, I believe. My trip to the Caucasus hangs on
it—and all my trips to come."

"Herr Je! Du lieber——!"

"I know. It's a queer thing. Nothing seemed to
hang upon anything this morning, and now everything upon one thing. It's no good, my dear man,
I can't explain. Trust me, I'll telegraph to you from
Exeter and wait for you there."

"Bod—" said Herr Löffner out of his chest. "If
you haf here a life-and-death-works—I cannot understand. If you make of it life-works, you telegraph and I come. But if it is a death-works—what
then?"

"It won't be," said Senhouse. "It can't be.
Good-bye." Herr Löffner went to his dinner.

At Wraybrook Park his lean face was announced
to Duplessis at half-past ten in the morning, at the
breakfast-table, by a respectful butler. It was not
told him that it had awaited him since eight o'clock.

"Some one to see me—in the drive?" he had
asked, suspecting nothing. "Why in the drive?"

"The gentleman preferred to be outside, Sir. He
had a dog with him."

Duplessis stared at his plate. "All right. I'll
come in a minute," he said, and resumed his meal.

At eleven he came out of the front door, cigar in
mouth, and saw immediately what was in store for
him. The carriage drive at Wraybrook sweeps

round the lake, which is the great feature of the
place. On the edge of that he had seen in a moment
the tall man in grey, bareheaded, talking with one of
the gardeners, and had flushed. His eyes narrowed,
and glittered; he paused perceptibly, then drew a
breath and went down over the lawn.

Bingo, sitting up on his haunches, gave a short
yap of warning, then apologized to his master.
Senhouse finished what he had to say to the gardener, nodded and went up to meet his man.

They encountered without recognition: Bingo,
with lifted forefoot, reserved his judgment. His
custom was to run in and apply the test of nose to
calf; but in this case he stayed behind.

"You wish to see me, I'm told." Duplessis spoke
first.

"Yes," said Senhouse, "I do. I have to trouble
you. I have just heard of John Germain's death."

In some sort Duplessis had been prepared for this
—but in no way which could have been explained.
He was able to take it quietly.

"News travels slowly your way," he said. "Germain died in July."

"So I have learned; but it must have been sudden. I happen to know that he was quite well at the
beginning of that month; and had not the least
reason to expect any such thing."

"Why should you?" Duplessis was rather famous for impertinence.

Senhouse said, "I'll tell you. I saw Mrs. Germain early in July"—Duplessis grew red—"In fact,

she must have gone directly from the North, where I met her, to her husband's bedside."

"I think I'll interrupt you for one moment," Duplessis said. "You are probably as interested in saving time as I am. Therefore the sooner I know how I can serve you the better for both of us." Bingo who had been looking with gloomy interest at the root of his tail, here attacked it with ferocity. Senhouse laughed.

"I'll tell you. Mrs. Germain has disappeared."

Duplessis asked, "Do you want me to find her for you?"

"I want you," said Senhouse, "to tell me where she is."

Duplessis looked him full in the face. "Really, I don't know what business you have to ask me that."

"Then I'll tell you, if you please," said Senhouse. "When she left the North she did not, I believe, go directly to London. She went to Blackheath, to her people. There she saw you."

"Who told you that, Sir?" Duplessis was angry.

"She told me that she should see you there. It had not been her intention; but she changed her mind."

"Then I have to thank you, Mr. Senhouse, for an insufferable interference in my affairs," said Duplessis.

"I advised her to see you—yes. Come, now," he said with a change of tone which Duplessis found hard to bear, "you have had your innings, I was careful not to touch on that. You have had more

than one, if I don't mistake you. I think now that
I go in."

Duplessis was not the man to give candour for
candour. His eyes were steady on his enemy. "I
don't give ladies' addresses without their leave, you
know."

"You may assume it here. When I saw Mrs.
Germain in Cumberland she gave me to understand
that she might wish to see me again."

"If she had wished it," said Duplessis, "I suppose she would have told you where she was. Apparently she does not wish it."

"Obviously you do not," Senhouse replied; "and
I have reasons for putting your wish and her action
together. And, as a matter of fact, she could not let
me know anything, because I have no certain address."

"Your addresses are nothing whatever to me,"
said Duplessis. "I decline to tell you anything."

"Very well," said Senhouse slowly. "Then you
must get what good you can out of that."

Duplessis turned on his heel and walked away.
Bingo, sleek and swift, ran after him and sniffed
daintily at his calves. Curiosity, so to speak, was
behind him, drove his tail in between his legs. It
wanted but a spark to kindle the smouldering young
man, and here it was. He turned again, blazing.
"Call in your cur, will you? They don't allow dogs
here."

"Bingo, heel," said Senhouse, and watched him,
smiling quietly.

XX

IN WHICH BINGO IS UNANSWERABLE

Swinging along his miles from Honiton back into Exeter he saw the *patteran* just within the two-mile-stone. "She wants me. She's here. Bless her wild heart." Then he walked into the city, sat in the tree-shaded alley of the inn by Exebridge, and break-fasted, as well he might. He had eaten nothing since yesterday's noon.

At two o'clock, as he leaned, smoking his pipe and looking at the river, he saw Duplessis in a dog-cart drive over the bridge. This was precisely what he had expected the moment he saw the *patteran* in the road. "He'll lunch before he moves; he'll treat himself handsomely. I'll give him till half-past three. Then we go together—the three of us." Bingo lowered his ears. Senhouse and he were too old friends for eye-service or tail-signals. Together they crossed the bridge and strolled up the curving street. The second inn-yard they visited showed them the Wraybrook dog-cart, high and yellow-wheeled. "He's put up. He goes back to-night. He's lunching. Now what shall we do? I think, a walk."

He addressed himself to the wooded heights which look down on Exeter. His spirits were high to meet the evening's battle; he urged Bingo to extend himself, infected him with the fray to come. "My friend, do you know who lives in this town? Do you know whom we are to see by-and-by? A gentle-handed acquaintance, my friend—a lover of yours, whose troubles have been told you and me by sigh. Not by words, Bingo, my boy; for words have not been made fine enough to voice her thoughts, half-thoughts and quarter-thoughts: no, but by a sigh scarcely heard, or a hand on your head, by caresses, and lingering touches, and suchlike pretty talk. That's how we know her, and what we love her for, Bingo; because she's timid and full of alarms—and on the edge of the real thing, hovering on the threshold of the cage."

Bingo pricked up his ears, then whined. He moved his head to acknowledge a friendly speech, but he was trembling and looking up the road.

"Bingo, come in," said Senhouse, and trembled, too. He saw Mary coming up the road, books under her arm. She was rosy with breasting the hill; and he could see that her eyes were very bright. He could see, from the gate at which he leaned, that she was charged with excitement; that her lips were never still, that she looked sideways for events. He had to put his hand on Bingo's head to keep him back—and to keep himself back. "I'll give him one more chance," he told himself, and stayed where he was. Mary passed him, all unconscious, went quickly up the road, stopped at a white gate, and slowly pushed it open. As she went in he saw her pause and look down the road by which she had come. Then she went in, and the gate swung to and fro, and clicked as the latch caught.

Senhouse inspected the gate, then his watch. "Rosemount Academy for Young Ladies—three o'clock. She's teaching till four. She expects him." He retired to his trees; but had to call Bingo twice. He was halfway up the drive, nosing out his friend.

Duplessis came up the hill at five minutes to four, and smoked three cigarettes one after another. He looked at his watch incessantly, as he walked up and down the road. Senhouse watched him calmly, not making any effort at concealment—but concealed, because, it was obvious, Duplessis had no notion of his whereabouts. Ladies—young ladies in straw hats—came out of Rosemount Academy in twos and threes and vanished up or down the road, as the case might be. Some rode bicycles, and waved the prouder farewells to their friends afoot. One was fetched in a brougham by a furred matron; two had a maid; and one joined a brother in a cricket cap. Ladies of severer mien, tightly jacketed and in black, came presently; a long-haired music-master —and Mary.

As she stood beyond the gate she saw Duplessis. Senhouse knew that by her look. She had a trick, when she was at a pass, of driving all expression from her eyes. They showed then as masks of black: it was her way of defence. You could not tell whether she was glad or afraid of you.

But she addressed herself to her task; completed, or allowed the young musician to complete, the conversation, bade him a smiling farewell which sent him happily on his way, and then waited, blankly, but with colour, for Duplessis. The road was now empty but for these two.

He came up, lifting his hat; he took her hand, and held it while he bent to speak to her. Senhouse saw her so held, but with averted face; saw that she was listening, that she was serious—too serious to be frightened. Once he saw her look up at the man, and frame No with her grave lips; once again look up and frame Yes. At that second answer Duplessis took her hand again—her left hand which had been idle by her side—and held it while he continued to talk vehemently, in low tones. He watched her now intently, as she fought these long odds; and had Bingo by the scruff—Bingo on his hind legs, shivering and whining in whispers—"Steady, boy; hold yourself——."

Mary was now pale, and in her eyes was the light of distress. They beaconed across the way: but no help came. As she listened she began to breathe quickly; he could see her bosom's unrest. Her hand was caught up to Tristram's lips—but she sprang away then, and her "Oh, no, no! Never, never—I could not do it," gave Senhouse the cue for which he shook. He loosed Bingo, who, like a streak of grey light, shot across the road.

Duplessis started violently; but a low glad cry came from Mary's heart. "Bingo! Oh, my dearest friend! Oh, Bingo!" She stooped in the road, and the two were one. Then she rose vividly bright and waited for Senhouse.

He crossed the road leisurely—with no looks for Duplessis. He held out the maple-branch. "My excuse," he said. She took it from him, and kept it in her hand. But she could not speak. In the presence of the two men she showed nothing common or mean—no consciousness. She was perhaps at her best: her colour high, but not painful, her eyes serious, but not veiled. Modesty had been jarring affectation here: modesty was not possible. Her left hand still held Bingo's head to her side: Bingo on his hind legs, revelling in her hand.

The two men, each in his way, put their fate to the touch. Neither took his eyes off her, neither gave an inch. Duplessis would not have compromised if he could. His sullen rage was patent: he let it smoulder. Senhouse smiled—all the faun showed in him: the stored secret knowledge, the power of the adept, of the seer into the dark, of him who would mock if he were not full of pity.

He spoke first. "It seems that you are to choose," he said. "I can ask you to do that."

Her soft eyes beamed, and her smile met his in the way. "Halfway House?" she said, asking.

He nodded. "Halfway House, we'll put it still."

Duplessis said nothing at all; but fixed her with his knit brows. A good ear might have heard three hearts beating. I think that Bingo's did, for he nozzled in Mary's hand.

She let him gently down, stooped over him, kissed his head, whispered in his ear. Then, rising to her assize, with a look divinely mild and a gesture of confidence which brought tears into one pair of eyes, she put her hand in Senhouse's, and stood by his side.

Duplessis stiffened and looked at the pair of them. "I take your answer," he said, bowed to her, and walked down the hill. Bingo, sitting sagely on his haunches, suddenly yawned.

Shyly they turned to each other, shyly kissed. Senhouse kissed her twice, then threw his head back and laughed his joy to the skies. "Oh, wonder of the world!" he cried, and took her to his heart.

Here's for the last of her. In the train, on their way to London and Löffner, Senhouse was commenting upon what lay before them: the Caucasus, the Schwarzwald. What would she do in the Caucasus, for example? That was easy. "I shall sit in the door of the tent, waiting for you," she told him. In the Black Forest? What else?

He believed her. "We are to leave Halfway House, then?" and then he looked out of the window at the rolling hills of Wilts. "At any rate, here I am a bondslave—yoked by Baden for five years. Make what you will of it."

She said nothing; she was always slow of speech with her betters when they talked above her head.

But she pondered the saying, it was clear, for presently she picked up his hand, stooped to it, and kissed it; then, lowering her head, put his arm over her neck, and looked at him from below it. It was a pretty act, one of her prettiest. He saw the beauty of her gentle rebuke.

It sent him to his knees. Bingo, sitting on her skirt, looked pityingly at his master, for a few seconds, and then up into her face.

THE END